A WARHAMMER 40,000 NOVEL

Gaunt's Ghosts

SALVATION'S REACH

Dan Abnett

BLACK LIBRARY

For Aaron and Katie, of course.

A BLACK LIBRARY PUBLICATION

First published in Great Britain in 2011.
Paperback edition published in 2012 by
Black Library,
Games Workshop Ltd.,
Willow Road, Nottingham,
NG7 2WS, UK.

10 9 8 7 6 5 4 3 2 1

Cover illustration by Stefan Kopinski.

A CIP record for this book is available from the British Library.

UK ISBN: 978 1 84970 203 4
US ISBN: 978 1 84970 204 1

See Black Library on the internet at
www.blacklibrary.com

Find out more about Games Workshop
and the world of Warhammer 40,000 at
www.games-workshop.com

Printed and bound by CPI Group (UK) Ltd, Croydon, CR0 4YY

IT IS THE 41st millennium. For more than a hundred centuries the Emperor has sat immobile on the Golden Throne of Earth. He is the master of mankind by the will of the gods, and master of a million worlds by the might of his inexhaustible armies. He is a rotting carcass writhing invisibly with power from the Dark Age of Technology. He is the Carrion Lord of the Imperium for whom a thousand souls are sacrificed every day, so that he may never truly die.

YET EVEN IN his deathless state, the Emperor continues his eternal vigilance. Mighty battlefleets cross the daemon-infested miasma of the warp, the only route between distant stars, their way lit by the Astronomican, the psychic manifestation of the Emperor's will. Vast armies give battle in His name on uncounted worlds. Greatest amongst his soldiers are the Adeptus Astartes, the Space Marines, bio-engineered super-warriors. Their comrades in arms are legion: the Imperial Guard and countless planetary defence forces, the ever-vigilant Inquisition and the tech-priests of the Adeptus Mechanicus to name only a few. But for all their multitudes, they are barely enough to hold off the ever-present threat from aliens, heretics, mutants - and worse.

TO BE A man in such times is to be one amongst untold billions. It is to live in the cruellest and most bloody regime imaginable. These are the tales of those times. Forget the power of technology and science, for so much has been forgotten, never to be re-learned. Forget the promise of progress and understanding, for in the grim dark future there is only war. There is no peace amongst the stars, only an eternity of carnage and slaughter, and the laughter of thirsting gods.

Came then he, a prisoner, into the
House of the Daemon, and he was bound about
and anointed so that his life could be
taken in offering, as was the custom.
But he slipped his bonds, and made a fire
burn inside the House of the Daemon,
and burned it he from the inside out,
and so the Daemon it was that
burned and was slain.

– from the Kinebrach myth of the Rath and the Hero

'Throughout the year 781.M41, Warmaster Macaroth's main battle groups remained deadlocked at the frontiers of the Erinyes Group, despite his strenuous efforts to force a breakthrough. Macaroth's primary crusading strength was held off by a formidable defensive line composed of the forces of Archon Gaur, the Archenemy overlord.

'Meanwhile, trailwards, the Warmaster's second battle group had repeatedly failed to dislodge the legions of Magister Anakwanar Sek, Gaur's most capable lieutenant, from the Cabal Systems. Senior advisors urged Macaroth to break off from his bull-headed prosecution of the Erinyes Line, and concentrate on quashing Sek at the Cabal Worlds. With the threat of Sek removed, they counselled, the Crusade could safely resume an assault of the Archon's position. But Macaroth rejected the notion, claiming it would give the Archon enough time – perhaps two or three years – to rebuild and retrench to such an extent that the Erinyes Line would become unassailable.

'Split between these two concentrations of resistance,

Macaroth's Crusade was haemorrhaging momentum and materiel. The Crusade had become two crusades, and even Macaroth's vast war-tithes, and massive support from the sector lords, could not sustain his ambitions. Furthermore, there was a general and growing fear that, if properly co-ordinated, the forces of Sek and Gaur might combine with such effect, the Sabbat Worlds Crusade force would actually be annihilated.

'During this critical period, a series of covert operations was planned and executed at key sites across the Sabbat Worlds. The most critical, and the one upon which all the others depended, was undertaken at Salvation's Reach in the remote Rimworld Marginals. Seen as a huge gamble, and with atrocious prospects for success, the mission was authorised by Macaroth on the basis that, if accomplished by some miracle, it could alter the balance of the war entirely.

'This was the twenty-sixth year of the Sabbat Worlds Crusade, and Macaroth was increasingly looking like a man prepared to try anything, and risk everything, to secure a victory.'

– from *A History of the Later Imperial Crusades*

ONE
Suicide Kings

SOMETHING, PERHAPS THE year of living by the skin of his teeth on occupied Gereon, or merely the fact of having been born a sly and ruthless son of a bitch, had given Major Rawne of the Tanith First a certain edge.

He could usually smell trouble coming. That morning, he could *definitely* smell trouble coming. As edges went, his was as fine and sharp as the one along the blade of his straight silver warknife.

At dawn, with the twin suns beginning to burn up through the petrochemical smog across the city bay, he left the regimental billet and walked down to the rockcrete wasteland of the bayside revetment. There, he wandered as far as the bridge, and crossed over to the pontoons in front of the island guardhouse.

The pontoon walkway clunked underfoot. Looking down through the mesh, he could see the water, toxic brown and frothy. The massive galvanic plants along the bay, Adeptus Mechanicus developments that powered and lit the hive city's core systems, had just flushed their heatsinks, and filled the coastline with its morning

11

dose of radioactive effluent. There was steam in the air, steam that stank of sulphur and rolled like a fog bank, white in the suns' light. The waters of the bay and estuary had been corrosively acidic for a thousand years. It was sobering to think that anything still lived in it.

But things did. Just below the surface, they squirmed and moved, leech-mouthed, slug-slick, with dentition like crowded pincushions and eyes like phlegm. Rawne could see them, following him beneath the surface; a dark, wriggling mass. What gave them their edge? Was it the sound of his footsteps, the passing heat signature of his body? Pheromones? His shadow on the water?

They were survivors. They had adapted to their environment instead of allowing it to kill them. And they killed anything that threatened them.

Just like him.

Three Urdeshi troopers were manning the guardhouse. They didn't know him, and he didn't know them. They weren't his concern. He had chosen that particular morning because it was pretty much the last chance he was going to get before the regiment shipped out. The point of no turning back had been reached.

But still, there was the nagging discomfort of his edge. Something was off. Something was wrong. He'd chosen the wrong day to try it. Maybe the troopers suspected him of something, maybe they were wired up for some reason. Maybe something had given away his true intent.

Under ordinary circumstances, the doubt would have been enough to make him abort, turn around, and go home. The uncertainty would have been sufficient to make him blow it off and try again another day when the odds were more favourable.

Except there weren't going to be any more *other days*. It was now, or it was never. There were no more chances. The monster, *that monster*, should have been dead long since. Justice and decency demanded it, and only the dedicated efforts of good men who ought to have known better were ensuring the monster's salvation.

Dedication. Rawne had always possessed a measure of dedication. He knew what was right and what was wrong. He knew when an order was a bad thing and needed to be ignored. He knew that sometimes a man had to be counter-intuitive. A man had to do what looked like a bad thing so that everything else would be right in the end.

The monster was destined to die. Its death was required, demanded. Efforts had already been made, by more than one interested party. Rawne couldn't stand by and let things carry on.

Rawne was a man of serious convictions, after all. Thankfully, they'd all been wiped from his record the day he joined the Imperial Guard.

The Urdeshi watched him as he approached. What did they suspect? Did they know what he had really come for?

He stopped at the outer cage gate. The Urdeshi troopers wore black metal pins that indicated they had been seconded to serve the Commissariat's S Company, the close protection and security detail. They asked him his name and his business, and studied the papers he passed through the metal letterbox. One of them took a long time over the Contact Permission document signed by Rawne's commanding officer, as though he had literacy problems.

They let him through. They checked his ID tags. They eyed his tattoos with scorn. He was some kind of heathen farm-head from an agri-world, an indentured barbarian, not a proper fighting man from a civilised place like Urdesh. Only his rank kept the insults at bay.

They took his sidearm, put it in the guardhouse locker, and made him sign for it. Then they patted him down.

The Urdeshi had been fairly thorough up until that point, but now the long night shift and a clutch of caffeine headaches began to show. Rawne had been patted down by the very best in his time. He knew precisely how to twist or turn, innocent movements that looked like balance-keeping, so that even somebody taking the pat-down seriously could be misled and misdirected. Rawne kept his hands raised. By the time they'd finished, they would believe they had methodically checked everywhere, where in fact he had kept them entirely clear of one or two areas.

They found the knife. Tanith warknife, straight silver, buckled to his right shin.

'What's this?' asked one.

'Back-up,' replied Rawne.

They took it, made him sign for it.

He'd wanted them to find it. It was the decoy. People believed they'd done a thorough job if they found something. People usually stopped searching at that point.

'You've got thirty minutes,' said one of the guards. 'That is the permitted duration authorised by your papers. You will be back here in twenty-nine minutes. If you're not, we will come looking for you and you will be considered a justified target.'

Rawne nodded.

They opened the inner cage gate. Its chain hoist clattered. He walked through the guardhouse and out onto the inner causeway of the pontoons. The tide clearly caught here between the vast stone piers of the island. There was a pronounced stink of sulphur, and a soupy mass of dissolving garbage lapped against the slimy walls of the inlet.

He left the pontoon walkway and climbed stone steps that brought him in under the archway entrance. The island was an artificial atoll of stone and rockcrete built to support a squat, formidable lighthouse tower. The bridge that had originally connected it to the shore had long since rotted away. It had been replaced by the metal pontoon and the walk span.

The lighthouse hadn't burned for a long time. Dark

and neglected, the tower's thick walls and inaccessibility had been put to other uses.

Once he was out of sight of the guardhouse, Rawne stepped back into the shadows. He reached down to his left calf, and removed the other Tanith warknife he was carrying. He had tied it around his shin with boot laces. The one he'd surrendered had been Meryn's. Rawne had taken it without asking. Meryn would probably be searching his billet for it already. It added to Rawne's enjoyment of the whole enterprise to think that, whatever else happened, Meryn would end up on a charge for misplacing his regimental dagger.

Rawne believed the knife would probably be enough. It certainly ought to be enough for any self-respecting Tanith-born to get the job done. But he wanted to cover all the variables.

Off to the side of the lowering entrance archway was a dim stone cistern. It had once been the chute of a garderobe, or a drain-away built to cope with heavy storm swells. The edge of his warknife, deftly applied, freed the lip of the cast iron cover. Rawne hooked his fingers around the bars of the cover and lifted it out. There was a damp stone well underneath, with water lurking in the darkness at the bottom. Other things lurked down there too, things with pincushion gums and egg-white eyes. He could hear them slopping and writhing gleefully, as if entertained by his cunning.

The cord had been attached to the underside of the drain cover, so that it hung down into the shaft of the well, weighted by the waxed burlap musette bag on the end. He pulled the line up, and the bag with it, opened the drawstring top, and took out the heavy object wrapped in vizzy cloth.

It was a collection of objects in fact, all of them dense and heavy. Machined metal components. Rawne spread the cloth on the stone floor beside the drain, and laid the parts out on it. He slotted them together, quickly and skilfully. He'd done it a thousand times before. He could have done it blindfold. Each piece clacked or wound into place. The smell of gun oil was sweet and strong in his nostrils.

Standard Munitorum-issue laspistol, Khulan V pattern. It was one of the original stamped blanks shipped from Khulan for finishing in the armouries of Tanith, prior to issue at the Tanith Founding. The palm-spur had been fitted with a handmade nalwood grip, and age and use had lent the figuring greater beauty than any varnish or lacquer could have achieved.

The pistol had been smuggled into the lighthouse over a period of weeks, one part at a time. It lacked a power cell, a flash sleeve and the side casings. Rawne reached into his belt pouch. Inside were two cigars rolled in black liquorice paper. The S Company sentries had taken them out, sniffed them, and given them back. Each cigar was in a little tin case. Except they weren't. One of the tin cases was actually a flash sleeve. Rawne blew out the traces of tobacco fibre and screwed the sleeve onto the end of the barrel.

The Urdeshi had also failed to notice that he was wearing four tags, not two. Rawne unlooped the two side plates from the slender chain, dropped the tags back down under the neckline of his vest, and slotted the side plates into position.

Then he struck the tip of his knife into the back of his boot heel, and pulled the heel block away from the upper. The power cell was secured in a cavity he'd hollowed out of the heel. Rawne stamped the heel back in place, then slapped the cell into the gun. He toggled off, armed it, got a tiny green light on the grip just above his thumb. He felt the ambient hum of a charged las weapon.

He dropped the drain cover back, slipped the knife into his belt, and walked up the steps from the entrance archway with the pistol down at his side in his right hand.

There was a semicircular stone chamber beyond, large and full of echoes. Munitorum-issue armoured window units had been bolted or heat-fused into the gaping stone sockets. Rawne passed on into a larger stone chamber, fully circular and three or four storeys high. It was the core of the lighthouse. In the base, dead centre, stood some of the old lampwork, a great, engineered brass contraption with a wick-mount, winding handles, and a reservoir feed from the promethium sump below. A huge frame of gearing and chainlines surrounded it to elevate the lamp to the beacon room at the apex of the tower once it was lit.

The brass lampwork was black with age and the chains had rusted. The gears and winders were so corroded they had frozen, blotched green and white, and would never turn again. Decades of dust had accreted on the black grease of the lamp head and wick assembly in such quantity it looked like some exotic, thickly furred animal mounted on display.

Rawne walked up the stairs that ran around the curve of the chamber wall. There was no rail, and he made no sound, though the latter was not even deliberate. Like many Tanith, he had been taught by that great educator, life, not to give himself away.

He smelled caffeine and the unmistakable aroma of fried nutrition fibre. Slab, staple of the common lasman's diet, cornerstone of Guard rations.

Rawne reached a landing space. There was a doorway ahead. A guard, another Urdeshi man, was sitting beside the doorway on a chair borrowed from another building. Rawne kept the laspistol against his hip so that the man wouldn't see it immediately. He kept walking. It was all about confidence. Confidence was the key to everything. Use enough of it and you could pull off any scam, win any fight, or bed any mamzel. The more you acted like you were absolutely supposed to be doing something, the less chance anyone would

ask what the hell you *were* up to, until it was too late,
and they were – depending on the circumstances –
financially worse off, dead, or surprisingly naked.

The guard didn't spare him a second look. Rawne
passed him, and went in through the doorway.

The room had originally been the tower master's
chamber. It was bare boards and grilled windows, and
the corkscrew staircase ran up the inside wall to the
platform levels higher in the tower. The room currently
contained a heavy wooden cot, a small trolley table and
an old wooden chair.

The cot was neatly made, the blanket and bedroll laid
out as if for a barrack hall inspection. On the table was
a small lumen lamp, some books and a cookhouse tray.
On the tray was a tin cup and a flask of caffeine, a salt
shaker, a mess dish with the remains of a serving of
slab cake, hard biscuits and refried bean paste, and a
worn metal spoon. Rawne was surprised they'd allowed
a spoon. A determined man could turn a spoon into a
weapon. He could sharpen it against stone, stab with
it. If he didn't have time to work its edge, he could
improvise. Even blunt, it could do damage to an eye or
a throat if driven with enough force.

Maybe it's me, Rawne thought. Maybe I just see
weapons in everything. Maybe to other people, that's
just a spoon.

The books were all Imperial tracts and trancemissionary pamphlets, stamp-printed on brown, low-quality
paper. It was all the monster ever seemed to read. He
said they helped to settle him and fortify his resolve.

The monster was sitting in the chair beside the table,
reading one of the tracts while he digested his breakfast.
He was wearing unmarked black fatigues, boots and a
brown hide jacket. His shaved scalp and face were covered in deliberate ritual scars, old and puckered, but the
hands holding the trancemissionary treatise were soft
and unmarked.

The monster became aware of Rawne's approach. He stopped reading and looked up.

'Major Rawne,' he said. 'I did not expect to see you this morning.'

So damn polite. Like a real person.

'Pheguth,' Rawne replied.

The monster looked startled for a second. It wasn't just the fact that he had been called *traitor* in his own, abhuman tongue. It was the fluency of it. Rawne's time on occupied Gereon had allowed him to acquire a conversational grasp of the Archenemy language. He didn't merely know the word for *betrayer*, he could deliver it with colloquial authenticity. It was as though a part of the monster's old life had come back to threaten him.

The monster saw the weapon. He saw Rawne raising the laspistol from the guarded place beside his hip.

'Major–' he began.

Rawne said nothing else. He took aim and fired.

The crack of the discharge echoed around the room. Rawne heard seabirds roosting in the upper parts of the lighthouse launch into the air at the sound of the shot. Nothing else.

Footsteps. There would be footsteps. Which side would they come from? What angle did he need to cover?

Rawne looked at the monster. The monster, Mabbon Etogaur, looked back at him.

'Come on, or you're a dead man,' Rawne said.

Mabbon got up out of his chair. Rawne's shot had severed the heavy iron chain that linked the etogaur's manacles to a hefty floor pin. He looped up the trailing, cut end of the chain around his right hand.

'I don't understand,' Mabbon said.

'No time to explain,' Rawne replied.

It was going to be from the right.

The sea window blew in, exploding in a spray of armoured glass fragments. There was a man outside, on the lighthouse's external walkway.

Rawne tackled Mabbon and brought him down behind the trolley table and the cot. Three more lasshots shrieked in through the blown window space and scorched holes in the opposite wall. Prone, Mabbon looked at Rawne.

Rawne gestured for him to keep down.

The shooter outside switched his lasrifle to full auto and unleashed a storm of rounds into the room. Several struck the side of the heavy cot, splintering the wood and slamming the frame backwards. Some hit the trolley table and knocked it over. Some punctured the back of the old chair and filled the air with dust and floating animal hair fibres.

Silence. Dust and smoke drifted in the sunlight. Mabbon looked set to move. Rawne, still flat on his belly, reached out and picked up the salt shaker that had been knocked off the tray. He used it like a pen, and drew on the stone floor in salt. The looping white lines formed the scratch symbol for 'play dead'. The *Blood Pact* scratch symbol. Some said Rawne had learned far more on Gereon than was entirely good for him.

Mabbon looked at the symbol and nodded.

The shooter was cautious. He had killed the guard at the door before Rawne's arrival: cut his throat and left him sitting in his chair. Then he'd gone out onto the walkway and circled around, probably intending to get up and fire at Mabbon from above. The noise of Rawne's shot had forced him to make his play earlier than he had intended.

A minute passed, a full minute. It felt like a year to the two men pressed down on the floor behind the cot as they tried not to twitch or breathe. A second minute was almost up before something moved against the light and a figure stepped in through the blown window.

An Urdeshi trooper, by his clothes and his lasrifle; uniforms and Guard-issue weapons could be stolen. The boots crunched on the broken glass.

Rawne let him get a metre or so into the room, then fired under the cot. The las-shot clipped the man's left calf and he toppled with a squeal. Rawne leapt up at once, bounding over the battered cot to finish things. He was hoping to take the man alive for interrogation, but he was also fully prepared to seal the deal with a kill shot if necessary.

He almost fell off the cot mid-bound as shots tore down from above. A second shooter was firing from high up inside the tower, perched on the rail-less spiral of the stairs.

Rawne landed on top of the first shooter. It was an accident, but he worked with it. The man fought back. Rawne saw his face, close-up, and recognised him. They wrestled. Shots from above struck the floor beside them. The man had Rawne's wrist. Rawne couldn't aim his pistol. The man's lasrifle, looped around the man's torso on its strap, was wedged between them.

Rawne threw a hooking punch. He couldn't aim with the pistol, so he struck with it. The butt collided with the man's cheek and snapped his head around, but the impact tore the pistol out of Rawne's grip, and it went skittering away across the floor.

More shots struck the ground around them from above. Rawne rolled over hard, dragging his dazed assailant with him, like two lovers tumbling. He couldn't pull the lasrifle off the shooter because of the strap, but he got his right hand around the barrel to direct it, and his left hand down and low to squeeze the trigger.

The weapon was still set on full auto. Las-shots hosed up the throat of the lighthouse, deflecting off the curved walls, blowing out chunks of brick and stonework. It wasn't the cleanest piece of shooting Rawne had ever executed, but he managed to drag the chasing wildfire across the section of screwstair where the second shooter was crouching.

Hit, though perhaps not fatally, the second shooter

yelped and fell. He somersaulted down a dozen steps, cracking off the stone edges, and then grazed against the curve of the wall and flew right off the staircase entirely. He dropped eight metres, straight down, onto the prisoner's wooden chair, which exploded into kindling and dust under the impact.

Rawne was up. There was no opportunity for respite. A third assassin had appeared, rushing in through the main doorway. Like the other two, he was dressed as an Urdeshi trooper. He had a lasrifle with a bayonet fixed. He, too, had a face Rawne knew.

Rawne's laspistol was out of reach. The lasrifle was tangled around the body of the first shooter on the floor. Rawne went at the third attacker instead, closing the distance between them as fast as he could, ripping out his warknife.

The third assassin fired, but Rawne's straight silver had already parried his bayonet and turned the muzzle aside. The shot went out through the blown window. The assassin tried to re-aim, but Rawne fenced with his blade again and deflected the bayonet so that the next shots went clean up the tower space.

The assassin tried to club Rawne with an underswing of his tilted rifle. Rawne spun his warknife so that the pommel was behind his thumb, then punched the blade sideways, knuckles up. The blow slashed the assassin's throat, left to right. Blood gouted into the air, as though someone had tossed a beaker of red ink. Rawne ripped back in the opposite direction, and tore a second cut across the man's torso, right to left. The assassin fell on his knees with a deadweight thump, his lifeblood exiting his body under pressure through the two huge splits. He collapsed onto his face.

Rawne stepped back, spinning the warknife back upright in his hand, and then swung around, alerted by a sound from behind him.

The first shooter had got back up on his hobbled leg,

raising his rifle to his broken cheek to shoot Rawne in the back. But Mabbon had seized him from behind. The etogaur's broken manacles were wrapped around the man's throat, crushing the life out of him. Mabbon's face was absolutely expressionless.

The man struggled and made a cracked choking noise. Mabbon slammed his face into the stone surround of the blown window and then let the chain go slack, dropping him dead on the floor.

'The timing of your visit was quite fortunate,' he remarked.

Rawne nodded, picking up the third assassin's rifle in case there were any further surprises.

The three dead assassins all had the same face.

'Rime wants you dead,' he said.

'Half the sector wants me dead,' Mabbon replied.

Rawne shrugged.

'So, did you get some kind of tip-off that Rime was sending his Sirkle after me today?'

'No,' said Rawne. 'This was a coincidence. I came here this morning to prove a point.'

'What point?'

'That the Tanith First can protect you better than the S Company details the Commissariat assigns to you. We've all used our visits in the last few weeks to test security, to look for weakness, to smuggle things in. Today, I was going to demonstrate that if we could get a weapon inside, so could anybody, and thus convince the Commissariat to assign S Company duties to my platoon so we could take over from the buffoons they've been using to watch you.'

'Because Gaunt would be happier that way, because he trusts his own to do the job properly?'

'Something like that,' said Rawne. 'And it's Colonel-Commissar Gaunt to you.'

'My apologies,' said Mabbon.

Rawne looked at the bodies. Outside, he could hear

men approaching, and an alarm started to sound.

'Still,' he said, 'as demonstrations go, this proved the point well enough.'

'I'm pleased that my security will be your business for the remainder of my stay here, major,' Mabbon said.

'The Suicide Kings will look after you,' said Rawne.

'Suicide Kings? Like the card game?'

'Never mind. It's a private joke,' said Rawne. 'Anyway, there won't be much of a remainder. That's why I had to make my point today. It's also why Rime had to make his move. That suggests he has good intelligence.'

'You're moving me. We're going to begin at last?'

'Approval has been granted,' said Rawne. 'The mission has been authorised. We make shift at nightfall tomorrow.'

'I take it that when we make shift, we will be en route to Salvation's Reach?' Mabbon Etogaur asked.

'That's classified,' said Rawne.

TWO
Elodie on the Shore

WITH JUST A day to go, the Makeshift Revels were well underway.

It was all new to Elodie, of course. Everything was new, even her surname. Dutana. Elodie Dutana. It was her mother's family name, a name that belonged to her but which she had never used. She'd left a number of temporary professional surnames behind her on Balhaut, and taken up her mother's name to help rid herself of older memories and unsuitable associations.

She was Elodie Dutana, and she was part of a regimental entourage, and she was the companion of a brave and handsome Imperial Guard officer. It was a new life, and she liked it, and she intended to make the most of it.

She'd been through the whole process of embarkation once before, back on Balhaut, but it had been a blur, and she hadn't taken much in. Besides, they had been shipping out to what Ban Daur described as a 'dispersal point', not a warzone. There had been no sense of apprehension.

Now there was. The dispersal point was a city called

25

Anzimar on a planet called Menazoid Sigma. It had taken sixteen weeks on a stinking troop-and-packet ship to reach it from Balhaut, and they had been there eleven months.

Balhaut, where Elodie had spent the rest of her life, had been a place of towering, majestic cities. It had been the site of the Famous Victory, and though the wounds of war were still healing during her lifetime, and it was still possible to walk past empty lots or the shells of buildings during a day's business, Balhaut seemed to retain its air of dignity and significance.

Menazoid Sigma, what little she had seen of it, had little of either. Anzimar was dirty and industrial, and sat on a polluted bay where galvanic reactor plants filled the air with smog. There were twin suns, which was unsettling. Everything was noisy and stained. Everywhere smelled of chemicals. Elodie wasn't sure if the troop-and-packet ship hadn't been a preferable place to spend some time.

Everyone said the same. It was an ugly place, and not a good posting. They were only there for a time, waiting for routing orders to come through. Menazoid Sigma was simply a place to stop and resupply, a place to make ready. Some of the Tanith men, the ones who had served the regiment longest, talked about Menazoid Epsilon, which was apparently a neighbouring system where they had fought many years before. There was no sense at all they were pleased to be back in this part of the Sabbat cluster.

She had become part of the community attached to the Tanith First regiment. There were at least as many hangers-on following the regiment in supporting roles as there were serving lasmen. Elodie was still getting used to her status, her role, her responsibilities. She was still learning who everyone was. Eleven months, even eleven months spent on a sinkhole like Menazoid Sigma, was enough time to serve as an apprenticeship.

She was, in effect, an officer's wife. Her man was Captain Ban Daur, commander of G Company. Like many of the regiment, he was from the industrial world Verghast. He was a good man. Elodie quickly found that her impression of him was one shared by most: Daur was a genuinely good man. He was handsome, intelligent and principled. He wasn't loved by the men, but he was admired for his fairness and determination. He was honourable, and he could be relied upon. He had prospects for advancement, and they weren't at all hurt by the fact that, unlike most of the Verghastites serving in the regiment, he was from a good, mid-hive family. He came from breeding. He was not some lowly miner or labourman. Juniper said he was a good catch.

None of which was why Elodie was with him. She was with him because he was the one, and she'd known that since the moment she'd first seen him that day in Zolunder's Club on Selwire Street.

They had not formally married. The matter hadn't really been discussed. Marriage was permitted, and simply required certain documents and certificates to be signed by the commanding officer. There was no reason to believe that Daur's commander would refuse his request.

But they had not got around to it. Just a few weeks spent with the regimental train had shown Elodie that formal bonds were unnecessary. Soldiers understood loyalty, and loyalty was the glue that held everything together. She was Ban's woman, and everyone respected that. They didn't need a piece of paper to prove it.

As an officer's woman, Elodie entered entourage society at a comparatively high level. She had certain automatic privileges. Her status earned her respect from the other women. She got to decorate Daur's arm at certain regimental suppers. Officers were courteous to her. Daur's rank often secured him his own quarters rather than a shared billet, and she got to share that. She was, she knew, envied by some. There was nothing she could do about that. Juniper called her a trophy, whatever that meant.

The entourage train was a curious community. At the uppermost level were the wives and the women, the wet nurses and the children. A regiment always bred offspring. There were the pleasure girls and the camp followers, the women who were not attached to the regiment by way of blood like a wife or a mother, but by way of reliance. Their living came from the regiment, so they had to follow the regiment wherever it went. And just as their living came from the regiment, so did the livings of the seamsters, the button-makers, the dentists, the potion-grinders, the launderers, the entertainers, the musicians, the portraitists, the cooks, the bottlemen, the victuallers, the errand boys, the knife-sharps, the menders and fixers, the polishers, the cobblers and all the rest, most of whom brought along families of their own. It was an ungainly, parasitic entity that lived so that its host could live, and went with it everywhere, the two dependent on one another for survival.

She spent most days in the entourage camp, talking to the other women. A few, like Juniper, had become her friends and confidantes. They had helped her to find her feet. Juniper had taught her to take certain duties away from Daur's adjutant. Uniform work was a good one. She could get them cleaned and mended, get the correct one laid out ready for him. She could learn where to go to get the right replacement button or piece of braid, who to ask for the right brass paste, where to take a pair of boots for resoling. Daur had objected at first, saying that it wasn't her place to wash his clothes. He hadn't brought her along to shine his boots. She insisted she wanted to. She needed a greater purpose than to look well on his arm by the light of chandeliers. An officer's woman and his adjutant often developed an elegant partnership. Daur's adjutant was a man named Mohr.

He would advise her, quietly, on expected dress regulations, or send her a note if something was needed from
Daur's quarters. In return, Elodie left service business
to Mohr and made sure she wasn't around or, worse,
undressed, in Daur's quarters when the adjutant took
the daily brief. Sometimes, she even advised Mohr of
Daur's mood at the start of a day, a courtesy Mohr often
reciprocated at day's end.

That morning, there was no question what kind of day
it was going to be. Before dawn, the cookfires had lit and
the musicians had begun turning up. The Makeshift Revels were a festival, a carnival that marked the departure
of a regiment from its station. As soon as rumours began
to circulate that a regiment was about to make shift, the
revels began. All manner of traders and peddlers came to
the shore and set up shop, bringing street entertainers,
beggars, whores and, inevitably, thieves. It was the last
chance for the soldiers to indulge before departure, the
last chance for the entourage to acquire items before the
next halt, the last chance for the host town to earn coin
from the visiting troops.

It felt to Elodie like the heady holiday fairs that led up
to a major feast day back on Balhaut. It was noisy and
brash and cheerful, and there were treats and tempta-
tions to savour. But there was a gaudy, apocalyptic air
about it too. The regiment was going to war. No one
yet knew where, or what kind of war, and no one even
knew the exact hour they would make shift. Such things
were classified. Certainly, though, they were not leaving
Menazoid Sigma the way they had left Balhaut. They
were not heading for a dispersal point or a holding station. This was the real thing, and some of those leaving
would never come back, not to here or anywhere.

She rose early. There were things to do. Daur hadn't
told her specifically, but it was probably the last day on
shore. She had kissed him while he was still shaving at
the mirror, and left their quarters. He was going to need

his number one jacket by lunchtime. There was some kind of reception. She'd left the jacket with a tailor on the fifth row the night before and she needed to collect it.

It was early still, the suns just rising in the smog, but it was busy already. The shore bustled around her. Because the Guard camp at Anzimar was literally on the shore, Elodie had assumed that was what 'the shore' meant. The camp was a large town of prefab and rockcrete barrack buildings and halls housing, at present, six different regiments including the Tanith. It was flanked on one side by the sprawl of the city, and on the other by vast rockcrete skirts, the huge soot-scorched platforms where the bulk landers waited, cargo doors open, to swallow up the regiment and carry them up to the ships in high anchor orbit. The landers were huge, monolithic craft. The landing skirts met the shoreline and, with their hold jaws open and the waters of the bay behind them, they looked like oceanic monsters that had come ashore to bask and eat.

Elodie had learned that 'the shore' was simply Guard slang for any camp they occupied before shipping out. The shore was a lasman's temporary connection to one world before he marched on to the next. Sometimes a shore was a real shore, like it was on Menazoid Sigma. Sometimes it was a hive top, or a desert platform, a forest town or an island base. Sometimes it was an orbital station, sometimes it was a dizzying metropolis.

One more thing to learn. There was always one more thing to learn.

She was wearing a simple dress and a shawl and an old pair of combat-issue boots. It was cool, but the temperature would increase as the suns came up, and the cold stink of chemicals would acquire a burning tang. Plumes of brown filth trailed from the peaks of the galvanic reactors across the bay. There was fog out on the water.

The revel camp was a temporary fair of stalls and traders

that had grown up between the barrack buildings at the landing skirts. Bright, hand-painted signs numbered the rows and thoroughfares to guide people around. Crowds were already growing. There were acrobats and tumblers, men hawking song sheets and hymnals, barrows selling hot slab fritters and fried biscuits, a smell of caffeine and sacra and lho-stick smoke, the tapping of tinkers and cobblers at work.

Trinkets were the most common purchases for the rabble crowd, parting gifts and keepsakes and forget-me-nots. Engravers at small stalls worked to mark names onto cheap jewellery and lockets. Ecclesiarchs and trancemissionaries sold safeguard charms and rosaries; prophylactics against harm, the eternal protection of the God-Emperor. They also handed out pamphlets and treatises for uplifting consolation during the voyage. Blessings were obtainable, and so were sermons, delivered from portable pulpits. Garlands and posies were sold in abundance, and the victuallers and black-marketeers did a busy trade in foodstuffs, drink and smokes, indulgences for the last night on shore or the long nights in transit.

The crowd parted and a jester came by, clown-masked, striding on stilts. Behind him came a gang of laughing children, most of them regimental offspring. Elodie recognised many of them. Some she knew by name. That little girl was Yoncy. She was one of the ones Juniper minded, so Elodie had come to hear the story. For a while, Yoncy and her brother had been minded by a woman called Aleksa, but Aleksa had passed away and Juniper had taken on the care of them. The children were orphans from Verghast, and they'd been adopted by Tona Criid, a woman officer who'd found them on the battlefield. It turned out later their father wasn't dead at all. He was Major Gol Kolea of C Company. He hadn't wanted to overturn their little lives any further by taking them away from their adoptive mother, so he'd stayed out of it, and just kept an eye on them through Aleksa. Now the boy, Dalin, was a trooper, the adjutant of E Company, and the girl was getting quite big. The regiment had become their family, and had provided for them.

Still, they had suffered and lost a lot. Tragedy had marked their lives. You could see it in them, especially the little girl. From the time she had first seen her, Elodie had detected the most haunting sadness in Yoncy's eyes.

The girl was a pretty little thing though. She raced past after the stilt-clown, giving Elodie a wave. Behind her, letting her run along, came the brother, Dalin. He was in uniform, a fine young man, watching his sister's enjoyment with a smile. A last hour of shore leave for him before duties began. He'd bought a little medal of the Saint on a ribbon, no doubt for his sister.

He saw Elodie.

'Mam,' he said.

'Dalin,' she returned.

'A good day,' he said.

'I would think almost any day is a good day to leave Anzimar,' she replied.

He laughed.

Elodie walked on, past a bottle stall. She saw two Tanith men purchasing flasks of amasec. One of them saw her and suddenly looked guilty. He put the bottle he had been studying back hastily.

'How are you today, mam?' he asked.

'Well, soldier,' she said. His name was Costin. She knew it, because Ban had pointed him out as a man who had known great trouble with drink over the years. He was embarrassed because an officer's woman had seen him buying liquor.

'I was considering a gift,' he said. 'For my good captain, Domor, to mark this making shift. I would otherwise not touch the stuff.'

'You don't have to explain yourself, soldier,' she said.

But perhaps he did. As a hostess in the clubs of Balhaut, Elodie had observed much about the relationship between men and their poisons. Costin was clearly a sot. The raw redness of his face told her that. He drank quantity, not quality, or his Guard pay would not stretch to cover his habit. He was the sort of man who would brew his own sacra to ensure a cheap supply.

So why would he be purchasing a fine bottle of amasec that ought to be locked in a colonel's tantalus? Was it truly a gift as he said? Where would a man like Costin get that sort of money?

She reached the tailor's stall on the fifth row and joined a short queue that was being entertained by a fire-eater. Sixteen Valkyrie assault carriers wailed overhead in formation. Elodie watched the entertainer, oiled and lithe, caper as he blew cones of flame from his burning wands.

'Quite a trick,' said a voice from beside her. 'I tried to learn it once, in the hope that it might impress the mamzels.'

She turned and found Commissar Blenner standing in the queue behind her. He smiled and doffed his cap.

'Good day, Lady Daur,' he said.

'Not quite lady yet, sir.'

'You should see about that,' he replied.

'Really?'

'Yes, before–'

Blenner paused, as if he had strayed into territory he regretted.

'I always believe,' he said, changing tack, 'that sensible provision is the greatest defence against the vagaries of war.'

'I'll bear that in mind, sir.'

'Please,' he said, 'a blind man could see you are no soldier, so there is no need to address me like one. Vaynom, I insist.'

Commissar Blenner had, like her, joined the regiment at Balhaut. He was, Ban had told her, an old friend of the commander's, and he'd been brought in to supplement the Tanith First's commissar strength, now that Commissar Hark's work had become so specialised.

Elodie had encountered Blenner at several formal dinners. He didn't look like a soldier. He seemed a little pudgy and unfit, a touch bloated from an easy life of inaction. He looked like an Administratum clerk dressed up as a soldier. He had, perhaps, been handsome once, but he was no longer as handsome as he thought he was, and his roguish manner was a little obnoxious. Elodie had met his type many times in the clubs of Balhaut. Privileged, silver-tongued, charming enough to like. But you'd always wonder where he was going to put his hands.

'You are here for the tailor?' she asked.

'Indeed,' he said. 'My coat is being stitched. I have an influx to greet. Duty calls us all.'

It was her turn. She took Daur's jacket from the tailor, inspected the work, and paid.

'Good day, sir,' she said to Blenner. 'May we all make shift safely.'

'The Emperor protects, dear lady,' he replied. He watched her walk away. The view was worth the effort.

'Now, where's my damn coat?' he said to the tailor.

BLENNER PUT ON his stormcoat as he walked through the crowd. No one, not even the enforcers' serjeants-at-arms policing the revels, got in a commissar's way. He crossed a small yard where men were playing camp ball, and entered the infirmary.

Inside, a big Tanith thug was stripped to the waist and sitting backwards on a wooden chair while one of the orderlies, a skinny fellow still wearing his medical smock, applied a tattoo to his shoulder blade with an outsized needle. Blenner stood for a moment, watching in fascination. The man was big and hairy, and smelled of liquid promethium. This wasn't his first piece of ink.

The new tattoo, half done, was a playing card, the King of Knives. Colour would be added later.

'Is that really an appropriate use of medical facilities?' Blenner asked.

The orderly jumped up, realising Blenner was there. His smock was clean, but his fingers were permanently stained with blue ink. He had a cup full of needles. The man receiving the tattoo turned his big, bearded face and looked over his shoulder at Blenner. He made no attempt to get up or show respect.

'I'm sorry sir, I had a moment,' said the orderly.

'You do this work?' Blenner asked, peering at the tattoo.

'I've always done it, sir.'

'He's good with needles,' said the big man.

'What's your name?' asked Blenner.

'Lesp, sir,' said the orderly.

Lesp. *Lesp.* So many new names and faces to remember.

'What is that?' Blenner asked, gesturing to the tattoo.

'King of Knives, sir,' said Lesp.

'The Suicide King,' growled the big man.

'And what's your name?' Blenner asked.

'Brostin,' he said.

'You know what, Trooper Brostin?' said Blenner. 'I think you should get up off your arse and show me some civility.'

Brostin got up. He looked down at Blenner. He stank of fire-grease.

'Don't you like my ink?' he asked.

'I don't like your attitude,' replied Blenner.

'Life's full of disappointments,' said Brostin. 'Sir,' he added.

'What does it signify, the King?' Blenner asked.

'It's what I'm going to be, isn't it?' said Brostin. 'B Company, first platoon. We're going to be the Suicide Kings.'

B Company, Blenner thought.

'You're one of Rawne's?'

'I belong to Rawne and I belong to the fire,' said Brostin. 'I have done since before I belonged to the Guard.'

Blenner looked at Lesp.

'This isn't a suitable place to conduct this kind of business,' he said.

'Sir.'

'I should have you both up on a damn charge.'

'Is there a problem?' asked a quiet voice.

Blenner turned, and found himself face to face with the regiment's new medicae. The man had joined the company at Balhaut, just like Blenner. Blenner didn't have much time for him. The man's name was Kolding, a civilian drafted in by Gaunt. He was an albino, which Blenner had a little trouble with. It was off-putting. Kolding's skin was pale, and his eyes were always hidden behind dark glasses. His voice was soft and colourless too.

Blenner's main problem with Kolding was that the man was a death doctor, a mortician, an examiner of corpses. In Blenner's considerable opinion, Kolding had no business practising on the living. Blenner couldn't fathom what Gaunt saw in the man.

'I came in here,' said Blenner, 'and I found this activity going on. It's not good enough.'

'Why?' asked Kolding quietly.

'Because–' Blenner began. '*Because.*'

Doctor Curth came into the room behind the albino.

'Lesp is one of the regiment's most sought-after inkers, commissar,' she said.

Doctor Curth had entered carrying a stainless steel tray of clean instruments. She was looking at him intently. Blenner liked her. She was a handsome, slender woman. He'd often imagined her looking at him with that sort of intensity. Except that this felt uncomfortable, as though she was deciding where to make an incision.

'This is filthy and unauthorised, doctor,' Blenner said.

'I'll handle this, doctor,' she said to Kolding, who nodded and walked out of the room.

'Let's talk about it in here,' Curth told Blenner. She glanced back at Lesp and Brostin, and said, 'You two, get on. Finish later.'

She led Blenner into her small consulting room.

'Lesp is an artist. Ink is important, especially to the Tanith, though the Verghast and Belladon men are taking to it.'

'There is a matter of uniform code–'

'Certain regulations have always been overlooked when it comes to the Tanith and their ink,' she said. 'There is a long established precedent. To make a discipline issue out of it now would be unwise.'

'There is a health issue,' he replied. 'Ink and needles… This is supposed to be a hygienic area.'

'I can't think of a better place to keep the tools sterile, can you?' she asked. 'I'd rather they did it here, where needles can be boiled and tattoos dressed than have to treat men for infections caught from filthy backroom work.'

Blenner opened his mouth, and then closed it again.

'I… see I have a good deal yet to learn about the operation of this regiment, doctor. Can I call you Ana?'

'No, commissar. That wouldn't be seemly. Now, how can I help you?'

'I just stopped by for a moment.'

'You did,' she said. 'You look stressed. Troubled.'

'Is that a medical opinion?'

'It's the only kind I give.'

'I was hoping to see the doctor.'

Curth hesitated, and pursed her lips.

'I *am* a doctor, commissar.'

'And quite the most fragrant I've ever seen,' he said. 'But I wanted to consult with a male doctor. Privately.'

Curth nodded. She wasn't surprised, especially with a lizard like Blenner. She honestly had no idea why Gaunt tolerated him. He undoubtedly needed powder for some pox he'd picked up, and was too ashamed to let her examine his pathetic genitals.

'Doctor Kolding is—'

'Doctor Dorden,' said Blenner firmly.

'I don't really want to disturb Doctor Dorden,' she said.

'I do,' he replied.

Curth sighed, and got up. She went to the door of Dorden's room and knocked.

'Commissar Blenner wants to see you,' she called.

'One moment. I was just about to step out.'

'He says it won't take long,' said Curth. She looked at Blenner, who nodded his head to concur.

'Send him in.'

Dorden, the regiment's chief medicae, was sitting behind his desk swallowing, with the aid of a glass of water, the last of the six pills he took every two hours. There was no longer any disguising his weight loss and the thinning of his hair. His illness was not a secret, but it was not discussed. All Blenner knew was that the man had already out-lived every prognosis.

Blenner closed the door behind him.

'How can I help you?' asked Dorden.

'I would like you to give me something,' said Blenner.

'What, exactly?'

'A tonic, sir, a remedy.'

'For what, commissar?'

'That which ails me, doctor.' Blenner forced out a merry laugh.

Dorden did not smile.

'I don't have all day,' Dorden said. 'Well, I hope I do, but I don't know how many more days after that I'll get. So if you'd cut to the matter directly.'

Blenner cleared his throat.

'I'm afraid,' he said.

'We're all afraid. Throne, I know I am.'

'Forgive me, but I am serious. I am quite un-manned by it.'

'So get a grip.'

'Doctor, I have to lead these men.'

'You've led men before,' said Dorden. 'You've had a long career. Who were you with before us? The Greygorians? You've seen action.'

'Look, between you and me,' said Blenner, sitting down opposite Dorden and leaning forwards, 'life with the Greygorians was pretty charmed. I mean, Throne! It was a ceremonial detail. We did marching and pomp and colour drills. It was a life of bloody luxury!'

'I've heard you talk, at length, about your exploits under fire,' said Dorden.

'Yes, well. I tell a good story.'

'Does Gaunt know this? He brought you into our company.'

'He must know. Throne, I don't know. He knew what I was like back when we were at scholam. I haven't changed. He must know.'

Dorden steepled his thin, white fingers.

'Vaynom,' he said, 'we are on the eve of making shift on a mission so significant, we haven't even been told the parameters yet. Everyone is apprehensive. It's perfectly natural.'

'But—'

'Vaynom, what are you scared of? Is it dying?'

'Throne, I'm not ready to die!' Blenner spluttered. 'I haven't made my peace yet! You might be braced for it, but I surely—'

He stopped and looked at the doctor.

'That was a terrible thing to say. I apologise.'

'No need. You're right. I'm ready. What we're heading for doesn't frighten me at all.'

'Well, I'd like a little of whatever you're having, then,' said Blenner.

'That can be arranged,' said Dorden. 'Look, Vaynom,

I wonder if this is actually not about dying. I wonder if what you're really afraid of is being found out. I wonder if you're scared about being put in the line of fire and letting him down.'

Blenner sighed.

'Damn,' he said, 'I hadn't even considered that. I was still hung up on the dying part.'

Dorden smiled. He got up and took a small brown bottle down from a crowded shelf. He handed it to Blenner. It was full of little oval pills.

'One of these every day, or when you feel agitated. They will improve your fortitude and help you think clearly. Come to me when you need more.'

'Thank you, doctor,' said Blenner. 'Now listen. I don't want this–'

'I can assure you that what's just passed between us will remain in confidence.'

'Thank you.'

'One last thing, commissar. If you really want to fortify yourself, you should do what I'm about to do.'

'Yes?' said Blenner.

'Prayer and worship, commissar. I have become a regular shrine-goer. I think it's kept me alive longer than any pills. Look after the soul, and it benefits the man built around it.'

SHORE SERVICES WERE usually held in the camp chapel, but during the Makeshift Revels, the ecclesiarchs had taken to preaching and blessing in the open, out in the fair.

Ayatani Zweil was just beginning his morning address when Dorden arrived. Zweil was standing on a munitions box, codex in hand, with two young boys from the camp train stood either side of him swinging censers. They looked bored, but he'd paid them to do it. He'd chosen a site at the end of one of the stall rows, and a crowd had gathered. Dorden joined the back of it.

'The Saint, Saint Sabbat, made these worlds,' Zweil

said. 'She made these worlds with her grace for us to live in, and that's why we're fighting to free them. She watches us, you see. When we work and fight and sleep and eat. She even watches us when we're on the privy, which is disconcerting, I know, yet reassuring. Where was I?'

The old priest's sermons were certainly unconventional. When he had finished, he came down through the dispersing crowd to find Dorden.

'I'm always happy every morning to see you in my congregation,' he said, taking Dorden's hands.

'Because I'm evidence of another soul brought into the fold?'

'No, just pleased you haven't died in your sleep. I had a dream.'

'You do have those...'

'Last night. Lovely young ladies in it. Very distracting. Then I had another dream. The Saint came to me.'

'Did she?' asked Dorden.

'No, she was busy with something else, so she sent a dog. The dog said, ayatani, it said, you have to pray and do good works. It's your job to make sure that Dorden outlives you.'

'I see.'

'Have I told you this before?'

'Yes, last week.'

'Ah, I ought to get some new material. Maybe a parable. Parables are good. I had one once, a very nice blue it was, but rather too tight.'

'You don't really know what a parable is, do you?'

'How obvious *is* that?'

'Father, coming to you each day to pray is doing me good. I know it. I have been granted more life than I had reason to expect.'

Zweil took him by the arm and they began to walk along the bustling row, two old men together. The boys with the censers followed.

'I'm going to look after you,' said Zweil. 'I am. It's only right. I sort of got you in this terrible pickle. If I hadn't swapped blood samples on you, it would have been me with the cancer.'

'Father, medicine's not really a strong field of expertise for you either, is it?'

'Balls. I know what I mean. I'm going to look after you. Of course, taking you to war's probably not the best plan in that case.'

'I've always liked the Makeshift Revels,' said Dorden. 'Great spirit to them. Great anticipation.'

'Bag o'nails.'

'What?'

'Bag o'nails. It's another name for these revels. A corruption, you see, from "bacchanals". I'm thinking of getting a tattoo. The face of the beati. Your boy Lesp, he does ink, doesn't he?'

'Yes.'

'Good. The beati. With illumined clouds.'

'Where are you going to get it?'

'Here on Menazoid Sigma,' said Zweil. 'Oh, now doesn't *he* look disturbingly smart!'

They had crossed the path of trooper Wes Maggs. Maggs was wearing full dress uniform and looked very uncomfortable.

'Don't mock me, father,' he said. 'I hate getting gussied up.' The uniform was a blue so dark it was almost black, with silver braiding and insignia, including the old 81st emblem. There was a red sash, silver aiguillettes and, on the left breast, the formal medal of Belladon: the belladonna flower, its stylised scarlet petals shedding a single drop of blood like a tear.

'What's this all in aid of?' asked Dorden.

'I'm part of the honour guard,' said Maggs. 'For the influx. I don't know why they picked me. I don't do ceremonial.'

'Which influx?' asked Dorden.

'The Belladon one,' said Maggs.

'Don't keep them waiting,' said Zweil.

'Is it true?' asked Dorden.

'Is what true, doctor?' asked Maggs, fiddling with his cap band.

'About Wilder?'

'So I hear,' Maggs called as he hurried away.

'YOU'RE LATE,' SAID Major Baskevyl as Maggs ran up.

'Sorry, sir.'

'Take your place.'

Two full companies had assembled on the landing skirts in dress uniform. Banners were flapping in the wind. There was the flower of Belladon and the Tanith crest. The landing ship had just come in.

'Stand ready,' said Baskevyl as he walked to join the other officers. D Company was his, and F belonged to Ferdy Kolosim. Both companies snapped to attention. Kolosim nodded as Baskevyl approached.

'A good day for us,' said Kolosim. 'A new company. A *Belladon* company. Yes, sir. Just the sort of reinforcements this regiment needs.'

'This regiment does all right,' said Baskevyl. 'But the point is well made.'

'Is it true? It's Wilder's brother?' asked Captain Sloman.

'That's what I hear,' Baskevyl replied. 'It's his brother. He personally requested the transfer to join us. They've been trying to catch up with us for three years.'

'Just in time for this show,' said Kolosim. 'Do we know what sort of strength he's bringing? A full company? What specialism?'

'We don't know anything,' said Baskevyl.

'We could use heavy infantry,' said Sloman. 'Maybe some serious crew weapons.'

'Start showing those damn Tanith scouts how to fight a war Belladon style,' said Kolosim.

They all heard something. A sudden loud crash and blast.

'What the–?' murmured Baskevyl.

Drums. Marching drums, rattling and hissing, beating a perfect pace. Cymbals. The thud of bass kettles. Over that, suddenly like sirens, the bellow and parp of brass.

The reinforcement company came down the ramp of the landing ship into the suns-light to meet them.

'Is this a joke?' said Ferdy Kolosim.

It was a full colours band. They came out in match step, hammering their slung drums. The brass of their instruments gleamed. Their banners were bright and crisply new. At least half of the musicians were women.

'Fury of Belladon…' said Sloman.

'Quiet!' snapped Kolosim.

The band wheeled and marched until it was formed up and facing the reception guard. Their parade drill and formation work was certainly impeccable. They halted, and the bandmaster timed the music to a precise finish.

He stepped forwards beside his commanding officer to meet Baskevyl's group.

'Major Baskevyl, Tanith First,' said Baskevyl, taking the salute. 'With me, Captain Kolosim, Captain Sloman and Commissar Blenner. Commissar Blenner has been recently instructed to focus on discipline for the Belladon contingent.'

'An honour,' snapped Blenner.

Baskevyl was relieved to see Blenner. The commissar had arrived late, only taking his place during the band display.

'Captain Jakub Wilder,' said the commander. 'This is Bandmaster Sergeant Major Yerolemew.'

Baskevyl could see it. Wilder had the look of his late brother, the man who had led the 81st and been Baskevyl's commander and friend. Lucian Wilder, war hero, had given his last command on Ancreon Sextus more than five years earlier. Jakub looked like a younger, slighter version.

'We stand ready to join the Tanith First,' said Wilder. He held out a scrolled document with a red ribbon to Baskevyl. 'Our attachment paperwork is in order, and has been approved by the Munitorum.'

'You're a ceremonial band,' said Kolosim.

'Three sections, with a fourth reserve,' said Wilder.

'The thing is, we don't... we don't really need a marching band,' said Kolosim.

'Captain Kolosim means,' said Baskevyl quickly, 'that we weren't expecting to have the ceremonial aspect of our regiment enhanced in this way.'

'We don't just play instruments. We have weapons,' said Wilder, his mouth tight. 'We know how to fight.'

'No insult was intended,' said Baskevyl.

'If I may?' asked the bandmaster, stepping forwards. He was a tall, older man, with a lined face and a vague trace of white hair. He wore a mighty, square-cut beard and a monocle. In his left hand was his golden baton. He had no right hand. The right sleeve of his long tunic coat was pinned up, empty.

'Nearly seven years ago, we were instructed to join the 81st,' he said. 'Captain Wilder, my commander's brother, had requested us, for morale purposes.'

I remember, thought Baskevyl. I remember him saying 'I've written for them to send us a band, Bask. I think it'll put a spring in our step.' Throne, I thought he was joking.

'You know what transit connections can be like,' said Yerolemew. 'We were delayed. We arrived at Ancreon Sextus long after you had departed. I assumed we would be rerouted to join another Belladon regiment. But Captain Wilder here, he... he was very keen to join his late brother's command. He got himself assigned to us and pushed for the posting to be ratified.'

'It's difficult,' said Wilder. 'There were other delays. A squad of bandsmen and their instruments is easily subbed out for a combat team if transport is limited. We were always a lower priority. But I wanted to be here. *We* wanted to be here.'

He swallowed hard. Baskevyl saw a boy trying to do his best, desperate not to let down his big brother. He made the sign of the aquila and held out his hand.

'I knew your brother,' Baskevyl said. 'It was an honour to call him friend. And it's an honour to have you here. Welcome to the Tanith First, Captain Wilder.'

At his side, Commissar Blenner palmed another pill from the bottle in his stormcoat pocket, dry-swallowed it behind a pretend cough, and then smiled.

He felt better already. Whatever the poor doctor had given him was splendid stuff.

A colours band. A *colours band*. He could manage that. It was precisely his kind of thing. Soldiers, but without the annoying *fighting* part.

'WHAT THE FETH?' murmured Larkin. 'Is that a band?'

'Nah, you've been at the hard stuff again, you mad old bugger,' replied Jessi Banda. 'It's a hallucination.'

'Actually,' said Raess, 'Larks is right. It's a fething colours band.'

With Larkin in the lead, ten company marksmen, the ten best, had been making their way through the revel crowds together. The going was slow, because the old sniper wasn't as fast on his feet as he used to be. He limped on the artificial foot. Mad or not, they were all deferential to him, even the cocky Verghastite Banda and the hard-as-nails Belladon Questa. They all had lanyards, but Larkin could outshoot any of them.

The crowd had parted, affording them a brief view down onto the landing skirts where the transports were coming and going. They could see the Belladon banners, the flash of suns-light on brass.

'Throne,' muttered Lyndon Questa. 'My lot have brought a bloody band with them.'

'Good to see the Belladon adding to the combat

strength of the regiment,' said Banda.

'Screw you,' said Questa.

'In your dreams,' she smiled.

Nessa signed a question, and Larkin signed back, pointing her towards the scene below. She hadn't heard the drumming.

A smile crossed her face.

'Do they sound good?' she asked.

'Yes, that's the important bit to focus on, Nessa,' said Banda.

They left the crowd and entered a loading dock hall where Munitorum crews and servitors were unloading supply crates from long-bed trucks.

'What are we gn... gn... gn... doing here, Larkin?' asked Merrt, his crude augmetic jaw forcing his trade-mark stammer.

'It's a surprise,' said Larkin. 'Gather round.'

A group of Tanith lasmen were already present, led by Captain Domor.

'Morning, Shoggy,' said Larkin.

'What's this all about?' asked Domor.

'Well,' said Larkin. 'Commander said we're going to be doing some specialist training, didn't he? My shooters, your boys?'

'Yes, but he didn't say what, and he didn't say why,' said Domor.

'Ah, but one has got to be smart,' said Larkin. 'One has got to sneak past Gaunt's adjutant, perhaps by distract-ing him. I find Banda works well.'

'Beltayn's putty in my hands,' purred Banda.

'Then, while Bel's got his hands full–' said Larkin.

'Metaphorically speaking,' Banda put in.

'–one has got to take a look at the regimental supply manifests. See what sort of kit is coming in, and who it's been assigned to. One can then build a picture.'

'Is one going to share this picture,' asked Raglon, 'or is one going to get a punch in the mouth?'

'Patience, Rags,' said Larkin. He hobbled over to a stack of crates. 'These are yours, Shoggy. Full of kit for your boys. These are mine. Give me that crowbar, Raess.'

Raess handed Larkin the bar. The old marksman began to lever the lip off one crate.

'You can't do that!' a Munitorum tech exclaimed.

'Feth off,' Banda growled at him. The man scurried away.

'Well, look at that,' said Larkin, lifting the first item out of the packing crate with a smile.

'What in the name of the God-Emperor is this?' asked Raess.

'Hard-round rifles,' said Banda, taking one for herself. 'Old, shoddy, bolt action hard-round rifles. What the gak?'

'What's this ammo?' asked Questa. He held up a large calibre round. It had a brass firing cap and a head that looked like it was made of glass.

'I want my longlas,' said Banda. 'I don't want this.'

'What are we supposed to be hunting?' asked Nessa.

Larkin tucked the rifle he was holding up to his cheek, eased the old but well-maintained bolt action, and took a sample aim.

'Larisel,' he said. 'Like in the old days.'

'The old coot's finally lost it,' said Banda.

Larkin swept his aim, and suddenly found he had a target squared in his iron sights.

'Sorry!' he exclaimed, lowering the rifle. 'Didn't see you there, mam.'

'I'm looking for Captain Daur,' said Elodie.

'He's down at hall two, mam,' said Domor. 'For the influx reception.'

'Oh, right,' said Elodie. She was holding the dress jacket. 'I thought he said four. Thank you.'

She hurried back out into the suns-light.

'Are you going to explain?' Raess asked Larkin.

'Certainly,' said Larkin, still savouring the feel of the weapon.

'And why am I here, exactly?' asked Merrt. 'You know I can't gn… gn… gn… shoot any more.'

'Merrt, my friend,' said Larkin. 'You were the best shot I ever saw. I've decided I'm going to teach you how to do it again.'

'I'M SORRY I'M late,' said Elodie. 'I got lost.'

'It doesn't matter,' said Daur. He took the jacket from her and kissed her cheek. 'I've got time yet.'

'Do you need me?'

'No,' he said. 'I can take it from here.'

'I'll see you later, then,' said Elodie.

'There is one thing I wanted to talk to you about,' he said.

'It can wait until you're done with this,' she said, and slipped away.

Back at their quarters, she tidied a few things away. She hoped she hadn't caused a problem by being tardy with the jacket.

Elodie started packing. Under a small pile of books in a locker drawer, she found a small set of documents.

Petition for Allowance to Marry, the papers said.

BAN DAUR PUT on his dress jacket and buttoned it up. Then he put on his cap and buckled on his officer's strap and holster.

Major Kolea appeared in the doorway, flanked by Commissar Ludd. Both were in full dress too.

'Are you ready now?' asked Kolea.

'Yes.'

They walked out through the depot hall on top of the oil-stained landing apron in front of it. The Arvus lighter had just set down. Steam was weeping from its drive vents.

Flanked by a small honour guard of Tanith and Verghastite troopers, Daur, Kolea and Ludd approached the small craft. Its hatch was opening.

Six figures stepped out. The four leading the way were dressed in a uniform that made Daur's heart swell with unexpected pride. Blue, with a spiked helmet. Verghastite Hive Guard, very similar to the PDF uniform he'd worn back in the day at Vervunhive.

Two were Guard escorts, one of whom was carrying a double-headed eagle on a leather gauntlet. The eagle, cybernetically modified, was hooded. It twitched and ruffled its feathers.

The tallest figure was a woman, wearing the rank pins of a major. She was older, strong and slightly haggard. The other, shorter, was a female captain.

'Major Pasha Petrushkevskaya,' said the older woman. She made the sign of the aquila. 'Reporting for duty to serve the Tanith First.'

'Welcome,' said Kolea.

'I have six full companies,' Petrushkevskaya said. 'All Verghast-born and founded. They await in orbit to transfer to your vessels. They are bursting with pride to follow in the great tradition and join, at last, the regiment of the People's Hero.'

'I am Major Gol Kolea.'

Petrushkevskaya saluted.

'Your name is also celebrated,' she said. 'The great scratch company hero. It is an honour.'

'Thank you,' said Kolea. 'Though I understand you also served in the scratch companies during the Zoican War.'

'We never met,' said Petrushkevskaya.

'It was a big war,' said Kolea.

She nodded.

'This is my second in command,' she said, gesturing to the smaller, younger woman at her side. 'Captain Ornella Zhukova.'

'Once of the Hass West PDF Command,' said Daur. He smiled broadly.

'I wasn't sure you'd remember me,' said Zhukova. She was very neatly pretty, with olive skin and short black hair tied in a ponytail. Her features were elegantly symmetrical. 'I was just a junior, and you were a captain.'

'You know each other then?' smiled Kolea.

'A pleasant reunion,' said Zhukova.

Petrushkevskaya stepped back to introduce the other two figures in her party. One was a lithe woman of startling beauty. Her head was shaved to a fine down of hair, emphasising the sculptural arch of her skull. She was wearing an armoured bodyglove and had an astonishingly crafted steel rose in her lapel. The weapon at her hip was shrouded with a red cloth, as was the Verghast custom. She was a civilian, an up-hive lifeguard, Daur realised, a very expensive and capable employee.

The other figure was clearly her principal. He was wearing a plain black bodysuit and boots, a young man no more than fifteen or sixteen years old who had not yet lost the frailty of adolescence. His thin face was striking and narrow, almost feminine in its beauty. His hair was blond.

'This is Meritous Felyx Chass of House Chass,' said Petrushkevskaya.

'Sir,' Kolea and Daur said in unison.

The boy regarded them haughtily.

'Where is Gaunt?' he asked.

'We were sent to greet you,' said Kolea, 'and express the warm–'

'It's not good enough,' said the lifeguard. Her accent was the very hardest end of Verghast. Her lips were as red as the shroud covering her gun.

'It's all right, Maddalena,' said the boy.

'It's certainly not all right,' the lifeguard said. She stepped up to Kolea, face to face.

'Verghast sends six companies to reinforce your regiment,' she said, 'in honour of the debt owed to your commander by our hive, and the People's Hero can't be bothered to receive us in person?'

'That is, unfortunately, the case,' said Kolea.

'This young man,' said the lifeguard, gesturing to the slender boy, 'is Meritous Felyx Chass, of House Chass, grandson of Lord Chass himself. His mother is heir to the House entire. He has come to honour your regiment by joining it as a junior commander. Are you telling me that Ibram Gaunt has something more important to do than greet him?'

'Two things,' said Kolea, his voice perfectly calm. 'First, it's *Colonel-Commissar* Gaunt to you, you arrogant up-hive bitch. And second, yes, on this occasion, he does.'

THREE
Silver, Snake and Scar

TALL DOUBLE DOORS burst open as though they had been rammed by a siege clearance squad, and the band of officers continued on their way down the long colonnade. They were striding swiftly, boots clattering on the marble floor, coat tails trailing, not in step but at the speed of a forced march. Any faster and they would have broken into a run. To either side, along the imposing route, the sentinel guards snapped to rigid attention as the determined figures swept past.

They were officers, with a gaggle of ceremonial guardsmen trotting to keep at their heels. The ceremonials were struggling with sheathed sabres, lances, pennants, standards and pole honours that hadn't been designed to be ported in haste.

The main group was led by a formidable augmented human, his towering frame elongated and buttressed by the frames of bionic articulation that cradled his once virile form. He wore emblems of black carrion birds. Lord Militant Cybon was one of the great architects of the Crusade, and his war record needed no

53

interpretation or explanatory notes. He was a conqueror
of worlds, a Guard commander of the highest distinc-
tion, and had served the great Sabbat Worlds theatre
since the very instigation, at Warmaster Slaydo's side.
He was famously ruthless, and he was famously out of
favour now the warmastery was held by Macaroth, who
looked to younger blood.

Almost at Cybon's side was Isiah Mercure, a senior figure in the sector's Commissariat, head of the Intelligence
Division. Far shorter than Cybon, upholstered in sallow
flesh, Mercure was a grey-haired man with pock-marked
skin. He somehow radiated just as much presence and
authority as the regal lord militant.

Behind those two came four figures in pristine Com-
missariat uniforms, three males and a female: Viktor
Hark, the robust and powerful senior commissar of the
Tanith First; Nahum Ludd, his young and earnest junior;
Usain Edur, the regal, dark-skinned commissar serving
Mercure as his aide; Luna Fazekiel, a senior commissar
from Mercure's division.

Behind them, and in front of the struggling ceremonial
guard, strode a man whose stark, black garb combined
the uniform of an Imperial commissar and the authority
of a colonel of the Guard. He was tall and lean, and his
narrow face, made hollow by care, had the steel threat of
an unsheathed weapon about it because of the peculiar
quality of his eyes.

The man's name was Ibram Gaunt.

Without even breaking stride, Cybon raised his left
hand and delivered it like a breaching post. The blow
opened another set of double doors, which slammed
against the colonnade walls. Another line of sentinel
guards flew to attention, eyes front. The party swept on.

'Should we wait for the Administratum envoys?' Edur
called.

'Screw them,' Cybon growled.

'There are formalities, protocols,' Edur said.

'Screw protocols,' said Cybon.

To the left of them, a row of tall windows looked out onto the Anzimar Landing Fields. Lighters and transports hove in through the morning smog towards the main rockcrete aprons. Vendetta gunships roosted like hawks on the sky shield platforms that sprouted around the defence work of the field perimeter like a wreath. Gaunt saw the ship, the armoured ship, out on its own at one corner of the apron, re-entry heat still fuming off its hull in the damp air. The field crews were keeping a respectful distance. It was an Imperial machine, but it wasn't a pattern used by the Guard or the Navy.

Another set of doors smashed open. Ahead of them lay the entrance to the audience hall. Gilded doors, four times the height of a man, wrought with bas relief lions and carnodons, eagles and angels. Angels of death.

Appropriate, thought Ibram Gaunt.

It was the first set of doors they had come to that Cybon hadn't smashed open as if he was conducting an insertion raid. He and Mercure simply halted. After a half-second for the cue to sink in, Hark and Edur stepped around them, and opened the doors.

The room beyond the doors was vast, stone flagged and dressed with tall, stained-glass windows that turned the light into autumnal colours. High, clerestory levels stole more daylight from above the morning smog, and shed it down in silver beams between dark vault arches. A giant brass aquila had been inlaid into the centre of the floor.

Three figures awaited them under the chamber's largest window, a vast roundel rendering the Golden Throne in multicoloured glass.

One sat on a wooden bench seat, brooding. The second had his back to the door, gazing up at the stained glass vision. The third loitered nearby, examining some food and drink that had been presented on a small table. It was hard to tell whether the third figure was debating

if he was in need of refreshment, or simply puzzling as
to what food was for.

All three were male, but none of them were men.
None of them were even slightly men.

'Holy Terra,' whispered Ludd.

'That's the general idea,' muttered Hark.

The lord militant stepped forwards.

'I am Cybon,' he declared, altering the volume of his
augmetic voice box to declamatory mode. 'Who am I
addressing?'

The three figures looked up. Their eyes locked onto
him like targeting systems. This was not a fanciful
impression. Their eyes were literally biologic, autonomic
targeting systems, their scrutiny instantly assessing range,
movement, identity and armour. To be stared at was to
be in crosshairs.

'I am Cybon, the lord militant repeated firmly.

'Not you,' replied the figure on the bench, without getting up. His accent was thick, as though his language and
inflection had been worn away by dry winds in some
very distant reach of Imperial space.

'I don't think you appreciate who you're speaking to,'
said Cybon.

'I *know* you don't,' replied the figure on the bench. His
massive plate armour was dirty white, edged in crimson.
Ropes of beads and small fetish trophies, along with
what looked like scalps, hung off the plates. His war
helm rested on the bench beside him, his elbows rested
on his knees. His bared head was immaculately shaven
apart from a forked chin beard and a plume topknot of
the blackest hair.

The figure who had been examining the refreshments
was clad in grey plate, with a golden chest ornament
and his Chapter symbol in blue on a red-edged white
field upon his vast shoulder guards. Parts of his armour
were decorated in blue teardrop shapes. He held his
war helm under his arm. He was clean shaven, with

close-cropped black hair that formed small ringlets on his high forehead.

'Him,' he stated, pointing directly past Cybon at Gaunt. His gauntleted fist was huge, the pointing finger like a rifle muzzle with a suppressor attached.

'He's why we're here,' he said, and lowered his hand. His voice was softer than the seated giant's, and his accent more clipped.

'There is a protocol–' Cybon began.

'We care not for your protocol,' said the third figure. His armour was gleaming silver with traceries of white enamel. His voice was just an augmetic rasp. 'He's why we're here. He's the one we will deal with.'

Cybon hesitated, but decided not to reply. Mercure glowered and scratched his neck. Fazekiel swallowed hard. Edur, Hark and Ludd glanced back at Gaunt. The ceremonial guard had decided that it might be better to hover in the doorway than actually enter the chamber.

Gaunt stepped past the members of his party and walked across the chamber towards the three figures. He walked directly across the brass eagle scored into the flagstones and stopped face to face with the third figure in front of the window. He took off his cap, tucked it under his left arm, and made the sign of the aquila across his breast.

'Colonel-Commissar Ibram Gaunt,' he said.

The third figure glared down at him.

'Veegum said you'd seem small,' he rumbled. 'I forget how small human small is.'

'I didn't know if the Chapter Master would even consider my request,' said Gaunt. 'The fact that three of you–'

'Three's all you get,' murmured the figure in grey.

'We don't want to be here,' said the figure on the bench, rising. The bench creaked painfully.

'There are more significant actions we should be involved in,' said the figure in silver. 'This is a waste of our strength, even just three of us. But my Chapter Master made the petition personally. Your estimation is six weeks' operational time?'

'Yes,' said Gaunt. 'Transit included. And transit time permitting.'

'And we make shift tonight?' asked the figure in white.

'Yes,' said Gaunt. He took an encrypted memory wafer out of his coat pocket and handed it to the silver giant. 'Strategic evaluation. Everything we have so far, plus tactical proposals.'

The silver giant took the tiny sliver and passed it to the giant in white without looking at it. The bearded figure slotted the wafer into a data processor on the cuff of his vambrace. There was a low hum, and small hololithic images began to generate and rotate in the palm of his hand.

'May I know you?' asked Gaunt.

'Brother-Sergeant Eadwine, Silver Guard,' said the silver giant, tapping his own chestplate. He gestured at the giant in grey.

'Brother Kater Holofurnace, Iron Snakes.'

He indicated the figure in white.

'Brother Sar Af, White Scars.'

'Who made these tactical assessments?' asked the White Scar, still reading the hololith display.

'The basics were drafted by Strategic Operations,' replied Gaunt, 'but the better parts were modifications made by my men. The regimental scouts, in particular.'

'Is it the usual nonsense?' asked the Iron Snake.

Sar Af, the White Scar, ejected the wafer and handed it back to Gaunt.

'It's not actually useless,' he said. 'I've made some initial adjustments. There will be more notes.'

'I look forward to discussing them,' said Gaunt.

'There won't be a discussion,' said Sar Af. 'There will simply be notes.'

'Then I look forward to adjusting them,' said Gaunt.

'You can't do this without us,' said Sar Af, a shadow passing across his face. 'In truth, few can see why this would even be attempted. The odds are long, the risks unrewarding, the objective insubstantial. It's a tiny and extravagant sideshow, and Brother Eadwine's Chapter Master is clearly growing sentimental in his dotage to even humour you over this.'

'If that were true,' said Gaunt, 'you wouldn't even be here.'

'THEY'RE SO...' LUDD whispered. 'They're hostile. Like we're not on the same side.'

'We're on the same side,' Hark muttered.

'But–'

'The Adeptus Astartes Space Marines operate on a different level to us, boy,' said Mercure quietly. 'We fight the same war, wage the same crusade, but their operational context is far removed. They attempt what we cannot even consider. They undertake what unmodified humans cannot. We are brothers in arms, but our paths and concerns seldom overlap. It's simply the Imperial way of war.'

'So if they're here...' Ludd began.

'If the angels of death have come,' hissed Cybon, 'because they deem this operation worthy of their attention, it means Salvation's Reach is going to be an unimaginably bloody hell.'

FOUR
Bonding

LAMPS HAD BEEN lit throughout the complex of the Anzimar Barracks, partly to add to the festival nature of the
Makeshift Revels, mostly to combat the gloom of the
afternoon smog. It was especially oppressive that day,
and would not clear before nightfall. Already, the camp
and landing fields felt as though they were cast in an
evening shade.

Gaunt returned across the outer quadrangle with
Hark, Ludd, Edur and Fazekiel. They could hear exuber-
ant music playing from the halls, the clatter of dishes
and glasses from the refectory. The influx reception was
underway.

'At least we're dressed for it,' said Hark.

'I thought the lord militant was going to become apo-
plectic,' said Ludd, who was still processing the meeting
they were coming from.

'Lords militant don't like to be slighted, Ludd,' said
Hark. 'Not in favour of mere colonels. Not even for that
rare beast the colonel-commissar.'

'Cybon understood the game,' replied Gaunt. 'He was

playing a part too. He knew they would want to make the bond personally, with me. But the Chapter Master wouldn't have looked at my petition if it hadn't come with the explicit backing of Crusade high echelon and a lord militant or two. Cybon was an enabler. He had to be present for form's sake, even if it was just so they could belittle him.'

'Are they ever polite?' asked Ludd.

'They're Space Marines,' said Gaunt.

'But to be so disrespectful to a lord militant–'

'They're powerful beings,' said Gaunt. 'They like to remind people where that power lies.'

'So they're never cordial or–'

'I don't know them, Ludd,' said Gaunt. He stopped sharply and turned to look at the junior. The others came to a halt around them, in the middle of the quad square. 'I've made no particular study of their etiquette.'

'No one knows them,' said Edur quietly.

'They know you, sir,' said Ludd to Gaunt. 'That's what that was about. You're calling in some kind of favour.'

Gaunt's jaw tightened. In the gloom, his eyes seemed haunted by an uncanny light.

'Not a favour,' he said. 'You don't ask the Adeptus Astartes Space Marines for favours. It's about compacts and alliances. It's about doing enough to simply get noticed, so that when you ask them for something, they care who you are.'

'You realise we all look alike to them, don't you?' said Hark.

Ludd laughed, and then realised it wasn't supposed to be a joke.

'What did you do?' he asked.

'What?' asked Gaunt, turning to start walking again.

'What did you do to get noticed?'

'Just enough,' said Gaunt and walked away.

'Balhaut,' said Fazekiel. The others looked at her. 'The Tower of the Plutocrat. The Oligarchy Gate. The infamous Ninth Day,' she said. 'Gaunt's Hyrkans stood alongside the Silver Guard at the height of the battle. He certainly would have had dealings with them, possibly with Veegum himself. His achievements would have brought him to their attention. Perhaps even won their respect. Certainly, made enough of a mark so that years later, when he asked them for help, they would bother considering it.'

She looked at Ludd. She was only a few years his senior, but there seemed a gulf of maturity between them.

'It's all in his case file,' she said. 'Standard biographic data. There's more detail, some of it classified, but not hard for someone with Commissariat clearance to get if they're prepared to dig.'

'You've made a study of him?' asked Ludd.

'You seem surprised,' said Fazekiel. 'I am going to serve under him. I want to know about him so I know what to expect and how best to perform my duty. Any commissar would do the same before attachment to a new command. The surprise, really, would be that you *haven't*.'

'I don't know why I would,' said Ludd, blushing slightly.

'So you don't ask stupid questions at the wrong moment?' Fazekiel suggested.

'I think Nahum is probably a more intuitive servant of the Throne than you, Luna,' said Edur gently.

'It's not a matter of intuition,' she replied. 'It's not a privacy issue, either. It is in no way invasive to study and understand the career record of an officer you're serving. It improves your performance. It's common sense.'

A despatch officer ran up, saluted, and handed Hark a message wafer. Hark acknowledged receipt with a press of his biocoded signet ring. He read the wafer, and then put it in his pocket.

'We should get to work,' he said. 'There are newcomers to accommodate, and final arrangements to be made.

Here's something for you to ponder, Ludd. Fazekiel has accounted for the Silver Guard's presence. But the other two. An Iron Snake and a White Scar. Why three Chapters?'

'I'll find out,' said Ludd. 'Meanwhile, when do the rest arrive?'

'The rest of what?'

'The Space Marines?'

Hark smiled. 'We get three Space Marines, Ludd. Just three. They are rare and they are precious. Long gone are the ages when they marched across the stars in their hundreds or thousands. We're lucky to have three.'

'Under most circumstances,' said Edur, 'three is more than enough.'

'Let's hope this is one of those circumstances,' replied Hark.

'How will you find out, Ludd?' Fazekiel asked.

'I'll ask them,' Ludd replied.

'Why is *that* funny?' he added.

CROWDS HAD GATHERED around the infirmary, forming queues. Most of the regimental community wanted to get out and enjoy the last few hours of the Revels or, if they were permitted, join the influx reception in the barracks hall. They could hear the band music all the way from the infirmary. But there were certificates to get, and that meant getting your shots.

Elodie joined the queue. The regiment's medicaes were administering inoculations to all members of the retinue. The shots were a mix of anti-virals and counterbiotics, and emperythetical electrolytes, intended to protect them from foreign infection and cushion some of the traumas of shift travel. If you didn't have a certificate from the medicaes proving you'd had your shots, you couldn't embark. This time around, Elodie had been told, you also needed a bond.

They were all talking about it in the queue around her.

An accompany bond was a document of disclaimer issued by the Munitorum that showed the bearer understood that he or she was transiting into a warzone. Regimental retinues usually followed their units to reserve line camps or waystations adjacent to the battlefield. For a bond to be necessary this time, it indicated that, for whatever reason, the retinue would be following the Tanith First directly into the line of danger. They would be at risk. Their safety could not be guaranteed. They had to sign a bond to say they understood and accepted this jeopardy, or they could elect to remain behind. The Munitorum hadn't required the Tanith retinue to be bonded since Ouranberg in 771.

It was a hard choice, because remaining behind was a tricky option. For a spouse or a child, or for a tradesman whose livelihood had come to depend on a regiment, remaining behind meant risking never being able to reconnect with the unit. If you missed the shift, you might never get passage to wherever the regiment got posted next. You could spend months or even years trying to catch up with a unit on the move, like that ridiculous band had, so she understood.

For Elodie, it was no choice at all.

'Are you quite well, Mamzel Dutana?' the old doctor, Dorden, asked her when her turn came. He swabbed the crook of her elbow with rubbing alcohol while his orderly prepared a syringe.

'I am, doctor. But there are things on my mind.'

'You are anxious, no doubt, about what awaits us. War wounds us with anxiety from beyond the range of any weapon.'

She nodded.

'You seem untroubled, if I may say so,' she said to the old man. He seemed very frail, but his hands were rock steady, and she felt only a tiny pinch as the needle went in. 'I can only suppose it is because you have done this before?'

'You're not my first patient, Mamzel Dutana.'

'I meant war, doctor.'

'Ah. No, you never get used to that. But you're right, I can't for the life of me recall where I've left my trepidation.'

Elodie went back along the shore, through the revel crowds, a small wad of cotton pressed to her needle mark. She went to the hab shelters that stood in a row behind the laundry tents. It seemed actually to be getting dark, as though true evening was extending through the murky smog.

'Juniper?' she called. 'Juniper?'

The tents smelled strongly of carbolic soap and damp rockcrete.

'Juniper? Are you here?'

She ducked into Juniper's hab and came up short. The woman fuelling the small stove inside wasn't Juniper.

She was a soldier, a sergeant, lean and powerful with cropped white-blonde hair.

'Oh, I'm sorry,' said Elodie.

'You looking for Juniper?' asked Tona Criid.

'Yes.'

'She just stepped away to get bonded,' said Criid. 'I'd come to see Yoncy, so I said I'd stay while she got sorted.'

The little girl that Elodie had seen in the crowd earlier was in the corner of the hab, eating beans from a bowl. She had the medal of the Saint on its ribbon around her neck. Elodie could see that Yoncy wasn't going to be a child for much longer. She was small for her age, and appeared no older than a seven- or eight-year old, but she had to be eleven or twelve at least. Perhaps a life of slab and Guard rations had stunted her growth a bit. Perhaps she was one of those children who would suddenly become a young woman in one adolescent explosion. There was something quite knowing about her, Elodie felt. She still wore her hair in bunches, and swung her feet when she sat on an adult chair to emphasise her size. But it was as though she was slightly playing up the childlike effect, as if she knew it got her treats and favours. Everyone was her uncle or her aunt.

'I wanted to ask her something,' said Elodie. 'I'll come back.'

Criid shrugged as if that was good enough. There was a slight awkwardness, as if they didn't know what to say to each other.

'Actually,' said Elodie, 'can I ask you something?'

Criid closed the stove door, took a look at Yoncy to make sure she was tucking into her food, and then walked over to Elodie.

'For what reason would a soldier take a wife?'

'Apart from the obvious, you mean?' asked Criid.

'Yes, apart from that.'

'There's no better reason than that,' said Criid. 'None of my business, I'm sure, but how you feel is the only important reason.'

Elodie nodded.

'Has Ban asked you a question?' Criid asked.

Elodie shook her head.

Criid shrugged.

'Like I said, not any of my business.'

Elodie took the small fold of papers out of her dress pocket.

'Look at this,' she said quietly.

'Petition for allowance,' said Criid, reading.

'He hasn't said anything. Nothing. But he's got the paperwork. He's filled it in.'

'So what's the problem?' asked Criid, handing the papers back. 'Too fast? You going to say no?'

'No.'

'Good. It'd be bad in all sorts of ways if we go into this with a senior captain nursing a broken heart. Wait, is this about the accompany bond? You don't want to be bonded? Are you staying here?'

'No, no. That's fine. I've got mine.'

'So?' Criid asked.

'I don't know why he hasn't told me.'

'We're moving out in a hurry. It's not romantic, but he wants to get it squared away before we dig in.'

'It just feels like there's another reason,' said Elodie. 'Another reason why he wants to.'

'Is it because he might die?' said the little girl from the other side of the room. They both looked at her. Yoncy had lowered her spoon and was staring at them, half a smile on her face.

'Is it because he might die?' Yoncy repeated. 'He wants to get married in case he dies.'

'Go wash your face,' said Criid. 'You've got gravy all round your mouth.'

Yoncy laughed, and slid down off her chair. She ran into the washroom at the back of the little hab.

'Sorry about that,' said Criid.

'No, I'm sorry. I should have thought about what I was saying. It was insensitive.'

Criid frowned.

'Insensitive? What? Oh, you mean because of Caffran?'

She shrugged as if it was nothing.

'It hurts me he died, not that I didn't get to marry him first. It wouldn't have made a difference to us, a piece of paper. Though it does to some. Some marry, you know, to provide.'

'What do you mean?' asked Elodie.

'If you're not actually married, with a piece of paper to show for it,' said Criid, 'then the Munitorum doesn't recognise you as a widow. So some lasmen marry just to qualify for the viduity benefit. It's not much. Just a few crowns a year, I think, a widow's pension. But it matters to some people.'

'Not to me,' said Elodie. 'Do you think that's why he wants to do this?'

'I don't know. It might matter to him to know that

you'd be provided for. A captain's widow probably gets a better allowance.'

Elodie folded up the papers and put them away.

'Are you all right?' asked Criid.

'Yes. Yes, I'm fine.'

'You look pale. I've said too much.'

'No.'

'You haven't really thought about any of this, have you?' asked Criid.

'I thought I had. It seems I hadn't.'

'Then you'd better,' said Criid. 'He's a soldier. Soldiers die.'

'We all die,' said Elodie.

'Yes,' Criid nodded. 'But not as fast as soldiers.'

GAUNT WALKED UP the steps towards the entrance of the barracks hall. Smog and approaching evening had combined to create a gloom like twilight. The hall windows shone with lamplight.

Beltayn was waiting for him in the entrance way.

'Something's awry,' said Gaunt.

'It's a band, sir,' said Beltayn.

'I can hear what it is, I just couldn't for the life of me explain why.'

'I'll leave that pleasure to Major Baskevyl, sir,' said the adjutant.

'Anything else?' asked Gaunt.

'The new seniors are keen to meet you.'

'Of course. You explained that I was unavoidably detained?'

'I did, sir. Some took it better than others.'

'Anything else?' asked Gaunt.

'Transfers behind just before midnight local,' said Beltayn. He handed Gaunt a data-slate. 'Our transport has been confirmed as the *Highness Ser Armaduke*. It's a frigate, Tempest-class. Whatever that means.'

'So the Fleet couldn't spare a battle cruiser after all.'

'No, sir. Actually, the Fleet didn't spare this either. As I understand it, the *Highness Ser Armaduke* was substantially damaged during the Khulan Wars and has been in the depot reserve for the last twenty-seven years. It's had what I've been told is called "modification refit", but its performance still doesn't allow it to be fully Fleet certified.'

'You're saying it's a piece of scrap that would otherwise have gone to the breakers?'

'I'm not saying that, sir,' said Beltayn, 'because I know nothing about the Navy or shiftship doings. I'm just a common lasman, sir.'

Gaunt looked at the documents on the slate.

'Oh, the faith they show in us. Giving us a ship they don't mind losing because they're pretty certain it's going to be lost.'

'I'll remember to keep that insight to myself, shall I?' asked Beltayn.

'Yes, please,' said Gaunt handing the slate back. 'Anything else?'

'No, sir.'

Gaunt gestured up in the direction of the double-headed eagle that was perched on the head of a large statue of Saint Kiodrus nearby. The eagle ruffled its wings and shuffled on its marble perch.

'Not even that?'

'Doesn't belong to me, sir,' said Beltayn, 'and I didn't put it there.'

Gaunt went into the hall. Long, candle-lit tables were set for dinner, but the assembled guests were generally standing, talking in groups, drinks in their hands. Servitors whirred through the press. Regimental colours – Tanith, Verghastite and Belladon – were in abundant display. On a low stage to one side, the band was playing vigorously.

'Where have you been?' asked Blenner, intercepting him almost at once.

'Oh, you know, colonel-ing and stuff,' said Gaunt.

Blenner had a drink in his hand.

'I hate bashes like this,' he said, leaning close to Gaunt so he could whisper and still be heard over the band.

'The band wasn't your idea, was it?' asked Gaunt.

'Why would you think that?' asked Blenner, looking wounded.

'I don't know,' said Gaunt. 'There's something about it that feels like an elaborate practical joke.'

'Oh, thank you,' said Blenner. He took what appeared to be a pill from his stormcoat pocket and knocked it back with a sip of amasec. He saw Gaunt looking at him.

'What?' he said. 'I've got a headache.'

Kolea was approaching with several officers Gaunt didn't recognise.

'Commander,' said Kolea, 'it's my honour to introduce the senior officers of the new Verghastite influx. Major Pasha Petrushkevskaya and Captain Ornella Zhukova.'

Gaunt saluted them both.

'It's my shame,' he said, 'that I wasn't here to greet you. You've come a long way and you're contributing a great deal.'

'We understand,' said Petrushkevskaya. 'Major Kolea was good enough to explain that you were detained by an important strategic briefing.'

'I was. I am still sorry. Vervunhive has a very, very important place in this regiment. It is an honour to receive reinforcements from Verghast.'

'It is an honour to serve under the People's Hero,' said Zhukova.

'I don't know about that,' said Gaunt.

'Oh, yes,' said Zhukova, bright-eyed. 'To this day, your name is spoken with honour and respect at every level of hive life. Did you know that in Hess West Sector alone, there are four public statues of you? I have picts, if you would like to see them.'

'Thank you, but I'm confident I know what I look like,' said Gaunt.

Zhukova laughed.

'You are certainly more handsome in person,' she said.

'Now, I *really* like her already,' said Blenner, stepping forwards. 'Don't you, Ibram? I really like you, Captain Zhukova. The colonel-commissar is a terrible old bore, and pretends he doesn't like people going on about his heroism, or how handsome he is. But we can all see that for ourselves, can't we? Between you and me, he secretly loves it, and I recommend you do it as often as possible, no matter how much he protests.'

'Blenner,' Gaunt hissed.

'In fact,' Blenner went on, 'the more he protests, the more he secretly likes it.'

'Really?' laughed Zhukova.

'Oh, yes,' said Blenner. 'I should know. I've known him all my life.'

'Have you?' asked Zhukova. This seemed to impress her. 'That must be wonderful. What an example he must have set.'

'I can't begin to tell you,' said Blenner, placing one hand on his heart and tilting his head to the side. 'He's quite inspiring. Although, and few know it…' he dropped his voice and leaned forwards. Zhukova bent forwards to listen, her eyes even wider.

'…I taught him a great deal about life and the deportment of an officer,' said Blenner.

'Did you?' exclaimed Zhukova.

'I don't like to talk about it. It's not as if I'm looking for credit or recognition. It's enough to know that I've helped to shape the character of an Imperial hero.'

'Of course it is,' Zhukova agreed.

'Blenner!' Gaunt hissed, rather more emphatically.

'You're very comely, Captain Zhukova,' said Blenner.

'May I say that? I don't mean to speak out of turn, and I certainly mean nothing inappropriate by it. I speak only as a commissar, in a purely professional regard. My business is the morale and discipline of the fighting lasman, and in that regard, your captivating looks are quite a potent weapon to have in our arsenal. I mean this purely analytically! The men will follow you, obey you. They will be devoted to you, and–'

'Captain Zhukova is well aware of the effect of her looks on the male soldier,' said Petrushkevskaya. She was not smiling. 'Indeed, we have had conversations about it.'

'I'm sure you have, major, I'm sure you have,' said Blenner. 'You understand it too, don't you? The importance of something like that. Just in strategic terms. Now... *Pet-rush-kevs-kaya*... That's right, isn't it? Quite a mouthful. We should think about shortening that to something the men can get their tongues around.'

'Commissar Blenner,' growled Gaunt. 'Major Petrushkevskaya's name is Petrushkevskaya. That's what the men will call her. They'll damn well learn how to say it. Anything else would be disrespectful.'

'Of course,' said Blenner. 'I only meant–'

'It's all right, sir,' said Petrushkevskaya. 'Actually, it has been an issue. I'm generally known as Major Pasha. It's what I was called in the scratch companies, before my rank was official. Sort of an affectionate name, but it has its uses. Simplicity being one of them.'

Gaunt nodded.

'I see,' he said. 'Well, that's fine. Though I generally discourage the ranks from adopting informal names. A lack of discipline in anything, even the form of words, represents a lack of discipline that could spread.'

'That must be why we're called Gaunt's Ghosts,' said Blenner.

Zhukova laughed.

Gaunt had to bite his lip to prevent himself from

snapping at Blenner in front of them. He looked for another outlet to vent at.

'Where did that feth-awful band come from?' he asked.

'Uhm, sir?'

He turned. The others turned with him. Major Baskevyl had joined them, bringing another new face, an officer of Belladon extract. The man's face was oddly familiar, and clearly tinged by anger.

'Sir,' said Baskevyl, 'this is Captain–'

'It's *my* feth-awful band, sir,' said the officer. 'My command is a fighting unit of three sections that happens to carry the role of colours band for ceremonial occasions. Its presence is meant to reflect the martial prowess and splendour of Belladon, and to enhance this regiment. It is honourable and dignified. It has been devoted to the matter of joining this command for years, and has made considerable efforts to arrange transfers to do so. It is the marching band my brother personally requested.'

Gaunt waited a second before replying. He looked the man full in the face.

'You're Wilder's brother.'

'I am.'

'I meant no disrespect. I didn't know your brother–'

'No, you did not. And precious little trace of him remains here. When he took command of this regiment, the previous names were merged. I see all sign of the 81st has now vanished from the regimental title. A revision you made, I presume?'

'The new title was clumsy,' said Gaunt, showing no emotion. 'Belladon has, however, left a profound and positive mark on our ranks, and your brother's stewardship of this regiment, and his legacy, is not forgotten.'

Wilder jutted out his chin a little, but remained silent. Gaunt saluted him.

'Welcome to the Tanith First, Captain Wilder. The Emperor protects.'

Wilder returned the salute.

'Thank you, sir.'

'It must be said, captain, that we were not expecting to be reinforced by a colours band.'

'They're fighting troopers, damn you!' Wilder cried. He swung at Gaunt. His fist stopped dead, the wrist clamped tightly in Blenner's right hand. The speed with which Blenner had moved to intercept was quite impressive.

'I don't think, Captain Wilder,' said Blenner, holding the wrist firmly and speaking directly into Wilder's furious face, 'that striking your commanding officer would be a great way to end your first day in this regiment. It might even be a way of making it your first and *only* day.'

He laughed at his own joke. Zhukova laughed too, brightly and rather over-emphatically. The band had stopped playing and everyone in the hall was watching.

'But it is your first day,' said Blenner calmly and clearly, 'and this is an emotional moment. It has perhaps sharpened your grief over the memory of your brave brother. That's understandable. It's taken you a long time to get here, and you're standing here at last. We've all taken a drink. It's the end of a long day and there are longer ones ahead. So, why don't we make the fresh start here, and not five minutes ago?'

He looked at Gaunt.

'I think that would be a prudent idea,' said Gaunt.

Blenner let Wilder's wrist go. Wilder lowered his hand and straightened up. He smoothed the front of his jacket.

'Thank you,' he said quietly. 'I apologise. Thank you.'

'Nothing more will be said about it,' said Blenner. He raised his glass high and addressed the room.

'Welcome to the Ghosts. Fury of Belladon!'

Fury of Belladon! they all sang back, even Petrushkevskaya and Zhukova, and glasses clinked.

Gaunt turned to the band and gestured encouragingly.

'Play up! I was just getting used to it.'

Sergeant Yerolemew smiled, nodded, and brought the band back into full order. The music blasted out again.

'Deft,' Gaunt whispered to Blenner.

'I have my uses,' Blenner replied.

'I still don't need a band,' Gaunt added quietly. 'Can we see if we can at least lose their instruments in transit?'

'I'll have some people look into it,' whispered Blenner.

'And keep an eye on Wilder. He's trouble.'

'There's an old saying, Ibram. Keep your friends close, and the brother of the dead hero you replaced as commander closer. Or confined to quarters.'

THE UNDERCROFT OF the barrack hall was an extensive warren of vaulted wine cellars, pantries, larders and basements. Light shone out of the noisy scullery. The kitchens were filled with heat and steam and the smell of herbs and roasted meat, and kitchen staffers were loitering in the cool scullery entrance, beaded with sweat, as they took quick breaks between servings. From overhead, the boom and muffled clash of the enthusiastic band rang like a minor seismic disturbance.

Viktor Hark walked down the stairs beside the scullery, through a waiting group of overheated servers and pot boys, and turned left into the main undercroft space. The arched stone was whitewashed, and it was cool and dry, with just the hint of cold brick and the background top note of chemical smog that got into everything in Anzimar.

Lamps had been lit down here. Glow-globes and candles had been set at the long bench table.

First Platoon, B Company, had assembled. Varl and Brostin, Mach Bonin the scout, Kabry and Laydly, LaHurf, Mkaninch and Mktally, Judd Cardass and Cant the Belladonians, Mkrook, Senrab Nomis the Verghastite. Rawne, the presiding genius of B Company and the regiment's second officer, stood in a corner, leaning against the wall.

'Gentlemen,' said Hark, and held up his hand as they began to scrape back chairs and rise. 'As you were.'

There were bottles and glasses on the table, and an earthenware pitcher of water. None of the bottles had been opened.

'Trouble on the island this morning, so I hear,' Hark said to Rawne.

'I handled it,' said Rawne.

'You certainly did,' replied Hark. He reached into his coat, took out the message wafer that had been delivered to him in the quad, and handed it to Rawne.

Rawne unfolded it and read it.

'Congratulations, major,' Hark said.

Rawne allowed himself a small smile. The men began to whoop and pound their fists on the table.

'Further to the incident this morning,' said Hark over the row, 'and in light of the serious security failings demonstrated by Major Rawne, First Platoon, B Company, the Tanith First, is hereby charged with the secure management of the prisoner for the duration of this operation. In such respect, First Platoon, B Company, the Tanith First, will be designated an S Company by the Commissariat for purposes of authority and powers.'

The men whooped even more loudly.

'Major Rawne is supervising officer. I will consult directly on S Company procedure. That's "S" as in security.'

'I thought it was "S" as in special,' Cant called out.

'It's "S" for shut your hole,' replied Cardass. Men laughed.

'One word of advice,' Hark shouted over the hooting and thumping. 'Don't screw this up.'

'Would we, sir?' replied Varl. 'Would we screw anything up? Ever?'

'We screw some things up,' said Bonin.

Varl frowned. 'Yes, we do,' he admitted. He looked at Hark and grinned. 'We'll try really hard not to do that this time, sir,' he said.

'I don't know what I was worried about,' said Hark.

He started to walk towards the exit. 'I'll leave you to it,' he said over his shoulder. 'Your first duty shift starts tonight. You take over when the prisoner is transferred for embarkation.'

'Wait!' Rawne called after him. 'If you're our liaison officer, Commissar Hark, you ought to witness the whole of our little founding.'

The men had quietened down.

'Whose "founding"?' Hark asked, turning back.

Rawne smiled, and picked up an empty ammo box that had been standing on the floor at his feet. He shook it, and metal objects inside it clinked together.

'The Suicide Kings,' Rawne said.

The men whooped and hollered again.

'That's a card game, major,' said Hark.

'Lots of versions of that game around the sector,' Rawne said. He handed the ammo box to Cant, who reached in, rummaged, and took something out. The box then passed to Varl.

'Lots of versions,' Rawne repeated, watching the box get passed around, each man taking something out. 'Lots of variations. The version we call Suicide Kings, that came from Tanith in the first place, you know.'

'I didn't know that,' said Hark.

'The Suicide King himself,' said Rawne, 'in a standard deck, that's the King of Knives.'

'The King of Knives!' Brostin echoed lustily as the box reached him and he took something out of it.

'You see,' Rawne continued, 'the Tanith called the game Suicide Kings because of that card. The King of Knives. You know why?'

'No, but I am convinced you're about to tell me,' said Hark.

Rawne smiled. 'Back in the old times, ages past, the ruler of Tanith, the High King, was protected by a body-guard company. The finest warriors, Nalsheen. They were his close protection, his last line of defence. Instead of blade-tipped staffs, they used straight silver blades, just warknives, so they could close around the High King and protect him with their bodies, and not endanger him with the swings of long reach weapons. It was a great honour for a man to join the bodyguard company, but the chances were he'd die in that service. So when a man took up the duty, the Tanith granted him the powers of king in his own right. The High King was protected by men who had the authority of kings themselves. Absolute power in return for absolute service.'

Rawne looked at Hark.

'They were known as the Suicide Kings,' he said. 'They lived the lives of kings because their lives could end at any second, and they never questioned the sacrifice.'

The box had come back to him. There was one item left in it. Rawne took it out and held it up.

It was a Tanith cap badge, the skull and daggers, but it was dulled down to matt black to hide its glint, and the side daggers had not been snapped off, as was the Tanith custom. A letter 'S' had been etched onto the forehead of the skull. Every man in the room apart from Hark had one.

'That's what we'll be,' Rawne said. 'Suicide Kings. That's what the "S" stands for, and this'll be our mark.'

'You've left the side blades on,' said Hark.

'For this mark,' Rawne nodded. 'Surrounded by straight silver, the way a high king should be.'

'You surprise me with your sentimentality sometimes, major,' said Hark.

'Open the bottles,' Rawne said to Brostin. 'We'll celebrate. Except for the four men who have drawn a badge with a cross scratched on the back.'

The men turned their badges over. Bonin, Mkaninch, Nomis and Laydly had drawn the crosses.

'Water from the jug for you four, because you'll be taking the first turn of duty,' said Rawne. 'Luck of the draw. Sacra for the other kings. And one for the good commissar, I think.'

Hark took the small glass of eye-watering sacra that Mktally passed to him.

'Suicide Kings,' he said, tipping it back.

THOUGH NOT DRUNK, Jakub Wilder was by no means sober. The reception was dire and dull in equal measures, and he'd drunk a skinful to try to blot out the fool he'd made of himself with Gaunt. The man made him sick, made him angry. He should have landed that blow. He should go right back, take out his service pistol and shoot the arrogant bastard between the eyes.

They were serving junk too. Some kind of fortified wine. Wilder wanted a proper drink. A grown up drink.

He left the hall and stood in the open for a while to get some fresh air. When he started to feel cold, he went back inside. He bumped into a woman in the entrance-way. A damn fine looking woman, damn fine, in a blue dress. An officer's wife, probably. An officer's woman.

'I'm sorry, mam,' he said, and realised he was slurring slightly.

'Not at all,' she replied.

There were stairs down into the undercroft. Wilder had seen the servers bringing bottles up from the cellars. Maybe he could find himself some amasec, some of the stuff that had run out so damn fast at the start of the evening.

He went down the stairs. It was cool and gloomy. He could hear the main reception party, and also the sounds of men celebrating something in one of the undercroft spaces. Some private drinking party, no doubt. He'd avoid them.

Wilder found his way to the cage sections of the pantry where the bottles were racked. He shook the bars, but the cages were locked. The storekeeper would have the key. Damn.

'There's always a way to open things,' said a voice from behind him.

Wilder turned. There were three men behind him. They were sitting out of the way in a corner of the pantry area, crowded in around a small table under an arch. Coming in, he hadn't seen them.

'Excuse me?' he said.

They were Tanith. Two were Tanith born and bred. They had the pale skin and the black hair. One was a red-faced, drunken-looking bastard, the other... well, he just looked like a bastard. Handsome but hard-faced, like there was a bad smell right under his nose. He was a captain from his pins, the red-faced sot a common trooper. The third man wore the black uniform of the regiment, but he was fair-skinned and blond. His eyes were watery blue and his hair was thin, like white gold. There was an aristocratic air about him, a slight snootiness. A cross between a haughty aristo and a deep sea fish that never sees the light and becomes translucent.

'I said,' the captain spoke cooly, 'there's always a way to open things.'

'You got a key, have you?' asked Wilder.

'As it happens, I have.' The captain reached into his pocket and held up a small brass key.

'What are you... the pantry keeper?' asked Wilder.

'No,' said the captain. 'I'm the guy who knows how much money to pay the pantry master to get a second key cut.'

'You were looking for a drink?' asked the aristocratic fish, looking down his nose at Wilder with his milky blue eyes. That hair of his, it only looked white gold because it was so thin. It was pale, like his eyelashes. He'd probably been red-headed as a kid. A little snooty kid in the scholam.

'I was looking for a drop of proper amasec,' said Wilder.

'Then you don't even need the key,' said the captain. 'That is, if you'd care to join us.'

Wilder blinked. He realised he was swaying a little, so

he steadied himself against the cellar arch. He realised there was a very expensive bottle of amasec on the table between the three men.

'Don't mind if I do,' he said.

'Get another glass, Costin,' said the captain.

The red-faced drunk reached up onto a side shelf and took down a heavy lead-glass tumbler. He put it on the table and carefully filled all four from the bottle.

'You're Wilder, right?' asked the captain.

'Yes.'

'Welcome to the First,' the captain said. 'I knew your brother. He was a good man. I'm Captain Meryn, E Company. These gentlemen are friends of mine. Trooper Costin.'

The raddled Tanith nodded at Wilder.

'And this is Sergeant Gendler. Didi Gendler.'

'A pleasure,' said the aristo fish. The accent was strong, hard. Wilder had heard enough to know it wasn't Tanith, and it certainly wasn't Belladon.

'You're a Vervunhiver?' he asked.

'No, no,' said Meryn. 'Didi's not just a Vervunhiver. He's not some scum off the bottom of your boot. Are you, Didi?'

'Captain Meryn does like his little jokes,' said Gendler.

'Sergeant Gendler is better than the rest of us,' said Costin. 'It's well known. He's proper breeding, is Sergeant Gendler.'

'I'm just an honest soldier,' said Gendler.

'Didi is nobility,' said Meryn. 'He's up-hive blood. Noble-born to a good main-spine family.'

'Really?' asked Wilder. 'How'd you end up in a shit-hole like this, then?'

Gendler stiffened and his languid eyes narrowed.

'It's all right,' said Wilder. 'No offence meant. I ask myself the same question every morning.'

Meryn grinned. He held up one of the brimming little glasses.

'Come and join us, Captain Wilder.'

Wilder took the glass and pulled up a stool.

'What will we drink to?' he asked. 'What will we talk about?'

'Well, sir,' said Gendler, 'if you're down here and not upstairs, it rather suggests you don't want to be upstairs, or that you're not welcome. Which, in turn, suggests that we've already got something in common, the four of us.'

Wilder looked at the amasec in his glass, and licked his lips.

'I'm down here,' he said, 'because I was sick of that damn party, and I was looking for something to drink to wash away how much I bloody hate the guts of that bastard Gaunt.'

He paused and looked up at the three men sharply, suddenly aware of what he'd said out loud.

'Now, you see?' said Meryn. 'That's something else we have in common.'

FROM THE SHADOWS of an adjacent corner in the under-croft, eyes watched the four men in their huddle. Eszrah Ap Niht, known as Ezra Night, warrior of the Gereon Untill, kept himself in the darkness, and listened to them talk.

'LEAVING THE PARTY early, sir?' asked Elodie, passing Gaunt in the doorway of the barrack hall.

Gaunt stopped and saluted her.

'No, mam,' he said. 'I'm just stepping out to clear my head. The band can be...'

He faltered.

'I can hear what the band can be for myself,' said Elodie, smiling.

Gaunt nodded.

'I just need a moment to collect my thoughts. There are a few matters to attend to. You're looking, if I may be so bold as to say, quite stunning this evening.'

Elodie curtsied playfully. She was very pleased with the fit of her blue dress.

'Thank you, colonel-commissar,' she replied. 'You may be so bold.'

'You're looking for Captain Daur, no doubt?'

'I am. He's inside, isn't he?'

'Yes,' said Gaunt. 'Go join him, and have a very fine last evening on this world.'

ELODIE WENT INTO the hall. It was crowded and busy with noise. Music and conversation, laughter and the chink of glasses. There were several hundred people present, not counting the staff. The band was making an enormous sound.

'Have you seen Captain Daur?' she asked Corporal Chiria, Domor's adjutant.

'I think he's over there, mam,' said Chiria. She pointed.

Elodie looked. She caught sight of Daur. He was talking to a woman. They were clearly friends. They were laughing. The woman was very good looking. She was wearing an officer's uniform.

'Who's that he's talking to?' asked Elodie.

'Her?' answered Chiria. 'That's Captain Zhukova. She's influx, arrived today. From Vervunhive. Turns out she and Captain Daur knew each other really well, back in the old days, at the hive. Funny, isn't it?'

'It is,' said Elodie.

'Are you all right, mam?' Chiria asked. The corporal was a big woman, with a powerful frame. Her face was famously scarred, and it made her seem threatening, but Elodie knew she was very sweet-natured.

'Yes,' said Elodie. 'Of course. I think I just found out the answer to something.'

MERRT PULLED THE trigger. It was funny the things you didn't forget. Basic marksman skills, hunting skills, they never went away. Like how to pull a trigger. You didn't squeeze or jerk it, you didn't do anything that would shake or upset the fine balance you'd achieved between the weapon and your stance. Pulling the trigger, that most significant act in the art of shooting, was, at its best, the most minimal. A draw. A slow tightening of the finger during the exhale.

The old rifle cracked. Merrt felt the kick of it. He slotted back the bolt-action to eject the shell case.

'You missed,' said Larkin.

'I gn… gn… gn… know.'

'But you missed less terribly than you did the last ten shots,' Larkin grinned. He sat up, lifted his scope and took a look down the makeshift range. They'd set up on stretch of sea wall at the far end of the camp area, looking out down the plascrete shore to the filthy waters, with nothing between them and the far shore of Anzimar City three kilometres away except the toxic tide. There was a little jetty of rusting metal steps that led out from the end of the sea wall to a small stone derrick that was sometimes used as a beacon point. The jetty allowed Larkin to limp out to the stone platform and set up empty bottles and cans for practice. Effective range was about three hundred metres. Add in the strong breeze, the smoke and degrading light, plus the poor quality of the old rifle; it was quite a target to take.

Merrt slotted in another round, clacked back the bolt-action. Larkin took a sip of sacra from a flask. It was getting cold and the water stank.

'Best make the most of this,' said Larkin. 'After tonight, all practice is going to be shipside.'

Merrt sighed.

'It's not like I don't know what to do,' he said. 'I've always been able to remember what to do. I didn't forget how to shoot. I just stopped being gn… gn… gn… able to.'

Merrt had once been a crack shot, some said as good as Mad Larks, though it was impossible to make that assessment after so many years. On Monthax, a bitter lifetime ago, he'd taken a las-round in the mouth during the jungle-fight. The medicaes had rebuilt his lower face, fitting him with a crude and ugly prosthetic jaw. Apart from ruining his life, it had spoiled his aim. Larkin knew Merrt was right: you just had to watch him to see he knew what he was doing. He just couldn't translate technique into actual results. Throne knows, he'd tried. Merrt had spent years trying to re-qualify for his lanyard and get a longlas back.

'This trip's a shooting party,' said Larkin, taking another sip, 'so I need the best shooters I can get.'

'That's not me,' said Merrt. 'Not any more.'

'But you were, Rhen.'

'Exactly.'

Larkin sniffed.

'You know what your trouble is?' he asked.

Merrt tapped his jaw.

'Nope,' said Larkin, and reached out to tap a finger against the top of Merrt's head.

'Right,' said Merrt. 'It's gn... gn... gn... psychological.'

The jaw tripped him all the time. Apart from being ugly, it tended to seize and clamp, as if he were fighting the neural links the medicaes had wired it to. On some words, not even difficult ones, Merrt ground his jaw as if he were stuck in verbal quicksand. It got worse when he was edgy.

Larkin was no medicae, but life had given him some insight into head stuff. The stress factor suggested that it wasn't the physical impediment of the jaw so much as a nerve thing, like a nervous tic. Augmetics, especially bulk-fix battlefield stuff, could do strange things to you. Rhen Merrt, Emperor bless him, saw his problem as simply one of gross impairment. He was busted up, ergo he couldn't shoot any more. Larkin saw it was finer scale than that. The crude and halting neurodes of his augmetics were a constant reminder to Merrt that he was broken and imperfect, even during that one, serene, perfect moment of firing. He could never achieve full concentration. Result: shot ruined, every time.

That was Larkin's hunch. Except he couldn't prove it.

And even if he was able to, what could he do about it? Get them to remove Merrt's jaw?

'Take another pop,' said Larkin.

'So you gn… gn… gn… can watch me miss again?'

'No,' said Larkin. 'I'm not watching the bottles on the wall. I'm watching you. Take the shot.'

In the hall, Bandmaster Yerolemew had finally ushered the players to stop. It was time for them to break, to case their instruments, and enjoy some of the drink and food on offer. Two Tanith pipers on the opposite side of the hall had taken over entertaining the assembly.

The bandsmen came off stage, some carrying their instruments. Erish, one of the standard bearers, was helping Elway re-attach the drum banner to the frame of his field drum. Erish was a big guy, heavily muscled from carrying the weight of the colours staff. He had a back and shoulders that came out like a tulip bulb. On static parade, he played clash cymbals. Nearby, Ree Perday, one of the leads in the brass section, admired him appreciatively as she cased her brass helicon. Gorus, who played woodwind, was adjusting his reed.

'I need a drink,' said Gorus. 'I thought they were going to keep us playing all night.'

'Not like they even seemed to enjoy it,' replied Perday. She took off her high, crested cap and stroked her pinned-down hair.

'Who?' asked Erish, overhearing. He pushed past a pair of bandsmen with fanfare trumpets to join her. 'Point out a face, and I'll smack it.'

'He would, too,' said Gorus.

'Did anyone see where Cohran went?' Perday asked. 'He's been looking odd all day.'

'Odd?' asked Grous.

'Like he was sick.'

BANDSMAN POL COHRAN was less than two dozen metres away from Ree Perday when she asked after him. He had left the stage, and wandered into the latrine block behind the hall.

He was one of the youngest bandsmen, tall and well-made, good looking. He was especially handsome in the immaculate finery of his parade uniform.

The truth of it was that Pol Cohran was actually a kilometre away, floating in a sump-water tunnel under the groundworks of the main landing field, his white and bloating corpse providing a source of food for the gel-eyed, pin-toothed residents of the lightless ooze.

In the hall latrine, the other Pol Cohran caught his own reflection in the glass of the small window, cast by the lamp. He looked at himself. For a moment, his face rippled. There was a wet click and crack of bone movement as he relaxed the concentrated effort he had been sustaining, and cranial kinesis restored the normal structure of his skull. An entirely different face looked back.

He rested a second, enjoying the slackening of muscles and the loss of tension, then brought Cohran's face back with a muffled, gristly clack of bone.

GAUNT HAD BEEN using office quarters across the quad from the barracks hall. The night sky was smog-dark like stained velvet. There was an acrid back-note of pollution in the air.

He left the bright and noisy hall behind him and went up to his lodgings.

The door was unlocked. A lamp was on. Beltayn was the only one with a key, and Gaunt had just seen him in the hall.

He drew his power sword. The steel slid out of the scabbard silently. Peering through the crack in the door, he could see no sign of an intruder.

Gaunt stepped inside, sword ready. He was making no sound at all. A man didn't fight alongside the likes of Mkoll and Leyr all these years and not learn how to move like a ghost.

The office area was empty. Or had the papers on his bureau been disturbed? The bedchamber, then. Gaunt could *feel* that someone was there.

He moved around to the doorway. There was the tiniest flash of movement. His sword came around in a defensive block.

Something stopped it. Something parried his blade. It was moving fast and it was very strong. He reprised, a more aggressive blow. The slash was blocked, then something blurred into him. Gaunt sidestepped, but the attacker was too fast. He took a glancing blow across the shoulder and crashed sideways into a small library table which crashed over, spilling its load of books and data-slates.

Off-balance, he swept the sword around, now igniting its energy charge so that the already lethal cutting edge of the old weapon was enhanced by fierce blue fire. His attacker, still less than a blur, executed a handspring over the sizzling blade and landed behind him. One arm clamped his throat and another pinned his sword arm.

He head-butted backwards, then kicked back, smashing himself and the attacker locked to his back into the office wall. Objects fell off shelves. He used his left elbow and the heel of his boot to dislodge the attacker. The grip tightened, clamping the carotid arteries in his neck. He felt himself greying out. Before the chance went, he drove backwards with even more fury and he and his attacker collided with the desk and brought it over onto the floor with him.

He'd dropped his sword, but the throat-grip had gone. Gaunt came up with his bolt pistol aimed at his attacker's forehead.

She came up with a laspistol aimed at his face.

'Drop it,' he said. He didn't recognise her.

'You're Gaunt,' she said. Clipped accent. What was that?

'Yes.'

'Then this is an unfortunate mistake.'

'So drop the pistol,' said Gaunt, 'or I'll paint the wall behind you with your brains.'

She thought about it, pursed her lips, and then tossed the ornate and expensive laspistol onto the floor beside her.

'Identify yourself,' said Gaunt, his aim not flickering from her forehead.

'This is an unfortunate mistake,' she repeated.

'Not as unfortunate as making me repeat an order,' he replied.

She was lithe and extraordinarily beautiful. Her elegantly sculptural head was shaved to a fine down of hair. She was clad in an armoured bodyglove and the holster at her hip was shrouded with a red cloth.

'Maddalena Darebeloved,' she said. Her lips were very red. 'I am a licensed lifeguard of Imperial House Chass, Vervunhive.'

Gaunt eased his fingers on his gun-grip thoughtfully, but didn't move his aim.

'House Chass?' he repeated.

'You did not greet us this afternoon,' she said.

'I was detained,' replied Gaunt. 'Who's "us"?'

A second person emerged from the bedchamber. He was a young man of no more than fifteen or sixteen years dressed in a plain black bodysuit and boots.

'You did not come to greet us,' said the lifeguard. 'We came to your quarters to wait for you.'

'The door lock is gene-coded. Only my adjutant has a copy of the bio-key.'

'Any door can be opened,' said the woman.

'This is not how I wanted to meet you,' said the young

man. He had blond hair, and his youth lent him a feminine aspect.

'This is not how anyone wants to meet me,' said Gaunt. 'Who are you?'

'This,' said the lifeguard, indicating the slender boy, 'is Meritous Felyx Chass, of House Chass, grandson of Lord Chass himself. His mother is heir to the House entire. He has come to honour your regiment by joining it as a junior commander.'

'Really? Just like that?' asked Gaunt.

'He is part of the influx. The reinforcement effort provided by Great Vervunhive out of respect for you and your achievements.'

'All of which I appreciate,' said Gaunt. 'I just don't remember saying that highborns could just invite themselves into the command echelon.'

'It reflects great honour on both House Chass and this regiment,' said the lifeguard, 'if the son of the House serves in the Crusade in this capacity.'

'It won't reflect anything at all if he gets killed in the sort of Emperor-forsaken hole the scion of a Royal Verghastite House should never be seen in,' said Gaunt.

'That's why I'm here,' said the lifeguard.

Gaunt hesitated. He looked at the boy.

'Your mother. That would be Lady Merity Chass?'

'Yes,' said the boy. 'She asked me to convey her warmest greetings to you.'

'How old are you?'

'I am seventeen effective,' he said.

'I was on Verghast in 769. That's just twelve years ago. She had no children then. Even allowing for shift dilation–'

'I said I was seventeen effective,' replied Meritous Chass. 'I am eleven standard actual.'

'As is common with high status heirs and offspring on Verghast,' said the lifeguard, 'my charge's development has been slightly accelerated through juvenat and bio-maturation techniques so that he achieves functional majority as swiftly as possible.'

'So you were born just after the Vervunhive conflict?' asked Gaunt.

'Just after,' nodded the boy.

Gaunt blinked, and then lowered his pistol.

'Throne damn you,' he said, 'please don't say what I think you're about to say.'

'Colonel-commissar,' said the lifeguard, 'Meritous Felyx Chass is your son.'

FIVE
Highness Ser Armaduke

AT MIDNIGHT, LOCAL time, a new star woke in the skies above Anzimar. The city's population was hurrying to attend the day's *Sabbat Libera Nos* service, which had been held in the temples of the Beati every midnight since the Crusade began, in the hope of vouchsafing a brighter tomorrow. Some of the hundreds of thousands of citizens bustling from their homes, or even their beds, or suspending their labour, at that time may have turned their eyes skywards, for since the very origin of the species, mankind has entertained the notion that some ineffable source of providence may look down upon us. The upward glances were vain, involuntary wishes to glimpse the face of salvation.

No one saw the star light up. The smog that night was as thick as rockcrete.

SHIP BELLS RANG. At high anchor at the edge of the meso-pause, the Imperial Tempest-class frigate *Highness Ser Armaduke* lit its plasma engines. The drives ignited with a pulsing fibrillation before calming into a less intense, steady glow.

Below the ship lay the troposphere and the strato-
sphere. The shadow of the terminator lay heavily across
Menazoid Sigma, and the smog atmospherics were so
dense there were no visible light concentrations from the
night-side hives. Part of the world was in sunlight. The
foetid clouds, brown and cream, looked like infected
brain tissue.

Small ships buzzed around the *Armaduke* like flies
around a carcass. Fleet tenders nestled in close to its
flanks. Launches, lighters, cargo boats and shuttles
zipped in and out. The *Armaduke*'s hatches were all wide
open, like the beaks of impatient hatchlings. Entire sections of the frigate's densely armoured hull plate had
been peeled back or retracted to permit access. The old
ship, ancient and weathered, looked undignified, like a
grandam mamzel caught with her skirts hoisted.

Above the ship lay the exosphere. The vacuum was like
a clear but imperfect crystal, a window onto the hard
blackness of out-system space and the distant glimmer
of tiny, malicious stars.

The *Highness Ser Armaduke* was an old ship. It was
an artefact of considerable size. All ships of the fleet
were large. The *Armaduke* measured a kilometre and a
half from prow to stern, and a third of that dimension
abeam across the fins. Its realspace displacement was six
point two megatonnes, and it carried thirty-two thousand, four hundred and eleven lives, including the entire
Tanith First and its regimental retinue. It was like a slice
cut from a hive, formed into a spearhead shape and
mounted on engines.

It was built for close war. Its hull armour was pitted
and scorched, and triple-thickness along the flanks and
the prow. The prow cone was rutted with deep scars and
healed damage. The *Armaduke* was of a dogged breed of
Imperial ship that liked to get in tight with its foe, and
was prepared to get hurt in order to kill an enemy.

To Ibram Gaunt, closing towards it aboard one of the

last inbound launches, the ship had the character of a pit-fighter, or a fighting dog. Its scar-tissue was proud and deliberate.

Like the ritual marks of a blood-pacted soldier, he reflected.

The plasma engines pulsed again. Hold doors began to seal, and cantilevered armour sections extended back into position. Gaunt's craft was one of the last to enter the central landing bay before the main space doors shut. The swarm of small ships dispersed, either into the *Armaduke* to share its voyage, or away to planetside or the nearest orbital fortress. Formations of Fury- and Faustus-class attack craft had been circling the ship at a radius of five hundred kilometres to provide protection while she was exposed and vulnerable. Now they formed up to provide escort. Buoy lights blinked. Lines detached. Fleet tenders disengaged and rolled lazily away, like spent suitors or weary concubines. The *Armaduke* began to move.

Initial acceleration was painfully slow, even at maximum plasma power. It was as though an attempt was being made to slide a building – a basilica, a temple hall – by getting an army of slaves to push it. The ship protested. Its hull plates groaned. Its decks settled and creaked. Its superstructure twitched under the application of vast motive power.

The other ships at high anchor unhooded their lamps to salute the departing ship. Some were true giants of the fleet, grand cruisers and battleships six or seven kilometres long. Their vast shadows fell across the *Armaduke* as it accelerated along the line of anchorage. To them, it was a battered old relic, an orphan of the fleet they would most likely never see again.

The Fury flight dropped in around the ship in escort formation. The plasma drives grew brighter, their flare reflecting off the noctilucent clouds below, creating a shimmering airglow. Mesospheric ionisation caused bowsprite lightning to dance and flicker along the *Armaduke*'s crenellated topside until the advancing ship passed into the exosphere and the wash of the magneto-sphere's currents swept the lightshow away.

STEPPING OUT OF the launch into the excursion hold as the ship ran out, Gaunt sampled the odour of the vessel's atmosphere. Every ship had its own flavour. He'd travelled on enough of them to know that. Hundreds – or sometimes thousands – of years of recirculation and atmospheric processing allowed things to accumulate in a ship's lungs. Some smelled oddly sweet, others metallic, others rancid. You always got used to it. A ten- or twelve-week haul on a shiftship could get you used to anything. The *Armaduke* smelled of scorched fat, like grease in a kitchen's chimney.

He *would* get used to that. You could get used to the smell, the chemical tang of the recycled water, the oddly bland taste of shipboard food. You got used to the constant background grumble of the drives, to the odd noises from a vast superstructure constantly in tension. Once the drives were lit, the hull flexed; once the Geller Field was up and the ship had translated into the warp, the hull locked tight, like a well-muscled arm pumped and tensed. You got used to the acceleration sickness, the pervading cold, the odd, slippery displacement where the artificial gravity fields fluctuated and settled.

Once translation had been achieved, you got used to the ports being shuttered. You got used to ignoring whatever was outside. You got used to the baleful screams of the Empyrean, the sounds of hail on the hull, or burning firestorms, or typhoon winds, of fingernails scratching at the port shutters. You got used to the whispers, the shudders and rattles, the inexplicable periods of half-power lighting, the distant subterranean banging, the dreams, the footsteps in empty corridors, the sense that you were plunging further and further into your own subconscious and burning up your sanity to fuel the trip.

The one thing you never got used to was the scale. At high orbit, even with the vast extent of a planet close by for contrast, a starship seemed big. But as the planet dropped away to stern, first the size of an office globe, then a ball, until even the local sun was just a fleck of light no bigger than any other star, the embrace of the void became total. Space was endless and eternal, and the few suns no bigger than grains of salt. Alone in the bewildering emptiness, a starship was dwarfed, diminished until it was just a fragile metal casket alone in the monstrous prospect of night.

The *Armaduke* was accelerating so robustly now that the fighter escort was struggling to match it. Course was locked for the system's Mandeville point, where the warp engines would be started up to make an incision in the interstitial fabric of space. The warp awaited them.

The crew and control spaces of a starship tended to be kept separate from the areas used for transported material and passengers, even on a military operation. The transporters and those they were transporting needed very little contact during a voyage.

But the *Armaduke* was still twenty-six minutes from the translation point when Gaunt presented himself to the shipmaster. He did not come alone.

'No entry at this time,' said the midshipman manning the valve hatch. He had six armsmen with him, all with combat shot weapons for shipboard use.

Gaunt showed the midshipman his documentation, documentation that clearly showed he was the commanding officer of the troop units under conveyance.

'That's all very well,' said the midshipman, displaying that unerring knack of Navy types to avoid using Guard rank formalities, 'but the shipmaster is preparing for commitment to translation. He can't be interrupted. Perhaps in a week or so, he might find some time to–'

'Perhaps he's done it a thousand times before,' said

Gaunt's companion, stepping out of the bulkhead shadows, 'and doesn't need to do more than authorise the bridge crew to execute. Perhaps he ought to bear in mind that his ship is a vital component of this action and not just a means of transportation. Perhaps you should open this hatch.'

The midshipman went pale.

'Yes, sir,' he said, his voice as small as a shiftship in the open void.

THE SHIPMASTER'S NAME was Clemensew Spika. He had three Battlefleet commands behind him, but his career was in decline. A grizzled man of medium height, who conducted his command in full dress uniform, he was standing proudly at the gilded rail of the upper deck platform when they entered, gazing out across the bustling main bridge towards the vast forward viewer with a noble expression on his face. Gaunt wondered if he'd been standing there anyway, or if he'd struck the pose when he heard they were coming.

He turned as they came up to him, looking Gaunt in the eye, then tilting his head up to look at the Silver Guard warrior beside him.

'We are underway,' he said. 'Could this audience have waited?'

'No,' said Eadwine.

'Is this translation especially problematic?' asked Gaunt.

'No,' replied Spika. He gestured for them to follow him, and instructed his first officer to watch the steersmen. At the back of the upper deck was a small stateroom reserved for briefings or quiet counsel. Spika sat and indicated they should do the same. Eadwine remained standing.

Apart from one wall panel that displayed a detailed summary of ship function, the room was decorated with painted sections framed in scrolled gilt. Each painted panel showed a different view of Khulan: the Regal Palace, the Waterfalls at Hypson, the Tombs at Kalil, the Imperial Lodge in High Askian, the Smarnian Basilica.

'You understand how your vessel will be engaged in this venture?' asked Eadwine. His augmetic rasp had little colour or tone.

'Of course,' replied Spika. 'Rendezvous at Tavis Sun, resupply, then direct to the Marginals.'

'I mean there,' said Eadwine. 'In the Marginals.'

'Boarding action,' said Spika. 'I understand.'

'You will be required to stay on station,' said Gaunt.

'I know.'

'There will be no fleet support,' Gaunt added. 'The *Armaduke* will be vulnerable.'

'I know,' repeated Spika.

'There are several things we don't know,' said Eadwine. 'The dangers are considerable. We will be running silently for the last realspace section. There will be navigational hazards. Clearance and manoeuvre will be restricted. The deployment will be multi-point. Sustained. We do not know what we will find inside the target structure.'

'At all?' asked Spika. 'I understood that this mission was based on intelligence of–'

'It is,' said Gaunt. 'But it is limited. It may be out of date.'

'It may be a pack of lies,' said Eadwine.

'Encouraging,' said Spika.

'Depending on levels of opposition, you may be required to commit your armsmen,' said Eadwine.

'I wasn't told that,' said Spika.

'Is it a problem?'

'The armsmen of the *Highness Ser Armaduke* will fight for the life of the ship if necessary,' said the shipmaster firmly. He paused. 'But I have been given a complement of young recruits. Few have battle experience. I was given to expect that you would be doing the fighting.'

Gaunt glanced at the towering Space Marine.

Eadwine's helm hung from his belt. He was looking with what resembled interest at the painting of the Waterfalls at Hypson.

'The Navy has been economical with your briefing,' said Eadwine. 'What do you understand this mission to be about?'

'About a matter of strategic importance,' replied Spika. 'Specifically, from my point of view, the opportunity to put this newly refitted ship and its young crew through a proper shakedown prior to re-certification.'

Neither Gaunt nor Eadwine replied. Spika looked at them. There was something infinitely sad in his pale blue eyes, as if he had been trying for weeks now to overlook the obvious.

'A cynic might, I suppose, interpret this differently,' he said.

'How might that go?' asked Gaunt.

'An expendable and not entirely void-worthy ship and a young crew of little experiential value,' said Spika, 'given into the charge of a man who will never make admiral now and who asks the wrong questions of his superiors. A mission that is so likely to end in disaster, only scraps can be risked.'

'A good dose of cynicism is always healthy, I find,' said Eadwine.

'There were other clues,' said Spika, a hardness in his voice. He looked at Gaunt. 'I reviewed your file, those sections that were not restricted. Glorious moments early on, at Balhaut especially. Great favour. The achievements since have been considerable. I mean that. No one could fail to be impressed by your service record. But recognition has been scant since Balhaut. There is a sense that you have squandered great opportunities, and ended up achieving little credit for the expenditure of great courage and tenacity. Like me and my ship, you and your regiment are useful but disposable commodities.'

'A good dose of cynicism is always healthy,' replied Gaunt.

'I don't care who you are,' rumbled Eadwine. 'I don't care if you're the Warmaster himself. This is the Imperium of Mankind. We're all of us disposable commodities.'

The lights dipped. There was a shudder. The warp embraced them.

'I HATE THAT,' said Larkin. He froze and refused to continue walking until the ship lights returned to their original brilliance. There was an underdeck tremor. A distant exhalation.

'Worst part of any trip,' he added. The lights came back up, a frosty glare in the low deck companionway. He started walking again.

'The worst?' asked Domor.

'Yes,' said Larkin. 'Apart from getting there.'

'All true,' said Domor.

They had reached the armoured hatchway of a hold space originally designed as a magazine for explosive ordnance. Rawne and Brostin were waiting for them.

'I want a badge like that,' said Larkin.

'Well, you can't have one,' said Brostin. 'It's only for the kings.'

'The kings can kiss my arse,' said Larkin.

Domor looked at Rawne.

'This could continue all day, major,' he said.

'And it still wouldn't become amusing,' Rawne agreed.

'Gaunt wants us to see him,' said Domor. 'Is that all right?'

'Yes,' said Rawne. 'Provided you're who you say you are.'

Larkin winked at Rawne.

'Come on, Eli, these'd be pretty rubbish disguises, wouldn't they?'

'What are you suggesting?' asked Domor, a smile forming. 'We forced our own faces to change shape?'

'I've seen stranger things,' said Rawne.

'Nobody here is surprised,' said Larkin.

Rawne nodded to Brostin. The big man banged on the door, and then opened the outer hatch.

'Coming in, two visitors,' said Rawne over his microbead.

'Read that.'

A peephole slot in the inner door opened, and Rawne stood where the viewer could see his face.

The inner hatch opened. Rawne took Domor and Larkin through.

'Got anything he could use as a weapon?' asked Rawne.

'My rapier wit?' suggested Larkin.

Mabbon Etogaur was sitting on a folding bunk in one corner of the dank magazine compartment. The walls, deck and ceiling were reinforced ceramite, and the slot hatch for the loader mechanism had been welded shut. The prisoner was reading a trancemissionary pamphlet, one of a stack on his mattress. His right wrist was cuffed to a chain that was bolted to a floor pin.

Varl was sitting on a stool in the opposite corner, his lasrifle across his knees. Cant was standing in another corner, nibbling at the quick of his thumbnail.

Larkin and Domor came in and approached the etogaur.

He looked up.

'I don't know you,' he said.

'No, but I had you in my crosshairs once,' said Larkin.

'Where?'

'Balhaut.'

'Why didn't you take the shot?' asked Mabbon.

'And miss a touching moment like this?'

'That's Domor, that's Larkin,' said Rawne, pointing.

'Don't tell him our damn names!' Larkin hissed. 'He might do all sorts of fethed-up magic shit with them!'

'I won't,' said Mabbon.

'He won't,' Rawne agreed.

'He can't,' said Varl.

'Why not?' asked Larkin.

'Because how else would I be the punchline for another of Varl's jokes?' asked Cant wearily.

Larkin snorted.

'He won't because he's cooperating,' said Rawne, ignoring the others.

'And if I did,' said Mabbon, 'Rawne would gut me.'

'He does do that,' Larkin nodded.

'What did you need from me?' asked Mabbon.

'A consultation,' said Domor. He had a sheaf of rolled papers under his arm, and a data-slate in his hand.

'Go on,' said Mabbon.

Larkin took the pamphlet out of Mabbon's hand and glanced at it.

'Good read?' he asked.

'I enjoy the subject matter,' said Mabbon.

'A doctrine of conversion to the Imperial Creed?' asked Larkin.

'Fantasy,' replied Mabbon.

'He'd be a fething funny man if he didn't scare the shit out of me,' Larkin said to Rawne.

'We're leading the insertion effort,' said Domor. 'There's training to be done, planning. We want to use transit time to get as ready as possible.'

'Are you combat engineering?' asked Mabbon.

'Yes,' said Domor. 'Larks… Larkin, he's marksman squad.'

'I saw the lanyard.'

'We want to go over the deck plans and schematics you've supplied so far. It may mean several hours work over a period of days.'

'I'll try to build time into my schedule.'

'Some of the plans are vague,' said Larkin.

'So are some of my memories. It's all from memory.'

'If you go through them a few times,' said Rawne, 'maybe you can firm things up.'

The etogaur nodded.

'If you go through them so many times you're sick of them, maybe we'll actually do this right,' Rawne added.

'I've no problem with that,' said Mabbon. 'I offered this to you. I want it to happen.'

Domor showed him the data-slate.

'We want to talk about this too,' he said. 'This firing mechanism. We need to mock some up for practice purposes. You say this is fairly standard?'

'It's representative of the sort of firing mechanisms and trigger systems you're going to find,' said Mabbon, studying the slate image.

'It's just mechanical,' said Larkin.

'It has to be. They can't risk anything more… more complicated. They can't risk using anything that might interfere with, or be interfered with by, the devices under development at the target location. It's delicate. Any conflict in arcane processes or conjurations could be disastrous.'

'So just mechanical?' said Larkin.

'Complex and very delicate. Very sensitive. But, yes. Just mechanical.'

Larkin took the slate back.

'It looks very… It looks very much like the sort of thing we use,' he said. 'It looks pretty standard.'

'It's the sort of trigger mechanism I would rig,' Domor said.

'Of course,' said Mabbon. 'Tried and tested Guard practice. This is the sort of thing I taught them how to do. And I learned it the same place you did.'

Larkin looked at Domor. There was distaste on his face.

'Go get the folding table,' Rawne said to Varl. 'Let's look over these plans.'

IN BERTHING HOLD six, the lights stayed dim for a long time. When they came back up, it was without enthusiasm.

The air was fuggy. Too many bodies, too much breathing, not enough decent atmospheric processing.

'This is a dump,' remarked Ree Perday. The cots were stacked three deep and close together. It was a forest of prone bodies. There was virtually no room to stow the band's instruments.

'Well, it's our dump,' said Bandmaster Yerolemew. moving through the rows. He tapped an empty bunk with his baton.

'Who's not here?'

'Pol Cohran, sergeant major,' said Gorus.

'Where is he?'

'Acceleration sickness, sergeant major,' said Perday.

'Cohran doesn't get acceleration sickness,' said Yerolemew.

'He does this time,' said Erish.

'White as an undershirt,' muttered Gorus.

'Not one of your undershirts,' said Perday.

'Settle down,' said the bandmaster.

'Maybe the bandsman needs to see a medicae?' asked Commissar Blenner. He'd been watching from the end of a bunk row.

'Didn't see you there, sir!' snapped Yerolemew, straightening fast. The others began to move.

'Please don't,' said Blenner, coming forwards. He took off his cap. It always took the sting out, he thought, when the cap came off. 'This isn't an official inspection. I just came to greet you, make sure you were stowed.'

'That's kind of you, sir,' said Yerolemew.

'I can afford to be kind now, sergeant,' said Blenner. 'You can pay me back later by behaving yourselves.'

He crooked an eyebrow to the crowd and got a little chuckle.

'You'll find I'm a pretty fair sort, generally. Come to me in good faith and I'll always hear you out. Thank your lucky stars my name's not Hark.'

More laughter, and it was genuine.

'Anything to report so far? The facilities suiting your needs?'

'Pardon me, sir,' said Perday, 'but there's precious little room to store our instruments.'

'No, there isn't, is there?' said Blenner glancing around. 'Gaunt said something about storing them… where was it now? Airgate sixty.'

Still more laughter, some of it outraged.

'I know, I know!' said Blenner. 'No respect, is there? No respect for the simple, pure, uplifting decency that is a colours band. Am I right?'

It seemed he was.

'I tell you what we're going to do,' he said. 'This mission, it's pretty vital. It's dangerous too, I won't lie. But what we're going to do is spend the time proving that a marching unit is indispensable to the regiment. Indispensable! As soldiers and as musicians, you're going to prove your worth.'

That got a big cheer.

'Fury of Belladon!' Blenner tossed in for good measure, and circled his raised hand like a potentate on a balcony taking a march-past.

As they began to settle again, he turned to the sergeant major.

'I was looking for your commanding officer,' said Blenner.

'I can show you to his quarters,' Yerolemew replied. 'I was just settling the company.'

'You carry on, sergeant major,' said Blenner. 'I'm sure somebody else can show me. That young girl, for example. She seems very accommodating.'

'Perday?' called Yerolemew.

'Sir, yes, sir!'

'Kindly show Commissar Blenner through to Captain Wilder's quarters.'

Perday jumped up.

'This way, sir,' she said.

She led him off the bustling berthing deck and onto a rather more gloomy corridor where the officers had been given cabins. The deck was a mesh. Below, there was a maintenance trench and a sluice.

'What's your name, trooper?' asked Blenner.

'Ree Perday, sir.'

'Ree. Ree. And what's that short for?'

'Uhm, Ree, sir.'

'I see,' said Blenner. Not one to be deflected, he pressed on. 'And where are you from, Ree Perday?'

'Belladon, sir.'

'Yes, silly of me to ask.'

In the shadow of a maintenance hatch in the trench below, the thing with Pol Cohran's face watched them pass overhead. He had hidden so he could relax the tension in his face again. Bones clacked as cranial kinesis reasserted Cohran's visage.

'What was that?' asked Blenner.

'I didn't hear anything, sir,' said Perday.

'I hope it wasn't rats,' said Blenner. 'I do hate rats.'

'Oh, yes, sir.'

'Especially when you spot them leaving the ship first.'

Perday laughed, and knocked on a cabin door. It was open.

'Sir? Captain?' she called. She peered inside.

'Oh, Throne,' he heard her say.

Blenner pushed past her. The cabin was small and unfriendly. Wilder was sprawled on the deck. He'd been sick at least once. The smell of amasec was pungent.

Blenner rolled him over. He was bonelessly limp, but he was still breathing. There were fumes coming off him you could have lit with a lucifer.

'Oh, you bloody idiot,' Blenner muttered.

'What do we do, sir?' asked Perday.

'Go get a mop, Perday, and a pail of water,' said Blenner. 'Don't tell anybody why. When you come back, watch the door and don't let anybody in.'

She looked at him, helpless and anxious.

'Go on.'

She hurried out.

Blenner sighed, and then hoisted Wilder up and carried him over to the bunk. He groaned in his stupor.

'I could just shoot you for this, you realise that?' said Blenner.

Wilder opened his eyes, but there wasn't much of anything in there.

'You're a bloody fool,' said Blenner. 'I gave you a chance tonight, and you've already screwed it up. There's going to come a point when I can't help you any more, do you understand?'

Wilder closed his eyes.

'Can't and won't,' said Blenner.

Perday reappeared.

'Where's the mop, girl?' Blenner asked.

'Sir, I was just looking for one, sir, but I thought you should know. Company inspection, sir. Company inspection right now.'

'Throne, Wilder, you'll be the death of me,' said Blenner. He got up.

'Perday, use the jug of water there, and get a spare shirt or vest out of his holdall. Try to mop up this mess. Quickly, now.'

'Yes, sir.'

Blenner put his cap on and went to the cabin door. Baskevyl, Sloman and Edur had just appeared at the end of the corridor; walking, talking.

'Blenner,' said Edur. 'I was going to invite you to join us, but I couldn't find you.'

'I was already inspecting,' Blenner said. He pulled the cabin door shut behind him, so they couldn't see in past him.

'Inspecting?' asked Edur.

'More a meet and greet. I didn't know a surprise formal was due?'

'Standard Belladon practice to spring a surprise on a new intake during the first thirty-six hours,' said Baskevyl.

'Perhaps you should familiarise me with some standard Belladon practice,' said Blenner. 'Seeing as the Belladon are my special responsibility.'

'Yes, of course,' said Baskevyl. 'I didn't mean to cut you out of the process. I should have consulted you.'

'No harm done.'

'Would you like to walk in with us now? Maybe Captain Wilder too?'

Blenner pulled a face. He dropped his voice and leaned in close.

'There's a slight problem,' he said. 'The captain's been struck down with a nasty bout of acceleration sickness.'

'Really?' said Baskevyl.

'Nasty.' Blenner nodded. 'It's widespread, actually. More than one bandsman has got it. I'll be sending for a medicae to give everyone a check. The thing is, Wilder could join us, but he looks like death warmed over, and frankly I don't want him losing face by seeming weak in front of the men.'

'Quite right,' said Sloman.

'Here's an idea,' said Blenner, his voice still low. 'Why don't we do this inspection once I've had everybody checked? Give them a fighting chance to turn out properly on a first show. I mean, come on, between us, they're not going to get a fighting chance to do anything much more impressive, are they?'

Sloman laughed. Baskevyl tried not to.

'That's good policy, I think,' said Edur solemnly. 'This time tomorrow, maybe?'

They went back the way they'd come.

Blenner stepped into the cabin. He breathed deeply, and quickly necked one of Dorden's pills. Perday had done a good job of washing the deck. She was bagging the shirt she'd used for laundry.

'You're a kind man, sir,' she said. 'You said you were

fair and you clearly mean it. Others would have hung the captain out for this.'

'Don't tell me that,' said Blenner. He pointed at Wilder. 'Tell *him* that when he wakes up tomorrow morning.'

'The shipmaster seems reliable?' asked Lord Militant Cybon. 'This Spika? He was the Navy's choice.'

'He seemed agreeable enough,' said Gaunt. 'Sanguine.'

Cybon nodded.

'Amasec?'

'I'll take a small one, sir.'

Cybon's staterooms were some of the most comfortable passenger apartments on the *Armaduke*. Gaunt believed a senior helm officer had been rehoused to accommodate the lord militant for the voyage. Gaunt had opted for a standard officer's quarters of the lower deck beside the other Tanith seniors.

'Should I have seen him? He knows I'm aboard,' said Cybon as his aide marched off to get some amasec. The lord militant eased his augmetic frame down into a reclining flight throne. The chamber's desk was alive with hololithic displays. Cybon liked his information fresh and frequently renewed.

'I think I made the right noises,' said Gaunt, taking the small amasec that the aide offered him. The glass was from the lord militant's own travelling case. There was a small rook crest etched on the crystal.

'He knows you're aboard, but it's not general news,' Gaunt went on. 'And you'll be leaving us when we rendezvous with the fleet at Tavis Sun. So Spika needs to get used to me being the voice of authority.'

Cybon nodded and sipped his amasec pensively.

'You took a Space Marine with you?'

'Eadwine. Of the Silver Guard.'

'Sensible. That'll put the wind up him at least.'

There was a long pause.

'Times are changing, Gaunt,' said Cybon. His augmetic voice was a soft rumble.

'Sir?'

'It's been a long time since Balhaut. Moods change.
Fortunes shift. People go in and out of favour.'

'This has always been my experience, sir,' Gaunt said.
'Were you saying this in relation to anything particular?'

Cybon shrugged. Augmetics hissed. He steepled his
fingers around his glass, gazing at it. 'You and I were
ascendant at the same time, Gaunt. Before Balhaut.
Under Slaydo. It was a good time for us. We were
connected.'

'We were. I don't feel I've been unfairly treated since.'

'I don't feel you have either,' said Cybon. 'You made
your bed. You looked at the opportunities, and you
decided to stay in the field. You've made the best of that
choice. Throne knows, some part of me wishes I'd made
similar choices at certain points in my career.'

'Your career and command are enviable, sir. And it's
far from over.'

Cybon nodded.

'If this mission goes well, Gaunt, it could mean a lot. It
could mean a lot for the cause, but also for you, and for
everyone who supported the effort.'

'Which would include the Warmaster.'

'Naturally. But I doubt he's paid close attention to this
one. Do you know how many missions he is required
to scrutinise and approve every day? Across the sector?
Come on. This is one raid, part of a sequence, in a corner
of the Sabbat Worlds not seen as directly strategic. If it
fails, it's forgotten. If it succeeds…'

'It could make a man's career?'

'It could make the careers of many men, Gaunt. It
could alter the emphasis of operations. It could provoke
a… an overhaul. A much needed overhaul.'

'I see.'

Cybon wiped his lips with the back of his finger.

'I will remember you for this, Gaunt. I will credit you where credit is needed. I hope you will do the same.'

'Of course.'

Cybon looked at Gaunt. 'It's already begun, you know?' he said.

'Sir?'

'Four weeks ago, unadjusted, the first attack. There have been seven more since. In the space of these six months, sidereal, twenty-eight raids will take place at selected locations across the trailing portions of the Sabbat Worlds. All of them will work according to the philosophy cooked up by you and Mercure. The tactics. The clues left. The information broadcast. Some of those transmissions are very authentic.'

'They're as authentic as we could make them,' said Gaunt.

'Twenty-eight raids,' said Cybon. 'It's not even a massive commitment of men and materiel. Nothing so grand the Warmaster has to approve resourcing. The coordination, that's the clever part. It's smoke and mirrors.'

'It's *mostly* smoke and mirrors, sir,' said Gaunt. 'The effect will be very diluted if we don't pull off this attack.'

'Then that's what you'd better do, isn't it?' said Cybon.

MERITOUS FELYX CHASS had taken a seat in the corner of Gaunt's quarters and was reading a data-slate. He got up when Gaunt walked in. Gaunt gestured to him to sit again.

'Ravenor,' said Chass, indicating the book. 'I've never been particularly taken with his work.'

'Really?' said Gaunt.

'He died badly, didn't he?'

Gaunt shrugged. 'What matters is what he did first,' he said. He sat down at his desk. Maddalena Darebeloved was a silent presence in the far corner.

'You can always wait outside,' said Gaunt.

'He doesn't leave my sight,' she replied.

'I have a problem here,' said Gaunt. 'You tell me you're my son. That's both a surprise and a hindrance to a man in my particular circumstance.'

'I don't mean to be a–'

'What do you mean to be?' asked Gaunt.

'My mother thinks it would benefit me, as a future leader of House Chass, to learn from you.'

'Learn what? How to fight? Honour? Duty? You can learn all that from her.'

'My mother?'

'No, her,' said Gaunt, pointing at the lifeguard. 'But let's talk about your mother for a moment. According to you, you're her first and only son. That makes you heir to the House. Why is she risking your life like this? First sons, sometimes second sons too, they're kept closeted in protective custody to safeguard the bloodline. Getting sent out into the Imperium is usually the fate of subsequent offspring.'

'Verghastite philosophy is somewhat different–' Maddalena began.

'I wasn't talking to you,' said Gaunt. He was immediately annoyed with himself for snapping. He didn't know what it was, but the lifeguard really got under his skin.

'House Chass has always believed in experiential improvement,' said Chass. 'To see the Imperium, to learn about it, to learn from my father, these are all things that will benefit me when I finally take my place.'

'Your mother has never travelled, not as far as I know.'

'She would have,' said Chass. 'But she may be required to assume the House sooner than expected. My grandfather is ill.'

'I didn't know. I'm sorry.'

Gaunt got up, and began to pace thoughtfully. 'I'm afraid I think this is about prestige,' he said. 'You associate with the famous war hero of Vervunhive, and earn some glory of your own, you'll go back as more than just a popular heir to the House. That kind of borrowed gloss will get you a planetary seat, a governorship. I think House Chass has great ambitions to fulfil through you.'

'You are dismayingly arrogant,' said Maddalena.

'Just tell me I'm not also right,' said Gaunt.

There was a knock at the door. Maddalena instinctively reached towards her sidearm.

'Don't even think about it,' said Gaunt. 'Enter!'

Beltayn came in, with Nahum Ludd and Trooper Dalin.

'You sent for these men, sir?' he asked.

'I did. Come in. You might as well stay and hear this too, Beltayn.'

Chass had risen to his feet. Both Ludd and Dalin looked at him, curious.

'This, I have just discovered, is my son,' Gaunt said. He ignored their looks of surprise. 'I didn't know I had a son, and now I find myself compromised by the knowledge. This is a risky mission, and potentially none of us may come back. Taking the son I've just met along on what could be a suicidal venture hardly seems like the greatest exercise in parental responsibility.'

Gaunt looked at Ludd and Dalin.

'However, I could hardly leave him behind on Menazoid Sigma either. He wants to join us. He wants to serve with us. That's a reasonably admirable ambition.'

'I don't want special treatment,' said Chass.

'Good, because you're not getting any,' said Gaunt. 'Ludd, I hate to add to your existing workload, but I want you to prepare and process enlistment papers. If he wants to be a Guardsman, it had better be official.'

'And I take it you want me to keep an eye on him too, sir?' asked Ludd.

'No. Not at all,' said Gaunt. 'I want you to keep an eye on her.' He pointed to Maddalena.

'The young Lord Chass here,' said Gaunt, 'is noble born. He has a bodyguard. A good one. It's the only special favour I'll show him, allowing her to remain. She can look after him, but she will not get in the way of operations. The moment she does, you can remove her. My full authority. You can shoot her, if needs be.'

'He can try,' said Maddalena.

'Ludd is an Imperial commissar,' Gaunt said to her. 'If I were you, I wouldn't even *think* bad things about him.'

He turned back to the others.

'His lordship must not compromise my decision making, especially not on this mission. I cannot, *will* not, worry about him, or second guess my choices because of him. Dalin, you're about his age, so I want you to show him the ropes. There's no time for basic and induction. Let him shadow you, and teach him what he needs. I ask this as a favour, not a command. When the real fighting starts, we'll be keeping him away from the brunt of it.'

'I want to–' Chass began.

'Enough,' said Gaunt. 'Show him the ropes, please, Dalin. But I don't want him even compromising your duties as adjutant. He eats and sleeps like any common lasman.'

'He should receive a rank,' said Maddalena. 'Some privilege for–'

'If he wants to learn from me,' said Gaunt, 'he can do exactly what I did and start from the bottom. Take it or leave it. You asked for this, so don't complain now you've got it. If he doesn't like it, he can leave us at the fleet rendezvous and go home to his mother.'

He looked at them.

'That's all,' he said.

MKOLL, CHIEF SCOUT of the Tanith First, prowled silently through the vast and dark cargo decks of the *Armaduke*. He was hunting.

The engines rumbled distantly. He hadn't set out to look for anything in particular. He just wanted to get the lay of the land, learn the geography of the ship. Just in case.

He also wanted to get his equilibrium settled as fast as possible. Ship time unsettled him. He got through it by walking, and learning every obscure corner of whatever craft he was aboard. It was a form of meditation.

Half an hour into his first walk around, crossing a vehicle deck where mission equipment was secured under lash lines and the air smelled of disinfectant, he'd first seen the bird. It was moving through the cargo galleries, swooping from one set of hold rafters to the next. It looked as lost and as trapped as he felt.

He set to following it. It was big. A twin-headed eagle. At first, he wondered if it was some kind of vision, but it was real enough. He'd been told the intake had brought a psyber animal aboard with them. A mascot. It had evidently got loose.

It kept apace of him. He followed it through two of the small holds, then around an engineering deck where the few servitors didn't seem to notice it. It avoided the busy spaces, the troop decks, the vast and heated furnace rooms of the drive chambers where hundreds of crewmen toiled like slaves.

Like him, it sought the lonely parts of the ship.

He wondered how he could catch it without harming it. If it stayed loose, it could get lost or trapped, and die of starvation. The death of an aquila on the eve of a mission would not be the best omen.

Mkoll followed the bird into a vast hold space that had been left empty. Junk and spare plating had been piled up there. He heard a voice call out.

The eagle turned, surprised, and then immediately followed the voice down.

It settled on a metal spar beside two figures. They were sitting right out in the middle of the empty space, perched on scrap metal, a small fire burning in an oil can.

One of the men was Ezra Night. He was permitting his companion to examine the function of his reynbow.

Ezra saw Mkoll, and called out.

'Histye soule! Come join herein.'

Mkoll walked over to the fire.

The other figure lowered the reynbow and looked Mkoll up and down. He was a Space Marine of the White Scars Chapter. He was in full plate, his helm on the deck by his left foot.

'You are the master of the scouts?' he asked. 'I've heard all about you. Sit.'

SIX
Relativity

ABOARD THE *Highness Ser Armaduke*, only the ringing of ship bells marked the passage of time. There were no day or night shifts. Some vessels established a day/night cycle with their lighting systems, but this was evidently not Shipmaster Spika's habit. The *Armaduke* ploughed onwards in a state of twilight gloom, the decks morose and half lit. There was some talk of power conservation and economies of reserve, but few could avoid the suspicion that the habitat conditions were deliberate. On some decks, power went out completely and inexplicably, for hours at a time. The heating and air circulation of certain compartments and sections ceased and then, after a while, resumed with a bronchial rattle of ducts and flues. The agreed belief was that the *Armaduke*'s grim conditions had nothing to do with Shipmaster Spika's conservative approach to power consumption, and everything to do with mechanical decay and infirmity.

In the troop decks, the men and women of the company and its retinue gathered around lamps, or worked by wick-light. Most slept for many hours longer than necessary. Sensing a malaise, Hark initiated a program of fitness and training that involved free marches and squad runs around the outer perimeter of the main hold levels, a circuit of almost five kilometres.

Boredom and inactivity were the real dangers of warp travel. Confinement and idleness allowed minds to stagnate, allowed anxieties to fester. At one end of the scale there would be discontent and despair, and the scale moved up through spats and feuding, criminal activity and mutinous behaviour. Unhappy minds were also more easily preyed upon by the powers of the warp.

The confidential transit estimated at the point of departure suggested three to six days to Tavis Sun, for the fleet conjunction, and then another six to Salvation's Reach. There was no reliable science. Some warp routes remained stable for centuries. Others vanished into hectic maelstroms overnight. All sorts of variables affected the journey time, both appreciated shipboard and external sidereal. One could travel for a month and arrive the day before one's departure. One could set out for a three-day shift and never be seen again. If the bulk of the *Armaduke*'s rationed power was being diverted to turn the warp engine cogitators and assist the ship's Navigator to track the beacon of the Astronomicon and ascertain the best possible route vector, then the passengers and crew of the *Highness Ser Armaduke* would be grateful enough.

Only the chiming of the ship's bells marked the passage of time, but that was only the local time of the ship, a measurement of the turning of the clocks and horologs it took along with it into a hostile ocean outside time.

NAHUM LUDD HURRIED through the quarter decks with the dockets and enlistment papers he'd finally managed to prepare for Meritous Chass. He'd hoped to have them done by the end of the first night shift aboard, but it was now well into the second day. There had been inspections to run, the settlement of the quartered troops, and the usual discrepancies between pharmacological supplies and other materiel signed aboard, and those actually physically present. Since before the long sojourn on Balhaut, but especially since, the regiment had a chronic problem with misplaced drugs. Ludd and Hark had worked closely with Dorden and Curth to curtail the losses, to little avail. There was always a grey market of procurement inside the Imperial Guard, and sometimes it was downright black. In the early days, Rawne had been ringleader for unofficial activity, but he had made a visible effort to keep his hands clean. Either he was a good liar, or others had usurped his criminal enterprises. Ludd had his eyes on a few people. Men always looked for power and control, and rank was one way of securing it. There were others. The trouble with the Tanith First was that they were loyal. They were loyal to the Throne and they were loyal to Gaunt, but that loyalty was ingrained, so they were almost perniciously loyal to each other. That meant they closed ranks and kept secrets. The underhand dealings that went on at the heart of every regiment were especially stealthy in the Ghosts.

Ludd was quite unsettled by the appearance of Chass. He'd said as much, privately, to Hark.

'You're threatened,' Hark had said.

'How do you figure that?'

'Young man, young commissar, following in the master's footsteps, Gaunt's protégé,' said Hark. 'Then the actual son turns up.'

'In this version of reality you describe, I see myself as Gaunt's son?' asked Ludd.

Hark nodded. 'You even cut your hair the same way.'

'I thought I was your protégé,' said Ludd.

Hark had sniffed.

'You wish. I'm one of a kind.'

'This is just more of your systematic tormenting, to

keep me on my toes, isn't it?' Ludd had asked.

'If I told you that, it would have no beneficial effect whatsoever.'

Ludd wasn't convinced. It was, perhaps, slightly true that he didn't like the idea Gaunt might soon have a new favourite. But there was something else. Chass looked so much like Gaunt. Once you knew, it was painfully obvious. He was slender and gracefully slight by comparison, of course; just a boy, and a dainty, frail one at that, but Ludd recognised the likeness in him. If anything, Chass's youthful features were even more refined. In inheritance from his mother's side, perhaps. Gaunt was a well-made man. Chass, as an adult, would be more than just handsome.

It was the recognition that was difficult to deal with. Ludd saw Gaunt in Chass. It felt like he already knew him. It made him admire him, without even knowing him or wanting to. He responded to Chass, and he didn't like it.

Ludd's route took him down a grand companionway outside the Verghastite quarters, past the amusing spectacle of Mkoll presenting a double-headed eagle to the laughing Major Pasha. She was calling for her standard officer to take charge of the mascot, which flapped and clacked on Mkoll's raised wrist. Women from the retinue, laden with tubs for the laundry, had stopped to watch and laugh.

An archway to Ludd's left looked out over an assembly deck, a secondary hangar bay that could be brought into use by means of freight elevators from the primary excursion deck. It was the size of a parade ground. Out in the middle of it, he saw a single figure, training.

The figure was a blur. It was a close combat drill, executed using a bladed spear and a hovering practice remote.

He slowed and stopped. He watched. It was a genuinely terrifying display of speed, skill and aggression.

Though he had somewhere to be, Ludd took a deep breath and walked into the assembly space.

As he approached, the figure twisted and finally caught the drone, killing it with his spear's blade. It fell to the deck. The warrior bent down, picked up the broken drone, and tossed it into a bucket where other smashed remotes had accumulated. He took up another one from a box beside the bucket, and prepared to arm and launch it.

'What do you want?' he asked. He hadn't even looked at Ludd.

'I want to know if I'm permitted a question.'

Brother Kater Holofurnace of the Iron Snakes turned to look at him. He had his massive spear in one paw and the drone in the other. Ludd felt fear in his bowels, in his gut, in his throat.

'Commissar?'

'Yes. Ludd.'

'I do not care in any way about your name. You are a discipline officer?'

'Yes.'

'I will give you one answer,' said Holofurnace. 'Give me your question.'

'There are three of you. Three lent to us for this mission. Why three different Chapters?'

'That's your question?'

'It is.'

Holofurnace pursed his lips.

'You are a discipline officer. You should know it is improper and unprofitable to interrupt a man when he is schooling for war,' he said.

Ludd paused.

'Is that your answer?'

'It is.'

'But–'

'I never said my answer would match your question.'

Ludd opened his mouth, but didn't know what else to say.

'You can go away now,' said Holofurnace.

Ludd turned. He heard the remote hum as it was

launched. He heard the chop of the spear as it started to spin.

'THE TRUTH IS, I don't want to know,' said Elodie.

'That's not the truth at all,' said Juniper. The amusing distraction of the eagle had finished. The women were moving on towards the laundry.

'You're helping us with the wash today, are you Elodie?' asked Urlinta.

'No. Why are you doing laundry?' asked Elodie. 'We've only been in shift a day.'

'There's always washing and mending to do,' said Juniper.

'You can tell she's an officer's woman, can't you?' laughed Urlinta.

'As for this business,' said Juniper, 'you want to know about it.'

'I thought he was a decent man,' said Elodie.

'That is generally the opinion held of your nice captain,' said Juniper.

'Then again,' said Nilwen, 'he's a man. *And* he's a las-man. They'll stick it anywhere.'

'Nilwen isn't really helping,' Juniper told Elodie. 'So, he knows this woman, this officer? From Verghast, you say? So what?'

'She's very attractive,' said Elodie.

'Oh, case closed,' said Urlinta.

'Have you seen yourself?' asked Nilwen.

'He was going to ask me to marry him,' said Elodie. 'He had the papers. Then he didn't. He didn't the day she arrived. They've got a history, and it's made him think twice.'

'Sweetheart,' said Urlinta, 'if Daur was the sort who was going to drop you just like that the moment the next pair of tits–'

'*Officer* tits,' put in Nilwen.

'–*officer* tits came along,' Urlinta continued, 'he would

not have let you get bonded to come on a trip like this.'

'Urlinta is right,' said Juniper. 'He wouldn't have let you come along on an outing like this, not like this one, if he wasn't serious. That would just be unforgivable.'

'Unless,' said Nilwen, 'unless he's a man. *And* a lasman. In which case being a heartless bastard is standard operating procedure.'

'Nilwen–' Juniper began.

'I tell you, they will stick it anywhere.'

'I'll stick you anywhere,' said Urlinta.

'It's not helping,' Juniper said. 'We all know Daur. He's a fine man. One of the best. You can just tell.'

Elodie frowned.

'I was sure of that,' she said. 'I'd never have left Balhaut if I'd felt differently. I'd never have chosen this life. No offence.'

'None taken,' said Nilwen. 'None of us chose this life, did we ladies? It chose us.'

She and Urlinta cackled.

'Stop fretting about it,' Juniper said to Elodie. 'You'll give yourself frown lines, then he really will start looking elsewhere.'

'I just want to know about this woman,' said Elodie. 'How well did he know her?'

'Do you really want to know that?' asked Urlinta.

'Yes,' said Elodie.

'I wouldn't want to,' said Juniper. 'She's just a face from the past. You don't want to start obsessing, El. Really, you don't.'

'Actually, we don't mind,' said Nilwen, 'because we can gossip about it.'

'I tell you what,' said Juniper. 'I've been getting to know some of the girls from the new intake's retinue. The Vervunhivers. One of them might know something. I'll ask around.'

* * *

BLENNER STOPPED JUST outside Wilder's quarters, took the pill bottle out of his pocket, and shook it. There weren't many left. He was going to need more before long. He wasn't looking forward to the conversation with Dorden. The old doctor was bound to comment on the speed with which he had used the first supply. Well, screw him. It wasn't like he hadn't followed instructions. 'One of these, every day, or when you feel agitated'. Well, he'd been agitated quite a lot. A hell of a lot.

Maybe he could deal with one of the orderlies, show them the label, get them to fill out a scrip. He could avoid Dorden's awkward questions entirely. That ruled out the inker, then. Lesp, his name was. He'd already managed to piss him off. He couldn't go looking for favours there. Blenner thought about Curth for a moment. The idea of her made him smile, but not in any useful *I-can-help-you-get-more-pills* way. He just had an unbidden mental image of the good doctor Ana with nothing but a biomonitor and an encouraging bedside manner.

What about the freak, Kolding? Blenner didn't like him, but the man was new. Maybe he would respond to persuasion.

'Looking for me?' asked Wilder.

Blenner turned, deftly pocketing the bottle.

'I was about to knock.'

Wilder looked terrible. His eyes were hollow and he needed a shave.

'Come in,' he said.

They went into Wilder's quarters. There was still the faint smell of the counterseptic Perday had used to scrub the floor.

'How are you?' asked Blenner.

'What is this going to be?' asked Wilder. 'A formal reprimand? A quiet word?'

'Let's start with the latter, shall we?' asked Blenner. 'You made an arse of yourself last night. It could have been the end for you. It almost was. But you were covered.'

'So that's two I owe you?' asked Wilder. 'Is that what you're saying?'

'I gather Trooper Perday told you?'

Wilder nodded.

'She told me what the two of you did.'

'Don't mention it,' said Blenner.

Wilder sat down and rubbed his chin.

'I know how this goes,' he said. 'You want to make sure I know how much I depend upon you. I'm your man. You can call in favours.'

'Your experience of the Guard hasn't been particularly positive, has it?' Blenner said. 'Does it occur to you that I might just be trying to make sure a decent officer doesn't flush his career away? His career and his life?'

'Really? I don't believe you. Everyone's got an ulterior motive.'

'You really are a bitter man, Wilder. You think the worst of everybody.'

'And I'm never disappointed.' Wilder shrugged. 'Look at me, commissar. This was my brother's command. Now he's dead, and my face doesn't fit, and I'm a scum junior whose been a laughing stock since the moment he arrived because he brought a bloody band with him.'

'I know what it's like to be in someone's shadow,' said Blenner quietly. 'For you, your late brother. For me, my schoolboy friend. Ibram Gaunt. In a way, Gaunt for both of us, then. Hard acts to follow.'

'He's surprisingly unpopular,' said Wilder.

'The men love him.'

'Not all of them. Most, yes, but a few… a few malcontents, they loathe him. This isn't one big happy family.'

'Interesting,' said Blenner. He sat down facing Wilder.

'I'll deny I said it if you tell him.'

'I won't tell him,' said Blenner. 'Look, you expect me to have an ulterior motive. Fine. I'll have one. If it makes you feel better, Captain Wilder, I don't care about your

pathetic existence at all. I care about the fact that my
commissarial remit... my career, right now... is focused
on the Belladon in this regiment. And if I have to disgrace or execute their drunken bastard of an officer in
the first week, I'm never going to win them over. Make
sense?'

Wilder nodded.

'They said you'd tried hard last night.'

'Tried hard?'

'To make a good impression. I spoke to a few of the
men today. Commissars come in two flavours, the lasman's best friend and the lasman's worst enemy. It's an
odd fact, but in the long run, the rabble prefer the latter.'

Blenner took off his cap and finger-combed his hair.
He glared at the deck.

'They saw that's what I was doing, did they?'

'They're lasmen, commissar. Not idiots. Besides, they
liked you. They've heard all about Hark. Gaunt too. You
sound infinitely preferable.'

Blenner looked at him.

'So what's the problem?'

'In the end,' said Wilder, 'what they need is a bit of
steel. When the shooting starts, they don't want a friend.
They want someone they can absolutely depend on. The
shooting's going to start *soon*, commissar. Who would
you want at your side? The happy clown or the cold-
hearted bastard?'

Blenner's hands were shaking. He wanted to take a
pill, but he didn't want Wilder to see.

'We could–' he said, and faltered. He breathed deeply
and tried again. 'We could work together, captain. It
seems to me we could both use a little support. A little
mutual effort could clean your slate *and* strengthen my
position.'

Wilder nodded.

'We could try that. All right. Novobazky.'

'What?'

'Lucien had an excellent working relationship with his commissar,' said Wilder, 'Genadey Novobazky. They were together five years. The one before, Causkon, he was useless. But Novobazky was a real rabble rouser. He could talk, you understand me? Lucien used to write to me about him. The letters home. Novobazky could win a battle, he said, just by opening his damn mouth.'

'What happened to him?' asked Blenner.

'Died on Ancreon Sextus with Lucien.'

'So not *every* battle, then.'

'Don't be smart, commissar. Do yourself a favour and look up his service record. The text of his declarations.'

Blenner got up.

'Get your house in order, captain. We'll speak again.'

Wilder nodded. He didn't get up.

'I'll take your advice,' said Blenner at the door. 'So take some from me. Forget about your brother.'

'Really?'

'This is the Emperor's Imperial Guard, Wilder. It's about a lot of things, but family isn't one of them. Blood ties get in the way. They just get in the way. They are a weakness. Look at Gaunt and his son–'

'His what?'

Blenner hesitated.

'It'll be known soon enough. His bastard child arrived the same time you did. Vervunhive aristo with his own lifeguard. It was a surprise to Gaunt, and he's trying to treat it like it's nothing, but it will affect him. Don't let your brother do the same thing to you.'

'I see.'

'The Guard is the only family you ever need, captain. Blood relatives are just a complication.'

WILDER SAT ALONE for a while after Blenner left. He drifted off in thought, and then realised Didi Gendler was standing in the cabin doorway, grinning at him.

'You look a little the worse for wear,' said Gendler.

Wilder got up. Gendler exclaimed in surprise as Wilder grabbed him by the tunic front, dragged him into the cabin and slammed the door. He smashed Gendler back against the bulkhead.

'Are you out of your mind?' Gendler stammered.

'You bastards screwed with me! A friendly drink? I don't even remember getting on board!'

'I was under the impression you were a grown up, Captain Wilder,' snapped Gendler. 'It's not our job to moderate your drinking. Blenner stop by to put you on a charge, did he?'

Wilder looked away and let go. Gendler straightened himself up.

'You should thank us,' said Gendler.

'Why?'

'You only got to your cabin because of us. When we realised how much you'd tucked away, Captain Meryn had me and Costin smuggle you aboard. We were looking out for you. You'd have been shot for disgracing the uniform otherwise.'

Wilder didn't reply.

'In fact, the captain sent me to check on you. He told me to give you this.'

Gendler held out a small glass bottle.

'What is it?'

'A cure-all. Knocks back the effects of a hangover. From the captain's own supply.'

Wilder took it.

'This is from regimental stores,' he said, reading the label. 'Medicae supplies.'

'Don't be naive, captain. If you know the right people, you can get anything you need.'

'And who do you know, Gendler?'

'The right people.'

Wilder looked at the bottle again, and then unstoppered it and drank it.

'It's good stuff,' said Gendler. 'Costin swears by it. He's been functioning on it for years.'

'I take it you and Captain Meryn are businessmen,' said Wilder.

'We provide unofficial services. Someone has to. There's a demand. We're good at it.'

'It takes money. And organisation.'

'We have both,' said Gendler. 'Like I said, we're good at it. Time was, Rawne was the biggest noise in the shadow trade.'

'The second officer?'

'Right, you've met him?'

'Not yet,' said Wilder.

'He's rather more legitimate these days,' said Gendler. 'Legitimate and busy. Captain Meryn thought it was only fair and helpful to take some of the hard work off his plate.'

'Why?' asked Wilder.

'Oh, don't be dense,' said Gendler. 'There are winners and losers in any regiment. Rawne's becoming a bit of a winner. And he's always made sure Meryn lost out. Promotions. Advancements. Sometimes, you have to take charge of your own destiny. Meryn, me... *you*. We see a kindred spirit in you.'

'Someone to join your losers club?'

Gendler laughed without smiling.

'Thwarted men with ambition can do great things, Wilder. They can rise and make others fall. The privilege of rank, of opportunity. Failing either of those, the simple comfort of riches.'

'Is this about getting on, or revenge?' asked Wilder.

'Why can't it be about both?' smiled Gendler.

Wilder was feeling better. The cure-all had certainly been effective. He laughed.

'What do you and Meryn really want from me?' he asked.

'Cards on the table?' asked Gendler. 'All right. Friends

help each other. And everyone's got an angle. What's your angle? The most useful commodity is protection. Any shield that will let us operate unseen. It's early days, but you already seem to be on good terms with Blenner.'

'So?'

'He's a soft touch. A soft touch commissar. The best protection a Guardsman could ever ask for.'

'I don't know him at all,' said Wilder.

'That's not true. Besides, you could know him better. You could cultivate him. Find a weakness. Find his angle. Find leverage.'

'Could I?'

'It's what friends do,' said Gendler.

Wilder didn't reply. Gendler shrugged and turned to leave.

'I think he's got a habit,' said Wilder quietly.

'What?'

'Pills, I think. Anxiety is my guess. So, a narcotic.'

'How do you know?' asked Gendler, smiling.

'I've seen the habit before. He had a bottle. Didn't want me to see. Then he was twitchy. He wouldn't have tried to hide it if it was on the level or something he wasn't ashamed of.'

'Interesting.'

'Is it?' asked Wilder. 'It sounds like persecution to me. Is that the angle you were looking for? What will you do? Expose him? Control his supply and make him your puppet?'

'He's only useful if he stays in play,' said Gendler. 'We wouldn't want to strangle his supply. We would want to increase it. Become the friends he can rely on.'

'You're a bastard, Gendler,' said Wilder.

'An effective bastard.'

'You must feel right at home here,' said Wilder, shaking his head. 'Everyone's a bastard, one way or another. Even the mighty Gaunt has a bastard of his own.'

Gendler stopped, his smile vanishing.

'What did you just say?' he asked.

THE WOMAN'S NAME was Galayda. She was one of a group of Verghast intake that Juniper stopped in the laundry halls. Everybody was perspiring from the warm damp air. There was a hard chemical stink of ultra-processed water and cleaning chemicals.

'Ban Daur?' Galayda said. She was from Hass West, Vervunhive, a hab girl who had lost everything in the war and ended up attached to a scratch company man called Herzog, who was a sergeant in Major Pasha's brigade.

'He was PDF,' said Juniper.

'I didn't know any Hive Defence,' said Galayda. 'I fought for a while in the scratch company after I lost my ma and pa in the bombing. Gak, we all did. That's where I met Herzog.'

'But you put away the gun after the Zoican War?'

'I'm no soldier. A scratch company isn't soldiers. It's desperate people. A soldier's wife, though. That's more me.'

She looked at Juniper. Her sleeves were rolled up and her arms were stained and sore with chemical soaps.

'Sorry I can't help your friend.'

'No matter,' said Juniper. 'I'll find someone who can.'

'Stavik might know,' said the woman next to them.

'Yes, he might,' said Galayda.

'Stavik?' asked Juniper.

'He's one of the squad leaders under Major Pasha,' said Galayda. 'I think he was Hive Defence.'

'He was,' said the other woman. 'He was at the wall fort.'

'Or you could always ask Zhukova,' said Galayda.

'As if,' laughed Juniper.

'Yes, you want to watch Zhukova,' said the other woman, lifting another tub of sheets. 'She's awfully pretty, but she's a hard-nosed bitch.'

'Kolea,' said Galayda. 'He's one of the regiment, isn't he?'

'Major Kolea?' asked Juniper. 'Yes, he's the senior Verghastite officer.'

'The scratch company hero,' said the other woman. 'They still talk about him in the hive, like they talk about Gaunt.'

'You knew him?' asked Juniper.

'Only by reputation,' said Galayda. 'I think my Herzog might have met him a few times in the final days. But I knew his poor wife and her kids. Well, my ma and pa, they lived in the same hab block. I always thought that must have driven him on to be such a hero, losing his family. They died, didn't they? Her and her kids. They died a few days before the bombing took my ma and pa.'

'She died,' said Juniper. 'The children actually survived.'

'They did?' asked Galayda. She seemed genuinely amazed.

'They're with the company,' said Juniper. 'Captain Criid as she is now, she found them, looked after them. Adopted them, basically. It was only later we all found out that Kolea was their father.'

Galayda looked like she might cry.

'Oh, it's like a blessing from the Emperor,' she exclaimed. 'All this pain and sadness, and in the middle of it, a happy story! They both lived? I can't believe it!'

'I know them,' smiled Juniper. 'I look after the youngest sometimes. The boy is now a trooper himself.'

'The eldest, you mean?' asked Galayda.

'The boy,' said Juniper. 'Dalin.'

'They were both boys. Two boys,' said Galayda.

'No, a boy and girl,' said Juniper.

'I could have sworn they were both boys,' said Galayda. 'Oh well, isn't a happy ending a lovely thing?'

* * *

'I SHOULD NEVER have come here,' said Meritous Chass.

'It's your birthright,' replied Maddalena.

They were on a walkway overlooking a holdspace reserved for drill. Chass was watching the men parade. The great banks of lamps around them kept fizzling and fading in and out.

'I'm not really interested in that,' he said. 'This is dire. He doesn't want me here.'

'He's just surprised, Meritous.'

'I don't know how many times I have to tell you this, Maddalena, I hate that name. One of those stupid family traditions. Felyx, or sir.'

The lifeguard shrugged.

'He's just surprised,' she said. 'He has a child. He didn't know. He will need to process it.'

'How long will that take? What if he processes it and decides he's better off without me?'

'You're depressed.'

'It's hard not to be. Have you seen this rotting hulk? It's falling apart. We'll be lucky if the warp doesn't claim our souls. And the Tanith, I mean, the *real* Tanith. I know they helped defend the hive, and our House owes them, but they're like barbarian auxiliaries.'

'That's probably because they *are* barbarian auxiliaries,' said Maddalena. She suddenly snapped alert, her hand close to her weapon.

'Look,' she said, 'it's Trooper Dalin.'

Dalin was approaching them along the walkway. He seemed nervous.

'You know why Gaunt picked him, don't you?' whispered Maddalena.

'No.'

'He's Kolea's son. The son of the *other* great hero of Vervunhive.'

'It's all about image and reputation with these people, isn't it?' whispered Chass.

'Commissar Ludd sent me,' said Dalin. He looked like

he was deciding whether to salute or not. He couldn't look Chass in the eye. 'The enlistment papers are ready. Then I need to get you some kit, then a billet. It makes sense to attach you to E Company with me. I'm the captain's adjutant.'

'Show me the way,' said Chass.

Maddalena moved to follow him.

'Stay here,' Chass told her. 'Just for now, let me do this by myself.'

'Your mother charged me not to let you out of my sight.'

'He's on a shiftship in the warp,' said Dalin. 'Exactly where do you think he can go?'

SEVEN
Faces

CAVITY 29617 WAS a hold space, a long and slightly irregular chamber that ran beside and under one of the main plasma engine housings. It was low priority, and had only the rudiments of light and atmospheric processing. From the junk and dust, it was an attic or basement – or whatever they called such things on starships – that hadn't been used in a few centuries.

That suited Merrt.

Cavity 29617 was out of the way. It wasn't one of the big holds reserved for training exercise and technique work, and it was far smaller than the hangar decks used for parade and mass drill. It was narrow and long, which gave him some range. It had a breeze running through it from the processor vents, which gave it a cross-draught and made it feel a bit like outdoor conditions. And no one went there, so no one could see him being useless.

Since his injury on Monthax, years of practice had failed to yield any results. Merrt had tried: he'd shown a persistence and resolve rare even by marksman standards. He had worked to rebuild his shattered skill.

The only thing he was sure of was that he should have given up trying a long time ago.

But Larkin, his old friend and rival, was in another of his mad moods. He had invested his manic attention in Merrt, and Merrt didn't have the heart to let him down. He knew he *would* let him down, but he wanted to be seen to make an effort, so it didn't seem like he'd just let it happen. A few dozen hours' extra target practice, what could that hurt? It proved that Larkin was his friend, and he was willing to humour his friend's confidence. It meant that when he finally had to say he couldn't do it, he'd *know* that he couldn't do it. He had proof. Evidence. He'd tried, so the failure was softened.

Merrt had the bolt-action rifle Larkin was using to train him and a box of shells. Larkin had yet to explain the full significance of the old mech weapons in terms of the mission profile. A longlas was a far superior weapon. Only a few people in the Tanith First knew what they were heading into and what they might be expected to do when they got there. Merrt knew Larkin himself only understood bits of it. Just enough to train specialisms.

The one and only thing everybody knew was that they were not heading for a happy place. The next mission was going to be damn hard work.

Merrt had lined up some old tin cups, pots and lubricant canisters as targets, and set himself up in a seated position, his back against the cavity wall to take his weight, the rifle braced across a stand he'd rigged from an old metal bench. He'd then adjusted and finessed the rest using a couple of the sand socks every marksman carried in his pouch. He had a simple optic scope for range finding, but he used it separately, lining up an angle then putting the scope aside to take final aim along the iron sights of the gun.

He allowed for air drift, and the rifle's innate inclination to dip and rise on discharge. The weapon had a tiny left-hand bias, which Larkin had corrected for by

adjusting the sights with a watch maker's screwdriver.
Merrt let his tension out, then let all the air in his lungs
go, a long slow exhalation so that even the stir of respi-
ration or the tremble of suspended breathing wouldn't
affect the aim. The only thing he couldn't reduce was the
infinitesimal quake of his heartbeat, so he timed to fire
between beats. *Beat... line up the shot... beat... check the
line... beat... fire.*

The shot echoed down the cavity. The round clipped
the lip of a tin pot, and made it judder. He'd been aiming
for a mark on the pot about a middle finger's distance
away from what he'd actually hit.

Hopeless. Fething *hopeless.*

To even be considered for a lanyard, he'd have needed
to partially overlap the target spot.

'That is a poor shot.'

Merrt jumped. It wasn't so much that someone had
surprised him, it was that someone so big had miracu-
lously appeared in his line of sight.

He scrambled up, knocking over the stand.

'Gn! Gn! Gn!'

Surprise gave way to fear.

The White Scar squinted down the range, then looked
back at the human with the rifle.

'Very poor,' said Sar Af. 'Pathetic. Why do you even
bother?'

'Gn... gn... gn...'

'Speak up? Are you simple?'

'I'm gn... gn... gn... practising!'

Sar Af frowned. He coughed, and then rubbed the tip
of his nose with armoured fingers that could crush bone.

'You will be here a long time,' he said.

'I've been here a long gn... gn... gn... time already,'
said Merrt.

Sar Af nodded. He held out his hand.

'Give it to me.'

His voice reminded Merrt of Jago. Dry winds, gusting

forlornly through dusty valleys. Sandstone eroded by the air. Merrt handed him the rifle.

Sar Af took it; a stick, a toy. He sighted down the barrel, holding it one-handed, as if to check the barrel was actually straight. The trigger guard was entirely too small for his fingers.

He handed it back.

'I cannot use that. Shoot again.'

'Sir?'

'Again.'

Merrt reached to reset the stand and pick up the sand socks.

'Do not bother with that. Just take a good shot from where you are. Just aim and shoot.'

Merrt slunked the bolt, ejected the shell case, took another round out of the box at his feet, and chambered it. He glanced at the Space Marine. The giant was simply staring down at him, impassive.

Merrt put the gun up to his cheek, chose a tin cup, sighted, breathed out, and fired. The shot clipped the cup hard enough to spin it off the block. It made several dull, hollow sounds as it bounced on the hold deck.

'Still pathetic,' said Sar Af. He looked at Merrt. 'Good enough for Guard fire on a field, I suppose, but not precise enough for anything else.'

Merrt didn't know what to say.

The White Scar was still looking at him, but his mind was far away. It felt to Merrt like the Space Marine was precisely playing back at a painstakingly slow rate the memory of Merrt taking the shot so he could analyse it.

He stopped, looked back at Merrt, and then suddenly reached out a hand, grabbing Merrt by the jaw and throat. The hand turned Merrt's head to the side. Merrt struggled and choked.

'This jaw. This augmetic repair, it is your problem,' said Sar Af. 'You are being defeated by your own concentration. Your focus is so intense that as you fire the gun, it stimulates the neurodes in your jaw and you twitch.'

'I gn… gn… gn… twitch?'

'Just as you fire. Your jaw clenches.'

Sar Af let him go.

'It is physically impossible for you to shoot well.'

Merrt swallowed.

'Come back again tomorrow,' said Sar Af.

THE MAIN REFECTORY was in the mid decks. The walls and floor were plated with dull, galvanised steeling, and the metal tables and benches were bolted in place. There was a constant clatter of utensils and dishes against metal surfaces, and the air frequently fumed with steam from the galley.

Wilder picked at the slab on the plate in front of him.

Meryn sat down opposite. He had a covered dish of food and a tin beaker. Meryn drank the contents of the beaker in one swallow, then slid the empty beaker across the table to Wilder.

Wilder looked at the cup. Meryn took a fork out of his top pocket and began to eat.

'How's yours, Jakub?' he asked, pleasantly.

Wilder didn't reply. He picked up the empty beaker and looked in it. There was a little brown paper wrap in the bottom of the cup.

'What's that?'

'Happiness,' replied Meryn, still eating.

'For me?'

Meryn chewed to empty his mouth before replying.

'They'll make our mutual friend Blenner happy, which is the same thing.'

Wilder put the cup down again as if he had no intention of touching the little bag of narcotic pills.

'Where are they from?'

'Costin,' said Meryn.

'He grows them on a special tree, does he?'

'Do you want them or not?'

Meryn leant his elbow on the table, rocking the fork in his hand. He stared at Wilder, chewing another mouthful.

'Do you know where we're going?' he asked.

'No,' said Wilder.

Meryn sighed.

'Yes, I suppose if I don't get told, you certainly wouldn't.'

'What does that mean?'

'It means some people get on and some don't, Jakub. Some people enjoy favour. You were right, what you said to Gendler about Gaunt's brat.'

'Why would I have lied?' asked Wilder.

'No reason. Gaunt's got my adjutant running around looking after the spoiled little brat. The kid's no soldier. Not old enough. Doesn't look like he's done a hand's turn in his life. Certainly never fought. He'd blow away if the Archenemy so much as farted. Got his own cabin, though.'

'His own cabin...'

Meryn grinned.

'Can you believe that? Gaunt pretends he wants him treated like all the others, like every common lasman, but then his psychobitch *lifeguard* – because every common lasman has a lifeguard, don't they? Then his lifeguard says he can't share a general billet with other men. Oh no. She insists. She needs him behind a door she can defend.'

'She said this to Gaunt?'

'Of course not,' said Meryn. 'She says it to me. See how he did that? He declares that we're going to treat the brat like everyone else, then makes it my problem, so that the stink of favouritism doesn't stick to him.'

'What did you do?' asked Wilder.

'Gave him the small end cabin on the officer quarter block near mine.'

Wilder sat back, and sipped from his beaker.

'Doesn't that undermine Gaunt's wishes?' he asked.

'Gaunt's passive aggressive. He says one thing, but he means another. Come on, Wilder, you know how this goes. If I'd stuck to my guns and made the boy sleep in the general barrack, I'd have suddenly found myself getting all the shit details. It would have become E Company's turn to hose out the latrines, or spearhead the next attack.'

'So Gaunt gets his way and it looks like someone else's idea,' said Wilder.

'You're beginning to see the Imperial truth,' grinned Meryn.

'Why do you hate him so much?'

Meryn shrugged.

'He killed my world. My life. That deserves payback, sooner or later. But it's not that, so much. Everything I have, everything I've built up, I've made it for myself. Company command. Rank. Privilege. Influence. I did it all myself. I don't get things handed to me. I'm not part of his inner circle.'

'Who is?'

'Kolea. Baskevyl. Mkoll. Even Rawne these days, because apparently Rawne left his balls behind on Gereon. I don't owe Gaunt anything. He owes me everything. And he's never going to give it, so I'm taking everything I can.'

'What about Gendler?'

'Gendler's the same,' said Meryn, cutting another mouthful with the side of his fork, 'Gaunt took his life away. You have to understand, Didi was a rich man on Verghast. Up-spine. Noble blood. Lost it all in the Zoican War, family, property. And what choice did he get? Live in poverty in Vervunhive during the long years of post-war rebuild and deprivation, hoping that one day his legal claims for compensation might be heard in the assizes? Or take the Act of Consolation, where the dispossessed could join the Guard and start a new life?'

'Gendler made his choice,' said Wilder.

'Yes, he did. He said goodbye to his old life, to what family he had left, and came to serve Gaunt. And has Gaunt ever recognised him? Seen fit to make him more than sergeant? Didi cuts ties with his relatives forever, but Gaunt? They bring his fething son through the warp to be with him. *He* gets to bring his past with him. *He* gets to have a life. *He* gets to have a family. The Emperor's Imperial Guard makes sure of that. We sacrifice so he gets to be what he is. It's always about favour, Jakub, just like I said. It's always about favour and who you know.'

Wilder thought about it. Meryn watched his face.

'I know you feel it too, Jakub,' said Meryn. 'Just like us. Your brother. His command. His regiment. And look how they treat you. Like a joke.'

Wilder put down his fork.

'Life's unfair,' he said. 'That's all.'

'Right. So you make it fairer,' said Meryn.

'How?'

'Well Didi says we should kill Gaunt's kid,' said Meryn.

He smiled at the horrified expression on Wilder's face.

'Calm down. Didi's just a bit angry. It's the Vervunhive connection. Gaunt's not even up-spine blood, and he gets noble favour. Seriously, it's a joke. We're not going to murder anybody. Didi had sunk a few. He was just being toxic. There are less dramatic things we can do that will be just as satisfying.'

'Like what?' asked Wilder.

Meryn nodded to the beaker.

'You take those,' he said, 'you put them to work. That's a start.'

He got up, stepped off the bench and picked up his plate.

'Where I came from,' he said, 'men were raised as hunters. Hunters plan. They stalk. They take their time.

You know what a hunter's greatest weapon is, Jakub?'

'No.'

'Patience,' said Meryn.

EYES THAT WERE remarkably good copies of Trooper Pol Cohran's watched the shift change at the deep hold containment area.

It had taken a few hours to find out where on board the prisoner was being held. The armoured well of an old battery magazine had been converted into a cell. That was smart thinking. The battery magazines had thicker walls than the discipline brig.

The enemy had placed security measures in the hands of a dedicated squad. The squad, first platoon of E Company, had been granted Commissariat S status. They were also regimental veterans, die-hard Ghosts, so there was little chance of co-opting or turning one.

Cohran watched from the shadows. He checked the approaches, the ways to and from the cell, the routines. Where did food come from? How was it brought? How many times a shift? What opportunities were there to intercept and tamper with it? At any time, there were four of the S Company guards around: two outside the hatch, two in the tank.

Cohran, at least the thing that was playing the role of Pol Cohran, was patient. Observation times were limited, because Cohran's absence from the quarters deck would be noticed at certain times. He didn't want to give up the identity. More particularly, he didn't want the state of alert to be heightened because a trooper had gone missing.

But he was also keenly aware that his opportunities – and he had to choose one quickly – had fast-approaching expiry dates.

BLENNER POURED HIMSELF a second mug of caffeine and fantasised about slugging a dash of amasec in it. He had never been comfortable making shift, the day-less nights and night-less days, the dreams, the dislocation. He hadn't been sleeping well. The prospect of days or even weeks more did not fill him with relish. Give him a nice world and a straight fight instead. Actually, the fight could belong to someone else. Just a nice world would do.

He took another disdainful look at the data-slate he had been reading from. Excerpted pieces from the service record of Novobazky, pulled from the regimental archive. Wilder had been right. Novobazky could certainly talk. For hours at a time. It was giving Blenner a headache.

He took a pill. There were only a few of them rattling around in the bottle now. He didn't like to think of them as a crutch, but he really didn't like to think of facing life without them.

'You look terrible,' said Fazekiel, sitting down at his table in the staff section of the refectory.

'Is there no beginning to your charm?' asked Blenner.

She grinned, and began to arrange the food on her tray. She'd made them serve items like slab and veg paste on separate dishes. There was a lot of fibre, and a large canister of thick grey nutrient drink rather than caffeine.

'Healthy mind in a healthy body,' she said.

'In an entirely miserable and deprived body maybe,' he replied. He looked at her drink. 'What's wrong with caffeine? That stuff will kill you. And what's with the separate dishes?'

'I don't like things to touch,' said Fazekiel. 'It's messy and undisciplined.'

'Really?' Despite the hour and his heavy head, Blenner grinned. Luna Fazekiel was always immaculate. He'd never known anyone adhere to dress code so exactly, even by the demanding standards of the Commissariat.

She saw Blenner staring.

She was obsessively clean and punctual, obsessively regimented and organised.

'Something funny?' she asked. She was a handsome woman, and a highly effective commissar, but control smoked off her like blood fog off a power blade. There was no margin for error with her. No give. The troop mass saw that in her, and that's what made them respect her.

'No, no,' he said.

'Thought you'd be at the inspection,' she said.

He looked up.

'Weren't you the one who postponed it?' she asked.

'Ah,' he said.

'Where is this trooper?' asked Edur.

'Sir, I don't know, sir,' replied Yerolemew, rigidly at attention.

Edur looked at Wilder.

'Comment, captain?' he asked.

'The trooper's absence is unauthorised,' said Wilder, staring at the empty cot. In the hold space around him, the bandsmen of his command stood beside their made-up cots in perfect rows. He knew they would all have been looking at him if they hadn't had eyes front.

'There's the absence itself,' said Edur, 'and then there's your sergeant major's ignorance.'

'I think they're connected,' said Wilder. 'If Sergeant Major Yerolemew knew where the trooper was, the absence wouldn't be unauthorised.'

'Don't get clever, captain,' said Baskevyl.

Wilder could see that Major Baskevyl was uncomfortable. From what he'd heard, the major was a fair man who was probably unhappy seeing the good name of Belladon put under pressure.

'What's the trooper's name?' asked Edur.

'Cohran, sir,' said Yerolemew.

'I will issue a citation,' said Edur. 'It will be for both the trooper and–'

'Cohran is shift-sick,' said Blenner. He'd walked into the hall behind the inspection party.

'It's a bad case,' he added. 'Afflicted a lot of personnel this time out. You had a touch yourself, didn't you, captain?'

'Yes,' said Wilder.

'I signed a chit and sent Cohran along to the infirmary,' said Blenner.

'The sergeant major was unaware,' said Edur.

'Because I've only just done it, and I was coming to tell the sergeant major about it,' said Blenner.

Edur stared at him for a second.

'That's the thing about surprise inspections,' said Blenner pleasantly. 'They don't fall at neatly punctuated moments.'

'Very well,' said Edur. 'Let's carry on.'

THE INSPECTION CONTINUED for another forty minutes. When Edur and Baskevyl were gone, Blenner took Wilder to one side.

'Find two or three troopers you can trust. That girl, for example. Get them to find Cohran.'

Wilder nodded.

'You didn't send him to the medicae, did you?'

'No,' said Blenner. He wrote out a permission slip, tore it off his workbook, and folded it. 'Get this to him, and tell him where he was supposed to be. Fast. Then tell him to come and find me and we'll make sure this never happens again.'

'Thank you,' said Wilder.

'Don't thank me. My neck's on the line too.'

Wilder thought for a moment, and then took something out of his pocket.

'I wondered if you could do anything with these,' he said.

Blenner took the small bag of pills.

'What's this?' he asked.

'I found them,' said Wilder.

'Where?'

Wilder shrugged.

'Could there be... more of them?' asked Blenner.

'Probably,' said Wilder. 'Troopers are always finding a way of getting their hands on stuff. I'm sure some might turn up again.'

'I see,' said Blenner. He looked at the little bag and put it in his coat pocket. 'I'll take care of it, captain.'

'Good,' said Wilder. 'I thought that would be for the best. Just thought we should keep it quiet.'

They looked around as Sergeant Major Yerolemew approached them.

'Begging your pardon, sirs,' he said. 'Message just received. The full regiment's to assemble on the main excursion deck in an hour. The commander's going to address us.'

'I suppose now we're underway,' said Wilder, 'we get to find out where we're going.'

'I suppose we do,' said Blenner.

THERE WAS GREAT activity through the mid-decks of the ship as the regiment assembled for the address. At his bridge position, Shipmaster Spika watched his passengers bustling like hive insects through the oily tunnels and dank companionways. He adjusted settings and switched the pict view of several screens.

People intrigued him. People who didn't live in the void, like he did, seemed so contained by the fabric of the ship, so penned in. They were cattle, being transported to market. They did not inhabit the vessel the way he and his crew did.

His seat was a worn leather throne mounted in a gilded carriage. There were two big banks of control levers at the end of each armrest. The mechanisms were so old that many of the levers had been replaced: new metal bars and handle-tops seam-welded onto the eroded or broken spurs of the originals. Even some of the replacements had begun to wear. Spika adjusted the levers and his chair, mounted on a long, gimbal-jointed lifting arm, rose up out of the upper deck platform and extended out over the vast bridge. From there, he could sweep down and observe main console functions over the shoulders of key officers, or loft himself up into the domed roof to study the hololithic star-map projection or converse with the twitching, harnessed navigator.

He'd been invited to attend the address. A note had been delivered from the colonel-commissar fellow. He wouldn't attend. He knew where they were going.

Besides, the warp was rough and troubled. There was a lively tide and unusual levels of dispersion and turbulence.

He needed to be on the bridge, at his station, in case things got rough.

'WHAT'S GOING ON?' Elodie asked Daur, passing him in the bustling central line hall.

'Review,' he replied. 'Address. We get told our destination.'

'Really?' asked Elodie.

'This is the point of it all,' said Daur. 'The point where we commit. The real start of the mission. Look, I've got to get on and get G Company assembled. I'll come and tell you everything later.'

'Everything?' she asked.

'I promise.'

They moved off in opposite directions. Pol Cohran stepped out of the shadows of a colonnade arch and merged with the flow of hurrying figures, just another hustling trooper.

He'd heard what the captain had said.

We get told our destination.

Priorities had just changed again.

'You. You there!'

Cohran stopped, and turned slowly. Some of the personnel passing him bumped against him. Twenty paces behind him, Commissar Edur was glaring at him.

'Cohran? Trooper Cohran?'

'Yes, sir.'

'Come here, damn it!' Edur snapped, indicating a spot on the deck directly in front of him. The river of people around them parted and found other routes to take. No one wanted to get in the way of an Imperial commissar, especially not one who was clearly aggravated. Furthermore, no one had seen the newcomer Edur raise his voice yet.

'Right here, trooper!' Edur ordered.

Cohran hesitated a moment longer. He weighed his options, and realised they all depended on him maintaining his deception. In full view like this, in front of dozens of regimental personnel, his options were drastically limited.

He walked back to Edur, and stood in front of him, hands behind his back.

Edur wrinkled a lip.

'Under the circumstances,' said Edur quietly, 'I think an attitude of attention shows more respect.'

Cohran snapped to attention.

'This isn't the infirmary,' said Edur.

'Sir?'

'I said this is a long way from the infirmary, trooper.'

'Yes, sir.'

'Your acceleration sickness got better then, did it?' asked Edur. 'You don't look sick to me. Or did the grace of the beati and the God-Emperor shine forth upon you and heal you?'

'May they live forever in our hearts and our minds, sir,' said Cohran.

'Watch your tone.'

'Sir.'

'Let's see this slip, trooper,' said Edur.

'Slip, sir?'

'Your chit, trooper. The permission slip Commissar Blenner gave you.'

'I…' Cohran began. He paused. 'I believe I must have lost it, sir.'

'Let's go, trooper,' said Edur. 'This way.'

'I've got to report for the review and address, sir,' Cohran said.

'Move,' said Edur.

Edur pointed and walked Cohran off the central line hall into one of the transverse access corridors. Edur stayed close behind Cohran, a menacing escort. Two men ran past the other way, carrying a cargo crate between them.

'I should go to the address, sir,' said Cohran.

'Enough, trooper.' said Edur.

'It's mandatory. If I miss it, the captain will–'

'I said *enough*. You're already in trouble for not being where you were supposed to be.'

'But, I–'

'Seriously, how deep do you intend to dig your way into this, Cohran? Punishment squad deep? Flogging deep?'

More men went by in the other direction, hurrying, buttoning up their jackets.

'I just went to the infirmary, sir,' said Cohran. 'I can't miss the review.'

'I'm about out of patience with you, Cohran,' said Edur. 'I think you'll be looking at the inside of the brig for quite a time, while I fathom out why Commissar Blenner tried to protect you. People like you frustrate me, Cohran. If you'd just faced up when I confronted you, I'd have probably let you off with a citation. But this blather, this effort to wriggle out. It's what dilutes the Guard, you hear me? It's the kind of rot-thinking that eats out the heart of a good regiment. You're a weak man, Cohran, and there's no excuse for it.'

'I'm sick, sir,' said Cohran. He stopped walking.

'You're not sick. Get on.'

Cohran shivered and groaned, as though something unpleasant had just undermined him on a gastric level.

'Cohran?'

'I'm going to throw up...' gasped Cohran. He turned and blundered off the transverse into the narrow access tunnel of a engineering inspection bay, clinging to the wall and heaving.

'Cohran!' Edur strode after him. His hand went to his holster.

Cohran had gone a short way down the dank metal tunnel. There was a purr of heavy machinery from the bay up ahead. The light levels were much lower than out in the transverse, where people were still hurrying by. Cohran leaned his forearm and his head against the machined metal wall plate, breathing hard.

Edur drew his pistol and aimed it at the side of Cohran's head.

'You must think I'm a Throne-damned idiot if you think I'm going to fall for this play-acting,' he said. 'This just escalated to serious charges, you worthless–'

Cohran snapped around. With a speed Edur could not explain or anticipate, Cohran's raised hand caught his wrist, knocked the aim aside, and propelled Edur backwards into the opposite wall of the tunnel. He hit hard, grazing the back of his head and driving the wind out of his lungs.

Cohran reversed his turn, embraced Edur's gun-arm, extended it, and then broke the wrist.

Edur howled in pain. Cohran took the pistol out of the limp hand and tossed it into the engineering bay behind him.

It was done. Pain-shock alone would floor the commissar and–

Usain Edur was a strong man. A deep sense of right-
eous indignation broke through his wash of pain and
surprise. It was a reserve that had kept him alive on
several battlefields, a focus that allowed him to push
past the undermining fog of injury or confusion.

He threw himself at Cohran, leading with his left
shoulder. They cannoned together, and Edur dragged
Cohran along a section of wall plate, splitting his lip
and gouging his cheek. Cohran barked out a snarl and
drove his elbow back into Edur's collar-bone. Edur
smacked back against the opposite tunnel wall.

He came at Cohran again, leading with his good
hand. Cohran had turned to square up, head down,
fists raised. As Edur surged forwards, Cohran swung
a punch that caught Edur across the ear and drove
him sideways. He stumbled into the end of the tunnel
wall, and staggered off it into the engineering bay.

Cohran came after him. He needed to control things
again, quickly, before somebody passing along the
traverse heard or saw what was happening. The bay
was more out of the way than the tunnel. The purr of
the machinery masked their sounds. A single servitor
menial turned from an inspection panel to note the
visitors to his workspace with uncomprehending eyes.
Caliper digits flexed as it tried to process the interruption to its basic task functions.

The centre of the bay area was a deep through-deck
shaft that accommodated the rising spire of an accu-
mulator stack. The ancient brass rings and steel-cased
capacitor rods whirred and rotated. Fronds of energy
crackled down in the shaft below the iron handrail.

Cohran barged Edur across the bay and into the rail,
twisting his back and damaging his lower spine. Edur
cried out in pain, lashed out, and connected with his
broken hand. The blow, to the forehead, was enough
to make Cohran flinch backwards, but the pain from
the grinding bone made Edur gag and slump, his eyes

and mouth wide, gasping like a landed fish.

Cohran kicked him in the chest, then again in the face, smashing Edur's head back so it bounced off the guardrail. Edur collapsed in an awkward heap against the rail, his legs bent under him.

Cohran stepped forwards to snap his neck and finish the game.

He stopped dead, looking down the snout of Edur's pistol. Somewhere during the scramble, the commissar had got hold of it again. He was aiming it with his good hand, his broken hand curled like a dead fledgling against his chest. His head was swaying and blood was drooling from his mouth. He'd lost some teeth, and one eye was beginning to swell shut.

'Little bastard...' Edur slurred.

The surprise reversal made Cohran lose control of his face for a second. The features rippled.

'What the hell are you?' Edur asked.

It was enough of a distraction. Cohran punched, his fingers gathered into a beak-shape. The inhuman force of the blow demolished Edur's face and exploded the nasal and brow bones back into his brain. The hand holding the pistol dropped heavily. Edur's pulverised face bowed forwards as if in prayer. Blood pattered out of it in three or four separate streams.

Cohran straightened up. He could feel blood running from his own cheek and lip. He turned. The servitor had risen to its feet, agitated. Cohran stepped forwards, grasped it by its ceramite jaw and cranium, and snapped its neck. He broke off one of the servitor's digital tools and used it to gouge out the unit's optics and burn out its visual memory core.

Cohran looked around. He peered over the rail and saw the long drop into the gloom of the exhaust sump at the foot of the stack. Without prevarication, he tipped Edur's body down the shaft, watched it tumble and deflect off lower guard rails and then disappear.

He threw the servitor in after it.

He needed to get cleaned up. He needed to get to the excursion deck.

'THEY'RE PRESENT AND correct,' said Beltayn.

Gaunt nodded. He put on his cap, peak first, adjusted it, and took a calming breath. Then he walked in through the vast entry hatch. Beltayn fell into step behind him, with an escort squad from A Company led by Criid and Mkoll.

The *Armaduke's* main excursion deck was a vast hangar space with a floor plan equal to several parade grounds set end to end. Light shafted down from the lantern arrays bolted in amongst the girder ribs of the roof. Large craft, such as troop carrier landers and cargo runners, had been towed to the far end, away from the forward space doors. Some were enclosed in cages of gantry scaffolding so that servitors and Mechanicus crews could work on their maintenance. Small craft – the lighters and shuttles – had been hoisted up into the rafters on magnetic clamps and hung overhead like hunting trophies. On the port wing-hinge assembly of one suspended Arvus, a two-headed eagle perched and glared balefully down at Gaunt as he advanced out into the open space of the deck.

The entire regiment had assembled on the principal landing platform. The troopers were wearing operational uniforms rather than formal dress, but the clothes and kit had been cleaned and prepared to the highest standards. They were arranged in company blocks, with their officers to the fore of each section. A cantilevered through-deck elevator had been raised to form a podium in front of them. Company colours were displayed: Tanith, Verghast, Belladon.

The retinue had been permitted to attend. They clustered around the doorway or filled the second and third tier galleries of the deck's upper levels. As he walked out through them, Gaunt saw two faces he recognised: Daur's girl, Elodie, aloof and vigilant; Maddalena Darebeloved.

'No representation from the Adeptus Astartes?' Gaunt asked Beltayn quietly as they walked.

'They seem constantly occupied, sir,' Beltayn whispered back. 'It is reported to me that the Iron Snake spends all his time in relentless combat practice, and the Silver Guard does nothing but study schematic simulations.'

'What about the White Scar?'

'No one knows, sir. He seems to be roaming the ship.'

'And no representation from Spika's crew?'

'I think they're busy doing ship-y things, sir.'

They came out onto the main platform ahead of the review, and Rawne, his eyes front, barked out a stern order. The regiment seamlessly came to attention with one ringing clash. At this signal, Sergeant Major Yerolemew raised his golden pace-stick, and Trooper Perday tilted her head back, raised her helicon, and blasted out a pure, clean, solo fanfare.

Gaunt winced slightly. The playing was fine. In fact, it was perfect, and the sound remarkably uplifting. He just wondered when the Tanith First had become that sort of regiment, and when he had become that sort of commander. It had never been about ceremony.

He stepped up on to the elevated platform, made the sign of the aquila and told the regiment to stand easy.

'With this new strength,' he said, in a voice that was used to carrying effortlessly, 'already welcomed into our fold, we stand together for the first time.'

His eyes drifted across the sea of faces. They were attentive and still, but only a few betrayed any emotion. Ban Daur could never hide that earnest hint of determination. Major Zhukova, a new face for Gaunt, was positively glowing with pride. There was something wry and mischievous in Hlaine Larkin's eyes, and it was a distinctive and familiar as the ever-present hint of dissatisfaction on Viktor Hark's.

Then there was Meritous Felyx Chass. He was in the front rank of E, behind Meryn, flanked by Dalin Criid. Dalin or Ludd had procured a set of Tanith blacks and a camo-cloak for him. He looked breakable and frail, like a child dressed up as a soldier. It was almost as if Dalin had brought his little sister out onto the parade ground. Chass looked a good ten years younger than the youngest members of the company.

With a slight pang and a curious sensation of surprise, Gaunt realised who Chass reminded him of. With that expression of resolution not to fail or let anyone down, Chass looked like a boy, the Hyrkan Boy, the cadet in the corner of regimental picts of the fighting Hyrkan 8th, standing between Sergeant Tanhause and Commissar Oktar.

'We have embarked, and are underway,' said Gaunt. 'And, isolated by the shift, we no longer risk the dangers of loose talk in a home port. I can now tell you a little of the mission we are undertaking.'

No one moved, but he could sense their expectation.

'From the accompany bonds, you know this endeavour will be direct and risky. We will be making a shipboard attack on an enemy facility. That facility is located in the Rimward Marginals, at a place called Salvation's Reach. Specialism briefings will begin immediately after this address, and section leaders will be informed of specific mission requirements. We have, according to the revised estimate, about a week of lead time before we translate and begin deceleration approach of the target area. However, an estimated twenty-three hours from now, we will translate to effect a conjunction with other Battlefleet elements at Tavis Sun. This resupply is expected to last just a few hours, and is ship to ship. Unless this mission is altered or aborted, we will not see a friendly port until this work is complete.'

He raised his head slightly, regarding them all.

'I expect only the very best of you. I can't pretend I

can guarantee you will all return. But I ask you the one question I have always asked you. Do you want to live forever?'

There was a sudden, rousing cheer of approval from the ranks, like a close shell-burst, that made the double-headed eagle up on its perch flap its wings.

'Now get to your stations and begin preparation,' said Gaunt. 'Dismissed.'

As the congregation began to dissolve, Pol Cohran stepped out of the back rank of the band section and headed towards the nearest exit. A spray of synthetic skin had sealed his cuts and disguised the discoloration, but he had no wish to be in the company of others for longer than was necessary.

Now he had information, and it was essential he used it.

Beside the elevated platform, Gaunt turned to Hark and Fazekiel.

'The men seem to be in good spirits,' he remarked, watching them disperse.

'They were inactive on Balhaut for too long,' said Hark. 'And the newcomers are keen to prove themselves.'

'We are indeed,' said Fazekiel.

'By the way,' said Gaunt, 'where's Edur?'

'I haven't seen him since the start of day-cycle,' said Hark.

VAYNOM BLENNER WALKED into the infirmary section that had been reserved for the regiment's use. There were another three infirmary units aboard to administer to the crew. This suite was old and poorly maintained. It was clearly a back-up facility. The chrome and stainless steel surfaces and wall plates were stained with limescale deposits and other, less appealing, residues. Autoclaves chugged like poorly maintained generator engines. The central examination room radiated into a ward, two surgical theatres, and some side chambers for storage and supplies, along with private office spaces for the medicae personnel.

There was no sign of anybody. Blenner walked into the ward. One cot was occupied. Trooper Fulch from N Company had torn his shoulder unloading munitions boxes.

'Where are all the doctors?' Blenner asked.

'They were here just a minute ago, sir,' said Fulch.

Blenner walked back out into the central examination room. Kolding suddenly emerged from one of the rear chambers. He was looking for something. He saw Blenner.

'Can I help you?' he asked.

Blenner stared back at the albino levelly.

'Where's Dorden? I deal with Dorden.'

Kolding stared back at him. His eyes were unreadable behind those damn tinted lenses. He was worse than that damn native partisan Ibram insisted on keeping around.

'Dor-den,' said Blenner, elaborately separating the syllables as though Kolding was a simpleton.

'You'll have to come back,' said Kolding.

'Throne I will! I want to see Dorden now!'

'Kolding, what's taking so—'

Curth emerged from the back with an urgent demeanour. She stopped short as soon as she saw Blenner.

'Commissar.'

'I want to see Dorden,' Blenner said.

Curth looked quickly at Kolding. She took something out of a cabinet drawer and handed it to him.

'Go on,' she told him. 'I'll be right there.' Kolding disappeared back into the rear of the infirmary.

'That man needs training in interpersonal skills,' said Blenner.

'How can I help you?' asked Curth.

'And you need training in basic comprehension,' said Blenner. 'I want to see Dorden.'

He realised instantly that she wasn't in the mood for playful scolding. Her mood was hard and prickly, even by Ana Curth standards.

'There's an emergency,' she said. 'He can't attend you just now. How can I help you?'

Blenner pursed his lips. He wanted Dorden, but he quite liked the excuse to have to deal with her. His business with Dorden could probably wait.

He took the little bag Wilder had given him out of his coat pocket and tossed it to Curth. She caught it neatly, one-handed.

'What are these?' she asked.

'That's what I want you to tell me.'

She opened the bag, tipped a couple of the tablets out into her palm and squinted at them.

'It's a narcotic. Somnia. It's a morphiac derivative. That's a Munitorum pharmaceutical stamp. Where did you get them?'

'They… turned up during a routine search. Are they strong?'

'Pretty strong. I mean, I'd think twice about prescribing them. Effective, but addictive. I sometimes use the liquid version as palliative relief on very damaged patients.'

'So, to ease their last hours?'

'Yes. I'd have to have very compelling reasons to issue them otherwise. Perhaps to a patient in chronic pain who is allergic to safer compounds. You found one of the men with these?'

'Yes. You missing them?'

'I'd have to check, but I don't think so. We carry such small quantities of this as standard, Lesp or one of the other orderlies would have noticed.'

'There is an ongoing problem though, isn't there?' asked Blenner.

'Yes, and we're working on it. But it's usually milder sedatives that are easier to misplace. Harder stuff like this is rarer. It could have come out of the ship's supplies. Do you want me to ask the ship's chief medicae?'

'No,' he said. He paused, and then repeated the word. 'No, I just wanted them identified. Thank you.'

'Well, if that's all,' she said. She clearly had somewhere else she wanted to be.

'I'll take them with me,' he said, holding out his hand.

'I should dispose of them,' she replied. 'Oversight of pharmaceuticals is a medicae responsibility.'

'It's still a discipline matter for now,' he said. 'I'll need them back as evidence.'

She resealed the bag and tossed it across to him.

'Thank you,' he said. He thought about the almost empty bottle in his pocket, but couldn't bring himself to front her up with the question. He didn't want her knowing. He needed to speak to Dorden.

Blenner nodded politely and walked out of the infirmary. Curth issued a deep exhalation of tension and hurried away into the back rooms.

In the hallway outside, Blenner collided with the orderly, Lesp, who was rushing towards the infirmary, leading Ayatani Zweil by the arm.

'Watch where you're going!' Blenner exclaimed. He shot a look at Zweil, expecting some cantankerous barb back. Blenner had been around the regiment long enough to know that the old priest's mouth didn't possess a safety catch.

The look on Zweil's face took him by surprise. Care, anxiety, dread.

'What's going on?' Blenner asked. His mind put the pieces together. An empty infirmary. Kolding and Curth trying to get him to leave. The orderly bringing the priest in a hurry.

'Oh, Throne,' said Blenner, and turned back, striding through the infirmary into the back room.

'Wait. Please!' Lesp called after him.

'Vaynom, what's-your-name, Blenner. Show some Throne-damned respect and don't be an arsehole!' Zweil yelled. They were both rushing after him.

Blenner burst into the back office. Curth looked up from a tray of instruments in surprise, and the surprise quickly turned to despair at the sight of him. Kolding was on the far side of the room, administering a shot of something.

Dorden had brought a trolley table over when he fell. Gleaming instruments lay scattered across the deck mesh. They'd made him comfortable with bolsters from the day bed, but they hadn't dared lift him. He looked so thin and pale.

'This isn't the time,' said Curth.

'What's going on?' Blenner asked.

'Could you give the medicae some dignity and leave, please?' she said, coming over to Blenner. Lesp led Zweil past them to the old doctor's side.

'Yes, there's no need for you to be here,' said Zweil as he went by.

'Is he dying?' Blenner asked. Dorden was now partially obscured by the figures crouching around him. He hadn't even seemed conscious when Blenner walked in.

'You know he is,' Curth replied quietly. He could see she was battling to retain her professional composure.

'I mean now,' said Blenner.

'He's been well for the last week,' she said, her voice still low. 'Amazingly so. But I think the stress of making shift has taken its toll. He collapsed just now. I think we can stabilise him and get him some bed rest.'

'He shouldn't have come on this mission,' said Blenner.

'It would have been crueller to leave him behind,' Curth replied.

'Should Gaunt know? I should get Gaunt.'

'No!' she replied, fiercely. 'He doesn't want that. He doesn't want a fuss. Let him rest!'

'You've brought the damn priest to him,' said Blenner. 'If he's come to administer the Imperial Grace, then Ibram deserves to–'

'No,' she replied. 'Zweil's his friend. He's been supporting him through this. It seemed right to fetch him here. Gaunt doesn't need this on his mind just now.'

Blenner swallowed.

'I didn't mean to just burst in,' he said.

'It's all right.'

'You could have said something. I do have a few circumspect bones in my body.'

'I'll bear that in mind,' she said.

'I really should say something to Ibram,' said Blenner. 'If something happens, and he finds out I knew–'

'Then you don't know,' said Curth. 'You didn't see anything.'

Blenner thought about this, and nodded. He turned to go.

'Are you all right?' he asked.

A tiny flash of surprise crossed her face, as if it never occurred to anybody to ask her that.

'Yes, commissar. Now get along so we can work.'

Blenner left. Curth went to Dorden's side.

'I think he's stabilised,' said Kolding quietly.

'You should take things more easily,' said Curth.

'Why?' whispered Dorden. His voice was the vaguest whisper of dry leaves.

'Because doctors make the worst patients,' said Curth.

'Actually, carnodons make the worst patients,' said Zweil. 'I knew a tamer, a circus man, worked the bag o' nails on Hagia, and he owned this performing–'

He paused. He saw the looks he was getting.

'However, for now, I will stipulate that doctors, in fact, make worse patients that carnodons.'

Dorden managed a tiny smile.

'Even carnodons, let's say, with infected gums that haven't eaten for a week, and then you accidentally leave the cage door open...' Zweil trailed off into a mumble.

'Did I hear Blenner's voice?' Dorden asked.

'He's gone now.'

'I don't want a fuss,' said Dorden.

'He's gone,' Curth repeated. 'He won't say anything.'

'Nothing to say,' said Dorden. 'I'll be on my feet again in a moment. I'm just tired.'

Curth looked up and saw Lesp trying not to cry.

'He probably wants his pills,' said Dorden. His voice was so far away. He beckoned Curth closer with twig fingers. 'He comes to me for a little tonic. To settle him. Make sure you look after him, Ana.'

'I will,' she promised. 'But let's look after you first.'

CLOSE TO THE warp engines, the noise was immense. Everything, every surface, every wall panel, every tooth in a person's head, vibrated at an ultrafast frequency.

Layers of armour plate and bulkheads secured the drive chambers. Some sections were sealed chambers where only conditioned servitors or crewmen in protective armour could venture during drive function. Hard, hot yellow light shafted out through the letterbox viewing slits of the reinforced hatches like the glow from a furnace room port.

Vast engineering spaces were filled with dripping, frosty coolant systems, or the black-greased pistons of circulation pumps and galvanic generators. In sooty caverns full of smoke and flame, ogryn and servitor stokers shovelled granulated promethium resin into the chutes of the combustion generators, the huge conventional turbines that ran the *Armaduke*'s non-drive systems. In other, cooler chambers, ancient and perfectly machined empyroscopic rotors spun along horizontal axes, maintaining the ship's spatial equilibrium and helping to sustain the integrity of the Geller Field that protected the ship from the psychoreactive fabric of the immaterium.

The creature with Pol Cohran's face concealed the body of the engineering ensign he had just murdered in a tool locker, and entered the massive engineering chamber containing the *Armaduke*'s Geller field device. He'd had to kill three times to get this close. The ship's drive sections were not specifically secure or patrolled, but access or activity by anyone who wasn't officer class or engineering division was immediately noticed. The first crewman had died because he'd seen Cohran. His body was now incinerating in a promethium furnace and Cohran was wearing his grimy overalls. The second and third crewmen had died because Cohran had needed to extract deck plan specifics and information about the drive deck layout. One was now crumpled at the bottom of a coolant drain, and the other had just been hung by the throat from a hook between stoking shovels and furnace tongs.

Sound and vibration in the Geller field device chamber was oddly disconcerting. The air was dry, and there was a considerable static field that made his skin prickle. There were rubberised handrails around the chamber so that crewmen could earth themselves and not cause a shock or spark fire off the metal surfaces.

He could feel the throb of the machine in his gut, the pulsing of its operation in his sinuses and eyeballs. The device, a piece of technology vital to all warpship function, generated a subatomic field around the ship, a bubble of realspace that protected the vessel from the vicissitudes of the aether around it. Once the warp engines had breached the veil of the warp, a starship depended on its Geller field to insulate it from the lethal and corrupting touch of the immaterium by maintaining a psychic ward.

Cohran knew he was in a position to end it all. Sabotaging the Geller field device would take some doing, and would probably require the use of something explosive or combustible, but he was more than capable of procuring and using either. If he could collapse the Geller field while the *Armaduke* was still in the warp, then the ship would perish. It would be torn apart by the unreality storms of the raw aether, shredding in an instant. Either that, or the daemonic essence of the warp would find form and intrude into the ship, or the minds of the occupants.

Unwarded, the ship would be vulnerable to the spawn of the Realm of Chaos, and everyone aboard would know only the extremity of madness before the Ruinous Powers devoured them.

Then everything would be gone and done, and finished, the pheguth and his treachery, the threat that treachery represented, this whole vainglorious undertaking. The creature wearing Pol Cohran's face would have completed the mission he was charged to perform by his master, Rime, and his master's master, the Anarch. He would have finally stopped the Imperial Guard's determined efforts to deploy the pheguth Mabbon Etogaur against the armies of the Gaur.

But during his address, Gaunt had betrayed other secrets. The target was Salvation's Reach. That intelligence needed to be communicated. More importantly, they were due to make conjunction at Tavis Sun. They would be rendezvousing with Battlefleet elements, possibly one of the considerable crusade fleet packs that were maintaining Imperial superiority in this part of the sector.

To destroy the pheguth and his handlers, and the *Armaduke* along with it, that was a victory. To achieve all that *and* cripple a Battlefleet division, that was a truly worthy opportunity.

A more subtle form of sabotage was needed. A more insidious piece of manipulation. His master had taught him well, trained him to improvise imaginatively in just such circumstances, to make the best use of elements at his disposal for the greatest effect.

Cohran opened the casing of the control circuits that governed the empyroscopic rotors.

He was not going to collapse the Geller field. He was simply going to alter its rhythm.

SOMETHING, SOMEWHERE, TREMBLED.

'What was that?' asked Shipmaster Spika.

None of the bridge crew answered him directly. Copious

quantities of data shunted through their connective links and displayed across the monitor plates. The air was filled with the dry scratchy voices of vox links talking to each other.

He'd felt a minuscule vibration, an almost subliminal palsy. It had come to him through the deck, through the data-stream of the ship, one tiny aberrant shudder in a constant vortex of noises and rhythms and pulses and information.

He consulted his data viewers and asked questions of his cogitators. Nothing seemed wrong, nothing out of place, not within the margins of operation, and certainly not given the temperamental and mercurial nature of an old warship like the *Highness Ser Armaduke*.

Spika sat back and thought. It had probably been nothing, or a fleeting glitch that had corrected itself.

But it was a nothing he hadn't liked at all.

CAVITY 29617 WAS cold. Merrt had been waiting there for about half an hour, unwilling to practise or set up shots, unwilling to leave.

He sat at one end of the long chamber, arms hugged around the old rifle.

'You are here. Good.'

Sar Af was standing behind him. Merrt got up quickly.

'You gn… gn…. gn… told me to come back,' he said.

'And you have proven you can follow instruction,' said the White Scar.

He reached out a hand and grabbed Merrt by the jaw and throat, turning Merrt's head to the side. Merrt struggled again.

'Let me gn… gn… gn… go!'

'This jaw. It is definitely your problem,' said Sar Af. 'You are being defeated by your own concentration. Your focus is so intense that as you fire the gun, it stimulates–'

'Yes. Yes! You told me all this gn… gn… gn… yesterday!'

Sar Af let him go.

'It is physically impossible for you to shoot well.'

Merrt swallowed.

'Again, you told me so yesterday. Did you ask me back just so you could gn… gn… gn… humiliate me?'

Sar Af stuck out his chin, as if considering a response. He turned away.

'Set up a shot,' he said.

Merrt stood for a moment, then picked up several tin pots and walked the length of the cavity. He set the pots out along the top of the block and walked back to where the Space Marine was waiting.

Sar Af had produced something from an equipment pouch. Merrt realised that it was a disposable shot injector just a second before the White Scar grabbed his head again and jammed it into his jawline, behind his left ear.

The pain was considerable. Merrt cried out and staggered backwards, his eyes watering.

'What the feth are you gn… gn… gn… doing?' he asked.

'Just wait.'

Sar Af took the injector and tossed it away.

Merrt had a lancing pain in his ear and a horrible warmth spreading through the line of his throat and his jaw. He started to gag slightly as the numbness increased.

'Attend to yourself,' said Sar Af. 'You are drooling.'

'What have you gn… gn… gn… done to me? What gn… gn… gn… was that stuff?'

'Muscle relaxant,' said the White Scar innocently. 'Quite powerful, I suppose. A tranquiliser. The sort of stuff a medicae would use for pain control. During an amputation, for instance.'

Clutching his throbbing, disturbed face, Merrt looked at the Space Marine in horror.

'Pah, relax,' said Sar Af. 'I am not going to cut anything off. Not literally.'

Merrt tried to answer, but he only managed to make a deep and inhuman rumbling in his throat. His entire jaw and cheek was numbed and immobile. The lower half of his face was inert and paralysed.

'The jaw,' said Sar Af, gesturing towards Merrt. 'That jaw of yours. It is the root of your inability.'

The Space Marine went over and picked up the old rifle. 'You are being defeated by your own concentration,' he said as he came back, as though he were repeating some litany lesson that needed to be repeated so that an unwilling student might eventually learn it.

'Your focus is so intense that as you fire the gun, you twitch. So we need to remove the jaw from the equation. It cannot twitch if it cannot twitch.'

Merrt felt ill. The paralysis was so unpleasant that he felt he might be sick, except he couldn't guarantee that his mouth would open to allow it. Visions of choking on his own vomit filled his head and made things worse.

'Take the shot,' said Sar Af, handing him the rifle.

Merrt glared back at him, hoping his toxic stare might communicate what his voice could not.

'Take the shot,' Sar Af repeated.

Merrt took a deep breath. He pulled back the bolt, took a round from his pocket, slipped it into the breach, locked the bolt back into place, then turned and lined up on the row of pots. A standing stance, unbraced apart from his own posture. No rest, no sand-sock, no tripod, no back brace: neither a recommended nor reliable position. He didn't care.

'Go on,' said Sar Af. 'Take the shot.'

Merrt settled his shoulders. He felt spittle on his lip, the dull throb of numbness under his ear. He took aim along the iron sights.

He breathed out.

He fired.

EIGHT
Conjunction

DEAD SPACE. THE visible universe was a weathered brown blackness, as if the void was somehow filled with a fog of dirty starlight. Nebulous beige streamers of some exotic matter streaked the depths. More than anything else, there was distance, the unfathomable distance of gazing out from the bounds of a harsh and inhospitable solar system, a few lonely rocks tumbling around a dull, grinding, electromagnetic light source into the humiliating immensity of the interstellar gulf.

Then lightning struck.

The lightning was a spear one thousand kilometres long. At the heart of its blinding shock-light was a twisting vein of toxic yellow, like scorched ceramic. At its origin point, an interspatial bubble of rupturing subatomics, the root of the lightning was brighter than any star, and shot through with threads of sour green and galvanic blue.

The lightning flashed and died, then another spear flashed, and then a third that was twice as long as the first two. It scored a line of light across the dark firmament, and left a fading afterimage like a jagged fault line.

A fourth flash followed, this one finally puncturing realspace and eating a hole through it, like a hungry flame

171

burning through a sheet of paper. Suffixed by a halo of aftershock lighting, the *Highness Ser Armaduke* translated through the puncture, leaving the warp behind and coasting slowly out into the materium. Aetheric energies coursed off its flanks like thawing ice, shredding away in its wake and disintegrating.

The translation point behind it popped and crackled as it healed and faded, puffing and cracking like a membrane under pulses of thumping pressure. The *Armaduke* stabilised and adjusted its realspace passage. Its auspex and detector grids began to pattern-search and composite the visible starfields to verify the navigation plot. Vox systems were enabled.

Six minutes after achieving translation, a deck officer brought a data-slate to Shipmaster Spika.

Spika adjusted his silver-plated voice-horn on its stalk.

'Translation complete,' he announced, his voice ringing through the ship. 'Tavis Sun. Tavis Sun. Approach now factoring for fleet conjunction.'

He turned off the speaker and looked at his deck officer.

'Have we detected the elements?'

'Not yet, sir,' said the officer. 'If they have made the schedule, we expect to track them in the next twenty minutes.'

'Has engineering come back on that consultation I requested?' Spika asked. Since that first anomalous tremble hours before, he had been attempting to trace the aberration.

'I understand a full field-and-rate diagnostic is on its way up,' said the officer.

'Hurry them, please,' said Spika.

A klaxon sounded.

'Battlefleet elements detected,' another officer called out. 'Holding position around the local star. Close, and preparing for vox-hail.'

* * *

THEY WERE BACK in realspace. Cohran could feel it. He had attempted to slip up-deck towards the main vox-caster assembly, but it was proving too difficult. There was too much activity, too many people who would see him and question his business in a crew section. He wouldn't be able to stay in the vox room long enough to achieve his goals.

Instead, ever pragmatic, he headed back down towards the old munitions magazine that was serving as a cell. From his observations, the guard detail would be approaching a shift change. The men would be tired.

And there were only two of them at the hatch.

A FULL INTERDICTION flotilla was waiting for the *Armaduke*. It was a patrol group from Battlefleet Khulan: four frigates and two cruisers supported the *Aggressor Libertus*, an Exorcist-class grand cruiser, and the *Sepiterna*, an Oberon-class battleship. In their train was a family of bulk transports and fleet tenders. As soon as they identified the *Armaduke* making its long curve approach in from the system rim along the invariable plane a barrage of vox-hails went up. Several squadrons of fighters were launched from the flight decks of the capital ships, and one of the escort frigates, the *Benedicamus Domino*, impelled forwards, void shields up, to meet the approaching vessel while its identity was confirmed.

Tavis Sun glowered behind the fleet spread, a malevolent red coal. The immense ships were just blowfly dots against its hot, dark mass. It was an old star, rheumy and frail, bloated and throbbing with wheezing electromagnetic gasps, like a feast-day fire dying in its grate at the end of the night. Its rasping, radiostatic voice blurred and chopped the vox transmissions, sandpapering the communication links. The star was bleeding cold gas and hot radiation into its lifeless system as it used up the last few millennia of its fuel mass. Dark spots like tumours appeared in its flushed coronasphere. Occasional septic pulses of energy and flame flared out into its stellar shadow. The planetary bodies that orbited it were scorched dead rocks or rings of debris, the residue of the ferocious burn the star had suffered a million years earlier at the start of its terminal decline.

The *Highness Ser Armaduke* gunned in, riding the gravitic slope, twenty million kilometres out and closing. Its flight decks and excursion bays began to prepare for open cycle. Tender boats and suppliers scooted forwards from the fleet line and fell in behind the *Benedicamus Domino*.

At the master station, Spika took the report from his deck officer.

'Incoming hail from Cragoe, Master of the Fleet,' said a vox herald.

'One moment,' said Spika, reading, speeding his way through the data-slate.

'What is it, sir?' asked the deck officer.

'Fleetmaster Cragoe is hailing again,' called the herald.

'Look, look at this,' said Spika. The deck officer peered at the hololithic displays Spika was consulting. They were field effect summaries from the immaterium leg. The deck officer had seen similar profile reports a thousand times.

'What am I looking at?' he asked.

'Fleetmaster Cragoe is hailing again!' called the herald.

'Wait,' Spika growled. 'Look, here. You see?'

'I see a Geller field profile,' said the deck officer.

'Nothing untoward,' Spika agreed, 'until you see how it compares to the one at the previous interval and the one at the interval that followed.'

'I still don't see, sir.'

'The Geller field was altering during transit. Its configuration was changing.'

'Within tolerances,' said the deck officer. 'Isn't that normal fluctuation?'

'It repeats,' said Spika, his voice tight and unhappy. 'It repeats, you see? There is a pattern to it, but you only see it when you run the sampled profiles one after another. That's not normal field variance. That's an artificial repetition.'

'Artificial, sir?' asked the deck officer.

ALONG THE DECK frame of the launch platform, hazard lamps were cycling and the chamber was shuddering with the din of airgate alarms. A massive overhead clamp had just positioned the elegant blue and white Aquila lander on the blast deck, and servitor teams were detaching the cradle lines and feeders with power tools.

Gaunt walked with Lord Militant Cybon towards the boarding ramp. Over their heads, a series of hard metal thumps accompanied the retracting hoist, and the thick delivery hatch that led up into the *Armaduke*'s starboard small ship hangar rumbled shut.

Staff aides hurried past them, carrying the lord militant's luggage. A duty officer approached, and saluted.

'Transfer standing by, sir,' he said. Cybon acknowledged him with a slight nod.

'The *Sepiterna* awaits,' said Gaunt.

'As does the Warmaster,' replied Cybon. 'I should be with him in eighteen weeks, in time enough to communicate the essence of this plan in person. And in time to consider its success.'

'Or otherwise,' said Gaunt.

Cybon studied him. The lord militant's eyes seemed very old, as though they had seen too much. Gaunt's, by comparison, were very new for precisely the same reason.

'I never took you to be a pessimist, Gaunt,' rumbled Cybon.

'I'm not, sir,' Gaunt replied. 'Just a pragmatist.'

'The Emperor protects,' said Cybon.

'That's just what I tell the men,' said Gaunt.

'And if he doesn't protect you, you don't need protecting,' Cybon added.

'I'm not sure if that's entirely reassuring,' said Gaunt.

'It's not supposed to be,' said Cybon. 'Do I look like a sentimental old bastard to you? I'm simply passing on what experience has shown me.'

He turned to board the lander. Gaunt could feel the air pressure in the bay begin to change as the airgate began to cycle to release.

'Safe voyage,' said Gaunt. He regretted it instantly. Sentiment didn't sit well with either of them. Cybon snorted derisively.

Halfway up the ramp, he turned to look back at Gaunt.

He made the sign of the aquila, nodded, and disappeared into the shuttle.

'Clear the deck space,' shouted the launch officer. 'Clear the deck space!'

THE ARMADUKE CONTINUED to decelerate towards the ships sent out to greet it. They were entering the close approach phase, with the Battlefleet's fighter screen spreading out wide around the newcomer. A small speck, bright and fast moving, left the starboard flank of the coasting *Armaduke* like a launched flare and began to accelerate away towards the main fleet grouping.

From an observation bay, Gaunt watched the Aquila on its way. He turned, descended the steps and pushed through the busy deck crews and launch personnel to reach the nearest access hallway.

He met Hark and Kolea coming the other way. They didn't have to say anything for him to know they were looking for him and the news was going to be bad.

'Edur's dead,' said Hark.

'How?' Gaunt asked, immediately imagining some shipboard accident.

'A maintenance crew found his body at the bottom

of an inspection hatch fifteen minutes ago,' said Kolea. 'Injuries consistent with a fall.'

'A fall?' asked Gaunt.

'The sort of fall you might have if you'd already been beaten to death,' said Kolea.

'Throne,' Gaunt murmured. 'Viktor, mobilise the regiment. We're going to find the killer immediately. I'll go directly to the shipmaster and inform him of the situation. We're going to need the cooperation of him and his crew if we're going to section the ship.'

He looked at Kolea.

'Gol, get to Rawne. Fast as you can. Tell him security has been compromised.'

RAWNE APPROACHED THE armoured hatchway of the magazine-turned-cell. Cant and Mktally were waiting for him.

'Open it,' Rawne said.

'You're not due for another two hours–' Cant began.

'There's a problem. Open it.'

Cant turned to bang on the outer hatch. Mktally hoisted his lasrifle and covered the approach hall.

Coming in right behind Cant, Rawne already had his straight silver drawn in his right hand, the blade up his sleeve. His left hand deftly slipped the loop out of his hip pocket.

'Where's your badge, sir?' asked Mktally.

'What?' asked Rawne.

'Your badge? You said we should all wear them.'

Without hesitation, Rawne threw the knife. He delivered the straight silver with a vicious and expert underhand throw, and the blade buried itself in Mktally's heart.

He fell back against the corridor wall, and slid down, instantly dead. Before he'd even begun to topple, Rawne had hooked the loop over Cant's head from behind.

It was a steel string from a colours band lyre. Cant had barely time to notice it was there when Rawne twisted

the loop to tighten it. The string cut into his neck like a
cheese wire. Cant toppled backwards into Rawne, blood
pouring from an almost three hundred and sixty degree
throat wound, his mouth wide open, unable to breathe
or cry out.

Rawne let Cant go. The trooper's legs were still twitching. There was a considerable pool of blood. Rawne drew
his laspistol. He took one last look at Cant's beached fish
expression, and rearranged his own features. There was a
hideous and painful scrunch of bone and muscle, and a
second Cant faced the entrance. He banged on the door,
then opened the outer hatch.

'Coming in, one visitor,' he said over his microbead.

'Read that.'

The peephole slot in the inner door opened, and Cant
stood where the guard inside could clearly see the face
he had made for the occasion.

The inner hatch began to unbolt.

'What's the matter with you, Cant?' asked Kabry, looking out at him. 'You're supposed to stay outside.'

Cant shot him in the face and kicked the hatch wide
open.

'Fleetmaster Cragoe demands that you issue a full
response, sir!' the vox herald pleaded.

'Shut that man up,' Spika snapped to his number one.
'I'm trying to think.'

There was a commotion behind him. He glanced
around to see the Guard commander, Gaunt, pushing
his way onto the master station platform, ignoring the
attempts of the deck officers to head him off.

'Shipmaster Spika has no time to deal with you now!'
one of the officers was repeating in a whining tone.

Gaunt punched him in the mouth and laid him out
on the deck.

'Sorry,' he told the man in what seemed like a genuine
tone of remorse. He reached Spika's side.

'We've got a serious problem.'

'How do you know about the Geller field?' asked the shipmaster.

'I–' Gaunt began. 'What about the Geller field? I'm talking about a security breach. A killing.'

Spika blinked slowly.

'It's so they know we're here,' he said quietly.

'It's what? ' asked Gaunt. 'What is?'

'It's so they know we're here. It's a trail they can track...' Spika's pitch was rising. 'Oh, Holy Throne of Terra.'

He wrenched his silver-plated voice-horn up close to his mouth.

'Alert! Alert stations. Shields up. Shields up. Shields up!

The bridge personnel turned from their positions and stared at him. They were young. Painfully inexperienced. A few of them clearly thought it was a surprise drill.

'Don't gawp at me, you mindless idiots! Do it now!' Spika yelled.

Multiple alarms and bells began to sound. The bridge crew went into a kind of overdrive, dashing in all directions. Light levels dipped as the shields woke up. Squealing and clattering, ceramite shutters began to close like eyelids across the realspace ports.

'Are we under attack?' asked Gaunt.

'I think the prospects are very likely,' replied Spika.

'Lord Militant Cybon is out there in a small unescorted ship,' said Gaunt.

Spika ran his tongue around the inside of his lips as he thought about this.

'Damn him,' he said. He looked at the Officer of Detection, whose seat was surrounded by dead-eyed auxiliary servitors spinally hardwired into the deck.

'Full sensory sweep,' Spika said. 'Locate the lord militant's ship, track it, and prepare to put us between it and any attack if necessary.'

A different series of alarms sounded.

'Contact! Contact!' the officer of detection announced. 'Translation signature three AU to port.'

'A ship? Identify!' yelled Spika.

'Tracking one signature. Tracking a second signature. Tracking a third.'

'Three?' asked Spika.

'Tracking a fourth!'

LIGHTNING STRUCK.

The lightning was a spear one thousand kilometres long. This time it was red, like the most malignant hatred, and shot through with snakes of yellow and coral-pink.

The lightning flashed, puncturing realspace and eating a hole through it, like acid eating through a plate of steel. Surrounded by a crown of thorns of aftershock lightning, four starships translated through the corroded wound, ploughing out into the materium like missiles fired from a launcher.

The first two were Destroyer-class escorts. The third, close behind them, was a much larger cruiser.

The fourth, trailing slower and more ponderously still, was a monster, a vast battleship.

All four vessels were blackened as if they had spent too long scorching in the heart of a sun's furnace. A volcanic red light lit them from within, glaring from their window ports and coiling across their surfaces like veins filled with magma. They had once been Imperial ships, all of them of the most ancient patterns and design. But that identity, and those lives led in Imperial service, were distant memories. Gross corruption had stolen them from the Imperial fold aeons before and transformed their adamantine carcasses to the whim of the Ruinous Powers.

The ships began to scream. Hellish noises and foetid transmissions blasted out through their vox networks as though each one possessed a voice, part animal howl, part augmetic rasp. On the Imperial ships, vox heralds collapsed at their consoles, their brains bursting as the amplified shrieks burned through their systems and shorted them out.

Each Archenemy ship howled out its name as it gunned in; gut-howls that came from their inner cores, from the smoking hearts of their reactors. It was like the bellowing of mindless, stampeding cattle, or the idiot shouting of lobotomised bulk servitors that knew nothing but their own names.

Ominator! Ominator! raged the first destroyer.

Gorehead! spat the shredded vox-casters of its twin. *Gorehead! Gorehead!*

Necrostar Antiversal! declared the blood-shot cruiser.

Last of all, deepest, and most awful, the voice of the monstrous capital ship, like the deathscream of a black hole.

Tormaggedon Monstrum Rex!

NINE
The Fight at Tavis Sun

KABRY FELL BACKWARDS into the pheguth's cell, the back of his skull blown out. A sticky sheen of blood and tissue coated the wall and floor surfaces behind him. Cant forced his way into the cell, laspistol drawn.

It had all happened in a second. Chained at his seat, Mabbon Etogaur looked up, saw Kabry twist over dead, and dropped the trancemissionary text he was reading.

The other guard on duty inside the cell that shift was Varl. He screamed at Mabbon to get on the floor, and threw himself at the open hatch door. His lasrifle was still strapped around his body.

Varl's weight hit the hatch and swung it hard into Cant. The impact staggered Cant halfway back out of the hatchway, but his chest and shoulder prevented the hatch from fully closing so that Varl could bolt it.

Varl put the full yield of his augmetic shoulder into keeping the hatch pinned on the attacker, but with his body wedged against the door, he couldn't unship his rifle. He yelled a few savage curses as he rammed the hatch repeatedly.

Cant had his right arm and shoulder inside the cell. He was pushing back, his left hand and cheek pressed against the outside of the hatch.

His laspistol was in his right hand.

He raised it and fired into the cell, shooting blind. Shots smacked off the rear wall and the floor. One grazed the ceiling. Two of the bolts ricocheted like cometary fragments off the dull metal surfaces. One punched clean through the back of the pheguth's seat. Mabbon was face down on the floor, as far out of the firing line as the chain would allow.

Cant fired again, intent on filling the interior of the cell with sizzling, rebounding las bolts.

Calling Cant a name that would not have impressed his poor, dead mother, Varl stabbed him through the forearm with his warknife. The blade cleaved through muscle and bone and bit into the steel liner of the cell, staking Cant's right arm against the wall inside the hatch, so he was pinned like a specimen. Pain forced Cant to drop his pistol.

Varl redoubled his efforts to shove the door, hoping to crush or crack bone. Cant growled in discomfort.

'You like that, you bastard?' Varl shouted. He stepped back and threw the hatch wide so he could gun the assassin down.

Cant faced him.

Varl hesitated, seeing the face of a friend and comrade. He didn't hesitate long, but it was just enough for Cant to form a beak with the fingers of his left hand and smash Varl in the chest. Varl was thrown clear across the cell.

Alarms started to shriek. The bracket lamps in the approach corridor began to flash and cycle. *Battle stations.* There was a strong ozone whiff as the void shield generators lit up.

Cant yanked Varl's warknife out of the wall and freed his pinned arm. Blood ran down his wrist and dripped off his fingers. He took a step forwards.

Varl was trying to get up, gulping in air as he tried to fill lungs that had been pressed empty. His face was bright red, his eyes wet with tears.

Lasfire ripped up the approach hallway and spanked off the hatch and the hatch surround, causing Cant to duck in alarm. Cowering, he turned. At the far end of the hallway, Kolea was approaching, firing his rifle from the hip.

The assassin threw himself flat, rolled close to Mktally's corpse outside the hatch, and tore the lasrifle away from the dead Tanith. Sitting up, the assassin returned fire down the approach. Kolea dived behind a bulkhead to avoid the hail of bright las rounds.

'Varl!' Kolea yelled. 'Varl, close the hatch.'

The assassin was no longer wearing Cant's face, nor Rawne's. Pain, and the necessity of redirecting his strength into the fight, had obliged him to revert to his own face. It wasn't the one he'd been born with, but it was what amounted to his true identity. It was the face of Sirkle. All of the rogue Inquisitor Rime's minions had the same visage.

Kolea fired again, two or three loose bursts. The shots spattered around the hatch end of the approach. Sirkle fired back, full auto, his rifle lighting up with bright petals of muzzle flash. The barrage caused Kolea to duck back into cover. Sirkle turned around to unload into the cell and finish his mission.

He was just in time to see the pained, red-faced Varl slamming the cell door in his face.

The hatch locked. Sirkle roared in frustration. He turned back and began blasting down the hallway again, walking forwards, preventing Kolea from getting out of cover or returning fire.

Head down behind the bulkhead rim as shots hammered against it, Kolea yelled into his microbead.

'Holding level. This is Major Kolea in the holding level.

I need security here now! Security and medicae. Urgent!'

Kolea couldn't hear if there was any reply. The fury of the gunfire coming at him, combined with the shrill of the alarms, filled the boxy hallway.

Sirkle advanced, firing as he came.

THE INTERDICTION FLOTILLA didn't wait to be fired upon. There was no mistaking the intent or allegiance of the howling daemon ships that streaked in towards them from the disintegrated stretch of realspace fabric.

The *Aggressor Libertus* lit off first, rolling out of its line position ahead of the massive *Sepiterna*. Advancing at a crawl, it delivered a series of punch-fire barrages with its main batteries, which surrounded its steepled, armoured flanks with a corona of fire.

Benedicamus Domino also commenced firing. It began to come about out of its rendezvous heading with the *Armaduke* and retrained on the attacking group. Its turrets began to spark and crackle as it directed its fire forwards across the gulf. It was attempting to screen and support the decelerating *Armaduke*, which was all but aft-end on to the attack.

The other escorts, holding their places in the gunline relative to the capital ship, began their own rates of fire.

The range was considerable, but the Archenemy ships were closing rapidly, and they seemed to drink in the Imperial barrage. Firefly darts of light crackled around the ruddy glow of their shields. Even the formidable main weapon fire of the *Aggressor Libertus* flashed off their shields like rain.

They continued to howl out their names, throaty and malevolent, scorching out the Imperial vox systems, drowning their audio traffic, distorting their auspex returns.

Ominator! Ominator!
Gorehead! Gorehead!
Necrostar Antiversal!

Behind them all, the doom-voice of the daemon monster.

Tormaggedon Monstrum Rex!

'Have you located Cybon's launch?' Gaunt demanded.

'I'm trying to,' replied Spika. With the vox system compromised by the daemon ships' relentless aural assault, the bridge crew of the *Armaduke* had switched to voice relay, shouting commands, instruction and data from position to position. Gaunt realised that the shipmaster was doing a thousand tasks simultaneously. Spika was watching every single bridge position, and the main board of his station, plus the strategium's tactical plot. He was listening to every shouted relay, every nuance of dialogue, and chipping in with orders that sent crewmen rushing to obey. He had both hands on his master systems, operating dials and power-modulation levers without looking. He was feeling the soul and motive energy of the *Armaduke* as it spoke to him through the deck, the seat, the metal controls.

'Coming about,' he said.

'You're turning to face them?' asked Gaunt.

Not even looking at Gaunt, Spika manipulated another control and reeled off a string of corrective heading numbers. Below, the steersmen hurried to obey his command.

'How do you usually fight, colonel-commissar?' Spika asked. 'With your back to the enemy?'

Gaunt didn't reply.

'I can mark more of my batteries as status effective if I present head-on or broadside,' said Spika.

'Side-on makes us a bigger target,' said Gaunt.

'Only while we're turning.'

'Shouldn't we run in alongside the *Sepiterna*?' Gaunt asked. In truth, he had very little idea of the fight's comparative geography. The three-dimensional strategium displays were moving too swiftly, and the type of detail they were processing was far removed from the tactical flows he was used to reading. They made the essentially flat plane of a battlefield seem elegant and pure.

But he knew enough to know that the *Armaduke* was turning into the line of fire, and that, along with the *Benedicamus Domino*, they were placing themselves ahead of the flotilla's main strength and directly in the path of the howling daemon ships.

'I'm not going to leave the *Domino* alone to face this,' said Spika, working his controls. 'Two frigates, side by side. They can harm a lot of hull between them.'

'But–'

Spika looked at him for the first time. It was just a brief glance, but Gaunt was struck by the singleness of purpose he saw in Spika's eyes, the fortitude and, in a tiny measure, the anticipation.

Shipmaster Spika had been too long away from fights worthy of his talents. He wasn't going to run or back down.

Gaunt raised one hand in a gesture of submission.

'You don't come down to the surface and tell me how to deploy my men,' he admitted.

'I certainly do not,' replied Spika. 'I imagine I would be tremendously bad at it.'

'You're enjoying this, aren't you?' asked Gaunt.

'Wouldn't you?' asked Spika. 'Now keep quiet or I'll have you ejected from my bridge.'

He stood up.

'Enhance the strength of the port voids as we turn. Artificers, power to the primary batteries. Bombardiers, load up. Detection, find us a target we can burn. And find the thrice-damned lord militant so we can screen him!'

Gaunt had seen Spika's spirit before. It was an old warrior's lust to achieve one last hoorah, to prove he was still worthy of the uniform. It was a desire that often manifested in suicidal decisions.

Given what was bearing down on them, a man

prepared to take potentially suicidal risks might be their only hope.

THE ARMADUKE BEGAN to turn. Once fully executed, the manoeuvre would put it in a modest gunline formation with the eager *Benedicamus Domino*, which had slowed to a dogmatic attitude of confrontation and was blitzing with all weapons. Huge volleys of main battery fire were ripping past and above both ships from the main gunline thousands of kilometres astern.

The *Sepiterna* had begun to spit huge, ship-killing bolts from its primary batteries.

The onrushing daemon ships wore the fusillade. Their shields wobbled like wet glass as they soaked up the punishment. They were half a million kilometres out, closing at a sharp angle to the system plane, as if they intended to perform a slashing strike down and across the Imperial gunline.

Then the black shape proclaiming itself *Necrostar Antiversal* began to glow brightly from within, a red glare that started in its heart and spread through its tracery of red veins, straining with light and heat like a charred volcanic cone about to split and blow open under pressure from within.

A vast froth of red corposant enveloped the daemon ship's prow, chained lightning that crackled and coiled like live snakes. With a sudden flash, the lightning boiled over and lanced a jagged red bolt out ahead of the ship, a whiplash discharge of immense aetheric energies.

The bolt wasn't even a direct platform-to-target strike like a main plasma or laser weapon. The lash of it flew out sideways, wild and frenzied, untamed and unaimed. It coiled madly out into void space and only then whipped back towards a target, like a lightning strike jumping as it hunted for something to earth itself against.

The jagged, blinding discharge struck the *Benedicamus Domino* like the vengeance of a displeased god, blowing out its forward shields and exploding its upper decks. There was no sound. A snap shockwave of heat and debris ripped out from the impact, followed by a slow, widening ball of white light that was too hard to look at. Bridge viewers dimmed automatically. When the glare died, the *Domino* was revealed on fire and listing, sections of its upper structure and hull architecture annihilated or left glowing gold along burned edges.

Spika maximised the magnification to get a look at the frigate. The pict image jumped on the bridge screens, fuzzed, and then steadied and resolved.

'By all that's sacred...' Gaunt breathed.

Screaming its name again, like a child driven to raving madness by a fever, the *Necrostar Antiversal* bled more corposant and unleashed another shot.

The second bolt of jagged red fury hit the *Armaduke* as it turned.

GOL KOLEA REALISED he might have actually passed out for a few seconds. He hoped it had only been seconds. Something had made the ship shake like a toy rattle, and he'd bounced off the hallway wall and deck.

It was dark as he came round, apart from the emergency lighting and the flashing hazards. The air was full of smoke, and it wasn't just the heat discharge from the fire fight. There was dark fuel smoke in the ship's air circulation system, like blood in water.

They'd been hurt.

He snapped awake and got up, clutching his lasrifle. There was no sign of the assassin. He could hear bewildered and rapid vox chatter coming out of every duct and wall-link as the crew tried to re-establish control of the pole-axed ship. He felt as if he were standing at a slight angle to the horizontal, as though the deck were tilted. That suggested the inertial systems had been damaged. Kolea didn't know much about warships, but he was sure it wasn't a terribly good sign.

The main lights blinked back on as power was restored. It made the smoke seem thicker. Kolea hurried down towards the cell hatch, keeping his aim up and wary. There was still no sign of the killer.

'Varl,' he yelled 'Varl, open up!'

He knelt down. Mktally looked like he was asleep, but he was stone dead, a warknife transfixing his heart. Cant was a mess of blood, so much blood it was hard to look at. What appeared to be a noose of wire had almost decapitated him.

'Oh, Throne,' Kolea whispered.

Cant was alive.

'Varl! Open the door!' Kolea yelled, clamping his left hand around Cant's throat to try to staunch the bloodflow. Cant was unconscious, but he was trembling with pain.

'I'm not falling for that again,' Varl yelled from behind the hatch.

'Open the fething hatch, Varl. It's Gol!'

'Right, and last time it was Cant! I'm not an idiot. Suicide Kings, Gol. I've got a job to do! If you are Gol, you'll know I'm right. If you're not, go feth yourself!'

Kolea heard movement. He kept his left hand clenched around Cant's neck, but hoisted his lasrifle in his right.

'Identify!' he yelled.

Figures appeared in the approach hallway, moving towards him through the smoke wash. It was Bonin, with Cardass, Nomis and Brostin. Their guns were up.

'Kolea?' Bonin called.

'I need a medicae!'

Coughing, Zweil pushed past the B Company men and lowered himself beside Kolea.

'Oh, the poor boy's gone,' Zweil said.

'Are you a gakking medicae?' Kolea snapped.

'Not this week, major.'

'Then could we get a real medicae before we resort to last rites?' Kolea snarled.

'Just let me give the poor lad some consolation in case,' mumbled Zweil, fishing out a pocket icon of the Saint and a silver aquila on a chain.

'Let me through,' said Dorden. He looked down at Cant.

'Gol, I've got it,' Dorden said as he bent down and put his hand over Kolea's. 'On three, let me take the compression. Two, three.'

Kolea took his hand away. It was wet with blood.

'Will he live?' he asked.

'He shouldn't even be down here,' said Zweil. The old priest glanced at Dorden. 'Oh, you mean the boy. I get you.'

'We'll see,' said Dorden. He began working at Cant's throat, pulling back the neckline of the jacket. 'Where's my pack?'

Bonin ushered Kolding through. The albino was lugging a medicae supply kit.

'I need wadding and some sterile gauze,' said Dorden.

Kolding nodded, opening the kit and taking items out.

'Sacred feth,' Dorden murmured as he worked. 'Look at this.'

Kolding peered in.

'What?' asked Kolea.

'The badge,' said Kolding quietly. 'The Suicide Kings badge. This man had it fixed to his collar. It hooked under the garrotte. If it hadn't got in the way, the wire would have gone clean through to the spine.'

Kolea looked up at Bonin.

'Small mercies,' said Bonin.

'It's still a damn mess,' said Dorden. 'We need to release the wire, but it's pinching the carotids. If they're torn, taking the wire away will make him bleed out.'

'We can't patch him without taking the wire off,' said Kolding quietly.

'Damned either way,' said Dorden. 'I'm not even sure how we're going to patch the wound anyway.'

'Tape and carbon bond,' said Kolding.

Dorden looked at him.

'Not a procedure I've heard of, Doctor Kolding.'

'Not a medicae one,' admitted Kolding, 'but in the mortician's trade it works well. I suggest it because once we take off that wire we've got to move quickly.'

'You're not serious?' asked Kolea.

'It's the best suggestion I've heard,' said Dorden, 'and I'm senior medicae here.'

Kolea got up and looked at Bonin and the other troopers.

'The killer's got to be close by. He's hurt. He fled when everything went dark.'

Bonin nodded. He had already started to search the hallway.

'I've got a blood trail. Let's go.'

'Why did everything go dark?' asked Kolea. 'Did we hit something?'

'Something hit *us*,' said Judd Cardass. 'I think we're in some kind of battle.'

Kolea looked up at the ceiling. The superstructure of the ship was creaking and groaning.

'Seriously?' he asked. Apart from the bump, he wasn't sure how anyone could tell.

'REPORT,' SHIPMASTER SPIKA was yelling through the smoke. 'All departments report!'

The main lights of the bridge chamber stuttered and came back on. Damage klaxons were whooping. Some of the ornamental glass shades on the platform lights had been dislodged, and had shattered on the deck.

Voices peeled off reports from every direction. Spika listened, trying to adjust his console. The main display had frozen. He thumped it, and it hiccupped back into luminous green life.

'Shut up. Shut up!' he yelled above the conflicting voices. 'Artifice, do we have shields?'

'Negative, master. Void shields are down.'

'Get them operational. At once!' Spika thought hard. 'Position? Inertial station, I want our relative now.'

Data zapped onto his screen, the figures echoed aloud by the voice of the officer at the Inertial desk.

'Still side-on…' Spika murmured. The hit had wallowed the *Armaduke* like a heavy swell and halted the starship's lumbering turn. Not a good place to be, especially without an active shield system.

'Steersmen! Complete that turn.'

At the long, brass- and wood-cased helm station, the hardwired steersmen cranked the attitude controls.

'Shield status?'

'Repairs underway, master!'

'I want a two-minute corrective burn to these adjusteds. All plasma engines,' Spika declared, following his order with a string of four-dimensional coordinates.

'Plasma engine four reports fire. Output suspended,' said the duty officer at Spika's side.

Spika recalculated faster than his cogitator. He announced a corrected set of coordinates.

'Cap engine three, and boost five and six to compensate,' Spika ordered. 'Bring us about. Bring us about!'

'Corrective burn in five, four, three…' the duty officer announced.

'Tell the artificers to crack the whip!' Spika told another subordinate. 'The stokers must put their backs into it. Feed those damn furnaces. Death is the only excuse for not shovelling!'

'Sir.'

The deck shuddered and the lights dimmed as the burn began.

'Gunnery!' Spika yelled, selecting another pict screen. 'As soon as you have capacity, you may fire at will.'

'Aye, master!'

Spika looked at the strategium, assessing the proximity of the Archenemy line. It appeared that one of the unholy escorts – *Ominator* by its wild animal screams – was peeling towards the shield-less *Armaduke* to finish the duel while the others gunned directly for the main line. It had lofted attack ships from its carrier decks.

Spika's poor relic of a ship had survived the first knock, though the list rolling up the damage report display was chilling. Spika had a feeling it had been less of a case of their shields doing their job, and more a case that the *Necrostar Antiversal* had developed insufficient power for another blast so soon after crippling the *Domino*. The *Armaduke* had survived because the discharge had been underpowered.

Even underpowered, it had blown out their shields.

Spika could smell fear in the air. All of his young and inexperienced officers were ashen and shaken. The hard-wired servitors twitched in their sockets and plug-racks, neural links pulsing. Even the more veteran crewmen, like the Officer of Detection and the Chief Steersman, looked frantic.

They were terrified. His ship was terrified. Spika could taste the wash of cortisone and other stress hormones flooding the ship's neural and biological systems. There was a stink of terror mixing with the smoke in the air-circulation system. Thirty thousand souls, locked in a metal box, in the dark, under fire. Most of them had never known anything like it before.

He remembered his life as a bridge junior. It was the absence of information that really gnawed at you. Only the shipmaster and the officers with access to the strategium feed had any real notion of what was going on outside, and then only if the Officer of Detection was doing a decent job. In a void fight, realspace ports shuttered and closed, and everything became feed only. Even if the ports had remained open, there was nothing to see. You were brawling with – and being fired upon by – an object that might be thousands of kilometres away in the interstellar blackness, and moving at a considerable percentage of the speed of light. There was the shake and terror of impacts, the raging engines, the cacophony of voices and data-chatter, but everything else was blind and far-removed, separated from the realm of the senses. No wonder juniors lost their nerve, no wonder the helm servitors and data-serfs wept and moaned as they worked at their logic stations, no wonder the stokers wailed and lamented as they laboured in the fiery caves of the engine vaults. Every soul depended on the uniting perception, the singular view, of the shipmaster. He alone could appreciate the grand dance of a fleet action, the war going on outside the metal tomb inside which the crew toiled. Every man worked without even understanding what benefit his small contribution was making. If death came, it overwhelmed suddenly, utterly lacking in warning or explanation.

The world would come apart in light, and then fire and hard vacuum would annihilate you.

The Officer of Detection cried out. Spika checked the scope.

The monster *Ominator* had launched munitions at them. Deep-range warheads were rippling through the void at them on plasma wakes.

Spika swore. He expected some comment from Gaunt.

To his surprise, the colonel-commissar was no longer at his side.

ELODIE TRIED TO focus. She'd been doing something. Something really ordinary. That was it, she'd been signing something. The ship had just that minute shuddered, and a metallic voice had announced they were arriving at wherever it was they were supposed to be going.

Some men from the regiment had come into the transport decks with yet more Munitorum paperwork for the retinue to sign. They'd circulated. Costin, the drunkard, had brought stuff to her when it was her turn. He just needed her to make her mark. It was another disclaimer, all part of the accompany bond.

Elodie had barely paid attention. The sustained quake of re-translation had disquieted her, and some of the children and younger women had become upset. When the metallic voice made its announcement, there had been cheering, and loud prayers offered in thanks to the Saint and the Emperor. Lay preachers and men of faith got up to lead the retinue in hymns of deliverance from the warp.

Then other things had happened very quickly. Things she didn't understand. Sirens had begun to sound. Klaxons and bells. Sudden tension and fear had flashed through the hold habitats of the retinue company, an alarm born of ignorance. No one knew what was happening.

Realspace port shutters in the outer chambers that had only just begun to re-open after the immaterium transit were suddenly closing again. Old shutter motivators groaned at the sudden reverse. Members of the retinue had been waiting days to see out of the ship, if only to glimpse the brown darkness of space and the reassurance of distant stars, and now that solace was being denied them, all over again.

And the voice. The metallic voice. It was shouting words that sounded like *battle stations*.

How could they be in a battle? That seemed so unlikely.

Abruptly, as she was puzzling it out, something happened to the ship. Something hit the ship so hard everyone was thrown about, and the lights went out, and the air began to reek of smoke. When the lights began to flutter back on again, people were screaming. The children were wailing. Men and women had been hurt by the fall, bruised or bloodied by striking the deck or furniture fittings. Elodie struggled up, helping an older woman beside her. She was amazed at her fear. She'd never felt so numb and helpless. Costin had fallen too, spilling his papers all over the deck mesh. He was panicking. As she helped the older woman, Elodie glimpsed him taking a deep pull from a flask. The noise of panic in the chamber was almost overwhelming.

'We're in a fight! A fight!' someone shouted.

'We will perish in the void!' someone else shrieked.

'Be calm. Be calm!' Elodie heard herself saying to the people around her. She had no calm of her own to share. She wanted to know why she could smell smoke. She wanted to know if the world was about to turn upside down again, and if the lights would come back on if they went out again. The screech of the alarms seemed designed to promote acute anxiety.

She saw Juniper. The woman was frantic.

'Where's my little dear?' Juniper was crying. 'Where's my dear little girl? I lost her when the lights went out.'

Elodie put her arm around Juniper to steady her, and looked around, searching the seething crowd. People were rioting in every direction.

'Yoncy?' Elodie yelled. 'Yoncy, come here to us!'

'Where are you, Yoncy?' Juniper called.

Elodie saw Captain Meryn, who'd been supervising the troop of men on paperwork detail.

'Have you seen Yoncy?' she asked.

Meryn had an ugly expression on his face, a sick look of fear. He glared at her.

'Who?' he asked.

'Captain's Criid's little girl!' Juniper blurted, crying. 'The dear thing will be trampled!'

Meryn pushed past them. He said something that Elodie didn't hear properly.

She was pretty sure it was something like, *Do I look like I care?* Or words to that effect.

There was a sudden rekindling of panic as the ship's plasma engines began to thrash and rumble at an accelerated rate, making everything reverberate. Elodie clutched Juniper, who was sobbing and shaking.

'We'll find her,' she insisted. 'We'll find her.'

Elodie assumed that the trauma couldn't get any worse. But there was a sudden bark of cracking gunfire. Everyone flinched and ducked, and almost everyone screamed.

The crowd began scattering. Those who couldn't flee threw themselves flat onto the deck or took cover behind cots, crates or bunk blocks.

There was a Tanith trooper barging down the central hold space aisle towards Elodie and Juniper. Elodie didn't recognise him. There seemed to be something wrong with his face, as if it had become blurred. His right hand was soaked in blood and brandishing a lasrifle. As he advanced, the soldier was cracking off bursts of autofire above the heads of the crowd to scare them out of his way. The gunfire bursts pattered and sparked off the high hold ceiling.

His left hand was around the throat of the terrified child he had snatched up as a shield.

It was Yoncy.

TEN
Shields

SPIKA STARED AT his comparatives for a second. His plasma engines were burning hard, and he could feel the grav torque pulling at the ship's seams as it surged into the hard turn.

They were never going to make it. They were never going to turn in time. They were certainly not going to pull clear of the munitions spread rushing towards them. He had ordered counterfire to try to track and detonate some of the incoming torpedoes, but even with the detection systems on their side, it was like trying to hit an individual grain of sand with a bow and arrow during a hurricane. Another few moments and the enemy munitions would be sufficiently in-range to establish target lock and start to actively hunt them.

A warhead spread that large would demolish an unshielded hull like an eggshell.

Spika had one choice. In truth, he had two, but one of them was 'die', so there was little to discuss. *Ominator*, shrieking its name in grotesque pulses of noise through the void, like a wounded animal in a trap, was coming for them. *Aggressor Libertus* was racing away from the solid Imperial gunline to offer support, but it was six or seven minutes away from being any use.

Spika adjusted the heading values and added nineteen seconds to the burn duration.

The chief steersman glanced at him.

'Execute!' Spika yelled.

THROUGH THE GLASS, darkness.

'I can't see anything,' said Felyx.

'Get behind me,' hissed Maddalena Darebeloved.

Felyx glanced at her.

'You're ridiculous. Simply ridiculous,' he said. 'This isn't a street hit, this is a void fight. How is getting behind you going to protect me?'

He turned back to the realspace port. They'd found a stretch of hull-side hallway in the outer accommodation deck where the realspace shutters had failed to close properly. There was a limited view out into the blackness. Felyx was leaning close to the thickened armaglass to peer out, but he was seeing little more than his own reflection.

'I can't see anything,' he whispered. There was nothing visible outside, just darkness. Not even stars. For all the commotion going on inside the *Armaduke*, there was apparently nothing to warrant it.

Dalin watched Felyx and his lifeguard. There was a tremendous noise coming from the transport decks behind them, a palpable edge of panic. Dalin was anxious, and very distressed by the great surges of engine noise, and the rapid shifts and sways in mass and gravity. He felt like he was on a boat in a heavy sea.

'We should go to the bunker spaces,' he said.

'Someone speaks sense,' said Maddalena.

'Being in a bunker deck isn't going to help much if we're hit,' snapped Felyx. 'If the ship goes up, there's nowhere to hide.'

'Being in a bunker deck offers better chances of survival than standing beside an unarmoured window that could blow out to hard void at any moment,' said Maddalena. 'Don't make me pick you up and carry you.'

The shipwide alarms were still sounding, and personnel were running past them. The smell of smoke remained intense, but it had been partly obscured by a rising stink of heat. The engines were running hot. Furnaces were seething.

'My first void fight, and this is what I witness,' complained Felyx, peering out again, bobbing his head to try different angles. 'I suppose everything is too far away for us to see.'

'Really?' asked Dalin. He was honestly surprised. He'd never really thought about the scale in those terms. He understood that the void was big, but he'd never imagined a situation where ships the size of the one they were travelling aboard could engage without being able to see each other.

The ship was the size of a city! How ridiculous was it to fight something so far away you couldn't see it? A lasman had to appreciate his enemy, or at least his enemy's position, in order to fight. And what kind of gun could–

Somebody ran up to them, out of breath. Dalin turned, and suddenly stiffened. Maddalena also snapped around in surprise.

'What in the God-Emperor's name are you doing here?' asked Gaunt.

Felyx turned from the realspace port at the sound of Gaunt's voice.

'What the hell are you doing?' Gaunt snarled. Dalin blinked. There was something in Gaunt's manner, an agitation, that he had never seen before. 'Get to the bunker spaces. The shelter decks. Come on!'

'I–' Felyx began.

'Shut up and move,' Gaunt barked. He looked at Maddalena. 'Some lifeguard you are! Do your damn job! Get him into a shelter cavity! There are standing orders for this kind of situation. I could have you all on charges!'

He looked at Dalin.

'I'm disappointed in you, trooper. I thought you could be trusted to keep these people in line.'

Dalin stood to attention.

'No excuses, sir.'

Gaunt looked back at Felyx and his minder.

'No excuses, but they probably aren't cooperating, are they? Did you tell them to go to the bunker decks?'

'Yes, sir.'

Gaunt stared at Maddalena.

'Do your job.'

'What's happening?' asked Felyx.

Gaunt glanced at him.

'We're in a fight.'

'I can't see anything.'

'Of course you can't!' Gaunt snapped.

'How many ships? Are we winning?' Felyx asked.

'Go to the bunker, now!'

'What are you doing here?' asked Felyx. 'Aren't you supposed to be somewhere important?'

Gaunt hesitated.

'Go to the bunker,' he growled.

'Holy Throne!' Dalin blurted.

There was something to see outside. In the time they had been speaking, something had loomed silently, filling the realspace ports. They had indeed got the scale wrong, but in the opposite direction. The blackness they had been staring at had been the lightless shadow of another ship's flank. Now it resolved as they surged past it. They saw where the hard-edged light caught the upper hull and gun towers, saw the glowing lines of fusion burning where vast sections of deck had been scoured away. Clouds of debris, like glitter, filled the void. Brutal ribbons of escaping energy licked and flared from ruptured power plants in the ship's exposed entrails. Chunks of armoured hull wallowed past on slow, lazily spinning trajectories. They were right alongside another ship, but had been in its shadow and too close to see it before.

The other ship was stricken and all but dead. It looked like a burning hive, seen from the air.

'I will escort them to the bunker right away, sir,' said Dalin.

They all turned as they heard the same noise. A sharp, snapping report had come from the direction of the transport decks, a crackling chatter that for all the worlds of the Imperium sounded like gunfire.

'*Now* get behind me,' said Maddalena.

THE PLASMA ENGINES were exceeding the operational limit of their tolerances. Immeasurably old, and refitted more times than Spika cared to imagine, they were simply no longer able to develop maximum thrust from cold or low power at short notice.

The hull frame wasn't up to it either. The *Highness Ser Armaduke* had never been an elegant or graceful ship, not even in the heyday of its youth, millennia before. It was dogged and robust, not agile.

The hull, wrenched by the extreme forces of the manoeuvre Spika was attempting, was crying out in pain. Crew members, especially hardwired servitors and serfs, were screaming as waves of techno-empathic pain gripped them. Several dropped dead. The steel and plastek cranium of a high-function servitor at the environmental station burst apart in a spray of fire-fly sparks, the pressure slap shearing the metal plates from the skull beneath, revealing the bone and organic traces of the Imperial human who had forfeited his life to the augmetic processes of Navy service many stand-ard lifetimes before. Scorched rivets and yellow teeth scattered across the deck. An artificer's assistant with a porcelain face lay down beside the manifold console as if to sleep. It scrunched into a foetal position and died without reopening its optics. A bulk servitor, a loader in the upper forward starboard magazine, suffered some kind of cerebrovascular crisis, and beat its reinforced head apart against a munitions silo wall. Hyper-strain triggered a convulsive fit in a precision drone serving the strategium, and its subtle haptic limbs began to thrash so rapidly they became a humming bird blur.

Spika ignored the losses. He disregarded the rupturing seams of the outer armour, the inner frame sleeves, the hullskin compartments. He paid no attention to the atmospheric failures on four decks, the brownouts and blackouts, the energy drain as available resources were re-routed to the realspace engines and the shield repairs. He took no heed of the rank of realspace windows that blew out along a distorting hull ridge and opened sub deck 118 to hard vacuum. He ignored the critical alert hazards that were flashing at the top of the engine console, warnings that the frantic, red-lining plasma drives were close to failure and shut down.

By the Golden Throne of Terra, he had never seen a master's console alight with so many alarms at once. He knew he had a survival margin that could be measured in milliseconds.

The *Armaduke* could not outpace the free-running torpedoes delivered from the *Ominator*. It could only hope the warheads found something else first.

'May the God-Emperor forgive me,' said Spika.

The *Armaduke*, engines searing white hot, turned the ship in behind the listing bulk of the stricken *Benedicamus Domino*. The sundered hull of the wounded frigate eclipsed Spika's ship.

Spika knew that there were likely to be ten or even fifteen thousand crewmen still alive on the *Domino*. But the *Domino* was past saving. The *Armaduke* was still alive.

The warheads, thirty of them, rained into the starboard

side of the keeling ship, which had been knocked side-on into the path of the enemy by the first strike. Only wisps of shield remained. Two torpedoes detonated as they ploughed into the dense, glittering debris field that fogged the vacuum beside the *Domino* like a cloud of blood beside a floating body. Another triggered as it struck the hard, pressurised release of environment gases squirting through the *Domino*'s burst hull.

All three detonations, miniature starbursts too bright to look at, disappeared a moment later as the other twenty-seven warheads encountered the primary hull. Concentric rings of shockwave and overpressure criss-crossed, and twisted the fabric of the hull apart, like raindrops rippling the still surface of a pool. Light bloomed, a supernova, a ferocious pink-tinged white that scared away the blackness of the void like a sunrise and turned the *Benedicamus Domino* into a sharp-edged black silhouette.

The frigate perished. Disintegration crept through its structure from the blast point outwards, vaporising the hull's armour jacket, chewing away the superstructure, sloughing away surface plating like fish scales. Tidal waves of liquid flame poured and gurgled through each deck level, and then ate away the deck planes in between. Firestorms surged up connective shafts and access wells, boiled through environmental systems, and torched the ship's leaking atmosphere. Within a second of the main strike, geysers of fire and explosive shockwash were squirting out through the other side of the ship like exit wounds, blowing out shuttered ports, carrier deck doors, airgates and gun stations. Out flung debris, including several furies and cargo shutters washed out of the *Domino*'s bays, born along like flotsam in the blast, spattered against the *Armaduke*'s outer hull.

Then the shock pulse hit, a double hammer blow: first the electromagnetic punch then the kinetic rip. The *Armaduke* rode them out, shuddering, lurching.

The glare faded. The *Benedicamus Domino* was left as nothing but a blackened metal mass of fused and glowing scrap, an iron-rich asteroid fragment.

Shipmaster Spika fought back the urge to vomit. Adrenaline had spiked critically in his system: his augmetic neurides were overheating, and his vision had reduced to a grey tunnel. Dataflow assault was so intense his stomach was churning and he wanted to gag.

He yelled a new heading at the chief steersman. He entered the engine correctives manual at his master console, nursing the screaming plasma engines down to a more gentle roar, cooling and banking down their excessive output, swinging the *Armaduke* on a more gentle turn to avoid the *Domino*'s radioactive cadaver and square with the *Ominator*.

The *Ominator*'s jubilant, taunting shrieks had been briefly silenced by the electromagnetic pulse of the multiple detonation, but now it was back as the vox system recovered. It was crowing, almost laughing out its name in a voice scarred and scaled by vox distortion. The *Ominator* had direct-line speed, the proper momentum and attack rate of a charging predator. It had not been obliged to bleed valuable speed and energy through stumbling evasions and desperate antics, the way the *Armaduke* had.

'Gunnery!' Spika commanded. He used a haptic reader to communicate the munitions spread he desired. The *Ominator*'s attack squadrons were already rolling in on them, zipping over and under the smoking mass of the wrecked *Domino*.

'Shields as a matter of urgency,' said Spika, trying to clear his throat of rising acid. 'We're going at them, and we're going to burn them all the way back to hell.'

ELEVEN
The Clear Shot

EVERYBODY WAS DOWN on the deck, the women sobbing, the children bawling. Elodie was holding on to Juniper to stop her throwing herself at the man who had seized Yoncy. He had a gun, and he was shooting it wildly. Anyone who waved a gun, and was prepared to fire it in a crowded room, anyone who was prepared to snatch a little girl as a shield, that was someone you didn't try to tackle.

Elodie wrestled Juniper down, slapping her pawing hands aside. Elodie was moaning. Everyone was making some kind of sound: distress, fear, desperation.

Everyone except Yoncy. Elodie saw that Yoncy was still and expressionless. Trauma had clearly conquered her. She was like a doll in the crook of the gunman's arm.

The man rattled off a few more shots to keep them all ducking. More screams came from the womenfolk. He was backing towards the hatch under the portside walkway, coming right down past them. Elodie wished she could work out what was wrong with the man's face. It was twisted, distorted. It wasn't a proper face at all.

209

'Drop her! Drop the girl!'

More panicked screams. Elodie glanced around and saw three Ghosts rushing into the transport deck from the far end, rifles at their shoulders, covering the man and his hostage as they prowled through the rows of cowering retinue personnel.

The man who had shouted the order was a Belladon, Cardass. To his left was Bonin, the Tanith scout, weapon up and sighted. To Bonin's right was Gol Kolea.

Kolea's lasrifle was at his cheek. The expression in his eyes tore Elodie in half. It was part hatred, part anguish.

His daughter. His little girl.

'Drop her!' Cardass yelled again.

The gunman answered with some inarticulate noise as though his mouth wasn't working properly. His face seemed tangled.

Elodie felt her heart fluttering. She so wanted to get up, to tear the girl out of the maniac's grip.

She saw Captain Meryn. He was cowering right beside her, next to one of the cots. Costin was nearby too, his head in his hands, the documents he'd been carrying scattered around his knees. One of the gunman's wild shots had clipped his shoulder, leaving a grazed burn.

Meryn's eyes were bright with fear, like those of a cornered animal. He wasn't carrying his rifle, but Elodie could see the laspistol holstered at his waist.

'Shoot him,' she hissed, holding Juniper down. 'Captain, shoot him!'

Meryn ignored her.

'Shoot him!' Elodie repeated.

There was a clear angle. The gunman was side on to them, and he hadn't seen Meryn or his comrade. Any half-decent shot could have put a las bolt through his head or his torso, missing the girl entirely.

'Are you mad?' Meryn rasped back.

'You can take a clear shot!'

'Shut up!'

'Captain, shoot him!'

'Shut the feth up!' Meryn snarled.

'Put the girl down,' Kolea ordered. His voice cut the air and the panic like a scythe. It was toneless, as if the light had gone out in his heart.

'Back off! Back off!' the gunman yelled back, the words clawing, imperfectly shaped, out of his deformed mouth. The strain of his efforts had finally overcome the Sirkle's face-shifting abilities.

Kolea, Bonin and Cardass had him triangulated, all aiming straight for his head. They were squinting down the top sights of their weapons, shoulders hunched, trotting forwards with short, hurrying steps.

Elodie wondered if any of them would dare take the shot.

'Put the girl down!' Cardass demanded.

'Forget it,' Kolea said. 'Judd, forget it. He's got nothing to lose any more. He's not going to let us take him.'

He lowered his rifle to his chest, though he still kept it pointing at the gunman.

'Are you?' he asked. 'You bastard. You're going to make us kill you, and you're going to make us kill the girl to do it.'

The gunman said something. His lips were too slack and misshapen for the words to be intelligible.

The ship shook. It was violent and abrupt. There was no sound, and no light came through the sealed port shutters, but the ship juddered as though it had been dropped.

A moment's distraction.

Rawne dropped from the portside walkway onto the gunman's back. The impact felled the gunman and took Yoncy over too. Rawne's straight silver blade plunged into the killer's right shoulder. His weapon went off, spraying las bolts into the air.

All three of them tumbled. Rawne lost his grip on the warknife. The gunman kept his grip on Yoncy. With a

bellow that made the civilians sheltering around them
shriek, Rawne got hold of Yoncy and wrenched her out
of the killer's grasp. He simply hurled her into the air,
perhaps out of desperation, perhaps in the belief that a
fall injury would be preferable to letting her stay in the
killer's reach a moment longer. The killer lashed out and
clubbed Rawne in the face with the edge of his rifle.

Hoisted, Yoncy tumbled. Elodie sprang forwards, her
arms outstretched, and managed to catch her before
she bounced off the sheet metal deck. The little girl was
heavy. The impact tore muscles in Elodie's forearm.
She kept her grip, rolling, trying to shield Yoncy from
the landing. They crunched down onto Elodie's right
shoulder, Yoncy cushioned against Elodie's breasts and
stomach. The back of Elodie's head struck against the leg
of a cot and she blacked out for a second.

There was blood in her mouth, in her nose. She
blinked. Yoncy was yelling and thrashing on top of her,
squirming, kicking her heels. Pain flooded Elodie's skull
and her right arm.

The gunman was back on his feet. The warknife was
still wedged into his shoulder blade. Rawne was down,
flattened on the deck by the clubbing blow. The killer
pointed his lasrifle at Rawne to cut him apart.

Kolea's first shot blew the gunman's right arm off at
the elbow, causing the dismembered limb and the lasrifle it was aiming to spin like a slow propeller. Kolea's
second shot blew out his chest in a splash of burned
blood and splintered ribs.

Kolea's third shot traumatically deformed his head
far more significantly than anything the face-slip had
achieved.

The killer went down, full length, felled like an old
straight nalwood, leaving blood mist in the air behind
him.

Elodie's shoulder was busted. The pain speared into
her so sharply she couldn't move.

Meryn took Yoncy off her and turned to Kolea.

'She's all right,' Meryn said. 'She's safe, Gol. She's safe.'

THE OMINATOR'S ATTACK ships, ugly, cackling arrowhead craft, came in around the dead *Domino*. They were like miniature versions of their sire, a litter of squealing, ravening whelps.

'Shields?' suggested Spika, overcome by a terrible, analytical calm.

'Repairs still underway!' sang out an artificer's junior.

'Track them. Deterrent fire,' Spika ordered.

The *Armaduke*'s smaller, more nimble batteries and gun stations woke up, streaming beams and ripping, stuttering lines of las bolts up into the black. Barrels pumped in their arrestor sleeves as the gun mounts traversed hard, chasing the fast-moving attack ships. Through multiple viewers via multiple pict feeds, Spika watched the enemy pack rip over, darting along the flanks and underside of the *Armaduke*, banking between crenellated surface towers and engraved armour buttresses, hugging the lines of the ribbed prow, like aircraft flying low-level through the streets of a hive. Battery fire pursued them. Spika saw one attack ship engulfed in flame, tumbling like a firework wheel under its own momentum. He also saw a battery go up, strafed into oblivion. Lights began to go dark across his master console, tiny individual lights among the thousands of system indicators. *Prow battery 1123. Prow battery 96 (starboard). Keel battery 326 (centreline). Port tower 11. Environment hub 26 alpha (portside). Detection relay nine beta.*

A wave of target strikes rippled down the *Armaduke* as the enemy squadron raced aft, jinking, evading, gunning for weak spots.

There was a sudden electromagnetic crackle, a distort across most pict feeds, the fuzz-wash of serious las fire. As the pictures jumped and cycled back into life, Spika saw Furies. The Imperial void fighters, all of them

from the poor *Domino*'s fighter screen, were soaring
down the length of the *Armaduke*'s hull in the opposite direction, meeting the enemy squadron head-on.
Spika tracked almost three dozen individual dogfights,
acrobatic duels that were suddenly, bitterly in progress.
Furies banked after enemy craft around shield pylons
or detection towers, or harried them down around the
flanks and around the keel line. Like ascending birds,
Furies and foe-ships locked together, spiralling up and
away from the *Armaduke* as they tried to out-turn each
other and gain the kill shot. Some were tumbling. Others turned out in wide arcs, forced away from the frigate
in an effort to lose a pursuer, sometimes as far as the
glowing mass of the *Domino*. It was like an angry swarm
of insects mobbing the old ship.

'Shields in twenty seconds!' an artificer announced.

'Acknowledged,' Spika replied. 'Vox, do what you can
to signal the Furies. Warn them we are relighting and
they need to be clear when we do.'

'Aye, master!'

Spika's attention was on the *Ominator*. It had clearly
not grown tired of saying its own name. Instruments
estimated about nine minutes to firing point at their
current intercept rate. Spika shook that off. More like
seven or six and a half. The *Ominator* was hasty and
hungry. It wanted to get a lick in before the *Armaduke*
was shielded again, and before the storming bulk of the
Aggressor Libertus came charging in from the rear line.
The *Aggressor Libertus* was already trading long-range
punches with the *Necrostar Antiversal* as it accelerated. *Necrostar Antiversal*, realspace drives burning
orange-hot, clearly wanted to test its mettle against the
Sepiterna.

'Dammit, do we have any vox?' Spika asked.

'Routing available circuits to you, master.'

Spika pulled his silver speaker-horn close.

'Hailing, hailing, Master of the *Libertus*. Hailing,

hailing, Master of the *Libertus*. This is Spika, mastering the *Highness Ser Armaduke*.'

A crackle.

'This is *Libertus*, confirm.'

'Confirm, *Libertus*. Let the capital ship worry about that cruiser. We can crush this target with pinning fire and then turn together.'

A long pause, full of static.

'*Libertus*, confirm?'

'Agreed, *Armaduke*. You have guns effective and shields, confirm?'

'Confirm guns effective. Maintain positions relative. *Armaduke* now accelerating to close. Be ready to turn wide, repeat wide, if he proves reluctant to run between us.'

'Relative noted and matched. Acceleration matched. Let's slay the bastard, *Armaduke*.'

'Confirm.'

'Shields at your discretion!' the artificer announced.

'Light them,' said Spika.

There was a stuttering pulse as the void shield generators cycled into life. Deck lights dipped all the way into brown-out and back as onboard power was briefly refocused. Shielding crackled into being around the advancing *Armaduke*, forming blistering fields of immaterium distortion. Several Furies, late leaving the side of the *Armaduke*, tumbled, lights out and power gone, their systems temporarily blanked by contact with the defence fields. Four of the Archenemy's small hunter-ships detonated, crushed against the expanding shields, their drive plants destroyed by some allergic, alchemical interaction.

Shields raised, the *Armaduke* began to power past the *Domino* towards the onrushing *Ominator*. *Aggressor Libertus* followed on, about sixty kilometres astern and twenty to starboard.

'Clear the missile tubes!' Spika commanded. 'Main

batteries, main mounts – firing solutions on the designated target now.'

He focused the primary rangefinder on the *Ominator*.

THE AIR IN the system still smelled of smoke. At least this disguised the *Armaduke*'s pervading odour of kitchen grease.

Gaunt walked back towards the bridge, through corridors empty of life. All of the passenger complement was stowed in the bunker decks, and the crew personnel were at their battle stations. Occasionally, a junior rating or a servitor rushed past on some errand.

Gaunt had started out with little sense of the void fight, and now he had none at all. He wondered if they were close to winning, or close to dying. The ship was peaceful. It wasn't like being in a battle on the field, with the thump of guns, of artillery pummelling the skyline, with airborne overhead. Space was silent. There was no communication of nearby destruction.

But he could tell that a fight was going on. The deck creaked and the superstructure groaned, under tension. Every minute or so, the lights would dip and come back, or the engines would begin another frantic round of thrashing output. Static coated every surface; he presumed that was a side effect of the void shields. He'd seen it in buildings and ground vehicles close to active Titans.

Most of all he could feel the fight inside him, in his gut, his inner ear, his kinaesthetic sense. He could sense the soundless, invisible pull and twist and wrench of inertial compensation. The gravitic systems were fighting to maintain the environmental status quo as the ship lurched and came about. He felt as if he was standing in a quiet, swaying building: it flooded him with memories. Being in a high tower on Balhaut during the first firestorms. Being on the curtain walls of Vervunhive as the Heritor's woe-machines lumbered in.

At least, he reflected, he hoped it was the gravitic stresses. He hoped it was not the turbulence of his restless soul, troubled by a distress it had never expected.

The hatchway to a grand chamber lay open. Inside, under gently swinging lamp rigs, the Iron Snake Holofurnace was performing a fast sword drill against hololithic targets.

The sword work was devastatingly swift. Holofurnace was using a cross-stroke and rotational style Gaunt had not seen before, switching from one hand to a two-handed grip depending on the attitude of the sword.

Helmet off, Eadwine was sitting to one side, watching the rehearsal.

He didn't look up as Gaunt approached, but he knew the human was there.

'I thought you'd be cowering somewhere,' said Eadwine, his voice a machine rasp.

'No, you didn't,' replied Gaunt.

'No,' Eadwine admitted. He kept watching the Iron Snake's sword drill. The Iron Snake hadn't even acknowledged Gaunt's presence.

'He is getting sloppy,' said the Silver Guard warrior. 'I don't know what kind of blade-work they teach on Ithaka these days.'

'Aren't you concerned about the battle?' asked Gaunt. 'I thought you might have gone to the bridge.'

Eadwine turned to look at him.

'What would that achieve? There's no part for us to play. Not unless they board us. Are they likely to board us?'

'I don't think so.'

The Silver Guard shrugged.

'Then all we can do is bide our time until we are faced with our kind of fight.'

'You don't need to know what's going on?' asked Gaunt.

Holofurnace stopped slicing his sword and glanced over.

'Only if we live,' he said. 'If we die, why care about the detail?'

He went back about his training. The sword flashed fast, spinning and interweaving.

Gaunt realised that Eadwine was still staring at him.

'I do not read your face well,' said Eadwine. 'I do not read human micro expressions. They are too weak, insignificant.'

Gaunt didn't know how to reply.

'But you seem concerned,' the Silver Guard went on. 'Clearly, there is the stress factor of this fight, but you are a man who has known battles. Where is your resolution? There is, it seems to me, another element troubling you.'

'You read our faces well enough,' said Gaunt.

Eadwine frowned and nodded, as if quietly please with his achievement.

'So?'

'I find myself distracted,' said Gaunt. 'Without expecting to, I find myself concerned for the welfare of another person aboard. That concern has surprised me to an extent I find dismaying.'

'You question your focus.'

'I worry about maintaining it.'

'Is it a woman?' asked Eadwine. 'A woman? A sexual partner? I understand that can be very distracting for the emotionally compromised.'

'No,' said Gaunt. 'I have recently learned that I have a son.'

'Ah,' said Eadwine. 'Offspring. I know nothing about them either.'

He tilted his head, listening.

'You hear?' he asked.

Holofurnace had stopped drilling to listen too. Gaunt concentrated. He could make out a distant, repetitive thumping, masked by the engine throb, the steady chug of a machine rotating or cycling.

'That's the ship's primary magazine delivering

munitions at the fastest possible continuous pace,' said Eadwine. 'We are unloading everything we have at a sustained rate. We are trying to kill something very big.'

TWELVE
Kill Recorded

WHATEVER SENTIENCE CONTROLLED the daemon ship *Omi-nator*, its gleeful hunger for murder was so intense that it only belatedly became aware of the way the *Armaduke* and the *Libertus* had squeezed it into an untenable position.

They had met its headlong rush at the Imperial position with calm resolve, intercepting its trajectory so that the *Ominator* was obliged to pass between them. Such was the *Ominator's* fever to engage, it was over pacing itself. It became apparent that it was not going to be able to break off or execute an evasion in time, certainly not without rendering itself more vulnerable. Any attempt to hard turn out of the tactical lock would have consumed vast amounts of its power reserve and de-positioned it hopelessly in the battlesphere alignment.

It continued to shriek its name. The shielding around its prow and flanks began to throb with a sub-photonic gleam the colour of burst entrails. Mechanical organs along its spine and between the blades of its ribs began to throb as it gathered power for a main weapon strike.

Advancing steadily, the *Armaduke* and the *Libertus* exchanged a brief non-verbal signal and began to hose fire at the enemy ship. Two streams of bombardment ripped out from the Imperial pair, converging like the lines of some infernal diagram on the *Ominator*. The streams were traceries of pulsed and beamed energy weapons, the unified output of hundreds of batteries slaved to the master tracking cogitators. Heavy ordnance systems spat torrents of hard shell munitions, missiles, ship-to-ship ballistic charges and bombard rockets.

The *Ominator* soaked it up without breaking stride, taking the titanic barrage from the *Libertus* against its forward port shields and the destructive abuse of the slightly extended *Armaduke* across its starboard side and belly.

The two ships maintained their relentless assault. The *Ominator* advanced in the face of their sustained fury, apparently oblivious, as if the onslaught was entirely futile. The fire rate was stupendous. Two gunners aboard the *Libertus* were killed by recoil trying to service the hard batteries fast enough, and an artificer aboard the *Armaduke* was burned to death by an overheating laser assembly. From his command seat aboard the *Armaduke*, Spika believed he had never seen a ship take such relentless punishment.

The *Ominator* squealed its name and attempted to fire, but the hellish lightning failed to develop enough to whip out from the hull. It tried again, and then again: two or three more stuttering attempts at ignition.

Then its shields failed, and its hull tore open like a punctured membrane. Shielding energies billowed out into the void around it like ink in water, like ragged sailcloth carried along by a storm-borne ship, like a ruptured egg sac.

Something catastrophic happened deep inside the daemon ship's hull. There was a considerable though muffled explosion deep inside the ship about two-thirds of the way down its length. It was not a huge, satisfying sunburst of annihilation, but it blew out areas of deck plate and internal structure. Clouds of burning, toxic energy and atmosphere belched out. The mainframe shuddered.

Then the *Ominator* went dead. All of its onboard light sources died, even the infernal red glow from its core. Its energy output signature ceased, apart from the shreds of radiation and flame coming from the damaged sections. Its drive failed. Its plant failed. Its reactors failed. It became, in a second or two, an inert, dead lump of black machine junk, scorched and holed. Carried by its own forwards momentum, it began to tumble, prow tipping up, drive section rotating under, debris littering out of it like a spiral vapour trail.

The Imperial ships ceased fire. They waited, poised, in case it was a ruse, in case the daemon ship had decided to turn itself into a weapon and ram one of them.

It was lifeless. Blundering on, spinning like a discarded piece of scrap, it passed between them leaving a trickle of ejecta dispersing in its wake.

'Kill recorded,' cried out the Master of Detection.

'For the Emperor,' growled Spika.

As the Armaduke and the *Libertus* shared their kill, the vast *Sepiterna* had turned its guns against the *Necrostar Antiversal*. The enemy ship had crossed the main Imperial gunline, soaking up fire from the escorts as it paced a long, fast burn of an attack run across the battleship's bows, a diagonal slash across the alignment of the battlesphere.

Gorehead, a raging little beast, had fired in support of its keening brethren, trying to stifle the gunline's output and disrupt any aim at the *Necrostar*. A cloud of small craft had formed forward of the Imperial line, a massive dogfight swirl like pollen spilling from a flower head. Fury flights, along with heavier support squadrons

loosed by the Imperial ships, had ripped into the formations of Archenemy killships. One especially sustained
duel was being fought to keep the daemon interceptors
away from the Aquila bearing the lord militant.

Gorehead's primary weapons scored a decent hit against
an Imperial destroyer called *Phalanxor*, enough to impair
its void shields, and rendered it ineffective for long
enough to allow *Necrostar Antiversal* its passage. *Necrostar
Antiversal* was spitting massive hullcutter missiles at the
Imperial flagship, and its primary energy batteries were
cycling up to strike.

Sepiterna, an almost stationary island more than ten kilometres long, reached out to deny the obdurate intruder.
Beam weapons, red sparks in the brown twilight of the
void, found and neutralised the running missiles, igniting quick bright flashes of white fire. Then the principal
weapon fired, and slapped the charging Archenemy vessel sideways. *Necrostar Antiversal* spun away, all stability
control lost. Its port bow section glowed with a fierce
internal blaze, and atomised structural debris squirted
from its lurching bulk. It stopped screaming its name and
instead simply screamed. Demented with damage and
pain, the *Necrostar Antiversal* fell away, righted itself, and
then began to flee. The flight may have been caused by
a drive malfunction or a loss of helm. It was frantic and
headlong. The *Necrostar*'s realspace engines went to full
burn, one of them clearly misfiring and crippled to such
an extent the ship was leaving a dirty trail of burning fuel
and radioactive blowback behind it. It veered away like
a comet, and streaked towards the distant limits of the
system like a scolded hound, beaten and driven away
yelping.

Shipmaster Spika was aware that his artificers were
desperate to lower shields. Sustaining them at maximum
was depleting the reserves at a nightmarish rate. With fifty
per cent of the enemy strength dismissed, surely the fight
was done. Any grasp of tactical logic could tell you that.

Spika knew from bitter experience that when it came to void fighting with the Ruinous Powers, tactical logic had little or no place. He had, for many years as a more junior officer, studied the behavioural habits of large carnivores, particularly in such circumstances as hunting, protecting a kill or defending their family group or their young, as well as their actions when wounded or cornered. That, he had found, was most often how Archenemy ships performed. They did not make calculated strategic moves as though the battlesphere was a giant, three-dimensional regicide board. They did not observe the traditions and crafts of Battlefleet tactics as learned and studied by the officers of the Imperial Navy.

They fought like animals in traps, like wounded rogue beasts cornered in a canyon, like predators in the forest gloom. They ignored logic, or technical comparatives, or the output of threat assessment cogitators.

That, in the considered opinion of Clemensew Spika, an opinion not shared by the Departmento Tacticae of the Imperial Fleet, an opinion that had probably hindered the progress of his career over the years, that was why the Archenemy often won.

Tormaggedon Monstrum Rex, the behemoth capital ship of the enemy force, turned towards them. It had lost its appetite for a direct fight with the mighty *Sepiterna* and its resolved gunline, but it was evidently quite prepared to make a parthian shot or two at the *Armaduke* and the *Libertus*, pushed forwards and vulnerable as they were.

Spika ordered a hard evasive turn back towards the sun, and watched on the strategium display to see that *Libertus* was doing the same. If they could at least place themselves decently in the optimum reach of the main gunline, it might be enough to dissuade the monster from harrying them.

But the *Rex* was fast. It was the single biggest vessel involved in the fleet action; not as stately and deep through the waist as the majestic *Sepiterna*, but longer and of significantly greater tonnage. It accelerated, however, like a frigate. A light frigate. It was quite the nimblest supermassive Spika had seen since the Palodron Campaign against the diseased craftworld. Its internal glow, coal red, flared as if bellows had been applied. It powered in, weapon banks developing charge for a shot.

The *Sepiterna* spurred its whole gunline forwards, but it was a gesture that would have little practical effect in the timeframe. The *Aggressor Libertus*, a significant ship in its own right, began firing as it turned, loosing as much as it could at the oncoming monster. The daemon ship's shields held firm. The *Libertus*'s barrage, enough to strip a hive down to the mantle, spattered off the voidshields like firecrackers.

The *Rex* fired. The energy whiplash, so bright it was not any sort of colour at all, struck the *Libertus* in the small of the back, popped its shields like a soap bubble, shattered the hull jacket, and cored a hole down through the decks like someone cracking through decorative icing to slice open a layer cake. It was not one blast, one flash. The jerking, kinking coil of energy linked the two ships together like an electrical arc for almost twenty seconds. Its point of impact was brighter than a spot-welding torch. The burning force sheared through the *Libertus*, cutting it in a line that ran along its spine towards its prow. The cruiser was almost bisected lengthways. When the awful weapon finally shut off, the *Libertus* broke up, not cleanly in half like a nutshell, but into two large sections along a surgically straight line. Almost a third of the cruiser's tonnage sheared away along the port side from central environmental to the prow, armour splintering like glass, internal contents, crew and debris voiding in a cloud like smoke. The sectioning was so precise that Spika could see the cross-cut through the decks through his viewer, like a cross-section display in one of the glass cases at the Admiralty. He saw fires burning inside, pressure compartments blowing, bulkheads shredding, atmosphere venting, hydraulics and other fluids billowing out in quicksilver blobs. He saw slicks of debris litter and realised they were masses of weightless corpses.

A secondary blast blew out the *Libertus*'s ruptured plasma drives, sending the larger of the two hull portions spinning nose over tail out of a bright yellow explosion. The spinning section clipped the other hull portion and sent it tumbling out to one side, regurgitating material into the void.

The *Rex* brushed past its kill and closed on the *Armaduke*, dwarfing it. It was set to send the Imperial battlegroup home with at least three dead.

Its main weapons gathered charge, cracking fury in the reservoirs beneath the skin of the hull. It closed tighter still, perhaps intending to riddle the *Armaduke* to scrap with its small batteries rather than waste the main charge.

Spika felt its shadow on them. It overhauled them, blotting out the sun, a leviathan ten or twelve times their size. Every sensor on the *Armaduke*'s bridge screamed. Every alarm sounded. Spika instructed his gun crews to unload everything they had.

Tormaggedon Monstrum Rex boomed its name into the darkness. But it did not stop.

It passed so close by the *Armaduke*, the frigate shivered hard in its wake, and it kept accelerating, driving out along the unvariable and away, developing speed and translating into the warp. *Gorehead*, yapping at its heels, followed.

By then, the *Necrostar Antiversal* had fled through the outsystem and away, wailing in blind pain, and the corpse of the *Ominator* was tumbling down into the fires of Tavis Sun.

THIRTEEN
Turn Around

DORDEN TOOK A deep breath. Tension and fatigue had put a tiny tic in the corner of his right eye and a tremble in his liver-spotted hands. Rawne was struck by how grey the old doctor's skin had become. It reminded him, painfully, of the skin paint used by the sleepwalkers of the Gereon Untill, and of the wood-ash dust that the old nalwoodland communities of Tanith had used to anoint bodies for funerary rites. He'd never made that connection before. He made a point of not thinking about Tanith unless he had to.

'He'll live,' said Dorden.

Rawne nodded. He looked down at Cant. The trooper was unconscious, in a chemically-induced coma, his neck wrapped in bindings and counterseptic wadding. His face was drained of blood, colourless white rather than Dorden's dead grey. Dorden and the new man, Kolding, had worked for two intensive hours to save Cant's life. No one could yet tell what brain damage might accompany the catastrophic blood loss of the throat wound.

Rawne patted Dorden's arm.

'There's nothing I could do for the others,' Dorden said.

Rawne didn't turn to look at the wrapped corpses of Kabry and MkTally. Two Kings dead, another severely wounded. They had paid a high cost already guarding the pheguth etogaur. And that was without counting Edur and the crew personnel, and the poor bandsman fool that the Sirkle must have slain on Menazoid Sigma in order to worm his way into their midst.

'Get some rest,' said Rawne.

Dorden laughed. The infirmary was busy. In the aftermath of the void fight and the commotion aboard, there had been a lot of minor injuries: a few concussions and broken bones. There was still work to be done.

Kolding was nearby, washing Cant's blood off his hands in a metal sink in preparation for the next patient.

Rawne walked over to him.

'I understand the technique that saved him was your idea,' he said.

Kolding stared at Rawne. He wasn't used to being spoken to or even acknowledged by many of the regiment.

'It seemed expedient,' he managed to say.

Rawne nodded. He held out his hand. Kolding blinked. He hesitated for a moment, because he'd only just got his hands scrubbed ready again. The hesitation was too long. Rawne lowered his hand, and nodded.

'It's appreciated,' he said, and walked away.

Ban Daur entered the medicae suite, squeezing past the walking casualties queuing for treatment.

'Where is she?' he asked the orderly Chayker.

Chayker pointed.

Elodie was sitting on a cot in the corner, her arm in a tight, packed sling, a compress against the back of her head. Rawne watched Daur cross to her, kneel beside her, embrace her gently. Dorden had said that the woman had torn shoulder muscles and taken a mild concussion catching the child. Brave. Selfless. There were more reasons than just good looks to admire Elodie Dutana. Rawne kept watching as they spoke quietly. He assumed she was telling Daur what happened. Rawne tried to remember the last time anyone had looked him in the eyes the way she was looking at Daur.

Down the far end of the infirmary unit, where it was quieter, Criid and Juniper were sitting with Yoncy while Curth checked the child over. The little girl was perched on a cot and seemed to be enjoying the attention. There was no indication she had been remotely upset by her adventure.

'I owe you,' said Kolea, coming up beside Rawne quietly to stare at Yoncy.

Rawne shrugged.

'I was protecting the Archenemy feth-head, not the little girl,' said Rawne.

'Right.'

They both tensed. Meryn had just walked out of the side ward where he'd been checking on Costin's graze wound. Criid had crossed to Elodie and Daur to murmur a few words, and she turned as she saw Meryn.

'Ah shit,' said Kolea.

Criid walked right up into Meryn's face. They could feel the hatred radiating off her.

'You didn't take the shot,' she hissed.

'What? Tona?'

'Don't give me Tona, you spineless idiot. You had a shot and you didn't take it.'

'What? That bitch tell you that?' Meryn sneered back, jerked his head in Elodie's direction.

'No,' said Criid. 'Juniper told me. Juniper said you just kept your coward head down.'

'She's a fething liar.'

Criid went for his throat. They crashed into an instrument stand and scattered a stack of steel bowls. The bowls clattered across the deck. Some of the civilian casualties started to wail in alarm.

'Not in here!' Curth roared.

Kolea and Rawne stormed forwards and got hold of Criid. She fought back in a frenzy of arms and legs as they pulled her away from Meryn.

'Get off me!' she shrieked.

'He's not worth ten hours in the tank, Criid,' Rawne growled.

'He's not,' agreed Kolea.

Criid stopped thrashing and shrugged Kolea and Rawne off as they relaxed their grip. She glared at Meryn.

'You saw what she did!' Meryn cried. 'I want her charged!'

'Grow some testicles and shut the feth up, Meryn,' replied Rawne.

Meryn pointed angrily at Kolea.

'He didn't care! He's the fething blood-father. He didn't attack me!'

'I was just pulling Criid out of the way,' said Kolea.

'What?' asked Meryn, puzzled.

Kolea's axe-rake of a fist slammed Meryn into the infirmary wall. The impact demolished a wire shelf and smashed a row of glass bottles.

'Have you all lost your minds?' Curth yelled. 'This is a sick bay. Stop it!'

Working together, Criid and Rawne managed to pull Kolea's muscle-dense bulk off Meryn. Meryn had his arms over his head and face. Blood was squirting out of his nose. When he realised the fists were no longer raining down, he began to get up, slipped, and then rose to his feet. Kolea lunged at him again, but Daur had joined Criid and Rawne to act as anchors, and they wrenched Kolea back between them.

'What in Throne's name is going on in here?' Hark demanded as he pushed into the infirmary.

'It's just a misunderstanding,' said Rawne, hauling Kolea back.

'Yes,' Criid agreed. 'We thought Meryn was a human gakking being, but we misunderstood.'

'They were attacking me!' Meryn squawked. 'There are witnesses. Charge them!'

'It won't happen again,' Rawne said.

'There are witnesses!' Meryn insisted, outraged.

'Show me one,' said Rawne. He looked around the room, at the shocked faces of those present. 'Anyone?' he caught Curth's eye.

Curth shook her head.

Hark frowned.

'Will this happen again?' he asked.

'No,' said Kolea.

'No,' said Criid. 'We're done.'

Daur punched Meryn square in the face and laid him out on the deck.

'Call her a bitch again and I'll gut you, you Tanith bastard,' he said. He looked at Hark.

'*Now* we're done,' he said.

WITH THE FIGHT finished, the *Armaduke* had closed with the fleet. Packet and cargo exchanges were underway, with lighters ferrying supply loads across. Small ships were also attending the two wrecked Imperial ships in search of survivors.

Gaunt went to the ship's communication chamber. Spika was in attendance, along with Eadwine. Hololithic generation sockets built into the deck manufactured crackling full-size images of Lord Militant Cybon, Fleet-master Cragoe, and several senior Navy and Munitorum worthies from the fleet complement.

'I am gratified to see that you survived the transfer,' Gaunt said to the image of Cybon.

'The Emperor protects,' Cybon replied without enthusiasm.

'The question is,' said Cragoe, an immense being whose biological bulk appeared to have been reinforced and supported by massive augmetic armatures and plates, 'will this mission survive? Is your assignment still viable?'

'Yes,' said Eadwine simply.

Cragoe snorted.

'I believe you should abort and turn around.'

'Do you?'

'Your vessel was compromised and attacked from within. The conjunction was tracked and discovered. We took significant losses.'

'But we won,' said Gaunt. 'We drove them off. There is no reason to suspect that the fleeing enemy has any intelligence about our target.'

'And if they do?' asked Cragoe. 'If they have other agents aboard your ship?'

'Then we ride to our deaths, not you,' said Gaunt.

'It would be patently ridiculous to get this far and then turn around without solid evidence of compromise,' said Spika. 'We identified the means by which they detected us and tracked our position during shift. We will be alert for it in future.'

'Is there another issue here?' asked Eadwine.

'We must consider the obvious,' said Cybon. 'Why did their capital ship spare you when it had you cold?'

'It had exhausted its present charge on the poor *Libertus*,' said Spika.

'The answer is more obvious than that,' said Eadwine. 'I have replayed the data feeds of the fight's closing moments. Your gunline was eight seconds from range. The Archenemy capital ship had no wish to measure its worth against the *Sepiterna* and her warp escorts. The daemon ship ran rather than fight you. If it had stayed long enough to murder us, you would have achieved status effective and atomised her.'

'We would have tried,' said Cragoe.

'The Adeptus Astartes is paying the Navy a compliment, Fleetmaster,' said Cybon. 'I recommend you take it gracefully.'

Cragoe nodded his mountain peak of a head. The pict feed crackled and jumped slightly.

'It was no false flattery,' said Eadwine. 'I believe it perfectly explains the Archenemy ship's decision.'

'Then I approve the continuance of the assigned mission,' said Cragoe.

'Did all the specialist equipment survive?' asked Spika. 'I trust no part of the requisition order was aboard the *Domino* or the *Libertus*?'

'It is all intact,' said Cybon. 'We are transferring it now to your outer bays.'

'You'll need to clear a primary bay to take the Adeptus Astartes vehicle,' Cragoe told Spika. 'It's no bigger than a gun cutter, but it is massively armoured, and it will need a station of its own or your inertials and gravitics will suffer.'

'I'll redistribute the launch bay load,' said Spika.

'How long before you can make shift?' asked Cybon.

'We're running repairs now,' said Spika. 'The materiel transfer should take another five hours or so. We'll be ready then.'

When the hololithic presences blinked and dissolved away, Gaunt turned to Spika.

'My compliments on your combat command,' he said.

'Thank you for not getting in the way,' said Spika. He looked at the huge Silver Guard warrior.

'That was just flattery, wasn't it?' he asked. 'That bastard ship should have killed us dead.'

Eadwine shook his head.

'It was the truth as I saw it. I suppose it is possible that the enemy capital ship detected something or someone aboard this ship that it decided it did not want to kill.'

'If that's true, we'll find whatever they were sparing,' said Gaunt.

'Has it occurred to you it could be your prisoner?' asked Spika.

'The one they were trying to assassinate, you mean?' Gaunt replied.

'Were they?'

Gaunt laughed.

'What are you saying, shipmaster? This whole business was an elaborate ruse to make the pheguth's story more credible?'

'It is possible,' said Eadwine. He glanced at Gaunt. 'But I think they were running for their lives.'

THE CENTRAL LANDING deck had been cleared. Launch Artificer Goodchild, the senior flight deck officer aboard the *Armaduke*, saw the deck lamps begin to rotate and flash as the inbound craft approached. Pressure trembled as the environmental envelope adjusted. He signalled to his servitor crews to stand ready for landing attendance.

The craft sailed into the primary landing backlit by the local star, which was glowering outside the mouth of the bay. Goodchild had heard other flight artificers describe such vehicles, and he had reviewed the archived data, but he'd never seen one in the flesh before. Robust, like a flying tank, it was finished in the Chapter colours and insignia of the Silver Guard: silver-grey, white, and Imperial yellow.

'We used to go to war,' a voice said from beside him, 'and launch a thousand of these into the void, a hundred thousand, to demolish a fleet.'

Goodchild turned to find the massive Iron Snakes Space Marine standing beside him. He made to bow.

'Do not bother,' said Holofurnace.

They watched the Adeptus Astartes warcraft settle in to land on the arrestor clamps.

'But there are not many left,' Holofurnace said, uttering what seemed like a heartfelt sigh as he gazed at the craft. 'Like us, I suppose. I miss those days. The Great Wars. Can you imagine, ten thousand of those launching from a supermassive?'

'I cannot, sir,' Goodchild admitted.

'No,' agreed Holofurnace. 'Even the thought is too terrifying.'

'How old are you?' asked Goodchild.

'Old enough to remember,' replied the Iron Snake, 'and young enough not to care.'

'YOU SENT FOR me?' asked Felyx.

Gaunt looked up from his desk.

'No,' he said. 'I sent for her.' He pointed at Maddalena. 'You can wait outside,' he added. 'Shut the door.'

Felyx half-saluted, and backed out of Gaunt's quarters, closing the door. The lifeward was left alone, standing to attention, staring at Gaunt.

'And?' she asked.

Gaunt got up.

'There's something about you I can't–' he began.

'What?' she asked.

'Nothing. I was thinking aloud and it wasn't appropriate.'

'Not appropriate?'

'No,' said Gaunt. 'Do you want a drink?'

'No,' said Maddalena.

Gaunt poured himself a small sacra.

'Do you at least want to stand easy?'

Maddalena relaxed her pose slightly.

'Why did you want to speak to me?' she asked.

Gaunt looked thoughtfully at the untouched drink in his hand.

'He will ruin me,' he said.

'What?'

'The boy will ruin me. I want him gone. Pack your things and escort him off this ship. Transfer to the fleet and passage will be arranged back to Verghast. It will take some time, I'm afraid. The Battlefleet isn't in the business of passenger shifts.'

'Not acceptable,' said Maddalena.

'He will ruin me,' Gaunt repeated, 'so I hardly care for

your opinion. That fight began and suddenly all I could think of was that my son – my *son!* – might be in danger! The thought unmanned me. I came to find him. I–'

'It's understandable,' said Maddalena.

'I know it is,' Gaunt snapped. 'That's the point. He's my son and I'm going to care about him, even though I barely know him, and didn't know he even existed until this voyage began. He's my flesh and blood, and having him here damages me.'

'How?'

'Oh, please. Try imagining.'

Maddalena licked her lips with the tip of her tongue as she thought.

'Your concern for him will compromise your ability to lead. It will undermine your confidence. It will make you fallible and perhaps force command or tactical decisions that are unwise. It could weaken you, and soften you, and take your edge away.'

'There,' said Gaunt. 'That wasn't so hard, was it? So get him off my ship and take him home. I cannot have him on this mission.'

'Many of your men, your officers... they have brought family and loved ones with them. It is a calculated risk. The accompany bond indemnifies personal loyalty over personal safety and–'

'My men don't have to lead this mission.'

'True,' she said, 'though I think the issue is the same.'

'Thank you for your perspective. Now get the boy off this ship in the next three hours.'

'You will care about him wherever he goes,' said Maddalena.

'What?' asked Gaunt.

'Will he get home safely?' she said, shrugging. 'Will the fleet ship transporting him be attacked? If he returns to Vervunhive, will he survive the shame of being sent away by his famous father rather than being allowed to serve at his side? Will his chances for political advancement be forever undermined?'

'Be quiet,' said Gaunt. 'I don't need to hear that. Damn you. I didn't ask to know him. I didn't ask for him to be sent here.'

He shot his drink in one swallow. She walked over to him, took the empty glass from his hand, filled it, and took a sip.

'The point is, you *do* know him,' she said. 'Now you're aware he exists, you can't not know him again. Sending him away won't help. The humiliation certainly won't help him, personally or politically. Banishing him won't help you. This cannot be undone.'

'Yes, it–'

'No, colonel-commissar, it cannot. You know him. You know he exists. Whether he's at your side or a sector away, you will be concerned for his welfare. He's your son.'

Gaunt took the glass from her hand and knocked back the rest of it.

'So what you're saying is, you've ruined me anyway?'

Maddalena laughed. She took back the glass and refilled it, taking more of a sip for herself this time.

'I suppose so. It wasn't my decision, and I'm sorry for it. It wouldn't have been my choice to send him to you unannounced.'

She stared into his eyes.

'Better you keep him at your side than wonder where he is. Better he stays and learns something from you before you die. Better you fight for his life than anyone else's.'

Gaunt hesitated. There was an anger or a frustration he could barely articulate.

'I take it he'll be staying?' she asked.

Gaunt shook his head sadly.

'This stuff,' said Maddalena, holding up the glass and squinting at it. 'What is it?'

'Sacra.'

'It's not bad,' she said.

'There's something–' Gaunt began.

'About me? So you said. And I believe you said such thoughts were inappropriate.'

'They are,' said Gaunt. He kissed her mouth. She did not pull away.

'That's definitely inappropriate,' she said.

'I don't give a damn,' he replied.

FOURTEEN
Final Shift

TAVIS SUN WAS a memory four days behind the *Armaduke* when Dorden died.

Supplied and stocked with the last pieces of specialist equipment from the fleet group, the frigate had turned and translated away, running out through the murk of the warp towards the cold distances of the Rimworld Marginals.

Lord Militant Cybon had delivered a final broadcast from the *Sepiterna*, a valedictory address to the entire regiment. Zweil and the ship's cleric had held services of constancy and deliverance, but the mood on the ship had changed.

They were heading into the dark, into the bleak and underpopulated regions of the Sabbat Worlds, into dead space and zones of risk, into hazardous climes and marginal fields. Though they were thousands strong, together on the ship, they felt the isolation.

Blenner was observing the specialism rehearsals that were being conducted around the clock on several of the main hold decks. The large areas had been cleared, and floor plans had been marked out on the deck in paint. In places, the layouts resembled basic obstacle courses. Squads moved through the areas, reset the obstacles, and then ran the drills again. Most of them were chamber clearance exercises. Ranges had been set up for practice-firing breaching rounds, and the ship's artificers had rigged up a number of standard template door locks and hatch seals for teams to practise cutting. There was a lot of sweeper training going on too, and when he wasn't supervising that, Domor was in hold six with his best demolition men, running through methods for making safe explosive devices and triggers. Major Pasha was lecturing the regiment, one company at a time, on improvised explosives and booby traps, and the finer points of pressure pads. She knew her subjects. It seemed to Blenner that Major Pasha had learned a lot of dirty tricks in the scratch war at Vervunhive.

On another range set up in one of the holds, the regimental marksmen were drilling with their old bolt action rifles. They were firing the specially machined, glass-tipped rounds to acquaint themselves with the specific weight and pull of the unfamiliar ammunition. They were saline charges, non-lethal glass projectiles filled with inert salt water.

The accuracy rate required from marksmen like Questa, Banda, Raess and Nessa was painfully demanding. Blenner was, however, astonished at the performance score that Merrt was racking up.

'I thought Merrt was a lost cause,' he said to Hark.

'He was,' replied Hark. 'Larkin's been working with him, one-to-one. The real breakthrough was muscle relaxant.'

'What?'

'He's numbing his jaw,' said Hark. 'Apparently, that stops it twitching and ruining his aim. Of course, it means he can't talk.'

They watched Merrt finish a round of shots and then turn to the other shooters.

'I wondered why he was signing,' said Blenner, nodding at Merrt. Everyone in the regiment had learned basic sign language for stealth work. Blenner had assumed Merrt was using it in deference to the deaf troopers like Nessa.

'Where'd he get that idea from?' Blenner asked.

Hark shrugged. 'He hasn't really explained. Larkin hinted it had something to do with one of the Space Marines.'

Blenner shuddered. The Space Marines, though they were seldom seen around the ship, were a pretty constant reminder that this was going to be more than a pleasant ceremonial excursion. Inexorably, they were heading towards the sort of fate he had spent most of his career in the Guard trying to avoid, the sort of fate where polished buttons, impeccably buffed toe-caps and a winning way with mess-room banter would not matter one iota. It was getting to the point where Blenner couldn't laugh it off any more.

He'd spent a lot of time reading the stuff Wilder had recommended, the wit and wisdom of Novobazky. The speeches and mottos had survived Blenner's initial disdain. Novobazky, the Emperor protect and rest his soul, had clearly been a motivating and inspiring man. Blenner had attempted to memorise some of the proclamations. He'd even practised them out loud to the shaving mirror in his quarters.

The trouble was, he didn't believe them. He couldn't say them with any conviction. They didn't make him feel any better about dying, and, if he couldn't even convince himself, he stood no chance of putting fire into the bellies of his troops.

When he thought about it like that, Blenner felt the fear inside him grow. It made him want to throw back another pill or two, but he had exhausted his supply. There was the contraband he'd confiscated untouched in his desk, but Curth had warned him off that. His hands trembled.

'Heads up,' said Hark. A wall hatch had rumbled open and Rawne's Suicide Kings had entered, escorting the prisoner. Mabbon had been brought to observe and advise the operational drills. He was in shackles, and his face was without expression. Everybody in the hold space gazed at him.

They knew what he was. They knew the price the regiment had already paid simply having him there. They knew what kind of price they were going to pay if he was playing games with them.

Blenner felt an overwhelming urge to find a latrine. Space Marines were bad enough, but the pheguth was worse.

He got into the corridor outside, and found that his urge to crap his pants had diminished. His desire for pharmaceutical support had increased. If drugs could help Trooper Merrt improve his performance, then they would for Vaynom Blenner too.

That was how he came to be sitting with Dorden when he died.

'I'm worried that I might be taking too many,' said Blenner awkwardly. 'I've got through the ones you gave me rather quickly.'

'Don't worry, commissar,' said Dorden. 'You're a grown-up. I trust you not to abuse them. You're only taking them when your nerves demand it, aren't you?'

'Yes.'

'Good,' said Dorden. 'In fact, to make things simple, I'll sort you out a larger supply. To keep you going.'

The medicae office was very quiet. Blenner had passed Kolding and Curth on his way in. He breathed out.

'Can I ask you a question, doctor?' he asked.

'Of course,' said Dorden. He had got up to fetch a box of pills from a shelf. He was measuring loose pills out, a dozen at a time, into a small set of brass scales.

'Why aren't you afraid?'

'Afraid?'

'Yes,' said Blenner. He cleared his throat, nervously. 'Of... I'm sorry, of dying.'

Dorden smiled, still counting out pills.

'Death is nothing to be afraid of,' he said. 'It happens to everyone. It's ridiculous to think that the one thing everyone has in common, the one thing that unites us, is an object of fear. I am quite looking forward to it, actually. Duty ends. We are welcomed to the Emperor's side in some great place of triumph and glory. I imagine... I hope very much... that I will see my son again.'

'I wish,' said Blenner. 'I wish I wasn't afraid.'

'You're not afraid,' said Dorden. 'Not of death. You're afraid of living.'

'I'm sorry, what?'

'You're afraid of the things you'll have to do before death takes you. Pain, injury, fleeting things like that. You're afraid of life and the effort that life takes.'

'I'm pretty sure that death's the thing really bothering me,' said Blenner.

Dorden shook his head.

'You don't want to be found wanting,' he said. 'You don't want to die knowing those around you despise you or think you've let them down. You don't want to face the Emperor with question marks on the account of your life. You're not afraid of death, Vaynom. You're afraid of the things you're expected to do before you die. Courage. Fortitude. Sacrifice. Endurance. Those are the difficult things.'

Blenner sat back and wiped his hand across his mouth.

'If that's the way you see it,' he said. He stared at the deck. 'Those are sugar pills, aren't they? Sugar pills or salt tablets? It's a placebo.'

'You're quite mistaken,' said Dorden, measuring a last scoop.

'You would say that,' replied Blenner. 'That's the way they work. But you're handing them out like sweets. And you're not even remotely worried that I might end up with a dependency.'

Dorden turned around and looked at Blenner.

'Don't bother denying it,' he said. 'I can see it in your eyes. That expression. I'm good at telling when people are lying, doctor. It's my job. I know you don't want to spoil the effectiveness of the placebo, but just the way you're looking at me right now, I can... *doctor*?'

Dorden fell. His left elbow caught the rim of the brass pan on the little set of scales and flipped it, sending the white pills up into the air like chaff. They rained down across the deck like hailstones. Dorden had already slithered down the cabinet, pulling open two drawers, and subsided onto his back. His eyes were like glass. He seemed to be staring at something behind Blenner. Something *parsecs* behind Blenner.

'Doctor Curth!' Blenner screamed, leaping out of his chair so hard it fell over.

Curth ran in, followed by Kolding and Lesp. They crowded around Dorden's untidily folded form. Blenner didn't know what to do.

In the face of death, he was speechless.

CURTH'S HEAD WAS bowed. Her skin was pale, as though shock had sucked the blood out of her. She adjusted an intravenous drip.

Blenner stood at her shoulder and stared down at Dorden. The old man's eyes were closed. Fifteen minutes of furious activity had ended with Dorden on his back on the cart, Kolding and Curth working on him. Blenner had been able to do nothing except watch. He had been fascinated by the way Curth had wept through the entire process without making a sound or halting her work.

'He was dead for four minutes,' she said. 'We restarted his heart.'

'Is the machine keeping him alive?' asked Blenner.

'No,' she replied. 'It's just a precaution. He actually

started sustaining himself once we got meds into him and resuscitated.'

'Clinically dead for four minutes,' said Blenner. 'What about brain damage?'

'I don't know.'

'But the machine's not keeping him alive?'

'No,' she said. She turned to look at him. 'You are, actually.'

'What?'

'If you hadn't been with him,' she said, 'we might not have known he'd gone down. Not for minutes. It would have been too late to bring him back. We were lucky you were in there, badgering him for more of those wretched pills.'

'Hooray for me, then,' said Blenner. He paused. He felt like she could see the same faraway thing Dorden had been watching when he fell over. 'To be fair, I think they're placebos.'

'Of course they're placebos,' said Curth. 'Are you an idiot?'

'Steady on.'

'He's not going to prescribe something you scoff like candied fruit, is he?'

She stopped and composed herself.

'I'm sorry. I've just ruined their effect and all his hard work.'

'I should stop taking them, then.'

She looked him in the eye.

'I could be lying,' she said.

'You could. With you, Doctor Curth, it's much harder to tell. You could, of course, just be covering because you let it slip.'

'You'll never know.'

'Let's stop worrying about me, shall we,' he said, as brightly as he could manage. 'What about you? Do you need a moment? This is very trying. Can I offer you a shoulder to cry on? A warm embrace?'

'You never stop, do you?' Curth asked. 'One of these days I'm simply going to let you have your way, just to shut you up.'

'I– I don't know what to say–'

'Thank the Throne.'

He walked to the doorway.

'I think Gaunt needs to know.'

'No,' she said.

'Maybe not before, but he needs to know now. He'd want to know. Look, I'll go and tell him what happened, if you like.'

'I'll do it,' Curth said.

ELODIE WAS ALONE in Daur's quarters when Commissar Fazekiel knocked on the hatch.

'The captain's not here,' Elodie said. 'He's training in the hold.'

'It's you I wanted to see,' said Fazekiel.

'Me?'

Fazekiel came in, removed her cap, and pulled the hatch shut.

'There's a small problem, Mamzel Dutana. I'm sure it's nothing, so I wanted to see if I could get it squared away without a fuss.'

'What is it?' asked Elodie. She eased her arm, still in its sling. Her head was aching again.

The commissar pulled a couple of sheets of paper out of her coat pocket and unfolded them.

'We were clearing up after the incident with the gunman. My compliments, by the way, for saving that poor child.'

Elodie nodded.

'The transport deck hall was a mess. Furniture broken and overturned, clothes scattered,' said Fazekiel. 'We found these papers under a cot. They'd been dropped, and had slid under there. Forgive me, I had to read them to work out who they should be returned to. They belong to you. You've signed them here, and here.'

'Oh, yes,' Elodie said. She vaguely remembered the forms that had been thrust at her.

'I need to ask you a simple question,' said Fazekiel. 'Sometimes people wish to keep these things personal and private, in which case we can clear this up now, just between the two of us, and nothing else need be said about it. Are... are congratulations in order?'

'Congratulations? I don't understand.'

'Are you and Captain Daur married? Sometimes it's done in secret, I know. Perhaps before we left Menazoid Sigma?'

'Married?' Elodie asked. She swallowed. 'No. No, we're not.'

'You're not?' asked Fazekiel.

'No, unless I could be married and not know it. Could he have married me without me knowing it?'

Fazekiel smiled. 'No, mamzel.'

'Not even by filling out forms?'

'No.'

'Then we're not married.'

Fazekiel frowned, her face sad.

'Then we do have a problem. These papers, which you have signed, are part of a certificate for viduity benefits. The sort a wife would be able to claim after the death in service of her partner. A widow's pension, mamzel.'

'Oh.'

'If you're not married, then this is an illegal claim. An attempt to defraud the Munitorum. Unfortunately, this sort of fraud is quite common, given the large number of Guardsmen in service.'

'I don't know about this,' Elodie stammered. 'I was just given papers to sign. I was told it was something to do with the accompany bond. I wasn't trying to scam anything. Please, I wasn't.'

Fazekiel stared at her, eyes narrow.

'I believe you,' she said.

'I should hope so,' said Ban Daur.

They hadn't heard him enter the chamber. He was dripping with sweat and in need of a shower. His company's drill period was over for the day.

'Do I get to hear this from the start?' Daur asked.

'A fraudulent pension claim has come to light,' said Fazekiel. 'Your partner is involved, but appears to me to be innocent. I am obliged to investigate. Mamzel, who gave you these forms? Who told you to sign them?'

'I forget.' She thought for a moment. 'No... it was Costin.'

'What did he tell you they were?'

'They were to do with the accompany bond. There was him, and Captain Meryn. Some other troopers too, I'm sure. I can't remember who. They were moving through the retinue with the forms. They said it was routine paperwork. This was just before the man started shooting.'

Fazekiel nodded.

Elodie looked at Daur.

'We're not married, are we?' she asked.

Daur blinked. He laughed, and then stopped.

'No,' he said. 'I think you'd remember.'

Elodie wasn't laughing. She got up and walked over to one of the wall lockers. Clumsily, with only one hand working, she opened it, took out the petition forms and held them out to Daur.

'What does this mean, then?' she asked. She shook the documents. '*Petition for Allowance to Marry*. What does that mean? Why did you fill them out? If you were going to marry me, why didn't you ask me? Is it that bitch?'

'What? Who?'

'Zhukova! *Zhu-fething-kova!*'

'What?'

Fazekiel got to her feet.

'Captain, I'm going to go now. I have to look into this matter. I will be back with further questions. You clearly need to have a conversation with Mamzel Dutana that I don't have to be part of.'

ON THE FIFTH circuit of the drill course, Felyx Chass slipped and fell on a climbing slope. He was bone-tired, and didn't want to show it. He wanted to impress the other Guardsmen. He'd always considered himself fit, but the training was punishing.

The Ghosts, even influx troopers, seemed so much fitter and stronger. Even Dalin, who was staying close to keep an eye on him, possessed reserves of stamina that Felyx found alarming. The lasrifle was a dead weight in Felyx's hands. He felt himself lagging, stumbling on the ascents, fumbling through the crawls.

Then he fell.

'Probably not used to hard work, eh?' remarked Didi Gendler, helping Felyx up.

'I'm all right.'

'Probably comes as a bit of a shock after the life you've known,' Gendler added. There was a malicious look in his eyes.

'I'm fine,' said Felyx.

'No nice lifeguard to carry you around on her back today?' asked Gendler.

'She's busy.'

'Get on with it, Gendler,' said Ludd, coming over. 'Or I'll make you run the circuit again.'

'Just trying to help, sir,' said Gendler. He ran off, throwing a toxic look back at Felyx.

'Go rest on the bench,' Ludd said to Felyx.

'Why don't you just shoot me?' Felyx replied.

'What?'

'I've got everything to prove, so please don't make it harder for me. They think I'm nothing. A privileged brat.'

'They don't think that,' said Ludd.

'Screw them if they do. I'm going to continue, commissar. I don't want any favours.'

'I'll run the course with Chass,' said Dalin, coming up, lapping Felyx.

'Just carry on,' Ludd told him.

'The colonel-commissar asked me to keep an eye out,' said Dalin.

'On you go then, both of you,' said Ludd.

On the sidelines, watching the last of the shift's exercise drills, Hark came to a halt beside Kolea.

'Well, they're clearly both in love with him,' said Hark.

'Who?' asked Kolea.

'My boy and yours, Gol. Nahum and Dalin. Look at them trying to outdo each other to become Chass's new best friend.'

'They're not stupid,' said Kolea. 'Getting in tight with the commander's son, that's a fast track to advancement or decent favour.'

'The regiment doesn't work like that,' said Hark.

Kolea looked at him, and smiled. He patted Hark on the arm.

'For a smart man, you're surprisingly naive sometimes, Viktor,' he said. 'All regiments work like that, even the best ones. This is the Imperial Guard.'

'There you are,' said Luna Fazekiel, walking over to them.

'Is there a problem?' asked Hark.

'I don't know. I don't know what to make of it yet.' She handed Hark the folded slips of paper bearing Elodie Dutana's signature.

'I wanted to see where you think we should go with this,' she said.

'You were going to ask me to marry you, and then you didn't,' said Elodie.

'It's not quite like that,' said Daur.

'Then what are these papers for? This petition?'

'All right. It is like that. A little like that.'

Elodie took a deep breath.

'So, it's Zhukova,' she said, rather too fast. 'She turns up, and you rekindle your old romance, and suddenly marrying me doesn't seem like such a great idea–'

'Oh, Throne,' said Daur. 'Please, listen to me. Zhukova means nothing to me. I knew her years back, in the Hive Defence days on Verghast. She was incredibly young. Incredibly stupid, too. She had a crush on everybody.'

'Including you?' Elodie asked.

'Yes, including me. She likes… ambitious and successful men. Officers. I was in her sights for a while, but it was never reciprocated. It was just interesting to see her again. A reminder of old times, of mutual friends long gone. I was being polite.'

She sniffed.

'You were really that jealous?' asked Daur.

'Yes. I always will be.'

He nodded, half-shrugged.

'I'm honoured to be the subject of such jealousy,' he said.

'What about the petition?' she asked. 'Explain that.'

He was silent for a long time.

'I wanted to ask you to marry me,' he said at last, quietly. 'I got the paperwork organised, ready for written permission from Gaunt. Then I realised the timing was bad. You know, because of what it would look like.'

'What do you mean?'

'Guardsmen who get married on the eve of war, they only do it for one reason.'

'And what's that?' she asked.

'Because they assume they're going to die,' said Daur. 'They want to make sure their wife has the paperwork to support her claim for a widow's pension from the Munitorum. They do it so their spouse qualifies for the benefit. They do it because they're not coming back.'

He looked at her.

'I want to come back,' he said, 'and I didn't want you to think I wasn't going to.'

CURTH DIDN'T WANT to use the intership vox, or send a message through channels. It was too impersonal. She went to Gaunt's quarters and knocked quietly on the hatch.

When he didn't answer, she let herself in, intending to leave him a private note asking him to come and see her.

Maddalena was just coming out of the bedchamber. She was naked. When she saw Curth, she didn't grab clothes or anything to cover herself. She grabbed her weapon and aimed it at the doctor.

Curth yelped and leapt backwards, her hands raised.

Gaunt came in, pulling a sheet around his waist.

'Put that away,' he said to Maddalena. 'It's Doctor Curth.'

Maddalena lowered the weapon, put it aside, and disappeared, naked and long-limbed, into the bedchamber.

'This is awkward,' said Gaunt. 'Sorry.'

'Yes. I shouldn't have come in without permission.'

'I assume it is important, Ana.'

She nodded.

'Out of curiosity, how long has this been going on–'

She stopped herself.

'Forget it,' she said, closing her eyes and shaking her head. 'It's not my business, and it was inappropriate of me to ask.'

Gaunt looked uncomfortable. The scar across his abdominals was old and pale.

'You can ask,' he said. 'We've known each other a long time. It's been going on since the conjunction. I don't know what it is. It's just sex.'

'Oh, good,' said Curth, without any warmth.

Gaunt frowned. He looked lost for words.

'Just a hint,' she said, 'from a friend. If I was the girl in the bedchamber, overhearing this conversation, I don't think I'd be happy to hear it was "just sex".'

'If *you* were the girl in the bedchamber–' Gaunt began.

'Yes?'

'Ana, I–'

'You know what, Ibram. I always thought *I* might be the girl in the bedchamber one day. Funny that.'

He took a step towards her. The edge of the sheet snagged on the door frame. She held up a hand and turned away.

'Don't,' she said. 'Just get dressed and come down to the infirmary, please. I'll wait for you there. I came to find you because Dorden is dying. He's going now. There isn't much time left for him, and I think he needs you to be there.'

She paused.

'Actually, I'm not sure he does. He seems quite content. But I think *you* need you to be there.'

MOST OF THE regiment had gone to the dining halls for supper. Shift bells were ringing. She was walking back along a half-empty main spinal when Blenner saw her.

'Doctor Curth, has Dorden gone?' Blenner asked, crossing to her in concern.

'No. Not yet.'

'But you're crying.'

'Tension. It's a tension valve, commissar.'

'Dear lady, I told you I know very well when people are lying,' he said. 'It comes with the job.'

'It's the truth,' she said.

'It's not the whole truth, though.'

She snorted a laugh, wiping her eyes.

'Dorden's going to die. There's nothing I can do about it. He's part of this regiment's soul, and he's been my mentor and friend and everything else besides since I signed up. I don't know what I'll do without him, and that's only just hitting me. I've known for months, and it's only just making horrible sense now. He's going to leave us and we're supposed to carry on.'

Blenner nodded. He patted her shoulder.

'And that, on top of everything else, made me realise that nothing and no one lasts. Nothing lives forever, no matter how much we want it to. No matter how hard we fight. No matter how patiently we wait. I see that now.'

'You were… waiting for something?' he asked.

'And I waited too long. It's never going to happen. I understand that now.'

She wiped her eyes again and looked up at him.

'I have to go to the infirmary, to make sure Dorden's comfortable. I have to wait for Gaunt there, and brief him. Later on, I am going to need to be very seriously cheered up. I intend to get extremely drunk, Commissar Blenner. I believe you're the sort of person it's fun to get drunk with.'

'My reputation precedes me.'

'I will require sacra. I trust you'll be able to procure some?'

He nodded.

'I should warn you,' he added, 'I feel it's only fair. After a drink or two, I sometimes forget myself, Doctor Curth.'

She looked him dead in the eye.

'It's Ana,' she said.

FIFTEEN
The Marginals

SHIP BELLS RANG, and then a siren sounded, alerting every soul on board to the imminent translation.

A judder, a shake that rattled the bones of the ship, and they spat free and clear into realspace. New sirens blasted and a synthetic voice repeated the words 'Hostile zone, war footing' over the speaker system.

Spika had brought them to the target three days early.

'We're decelerating into the Rimworld Marginals,' Spika told Gaunt and Eadwine. 'Navigation has confirmed our realspace position and vector. Sixteen hours of deceleration into the gravimetric plane of this junk system, and then another five as we close on the target location. From this point we are running battle-ready and shields lit; this is a vox-silent phase. I suggest you begin final preparation. You should be ready to deploy from three hours out.'

'I'll make that five,' said Gaunt.

Spika nodded.

'I will issue half hourly notices to that point,' he said.

'What does it look like?' Gaunt asked.

Beside him, the Space Marine chuckled, as if the question was an idle whim.

Spika raised his eyebrows and called out to a deck officer. The realspace shutters covering the massive bridge ports rumbled open, and weak yellow light spilled in. There was nothing to see except a murky brown haze with a small bloom of light in its lower right corner, like a lens flare. White speckles, like grains of salt or flakes of snow, glittered past them, moving sternwards: a dingy emptiness where the frail available light looked like it was coloured with urine.

'You see?' asked Eadwine.

'I see nothing,' Gaunt replied.

'My point precisely,' the Silver Guard rasped, amused.

Spika reached out and adjusted some dials on his console. He barked another instruction or two to the observation and resolution officers at the sculptural cogitator stands below him.

A large, gridded sub-frame extended from the port sill to cover the bulk of the window space. It was made of thick armaglass, and inlaid with hololithic sensors and actuators. The frame was thick with armoured trunking and clusters of small repeater screens and secondary monitors. It lit, igniting a graphic overlay of luminous green across its grid, which quickly began to section and analyse. Bands of colour-coded sensory data spiked up the edges of the main grid and across the repeater screens. Columns of text data played out. Spika fine-tuned his controls, centred the main green crosshairs on the bloom of light, and began to enhance and magnify the area until the hololithic pict image filled the grid and blocked out the real view.

There was a little more detail. Magnified, the white bloom was a tangle of solids, rendered white by the reflected glare of the local star. It was still blurry and fuzzy, but Gaunt could see enough to tell it wasn't a planetoid. There was no regular geometric form. It was

like a knot, and skirts of tangled matter trailed out of it
to a great distance, like the broken ring of a gas giant. The
'snow' effect was more intense on this image. There was
a density of moving white specks, almost like static. The
image resembled some pallid, flaking, submerged thing
viewed under water that was thick with sediment and
microorganisms.

'That,' said Spika, 'is Salvation's Reach.'

The Space Marine seemed slightly interested.

'The specks?' asked Gaunt. 'Is that interference?'

'Debris,' Spika replied, shaking his head. 'The debris
field is exceptionally dense, and will grow denser the
closer we get to the target. Our shields will bear a lot of
it, but there will be manoeuvring, and that will degrade
our approach time.'

'Making us more vulnerable,' said Eadwine.

Spika shrugged.

'We will be visible for longer, yes,' he agreed, 'but the
debris belt will also disguise us. If I do my job right, we
can approach the main location and we'll appear to be
nothing more or less than another lump of tumbling
junk.'

'As we proceed from here,' said Gaunt, 'I'll need eyes
on this.'

'Why?' asked Eadwine.

'I have operational command, brother-sergeant. As we
progress with this raid, I want to be aware of all the information possible, interior and exterior. If the shipmaster
identifies a threat, I don't want to know about it later on.'

'You'll see it for yourself,' said Eadwine. 'The strategium will afford you quite enough–'

'I'm sorry,' said Gaunt, 'you seem to be labouring
under the misapprehension that I will be on the bridge
during the attack.'

'Of course,' said Spika, 'commanding the operation. I
have a place prepared for you. Where else would you be?'

'I will be leading Beta Strike from the front.'

'You… you're going in?' asked Spika.

Eadwine made a sound that approximated laughter.

'That has always been my practice,' said Gaunt. 'I will not send men in to do something I'm not prepared to do myself.'

'No wonder Veegum liked you,' said the Space Marine. 'There is a spot for you on Alpha Strike at my side.'

'Appreciated. But you know your business, and I know mine. Major Kolea and Major Baskevyl will lead the regiment with you at Alpha.'

'And Gamma Strike?' asked Eadwine.

'Major Petrushkevskaya and Captain Daur,' said Gaunt. He turned in his seat and pointed across the upper bridge area to the Tanith trooper waiting beside the main access hatch.

'That's my adjutant, Beltayn. I want him in my place here at the strategium, with access to your vox system.'

'My vox heralds can communicate all data between us,' said Spika.

'I have no doubt, but I require you to allow Beltayn's presence. If he translates an order to you from me, it carries my full authority.'

'I understand,' said Spika.

'You should also have your armsmen stand ready,' said Gaunt.

Spika frowned.

'Very well. For a boarding action?'

'Yes. But also for counter-boarding. We will be opening channels into that target. That means if things go wrong, they can get at us.'

Gaunt rose. The other two got up.

'Let us prepare,' said Gaunt.

Spika made the sign of the aquila.

'The Emperor protects,' rumbled Eadwine.

GAUNT WALKED OFF the bridge, Beltayn coming after him.

'You'll set up in there,' said Gaunt. 'He's not the most

accommodating person in the Imperium, but I've made it clear he has to cooperate. You have access. You relay everything. If he tries to fence you out, let me know and put me on speaker.'

Beltayn nodded.

'Major Rawne and Major Kolea said to let you know that preparation's begun, sir,' he said. 'We're arming up, and the assault vehicles are being serviced in the through deck hangars ready for loading. There's this to approve and sign.'

He handed Gaunt a data-slate.

Gaunt read it as he walked.

'Well, that's something to cherish,' he said, authoris-ing the document with a press of his biometric signet ring.

'Captain Daur wonders–' Beltayn began.

'We'll make time for it,' said Gaunt.

'Commissar Hark wants a word.'

'I see him,' said Gaunt.

Hark was waiting for them at the entrance to the spi-nal hallway.

'What is it, Viktor?' Gaunt asked.

'WE'VE UNCOVERED A disgrace,' said Hark. He had taken Gaunt to his quarters, where Ludd, Fazekiel and Rawne were waiting. It was quiet and private. The room was painstakingly neat and ordered, exactly the preserve one might expect of a man like Viktor Hark.

'I hesitate to use the word "scam",' said Hark, 'because that really doesn't adequately express how monstrous this is. It's an ingenious fraudulent scheme. I've no idea how long it's been running. Possibly since before I joined the regiment. Possibly since the Founding.'

Gaunt read his way across the paperwork that Hark and Fazekiel had spread out across the desk. Some of it was torn, or very old. Several pieces were fresh print-out copies from archive sources. His jaw clenched.

'We only stumbled across it by accident,' said Hark. 'Credit where credit's due, Luna found it. It's so insidious, it was nigh-on invisible.'

'What are we looking at?' Gaunt asked, still studying the various documents.

'As far as we can tell,' said Fazekiel, 'there are three main areas of fraud, but there is significant overlap. First of all, there are fraudulent claims for widows' benefit for women that don't exist.'

'They are all viduity allowances filled out in the names of dead troopers,' said Hark.

'In other words, fictional wives were being created, and paperwork retroactively completed, so that claims could be made on the names of deceased troopers,' said Fazekiel. 'But there are also viduity claims being made in the names of real wives and partners who are long dead. Women who died with Tanith, or on Verghast. Finally, there are real women, unmarried, like Elodie Dutana, whose identities are being used as spousal signatories. Better than an invented name, you see?'

'The individual viduity payments are minimal,' said Hark. 'But together, and in such numbers, and over such a length of time…'

He stopped and rubbed the bridge of his nose, eyes closed.

'Someone is generating a significant income stream,' he said. 'They are defrauding the Munitorum. It's quite possible that the Munitorum is already aware of the fraud, but it could take years, or decades, before an investigation catches up with the perpetrators.'

'That's probably what they're counting on,' said Rawne.

'Someone is making money out of the regiment's dead,' said Hark, 'from those fallen in combat, and from the civilian casualties. It's desecration. It's monstrous. Stealing from corpses. Robbing from graves.'

'Do we know who's behind this?' asked Gaunt. His face was white with rage.

'We're not yet sure how the money's being claimed,' said Fazekiel, 'or where the payments are put once they have been. They could be getting washed clean through the regimental accounts somehow. That would require collusion from low-grade Munitorum staffers. They could be getting laundered through gambling dens and the black market during shore leave.'

'They could be stuffed in a musette bag under a cot,' said Rawne.

'We've got one name,' said Hark. 'Costin.'

'That little bastard,' Gaunt murmured.

'He's definitely involved,' said Fazekiel. 'But Hark and I don't think he could have done this on his own. We suspect he has co-conspirators. And one of them might be quite senior.'

'It'd be hard to run this without a friendly officer to sign off the occasional card or petition,' said Ludd.

'Years ago,' said Gaunt, 'I nearly executed Costin.'

'Aexe Cardinal,' Rawne nodded.

'Drunkard. Idiot,' Gaunt hissed. 'He got men killed. Most of Raglon's platoon. I showed him mercy instead. Damn him.'

'We have a number of reports of Costin being conspicuously wealthy,' said Fazekiel. 'Off duty, he's always got money for good drink, good food, money to gamble. He gets his hands on better amasec than the senior staff.'

'He didn't do this alone,' said Gaunt. 'Who does he associate with?'

'Gendler,' said Hark.

'Meryn,' said Rawne.

'But we've nothing on either of them,' said Fazekiel. 'Costin's the only one with ink on his hands, and even then, it's circumstantial. We haven't interviewed. We haven't interrogated.'

'No interviews. I want to give the order for punishment execution,' said Gaunt. Ludd didn't think he'd ever seen such bitten-back fury in Gaunt before.

'I don't want to execute our only lead,' said Hark, 'even to make an example of him.'

'And do we want that kind of example a few hours before a raid?' asked Fazekiel.

'He's not walking away from this,' said Gaunt. 'Nobody involved in this is going to escape punishment.'

'I'm not suggesting they should,' said Hark, 'but I think we should make a move after the raid. If we execute Costin, or this comes out, it could destroy morale.'

'The only reason for keeping that little ghoul alive,' said Rawne quietly, 'is to crack him. With your permission, I'll get the truth out of him.'

Hark and Gaunt exchanged glances.

'It's the best way,' said Rawne, 'seeing as this was all my idea.'

He glanced up, scornful of the horror on their faces.

'Relax,' he said. 'I didn't do it. But the idea was mine. Years ago, just after we left Tanith behind. I remember getting drunk with Corbec and Larkin one night, joking how we could make a killing from the dead. It became a regular gag, how we could compensate ourselves for having such a fething shit existence by claiming for the lives lost on Tanith. In time, it turned into a standing sick joke, gallows humour. Never thought anyone would be so twisted they'd actually try it. I don't think anyone even thought I was capable, and that's saying something.'

Gaunt took his cap off and combed his hair back with his fingers.

'Do it,' he told Rawne. 'Whatever it is you do. I want to know who Costin's in bed with. Do you want us to look the other way, or would you like our help holding him down?'

Rawne shook his head.

'I can do it. I can put the fear of the Throne in him, and make him give up his confederates. And you won't have to look the other way. I'm not even going to touch him. It'll just take a word in his ear. Well, *two* words, actually.'

'I won't ask what they are,' said Fazekiel.

Gaunt picked up one of the documents from the table.

'The only reason I spared Costin on Aexe Cardinal was because Dorden pleaded with me,' he said.

He showed Rawne the paper.

It was a viduity form filled out to benefit Dorden's long-dead wife on Tanith.

THEY WERE SIX hours out. Ship bells rang to mark the half-hour. For the last two hours, there had been a regular series of thudding, tapping sounds. Debris from the immense Salvation's Reach junk belt was growing so thick it was bouncing off the *Armaduke*'s shields.

The regiment was almost battle-ready. There was a tension in the air like an electrical charge. Gaunt summoned the entire strength to the main excursion deck, and ordered the retinue in too. There was no formal order, no regularised ranks or echelons. The regimental assembly simply stood in a group facing Gaunt. All the Ghosts had stopped their preparation work to attend. Some had only half kit, or their hands were dark with gun grease. The women and children gathered in around the crowded deck. Gaunt saw Tona with Dalin and the little girl. Curth and Kolding arrived from the infirmary with Dorden. The old man, his skin the colour of ash, insisted on walking.

'You should be resting,' Gaunt said.

'What for?' asked Dorden.

'I still think–'

Dorden shook his head.

'Ana has administered a very strong opiate, Ibram,' he said. 'I find I can get out of bed and walk about. I'm not going to miss this. In fact, I have no intention of missing anything from now until I'm done.'

'I could order you to your bed,' said Gaunt.

'And I could disobey you,' replied Dorden. 'What would you do then? Shoot me?'

Gaunt laughed. Curth and Kolding were both trying not to smile, though Gaunt could tell that Curth was simultaneously riven with sadness.

'I just want to say–' Gaunt began.

'If it's goodbye,' said Dorden, 'I don't want to hear it.'

Some of the ship's crew, including several senior bridge officers, were attending the assembly too. Gaunt was about to clamber up onto a loading platform to address the crowd when the Space Marines arrived.

There was a hush. The three figures plodded into the hangar and across the deck like ogres, the crowd parting to let them through. The Space Marines had donned specialist armour that had been transferred aboard during the conjunction: ancient, ornate suits of boarding armour, precious relics from the most ancient times. Each suit of plate was decorated in the bearer's Chapter colours. They were the engraved, polished works of master artificers, worn and gleaming, massively layered and reinforced for defence; Gothic, crested and shivering with purity seals. Each warrior carried a huge boarding shield in the form of a half-aquila. Holofurnace carried a long power spear in the other hand, Eadwine a chainsword. Sar Af's huge right hand was free for his boltgun.

Their helms had visors like portcullis gates. They took up positions in front of Gaunt. Holofurnace held his spear horizontally at thigh level.

Gaunt nodded to them, and then looked at the body of the regiment. The double-headed psyber eagle shuffled and fluttered on its nearby perch.

Gaunt made a short address, just a few words. It didn't need much. They were ready. They had been waiting since Jago for a real fight, and now it was upon them.

When he was done, he made way for Zweil. The

ayatani led the assembly in a blessing and commenda-
tion. Just for once, Zweil was restrained and wandered
off topic barely at all.

At the end of Zweil's blessing, Gaunt nodded to Daur
and Elodie, and they came to the front. Gaunt read the
petition, and the marriage oath was sworn with the regiment as witnesses.

'The Emperor protects,' Gaunt told the couple. He
looked up at the assembly again and repeated the words.
The regiment cheered and clapped the union.

Gaunt looked at Wilder.

'Captain? Please?'

The bandsmen weren't in ceremonial rig. They were
dressed in duty uniforms for combat, but they had
brought their instruments. At Wilder's command, they
struck up a beloved battle hymn of the Imperium.

Daur and Elodie moved together through the crowd,
receiving congratulations. When they came to Captain
Zhukova, Elodie said, 'I'm sorry.'

'What for?' Zhukova asked, genuinely puzzled.

'Never mind,' said Daur.

Gaunt found Sar Af talking to Dorden. The old medicae looked especially fragile beside the vast Space Marine
in his heavy boarding armour.

'He is dying,' Sar Af said to Gaunt, as though this was
news and had just come up in the conversation.

'I know,' said Gaunt.

'But he is not afraid,' said Sar Af.

'I'm not,' Dorden said.

The White Scar nodded sagely.

He looked at Gaunt.

'And they shall know no fear,' he said.

THE BAND WAS still playing as the crowd began to disperse. Guardsmen said their farewells to members of
the support and retinue, and hurried off to finish their
preparations. Captain Daur said goodbye to his new

wife with a last kiss. Ezra walked into the open centre of the chamber, held up his arm, and the eagle obediently swooped to perch on his wrist. Carrying it as if he were a falconer, he walked out of the hangar at the heels of the scouts and the Space Marines.

Near one of the exits, in the bustle of the crowd, Rawne put out his hand and drew Costin to one side.

'How can I help you, sir?' Costin asked.

'They know,' said Rawne.

'What?'

Rawne nodded across the chamber at Gaunt, who was talking with Hark and Ludd.

'They know,' he repeated, his eyes hooded, a wicked smile on his face.

Costin blinked. He started to tremble.

'What do you mean? What the feth are you talking about? They know what? *What* do they know?'

Rawne's grin broadened.

'They *know*,' he repeated.

He turned and walked away, leaving Costin gazing after him, wide-eyed.

SIXTEEN
Countdown

THE CURRENTS OF realspace and the vagaries of the warp had condensed a vast cloud of material in the gravity pit of the Rimworld Marginals. The few pale suns fluttered like candles in the deep ditch of blackness and shone their thin light upon a prodigious pall of flotsam.

At the place known as Salvation's Reach, the junk belt was at its thickest: a monumental agglomeration of debris almost two hundred thousand kilometres deep at its thickest. Part of it was planetary debris: rocks, dust and other mineral effluent forming solid masses like gall-stones or bezoars. Some of it, however, was artificial in origin.

There was tech. There were machine parts. There were the hulks and shells of space machines: ships, barges, carriers, void habitats, supermassives, like some graveyard of wrecks. Craft lost and foundered down through the ages had washed up at Salvation's Reach, and there they had gathered, collected, mangled each other and, through the action of decay and gravitic pressure, fused into a great knot of material, accumulating like a metal reef.

Some of it was Imperial. Some of it was not. Some of it was of human or human-derivative manufacture. Some of it was not. Some ancient scraps, the carcasses of lost Imperial vessels, were relics of Terran tech that had not been seen for so long they were no longer recognisable to the Adeptus Mechanicus. Old template patterns, unrecoverably deformed, lurked in the silent residue.

Some of it was so old, so worn, so alien, it was impossible to discern the source or original function.

Mechanicus expeditions had been mounted down the years, along with Inquisitorial probe missions, and countless endeavours of salvage and scavenging.

But the Marginals were unstable, inhospitable and remote, and the secrets cast away there were too demanding to recover.

The *Armaduke*, adjusting its course by gentle realspace burns, slowly crept into this increasingly crowded environment, heading for the solid, planet-sized nugget at its heart.

DURING THE BEATI'S original crusade of liberation across the Sabbat Worlds, the Marginals had been the site of a significant fleet action, a turning point in the fortunes of the Imperium that had put the interests of the Sanguinary Worlds and their Archon into retreat. Legend said that Salvation's Reach had been the name of the Imperial flagship, a flagship that had stood its ground under astonishing enemy fire and died with all hands, holding the line long enough for the Saint's victory to be achieved. Legend said that the debris accumulated in the junk belt was the wreckage of that titanic fleet action, the battlefield litter of one of the Rim's greatest realspace engagements.

Other legends said that Salvation's Reach was the name of a planet, destroyed during that void fight. Different legends said it was the name of the Archenemy supermassive that had finally been scuppered just minutes before it target-locked the Saint's cruiser.

In Spika's opinion, none of the legends were any better than half-truths. The debris field included a great deal of space war junk, but it was the accumulated residue of thousands of fights accidentally clustered here, not the devastation left by one fight at this location. Besides, there were too many tech types, too many species variants. Cogitation analysis showed vast differences in the ages and decay of debris samples. Some pieces of scrap were just a few hundred years old. Some were a few hundred *thousand*.

Spika took the helm himself. This was rare, but his bridge officers did not question it. The insertion run required a shipmaster's finesse. It needed to be fast and quiet, but their speed was limited by manoeuvrability in the junk zone. Most of the junk could be dealt with by shields, but some pieces were two or three times the size of the *Armaduke* and required evasion. Obliterating pathway targets was an emergency option only. Spika did not want to draw attention to their approach by disintegrating a looming junk obstacle with battery fire.

Spika was also letting cold momentum take them in whenever possible. With an expert touch, he was allowing the *Armaduke* to drift from one corrective burn to the next, almost to the point where the old ship began to slide and tumble. Just one more piece of space machine wreckage, drifting towards the core. It was an artful simulation. If the forces dwelling within the metal core of Salvation's Reach had external sensors or detector grids, the *Armaduke's* approach would not be betrayed by a nonballistic trajectory. Spika kept his propulsion systems simmering, ready to breathe and squirt power at short notice to turn the ship or avoid some spinning mass.

Gaunt's adjutant, Beltayn, had arrived on the bridge and taken up a station near the shipmaster, with access to the strategium. Spika paid him little attention. He seemed a bright enough man, but he was just another drone, and Spika was sure he'd have difficulty picking him out of a squad in a day or two.

What he did pay attention to was the data that Beltayn had brought and loaded, with the help of the hololithic artificers, into the main strategium display. It was the most recent schematic of Salvation's Reach extracted by mnemonic probe from the mind of Gaunt's prisoner. This man, this *etogaur*, had been probed, interviewed and scanned on a daily basis since his capture.

As it had been explained to Spika, the man was a defector. A triple defector. It wasn't clear, but it seemed that the etogaur had once been an Imperial Guardsman. He had been captured and turned by the forces of the Archenemy, and drafted, because of his training and expertise, into the Archon's frightful cadre known as the Blood Pact. Later, for reasons Spika didn't even want to consider, Mabbon Etogaur had renounced that allegiance and broken his pact, joining the Sons of Sek, another martial fraternity. The Sons, as their name suggested, were a consanguinous echelon sworn to the Magister Anakwanar Sek, the Archon's principal ally and lieutenant.

He was a troubled soul, clearly, a restless heart. How, Spika wondered, did one man contain so much within one lifetime? Bonded into three different institutions that were ordinarily served unto death. Perhaps the original Imperial conditioning had won out in the end, driving Mabbon back to the Emperor despite everything.

If that were true, it was the most stupendous effort of fortitude and devotion. If it were false, they were heading to their deaths.

Mabbon had come to the Imperial side with vital data. He knew that the intelligence and insight he possessed would be the only things that would keep him alive and prevent summary execution. He had data, and he had the means to interpret that data. Despite the psionic scans and mind probes, he had kept certain things obscure. He was smart enough to know that he had to release the information he carried slowly. His life would become redundant the moment he gave it all up. He protected his mind through the conditioned resolve of someone who has both taken and broken the Bloody Pact, and through a variety of engrammatic codings. Before quitting the service of the Archenemy, he had layered into his mind data concerning the Salvation's Reach facility using a cerebral encrypter; information that could not simply be stripped out, but could only be recovered by methodical and repeated meditation. Since his capture, he had been slowly remembering and building a picture for his Imperium handlers.

The core of Salvation's Reach was a hulk habitat of considerable size, converted for use as a weapons development facility and manufactory. This facility had originally been set up by the Magister Heritor Asphodel under the instruction of the then Archon Nadzybar. It was remote and inconspicuous, and allowed for the enhancement and testing of weapon systems, be they systems developed by the mad genius Asphodel, recovered xeno artifacts, or gifts from the demented Chaos Gods.

Nadzybar had fallen on Balhaut. Asphodel had perished by Gaunt's hand on Verghast. The facility remained, inherited by the anarch, Sek. He was using it to strengthen his hand and develop weapon support for his Sons. It was an arsenal, a stockpile, a laboratory. According to Mabbon, Sek felt he should have taken on the mantle of Archon after Nadzybar. The anarch resented Gaur's rise to eminence and, though obliged by the martial politics of the Sanguinary Worlds to pact with him, had little respect for Gaur's command of the campaign since Balhaut. Sek envied Gaur's authority, and he envied Gaur's revolutionarily disciplined personal army, the Blood Pact. He press-ganged Blood Pact warriors like Mabbon to help him create his own force, the Sons of Sek, and set out to prove that he deserved the mantle of Archon.

It was a compelling claim. The previous decade had shown Urlock Gaur to be a savage chieftain, capable of extreme brutality, even by the standards of the Ruinous Powers. His Blood Pact was certainly supremely effective.

He was also sloppy, and lacked strategic insight. His blunt and ferocious style of warmaking had lost him as much as he had gained. It had driven him back all the way to the Erinyes Group in a series of catastrophic defeats, and only there had he managed to resist Macaroth's impetus.

In contrast, the Anarch Sek, a far more ingenious and mercurial tactician, had performed superbly along the Crusade's second front, securing and holding on to the Cabal Systems in the face of the Imperium's most determined efforts. It was entirely reasonable to expect that if, by means of facilities such as Salvation's Reach, Sek could show he was a better leader than Gaur, more able, better served and better equipped, the tribes of the Sanguinary Worlds might oust Gaur and look to Sek to take the crown of the Archon and break the stagnation.

Two consequences were clear. Sek's ambitions had to be stopped. The anarch was so capable that, if finally granted the supreme authority of Archon, he would make the continued prosecution of the Sabbat Worlds Crusade unviable. The Imperium would be forced to retreat and perhaps suspend operations entirely.

More particularly, what better result could the Imperium hope for than to have the fragile partnership of Archon and anarch fracture, and for Gaur and Sek to turn upon each other?

From time to time, Spika glanced at the slowly rotating schematic of Salvation's Reach projecting up from the main table of the strategium display. As they approached, actual detector readings over-mapped and refined the plans. So far, Mabbon's intelligence was remarkably precise.

Spika wondered how precise. What might be missing? What might have changed? Mabbon claimed to have visited the facility three times as part of the Sons force, and his memory engram of the structure had been copied from confidential files in the Palace of the Anarch. Details might have altered since then.

Ranged scanning had already indentified the three surface sites, preselected for the strike points: Alpha, Beta and Gamma.

A further question occurred to the shipmaster. It was actually one that had nagged him for days, and which he had been reluctant to voice.

The mission's credibility rested upon the belief that Mabbon Etogaur had defected back to the Imperial cause; that after taking a path from which there should have been no return, he had rediscovered his loyalty to the Imperium, and brought to them, as an act of contrition and recompense, the means to cripple and disarm their greatest present foe.

What if his defection had simply been back to the Blood Pact, and he was now manipulating the Imperium into doing Urlock Gaur's dirty work by taking out his chief rival?

GAUNT BUCKLED ON his belt, checked his bolt pistol, and slotted it into the holster. He finished buttoning up his tunic and then started to fasten on his sword belt.

Maddalena came out of the bedchamber. She had dressed in some expensive, lightweight and ornate partial combat armour.

'You're not coming along,' said Gaunt.

'I know, but if the fight spills this way, I want to be ready.'

She looked at Gaunt's power sword. It was clamped in its rack on top of the locker, ready to fit into the scabbard: the power sword of Heironymo Sondar, an emblem of Vervunhive and the great Verghast victory against the Ruinous Powers.

'You should show him that,' she said.

'Felyx?'

'Yes. You should show him that sword. Explain what you did to get it.'

'He already knows,' said Gaunt.

'Of course he does,' she said, 'but that doesn't mean it's not important for him to hear you tell it.'

Gaunt took down the sword, activated its field briefly, felt the throb of its power, then deactivated it and sheathed it.

'I'll bear that in mind,' he said.

There was a knock at the cabin door. Gaunt had begun to enjoy the way Maddalena's hand went for a weapon at the slightest cue, hardwired to fight and protect.

'Get in the bedroom,' he told her.

She raised her eyebrows.

'I really don't think we have time,' she said.

He laughed, though it felt like too serious a time. She got up and disappeared.

Gol Kolea was waiting at the door, in full kit, weapon slung. His salute let Gaunt know it was an official visit.

'Regiment battle ready and correct, sir,' he said. 'Strike Alpha is assembled on the main excursion deck. Strike Beta awaits you in lateral hold sixteen. Strike Gamma is assembled in lateral hold thirty-nine.'

'Thank you, major. Time on target?'

'Estimate is now five hours sixteen, sir.'

'Have the shipmaster informed we stand ready.'

'I will.'

'Anything else to report, Gol?'

Kolea shook his head.

'The mood's good,' he said. 'I mean, everything considered. All the build-up, the extremity of it. I think the Ghosts have been out of the fight too long. For some, it's

been so long they thought they'd never march again. We
need this.'

'We need to win this,' said Gaunt.

'Of course, sir. That's always true. In the grand scheme
of things, we need to win this. But for us, for the regiment, we just need to do it, win or lose. We have to get
bloody again or we'll be good for nothing.'

Gaunt nodded.

'Point taken. I think we're ready to get bloody.'

Kolea nodded at Gaunt's power sword.

'You might let the boy take a look at that sometime.'

Gaunt frowned sharply. Kolea held up his hands
peaceably.

'I know, I know,' Kolea said. 'I'm hardly the one to be
handing out advice on being an effective father.'

'It's not that,' said Gaunt. 'Have you been talking to
someone?'

'No.'

'You're not the first person to say that to me.'

Kolea shrugged.

'The Ghosts haven't taken to the boy yet, sir,' he said.
'It's a little strange for them, to be honest. But I think
they will. I think they'll respect him because he's yours.
But I think you need to show them you respect him too.'

Gaunt didn't reply. He put on his cap and picked up
his gloves.

'I'll walk down with you and inspect the assemblies,'
he said.

Kolea looked back into the apparently empty cabin
and pointed with his chin.

'Aren't you going to say goodbye first?' he asked.

Gaunt was forced into a half-smile.

'Not much gets past you, does it, Gol?'

Kolea laughed.

'I'm not disapproving, sir. Not my place. And she's a
handsome woman.'

'She'll also be here when I get back,' said Gaunt. He

closed the cabin door behind him and set off along the hallway with Kolea.

'That's what I like to hear,' said Kolea. 'Confidence.'

'That she'll still be there?'

'No,' he said. 'That you know you're coming back.'

THE SHEER SCALE of the debris mass became clearer as they approached. The *Armaduke* was just a speck, a speck amongst billions of specks surrounding the vast bolus of material. Salvation's Reach was a planetoid, a veritable *planet*, except that its mass was not spherical. It was a colossal lumpen ingot, flattening out to a disk form at its extremities, where gravity had moulded it.

Through the outer scopes and telepicts, Spika resolved surface detail akin to some ork ships he'd encountered. Except it was put together with less precision. He saw a compressed jumble of mechanical material, like machines mangled and intermingled by an industrial compactor. There were canyons and ravines, sharp peaks and plateaux, deep fissures and almost smooth plains of hull fabric. Swimming through the dense swarms of loose junk, the *Armaduke* found itself slipping through floating slicks of promethium and other liquids and particulates, substances that had seeped out of the main mass and bled into space.

Lateral holds sixteen and thirty-nine were situated about two-thirds of a kilometre apart on the port side of the *Armaduke*. They both had large armoured outer hatches equipped with atmospheric field generators. Prior to departure from Menazoid Sigma, the hatch surrounds of both hold apertures had been reinforced and built out with vulcanised buffer collars.

Spika initiated the final approach. Apart from orbital drydocks, the *Armaduke* had never been positioned this close to a larger object. It felt counterintuitive to him, though every system was green. A shiftship was built for the freedom of the open void, not to snuggle in against the outer layers of a megastructure, like a tick on the skin of a grox. Spika had been obliged to cancel and mute all the proximity alarms, and fundamentally adjust the ship's inertial stability to counteract the gravimetric load. The ship itself seemed to sense that the manoeuvre was wrong. Like Spika, the *Armaduke* was reluctant, as if it felt it was being deliberately crashed into the surface of a planet. The hull frame creaked and groaned uneasily. Burn corrections became hair's breadth subtle.

With a dull and protracted rumble, and an eerie screech of scraping hull that shuddered through the ship and seemed to issue from some immense, echoing cavity, the *Armaduke* settled against the skin of the Reach.

Spika killed the drives and correction thrusters. He activated the magnetic clamps and inertial anchors.

He turned to Beltayn.

'Inform your commander that the mission may now proceed,' he said.

IN LATERAL HOLDS sixteen and thirty-nine, artificer crews scrambled towards the outer doors, erecting protective screens and baffles around what would be their workspace. Several of them waited for the indicator lights on the control panels of the atmospheric field generators to show green. In order to assure the results, they anointed the panels and uttered the correct propitiations. Processors hummed and throbbed. Machinery was rolled forwards in front of the hatch gates, and power cables were played out. Servitor crews advanced and stood ready with pressure hoses that fed from the water reservoirs inside the *Armaduke*'s hullskin, water that was dark and sludgy with ice.

Behind the protective barriers in the main body of each holdspace, assembled with their equipment and weapons, the strike teams sat and waited. Some spoke quietly, some rechecked their kit or specialist equipment, some muttered blessings to themselves or smoked lho-sticks, some caught catnaps.

Some watched the artificers at work. The Ghosts were dubious. This wasn't their field of specialism. Every now and then, some pained metallic squeal would echo through the ship, a grinding shriek from where the cruiser's hull rested against the bulk of the scrap-metal world they had docked against. Ghosts jumped, made the sign of the aquila, and looked around for the source of the noise.

Just over twenty long, edgy minutes after the *Armaduke* snuggled itself in against the Reach, tell-tales flashed green in lateral sixteen and thirty-nine almost simultaneously. Gaunt had just arrived in sixteen, where Strike Beta had assembled. At a nod from the chief artificer, Gaunt took a handset from the waiting vox-officer and called through to Major Pasha in lateral thirty-nine.

'We have green here,' she reported.

'Fields stabilised,' Gaunt agreed. 'Give the order to open your hatch.'

'The Emperor protects,' Petrushkevskaya replied.

Gaunt looked at the chief artificer.

'Open,' he said.

The chief artificer nodded, turned and signalled to the bay gallery, where cargo officers activated the hatch gate controls.

There was a gentle clatter. Gaunt turned, and saw that Strike Beta had risen to its feet, en masse, weapons ready.

He knew full well that an almost identical scene was playing out in lateral thirty-nine.

There was thump, a hiss of compression seal pistons, a whirr of retractor motors, and the hold's massive outer hatch began to open. Effectively, the hull-side wall of the bay slid to one side.

Light from the hold revealed what was behind it: another wall, blackened and scabbed, worn by age and scoured by the void, lumpy and corroded, fused and blistered. This was the outer skin of the Reach.

Alarm lights flashed on and off, warning that the atmospheric field surrounding the docking buffers was fighting to maintain a seal. There was no danger of explosive decompression into the hard vacuum outside, but Gaunt could feel the sharp breeze of the slow leaks: air rushing out around the inexact seal.

'Can you stabilise it?' he asked.

The artificers were already making adjustments to the shape and size of the atmospheric field via the control station. Further prayers of efficacy were offered to the machine spirits. Slowly, the lights stopped winking and the sucking air leaks died away.

Silence. Silence apart from the very distant creak and squeal of metal on metal.

Gaunt walked past the protective screens right up to the face of the Reach's exposed outer skin. It was ugly, like blackened metal scar tissue, ridged and contorted beside the dank but clean hold structures of the *Armaduke*.

Gaunt took off his glove, put out his bare hand, and touched the alien metal. It was only just beginning to warm from the ambient heat of the hold's atmosphere. Gaunt felt an eternity of void cold, the legacy of airless dark. He felt the chill contours of threats and promises.

He looked at the chief artificer.

'Prepare to cut it,' he ordered.

The vox-officer was standing by. Gaunt relayed the same order to Major Pasha, and then switched channels to speak to Shipmaster Spika.

'Bridge.'

'Shipmaster, please signal Strike Alpha to launch. The order is given.'

'Understood.'

LAUNCH ARTIFICER GOODCHILD placed the vox-horn back on its hook, stood up and walked down the metal gangplank into his supervision gallery. The brass control board had been purified and blessed, and the votive seals, threads of inscribed paper attached by wax and red ribbons, had been removed from the lever controls and dials.

Goodchild had only to say one word. His servitors and technicians set to work. Greased pistons began to elevate sections of the deck. Exhaust vents clattered open. The main and secondary lighting systems of the principal excursion deck dimmed to cold blue and yellow hazard lamps began to flash. There was a pressure drop as the main airgates and outer space doors opened, hingeing out and away like the petals of a flower. The atmospheric envelope adjusted accordingly. Field strength peaked. Voices murmured all around him: the augmetic drone of servitors mindlessly pronouncing streams of technical calibration figures, and flight crew adepts monotonously repeating the catechisms of service and duty.

On the main deck below, gangs of ratings, many of them bulk-grown abhuman serfs, hauled away the cable lines and mooring wires, cranking them into the under deck drums. The first six boats on the primary landing were laden and waiting, lift systems running. Through-deck hoists were already lifting the next wave of craft up from the parking hangar. It was unusual for small craft like Arvus lighters and Falco atmospherics to be hoisted or repositioned with personnel on board, but the shipmaster had expressed to Goodchild the importance of rapid launch. Laden with lasmen and assault equipment, the landing craft were being loaded into the launch platform like ammunition into a gun.

The first craft lifted and began to accelerate towards the space doors. It was the heavyweight giant that Goodchild had seen aboard at Tavis Sun, a martial brute in the colours of the Silver Guard. Its pattern designation was *Caestus*, an assault ram vehicle of ancient Adeptus Astartes design, a machine built for boarding actions. Its rear burners lit hot yellow as it cleared the airgate and then turned wild green as it slipped through the hazy edge of the atmospheric field into hard space.

Behind it came the first of the assault carriers: Arvus-pattern craft, both long and standard body variants, followed by four Falco boats. They launched in pairs, their engines making shriller, thinner sounds compared to the guttural throb of the Caestus. The engine sounds died away as soon as the small ships left the atmospheric field.

The second launch wave was already sliding onto the ramp.

Goodchild walked back to his vox station and lifted the horn.

'We have launch conditions,' he reported. 'Launching in progress.'

Vox mic held ready in his hand, Beltayn watched the shipmaster and the other senior bridge officers gathered around the glowing strategium console. On the hololith, little patches of lights were spitting out of the imaged *Armaduke*, and whipping away in formation around the seam of the Reach structure. Spika had brought the resolution up, so not all of the Reach was being projected. Beltayn saw the little clusters of fast lights, like neon seeds, zipping across the ragged topography of the Reach's hull away from the *Armaduke*, flying very low, hugging the terrain to avoid detection. Beltayn noticed the way Spika was drumming his fingertips on the handrail of the strategium as he watched. There was a slightly sour odour on the bridge, the smell of adrenaline. It wasn't just the stressed crew: bio-wired into the neurosystems of the ship, the abhumans and serfs were reacting in tension too.

The ship itself was nervous.

'Strike Alpha eight minutes to target,' intoned one of the seniors.

Spika nodded. His fingertips drummed.

* * *

AT THE HELM of the Caestus, Pilot-servitor Terek-8-10 maintained a steady course. His biomechanical hands rested on the helm controls, though he was operating the heavy machine through the neural impulse linkage of his augmetic plugs. Manual control was for emergencies. The chambers of his hearts thrilled to the output of the engines either side of him. Forward view through the small window port was restricted. He was following a tight course through the broken geography of the target area's surface plotted by auspex and displayed via hololithic router. The Caestus was leading the assault flight, twisting around slopes of junk, banking over torn pylons, hugging the floors of metal ravines and chasms, even flying under accidentally created bridges and outcrops of shredded machinery.

Rear-projecting auspex showed the troop landers tight on his tail, following his lead. Terek-8-10 was also detecting steady vital readings from the three individuals strapped into the inertial suppression clamps in the armoured compartments of the twin hull booms below and ahead of him.

The vitals were impossibly slow, as though the individuals were so calm they were almost asleep.

Terek-8-10 woke up the weapon servitors and their fragile little sinus rhythms lit up alongside the three slow, heavy pulses.

'Four minutes,' the pilot-servitor intoned, each word clean and separate, each word significant.

IN LATERAL SIXTEEN, Gaunt watched the artificers roll the Hades breaching drill into position. Its vast cutting head was just a hair's breadth from the face of the Reach's exposed hull. The last few blessings were being made over its systems.

The chief artificer glanced at Gaunt.

Gaunt held up three fingers.

Three minutes remaining.

* * *

THE ARVUS WAS buffeting hard. Freak electromagnetics plagued the ravines and canyons scoring the metal skin of Salvation's Reach. It wasn't the most pleasant ride Gol Kolea had ever known.

The cargo hold of an Arvus lighter offered no visibility and precious little comfort. The bare metal box had been fitted out to afford bench-seating for combat-ready troops and enough room to stow their equipment. They were strapped in along facing rows, backs to the hull, feeling every jolt and shake down their spines. There were no windows, just a half-slit through to the tiny helm compartment. The Arvus was a workhorse, designed for loading and lugging. Comfort and luxury had never been considerations.

Kolea shifted in his seat. He had his lasrifle braced upright between his knees, and the harness of the rebreather mask buckled around his neck. Because of the way the boarding shields had been stowed, there was scarcely any room for his feet.

He was right by the rear drop-hatch, ready to lead the way out. He looked back along the cargo hold. Members of C Company were enduring the ride, most looking straight ahead or down at the deck: Caober and Wersun; Derin; Neith, Starck and the flametrooper Lyse; Bool and Mkan with the .30.

Facing him with his shoulder to the hatch was Rerval, Kolea's company adjutant.

'Two minutes,' said Rerval. 'We're almost there.'

'Yes,' said Kolea. 'Things will be so much better once they're shooting at us.'

THE LIQUID DRIPPING from the readied hoses stank of promethium and rust. The smell reminded Ban Daur of the rain that used to fall across Hass West and the fortress tops of Vervunhive. Dirty rain, soiled by the metal factories and engineering fab plants.

He walked the length of lateral thirty-nine, reviewing

the squads of Strike Gamma. The Ghosts were drawn up behind the line of protective barriers. There was edginess. Half of the assembled strength was Verghast, the influx from Major Petrushkevskaya's company. Despite their common bonds and origins, these troops had not fought alongside the Ghosts before, and they had yet to prove themselves worthy of the name.

He nodded to Vivvo, to Noa Vadim, to Pollo and Nirriam and Vahgner. He stopped to speak to Seena and Arilla with their heavy .30. He paused to exchange a joke with Spetnin, Major Pasha's number two.

Maggs was waiting with Haller, Raglon and the first-wave shooters, Merrt, Questa and Nessa. The marksmen carried their longlas pieces over their shoulders. The whole group was watching Daur's adjutant, Mohr, who was kneeling beside his voxcaster, listening.

'All set?' Daur asked.

'Have been for months now,' replied Haller.

Daur smiled. He'd known Haller a long time. They'd come up through Vervunhive Defence together. Haller undoubtedly recognised the rain-smell of Hass West too. Haller had never had the drive and ability to excel like Daur, but Daur knew how hard Haller had been training in the past few months to secure the leadership of one of Gamma's clearance teams.

Major Pasha joined them, with Hark. The commissar was setting his cap just right, ready for business. Daur noticed that the heavy leather holster of Hark's plasma pistol was unbuttoned.

'One minute,' said Mohr.

THE LIGHTING IN the Caestus's hull boom compartments turned red. Secured in their clamps, Holofurnace, Sar Af and Eadwine barely acknowledged the notification.

But steel-cased fists locked around the grips of weapons.

* * *

PILOT-SERVITOR TEREK-8-10 CHECKED his pict-screens. The final few seconds of data were streaming in, with actual real-time auspex scans and detection results superceding the predicted data and less accurate distance scans.

The Primary Ingress Target had, after detailed analysis, been designated prior to launch. It was a location that appeared on the distant resolutions to be a major airgate or docking hatch, one of the main entries to the Salvation's Reach facility. Now, as they were closing, the systems were showing the hatch to be a largely defunct ruin, part of the junked architecture. Thermal and energetic traces were showing a smaller airgate structure, still large enough for bulk cargo handling, to be the most recently and regularly used. This second gate was down and to the left of what the plan insisted should be the Primary Ingress Target. Density penetration scans showed the Primary to be both reinforced and back-filled with rubble and debris.

Terek-8-10 didn't make a conscious decision. The pilot-servitor processed the revised data and adjusted his mission profile for optimum effect. A deft manual adjustment, sixteen seconds from contact, steered the Caestus down and to the left. The secondary airgate locked up as the newly selected target, fixed in the crosshairs dead centre of the data-plates and monitors. It looked like a cliff-face, a cliff-face made of dark, stained and pitted metal.

Terek-8-10 triggered the afterburners.

The short-fire rocket burners lit, and the Caestus lurched as though it had been kicked from behind by a giant. Eight seconds from the cliff-face, the missile batteries mounted on the Caestus's wings unloaded their blistering shoals of micro-missiles. At the same time, the magna-melta cannon mounted between the ram booms discharged.

The radiant blast of the heat cannon puckered and warped the metal cliff face. The airgate hatch structure bubbled and liquefied, spurting a geyser of white-hot blobs into the void like silt disturbed from the bed of a pond. The epicentre of the hit was left as an oozing sore of white hot metal, a glowing crater that almost penetrated the reinforced hull skin.

Less than a second later, the spread of Firefury micro-warheads impacted, a saturation strike that annihilated the already compromised fabric of the airgate.

There was a light flash, which strobed ultra-rapidly with the multiple detonations, and the gate shredded: first blown in, and then instantly ejected as the pressurised bay behind it abruptly decompressed. In the last few seconds, the Caestus found itself flying into a swirling and exhaling fireball and a storm of debris that hailed off its prow shields and armoured hull, nicking and gouging and scraping. Terek-8-10 held the course firm, despite the monumental turbulence. Both visually blinded and scanner-blanked by the blast's extreme energy flare, Terek-8-10 fired the heat cannon twice more anyway, lancing devastating energy into the open wound of the blown-out docking bay.

The last seconds ran out. Their flight time was used up, with less than a single second of variation between predicted passage duration and actual elapsed time.

The Caestus was inside Salvation's Reach.

It punched through the expanding fireball, burning into the hold-space at maximum velocity. The docking bay area was of considerable size. The explosive decompression had thrown it into utter disarray. Half-glimpsed dock servitors, loading vehicles, cargo crates, even cartwheeling personnel, came spinning at them, carried by the riptide of escaping air. Some of them were on fire. A small lighter craft tumbled at them, snagged off a crane gantry, inverted, and met the starboard boom of the charging Caestus. The ram tore it in two, and it shredded back and away over the ram's drive section. The mangled boat bounced and rebounded off the dock ceiling, wing pieces and engine blocks disintegrating and scattering.

Terek-8-10's blind cannon blasts had gouged the interior of the bay, turning another two moored shuttles to molten slag. Two or three of the micro-warheads had also gone into the hangar, unimpeded by any obstacles. They detonated deep inside as they finally met solid objects. The Caestus tore through the gantry frame of a cargo loader, folding the girders and scaffolded structure around itself like a garland. The dragged framework ripped two small landers from their ceiling rack moorings.

The Caestus had almost run out of space. The far end of the docking bay was another gate hatch. Automatically triggered, blast-proof door skins were closing across the scored and grubby hatch.

Terek-8-10 fired the cannon, roasting a spear of energy out in front of the Caestus. The afterburners had finished their jolt, but the pilot-servitor fired them again, using reserve fuel, grabbing a last little bit of force and momentum.

The inner doors did not explode. They buckled under the melta-fire, forming pustules and scabs of molten chrome that spalled flakes of metal like dead skin. Still trailing shreds of twisted girderwork behind it like streamers, the Caestus hit the inner doors.

Now they exploded.

The impact stove the doors in. It folded one horizontally and punched it clean out of the hatch frame. The other, weakened more extensively than the first by the melta damage, ruptured like wet paper or damaged tissue, spattering the Caestus with superheated liquid metal.

The Caestus came through the doors into the secondary dock, bringing most of them with it. It had lost a considerable amount of momentum. Part of its port wing had been stripped away by the collision. Stability was impaired. Further explosive decompression caused gale-force cross-winds to wrestle with the heavy craft. The prow shields that had protected it thus far had finally burned out and failed.

It was more projectile than vehicle. It bore on, demolishing, one after another, three lighter shuttles that were suspended side by side above the dock floor on mooring clamps. Terek-8-10 saw sensor displays that told him the Reach's vast atmospheric processors were running at hyperactive levels as they attempted to compensate for the catastrophic pressure loss. Field generators were fighting to establish a cordon against hard space and seal the deep, gaping wound in the Reach's environmental integrity.

That was good. The Archenemy was too concerned about retaining its environment to consider the consequences. Atmospheric stability meant the Imperial Guard components following the Caestus in would be able to deploy directly.

The Caestus was almost out of room in the secondary bay. Terek-8-10 fired the magna-melta again and softened the end of the compartment enough to stab the ram-ship through it. The boom arms punched through hull plate, rock infill and inner skin compartment lining. This time, it left most of its other wing behind. Clipped and injured, ceramite armour blackened with firewash and molten metal, it tore through into the next chamber, an engineering depot. Almost all of its effective momentum had been robbed away.

Terek-8-10 stabilised the shuddering craft, slamming it sideways into the casing of a bulk processor as he fought it to a halt. He pulled the lever that dropped the boarding ramps.

'For the Emperor,' he howled in an amplified augmetic monotone. 'Kill them!'

Tell-tale lights on his main console showed him

that, down in the transport compartment, three inertial suppression clamps had been released.

SEVENTEEN
Boarding Action

'THEY'RE IN,' SAID Beltayn, over the vox. 'Contact reported.'

'Begin cutting!' Gaunt ordered. The artificers nearby had been poised for the order. The blessed engine of the ugly Hades breaching drill thundered into life, and the oily beast, like some giant promethean beetle from the lightless depths beneath some world's rocky crust, was coaxed forwards. Its heavy tracks clattered on the deck plates of lateral sixteen.

The Hades was a siege engine, a boring drill designed for sapping and trench warfare. Gaunt had seen the engineers of Krieg deploying such devices to great effect when he was still a cadet. Cutting through what amounted to the hull of a starship was not a conventional use, but it was the quickest and most expedient way in that the tactical planners had been able to devise. The Hades's huge cutting head, a four-part breaching instrument of interlocked, diamantine-tipped rotary power cutters, was mounted on the front of the tank chassis and adjusted by a powerful frame of piston drivers. The power cutters bit from the outside in, so that shredded material passed

into the maw between the cutters, down a conveyer belt
that ran through the middle of the machine like a diges-
tive tract, and was ejected as spoil through the rear. Seen
front-on, the Hades resembled the grotesque concentric
mouthparts of some deep sea sucker fish, with rows of
teeth surrounding a funnel throat. Deep in that throat,
above the belt, was a melta-cutter positioned to weaken
and blast the target solids into consumable slag.

The chassis snorted black exhaust fumes. The cutter bits
were spinning at maximum cycle. The operator triggered
the melta-array and fired several searing blasts into the skin
of the Reach.

The skin began to buckle and deform, filling the hold
space with a stink of pitch and scorched metal. Then the
whizzing teeth bit in.

The noise was painfully loud. It was the shrill scream of
a high-speed drill, but mixed with the deep throb and roar
of bulk industrial machinery. The heat blasts had softened
the hull skin enough for the grinding, rending drill heads
to find purchase. Hull metal wailed as it was abraded away.
Fine scrap began to tumble out of the belt ejector, shav-
ings polished almost silver by the rotary teeth. Fine dust
and smoke rose off the power cutters, which were already
super-heating from friction. The crew members standing
by unlocked their pressure hoses and began to spray the
advancing head with jets of dank water. The Hades operator still applied ferocious heat using the melta, because it
was essential for the hull fabric to be soft enough for the
teeth to bite. But it was also essential to keep the power cutters cool enough not to fuse and, more importantly, damp
down and emulsify the clouds of micro-fine, ultra-sharp
spalling that was coming off the cut in clouds like dust. If
that got into eyes or throats, if that was inhaled into lungs,
it would kill a man through catastrophic micro-laceration.
The cooked mineral stink was bad enough. Occasionally, a
flaw or imperfection in the hull fabric caused a large shard
of debris to splinter off and be flung out by the spinning

teeth. These pieces pinged and cracked off the protective screens and baffles. Gaunt knew what the Ghosts behind him were thinking. It sounded exactly like small-arms fire spanking off trench boarding.

One of the operators was struck by a piece of flying debris. It knocked him off his feet, but he got back up again, bruised and shaken. A few seconds later, another operator was hit by a sharpened sliver that went clean through his body armour and into his torso above the right hip. Colleagues pulled him clear, but he was already bleeding out by the time they got him to the hold doorway where the medicae teams were waiting.

'How thick?' Gaunt yelled over the howl of the drill.

'Density scans show just over three metres,' replied the chief artificer.

'Time?'

'Unless the composition changes, eighteen minutes.'

'How long?' asked Daur, shouting over the scream of the Hades in lateral thirty-nine.

'Twenty-eight minutes,' replied the head of the artificer crew.

'Strike Beta reports a significantly lower estimate than that,' said Major Pasha.

The artificer's face was half-hidden by a grimy protective mask.

'The alloy composite in this location is appreciably harder,' he explained. 'I have compared assay reports from the lateral sixteen cut. There is nine per cent more duracite in this location.'

Major Pasha looked at Daur.

'We'll be through when we're through,' she said over the noise of the cutting. He nodded glumly.

'What are you thinking about?' she asked.

'Alpha,' said Daur.

* * *

THEY EMERGED FROM the Caestus into a wracked, unstable atmosphere with flames leaping around them. Several huge fires blazed through the core of the engineering depot, and sections of the roof were collapsing because of the entry wound made by the boarding ram. Some form of fuel oil had spilled from a punctured tank and covered the deck. It was alight, like a field of bright corn: yellow flames, and their reflection in the black mirror of the oil.

Eadwine, Holofurnace and Sar Af strode through the fire, heedless. Their antique, crested helms made them seem especially tall; their ornate and bulky armour gave them an even more unnatural bulk. Flame light glittered off their gilded pectoral eagles and their barred faceplates, and sparkled off their massive half-aquila boarding shields. All three had their boltguns in their right fists, drawn up to rest on the right-angled corners of their shields.

They began to fire as they advanced, gaining speed, moving from a stride to a bounding jog. Bolt rounds banged out, destroying sensors, auto-defence units, potential items of cover. Spent shell cases tumbled in the air.

Behind them, the Caestus was disgorging the rest of its cargo, the weapon servitors. Two were tracked units with multi-laser mounts, the other four were perambulatory units, burnished silver and chrome in the colours of Eadwine's Chapter. They had faces of etched silver, wrought in the shapes of skulls, or at least the skulls of angelic beings. Their upper limbs were weapons mounts: autocannons, heavy bolters, rocket launchers. They came through the lakes of fire as obliviously as the Space Marines, advancing like reaping machines through tall crops, blasting as they came. Energy beams seared down the length of the depot space, and bright tracer shots stitched the air. Terek-8-10's directive scans had already identified the three access points at the far end of the chamber and fed them to the Space Marines via their visor displays.

'No human bio-traces in active opposition,' Terek-8-10 reported over the vox link. 'Several hundred detected trying to flee the chamber. Several dozen more detected beneath debris or rubble, fading.'

Almost immediately, as though the pilot-servitor's report had been tempting fate, the boarding force started to take fire. It rained down from a steep angle, bursting off boarding shields and the polished chromework of the gun-servitors. Sar Af took one kinetic blow across the side of his helm from a glancing shot that was hard enough to make him grunt.

Terek-8-10 was dismayed.

'Auspex does not read human bio-traces in opposition,' he declared.

'It does not have to be human to want us dead,' replied Eadwine.

He brought his shield up like a pavise, and fended off the rain of barbs. The other Space Marines did the same.

Sar Af noted the context of the impacts, the shrapnel marks and cuts, analysing instantly.

'Flechette rounds,' he said.

They sourced the origination, post-human eyes hunting the dark for muzzle flash, up in the chamber roof, up the dense framework of machinery and gantries.

Movement.

'Loxatl,' Eadwine reported. He had clearly glimpsed one of the long, sinuous xenos reptiles. The other Space Marines didn't reply. They were too busy trying to kill the creatures.

Terek-8-10 adjusted the parameters of his auspex scan to include the xenobiological element.

'Holy Throne of Terra,' he breathed.

The loxatl were pouring into the depot chamber via the ceiling vents, squirming down the girder work and vertical struts using their four grasping limbs and their tails, firing the murderous flechette blasters strapped to their bellies.

The auspex already showed sixty-eight of them, and the number was increasing with every passing second.

THE ASSAULT SHIPS of Strike Alpha followed the Caestus's headlong rampage into the heart of the Reach. The outer hatch of the reassigned Primary Target had been disintegrated entirely. The Arvus and Falco craft had to close up and enter one or two at a time to avoid the jagged tatters of metal framing the mouth of the eviscerated docking bay.

Decompression had stopped, so the air was free of flying debris. Generator fields had been re-established to seal the bay entrance, and each troop ship juddered as it popped the field edge and entered the contained atmosphere from hard space.

'Stand by!' the lead pilot sang out.

The main docking bay was a disaster area. It looked as though a flash flood had sucked through it, washing debris to the mouth in a deep sediment of jetsam. That debris included whole landing ships and shuttle craft. The flash flood had been followed by a fire storm that had left most of the space ablaze.

There was no way to set down.

The Arvus pilots were following the tracer signal from the Caestus. It had punched through into the next chamber.

'Throne, are we there yet?' groaned Rerval.

The inner dock was little better. The landers dropped speed again, circling towards the back of the chamber. The Caestus had smashed through into yet a third chamber, but this breach was too small and treacherously sharp for the thin-skinned lighters to risk navigating.

'Setting down!' the pilot yelled over the comm.

The first Arvus dropped on its thrust-fans, wing profile adjusting for landing. It landed with a bruising thump on the buckled, debris-littered decking.

The rear hatch dropped. Kolea, his rebreather up over his face, led the first squad out. He carried his lasrifle and a tall oblong boarding shield that looked like the lid of a coffin.

It took him a moment to get his bearings. It had been dark and cramped in the back of the utility lifter. Now it was bright, glaringly bright, and the space around them was vast, a primary scale docking facility. The air was almost freezing cold, but the heat from the various monumental fires scorched his skin. Machines and cargo-handling rigs destroyed by the Caestus's raid lay in their wake. Other ships were coming in through the smoke-wash and setting down behind Kolea's lander.

Rerval called out and indicated the source of the Caestus's tracer signal. Up ahead of them, there was another puncture in the wall, like a giant bullet hole, where the Caestus had gone through into the next compartment. Kolea ran forwards. Underfoot were burning scraps, lumps of debris and splattered organics from the dock personnel mushed by the pressure shock of the Caestus's strike.

The puncture was big, but the lower lip was four metres off the deck level, and the edges were still glowing red hot. Getting through was going to be entertaining. Kolea looked for a hatch they could force – a blast door, an airgate...

No time. Nothing in sight.

'Storm it!' he yelled. 'Grab some debris for scaling ladders. Move your arses. Living forever is not an option today!'

His squad broke away and gathered up sections of fallen gantry, dragging it over to the puncture. More sections were catching up with them, deposited by the next few landers. Baskevyl was among them. Kolea saw the concern in his eyes through the lenses of his breather mask.

'We've got a problem,' Baskevyl said.

'The breach?'

'Screw that, the landing. There's no space!'

Kolea assessed the options. There were now six lighters on the deck, and space for perhaps three more. The Falcos and longbodies coming in behind would soon be stacking up with no room to land.

'We have to get the empties up and away,' Kolea yelled to Baskevyl.

'Agreed!'

'Get the message through to the pilots,' Kolea ordered. 'They have to make room on the ground once they've discharged their complements, and the incomers have to make room in the air to let the outgoing pass through the dock area and get clear.'

'We can't keep them on station,' said Baskevyl.

'No, we can't,' Kolea agreed. 'Good thing we plan on staying here, huh?'

Baskevyl headed back towards the landing zone. Kolea joined his assault squad at the puncture. Under the supervision of Derin and Caober, sections of smouldering metal wreckage had been dragged up to the wall and hoisted to form makeshift scaling ramps into the puncture.

'Is it safe?' asked Kolea.

Derin just laughed.

'I know,' replied Kolea. 'Stupid question.' He lifted his boarding shield and clambered onto the tubular frame, going up hand and foot. As assault commander, he wasn't about to let anyone else show him how it was done.

'Come on!' he yelled at the men behind him. Most of them seemed particularly keen to help hold the debris steady.

'You heard the major,' Commissar Fazekiel yelled, arriving at a run from her transport. 'Get up that ramp!'

The Ghosts began to swarm up the girders behind Kolea.

Kolea reached the summit, and gazed through the massive tear in the compartment wall. He could see the fires burning in the depot space beyond, feel the back-wash heat. He could see the Space Marines across the vast floor. He could see what they were blasting at.

'Oh, holy gak,' he said.

'THEY'RE FETHING WELL waving them off!' Costin exclaimed, his voice sounding dull and stupid inside his rebreather. 'Look at them. Baskevyl's just waving them off!'

Meryn looked. He saw what Costin was talking about. E Company had just begun to deploy from their Falcos, and the landing zone was packed about as tightly as any-one would ever want. He could see Major Baskevyl and some of the other company officers signalling empty landers to lift off and clear the debris-strewn deck to make room for more.

That meant if they needed to pull out in a hurry, there wouldn't be enough transports waiting.

'Gak, that's just great,' snapped Gendler.

'I know! Fething marvellous, right?' Costin agreed.

Gendler didn't reply. Meryn pretended to be too busy shouting at some laggards to get down the ramp.

The truth was, Costin wasn't their best friend right then and there. Just before load up and launch, he'd come to them, shit-scared about something Rawne had said. The pathetic idiot had just dumped it on them, right in the middle of the pre-combat build up and the stress that brought with it. Costin was a liability. He couldn't handle a thing, least of all his drink any more. He was paranoid and raving. Best guess was Rawne had somehow sniffed out a trace of the sweet little deal they had been running. If that was true, then it sucked like a chest wound. It didn't suck quite as much as the assault run they were now in the middle of, but in the long term – provided there was going to be a long term – it could potentially suck even worse. If 'they' did know, things could turn very ugly for Meryn and his close confederates.

As ugly as Costin's face.

What had he done? What had the drunken shithead managed to do? How had he given them away? Loose talk over some sacra? Some dumb slip?

Whatever it was, Meryn was sure of one thing. 'They' had Costin. Rawne wouldn't have gone to Costin if he hadn't known for sure Costin was in it. Otherwise, it was probably a fishing trip. Costin was probably *all* they had, because only Costin was stupid enough to give himself away, and even then he wasn't stupid enough to blow the whole thing.

Rawne was baiting. Rawne was counting on Costin being so panicked he'd do anything he could to save his neck.

And he would. Costin *always* would.

So if they made it out of the Reach alive, Meryn had some serious damage-control to manage.

THE RAIN OF fire from the xenos became torrential. Flechette rounds detonated all around the advancing Space Marines in razorbursts. Eadwine felt ultra-sharp splinters slice off his armour. One actually punctured the ceramite. He felt it dig into the meat of his thigh. The sheer shot rate and penetrative effect of the loxatl blasters would finish them. Even three of the Adeptus Astartes would be brought to their knees, and then their deaths, by such a deluge.

His shield was still up. Sighting down his boltgun, he began to blast up into the roof space, blowing out rigs and gantries. Debris rained down. He saw one writhing reptile body tumble and burst on the deck. Scans now showed close to one hundred and eighty loxatl flooding down into the chamber. Some were racing down the chamber walls to attack from the ground. Eadwine directed the fields of fire of the weapon servitors as they pushed forwards in the face of the onslaught.

A large adult loxatl launched itself off an overhead gantry and dropped onto Holofurnace, dewclaws extended to slash. Holofurnace caught the animal on his shield and smashed it aside. It bounced off the deck, rolling, its blaster harness torn so that flechette ammunition scattered loose. Switching around, Sar Af put a single bolt through the loxatl's skull before it could rise. Its brain matter splattered across the deck, and its massive, blue-grey trunk and tail went into muscle spasms.

Another leapt. Sar Af blew it in half in the air. A third came down. Holofurnace had clamped his boltgun and drawn his spear off his back. He threw himself forwards to meet the close combat attack, decapitating the third loxatl with his circling spear blade.

'Ithaka!' the Iron Snake yelled.

The next loxatl to come at him lost its front limbs at the elbow joints in one fluid slice. The one after that died from an impaling wound. The next, which attacked as Holofurnace was ripping his spear out of his previous kill, had its back broken by a backhand smash of the Iron Snake's boarding shield.

It was something, but it was only a start. Auspex now showed two hundred and seventy-one xenos contacts in the chamber. There were so many coming down the roof pylons they were pushing the front runners off the hand holds, forcing them to drop, claws out, onto the Space Marines. Sar Af slugged them out of the air with bolt rounds, blowing open skulls and ribcages, severing whip tails, showering the fight zone with meat and viscera. Then two flechette rounds hit his right shoulder guard almost simultaneously and drove him down onto one knee.

Terek-8-10 raised the Caestus into the air behind them, ramps still gaping open. He got the damaged craft up to about eight metres, and swung it in over the heads of the advancing Space Marines. The armoured bulk of the Caestus formed a hefty shield, soaking up the majority of the blaster fire that had been raking the Space Marines and their servitors. In its shadow, Eadwine saw that the deck plates were peppered and grazed by the flechette fire to such an extent they resembled a lunar surface. The deck was also littered with bloody xenos meat and slimy, plum-coloured organs.

Flechette fire raked the Caestus. Loxatl dropped on to it, leaping down onto the hull booms, gripping onto the ragged wings. Some fell. Others clung on. They swarmed over the upper surface. Terek-8-10 retracted the open ramps, but several of them had already slithered inside, like lizards skipping across a rock in the sun. He could hear them skittering and chirring inside the vacated compartments. He could smell the stink of rancid milk and crushed mint that oozed from their flesh and breath. Another animal scrambled up the hull fairing right in front of him, and started firing its blaster point blank at the little armoured window port in front of the pilot's position. After eight frenetic shots, the armoured glass actually began to craze.

Terek-8-10 switched to manual control and began to swing the Caestus around. The increase in thrust sucked air into the atmospheric intakes, and the loxatl on the fairing was dislodged. It ripped past him, claws squealing on the metal, shrieking an inhuman scream as its tail and one hind leg vanished into the intake.

Terek-8-10 could hear the loxatls already aboard breaking through the compartment hatches under his position. The sickening stink of bad milk grew stronger. He adjusted the ram altitude again, tilting it more steeply, trying to train the magna-melta on the gantries overhead.

He got a decent angle.

'Cover yourselves,' he voxed.

Below the ram, the Space Marines backed off, shields raised.

Terek-8-10 had enough power in the heat cannon for

three more decent shots. He fired. Part of the overhead girderwork exploded, and droplets of molten metal rained down. The melta blast torched loxatl into blackened, shrivelled shreds that roasted off the gantries like scraps of burning paper.

He fired again. A huge section of the roof gantry, on fire and covered with burning loxatl, fell away, and glanced off the ram on its way to the chamber floor.

The creatures on board were in, right below him. They had torn open the compartment hatches. They fired up into the roof of the stowage bay and razor shrapnel from the flechette rounds burst through the floor of the pilot's position, shredding Terek-8-10's legs and groin. He felt the ice-pain of tiny hypervelocity metal shards travelling up through his torso, bursting organs, severing augmetics, and liquidising blood vessels. He felt them in the sacs of his hearts. He felt his lungs collapsing. Blood filled his throat. The loxatl underneath his position, chattering and squealing, kept shooting, blasting shot after shot up into the pilot's position.

With his last double heartbeat, the pilot-servitor triggered the afterburners.

KOLEA'S EYES OPENED wide. It was one of those sights he would never forget. He'd seen some things in his life as a Guardsman, seen some things before that too. This was a new brand on his memory.

He saw the Space Marines' boarding ram, the Caestus, damaged and blackened, crawling with loxatl. He saw it tilt, nose up, pointing at the tangled, complex ceiling structure of the depot chamber, a structure that was dripping with xenos. The loxatl were spilling out of the roof space like maggots out of bad meat.

Kolea was at the top of the makeshift scaling ladder, poised on the lip of the puncture hole. His men were behind him, yelling at him to go on, jump down, make way for them. He had to stick out his hand to steady himself. The ragged metal lip of the hole was hot.

'What can you see?' Rerval was yelling, from the girder behind him. 'Major, what can you see?'

He could see the tilted Caestus, engines pulsing, a writhing mass of loxatl across its upper hull, some falling off, tails lashing. He could see the Space Marines and their weapon servitors on the floor of the chamber below, blasting at the grey reptiles as they rushed in from all sides.

He could smell rancid milk and crushed mint.

'Major?'

Kolea watched as the Caestus shuddered. It fired up at the ceiling vault, bringing down huge chunks of machinery in showers of flame and sparks. Burning loxatl dropped like comets. It fired again. A massive pylon cylinder broke free of its ceiling mount and came crashing down, strung with fracturing gantries and doomed loxatl. The huge structure, streaming smoke and flames, barely missed the Caestus as it fell. It hit the chamber floor so hard that Kolea felt the shockwave shake the girders he was standing on. It almost crushed one of the Space Marines, the towering Silver Guard Eadwine.

Eadwine hurled himself full length to avoid the impact. He landed in the midst of recoiling loxatl, and immediately had to kill them to protect himself. The pylon cylinder toppled after the impact, and fell on its side with a second crash that kicked up sparks and a blizzard of burning scraps. It rolled, burning.

The Caestus was almost overwhelmed. Its afterburners lit. The rockets roared with scorching white heat. Laden with loxatl, the ram accelerated up into the roof.

That's when the real shockwave came. Kolea felt it in his lungs. He felt it punch his ribcage. He felt it hammer the deck and the compartment walls. He felt it knock his legs away.

The Caestus tore into the vault, triggering a vast fireball that ripped through the ceiling structures, destroying them. Macerated, burning loxatl were hurled in every direction. The expanding fireball, a rolling wave, lapped out across the ceiling of the vault and down the walls. Falling, Kolea felt the heat of it.

Wrecked but essentially still in one piece, the Caestus fell back out of the roof, bringing the ceiling down with it. Energy crackled and sparked like lightning around one of its twisted engine sections. A ramp door tumbled off. The air was full of flames.

The collapsing wreckage hit the chamber floor with a numbing crash.

Kolea hit the floor too. The blast had smacked him off the girder into the depot chamber. He jumped up, dazed, gazing at the devastation ahead of him.

'Major. Major Kolea. Respond!' Rerval was yelling over the link.

'Get in here!' Kolea yelled back. 'C Company get in here. Now!'

He raised his weapon and ran forwards. Behind him, Ghosts were leaping in from the rim of the puncture.

EADWINE GOT UP, throwing wreckage aside. A loxatl reared up at him, and he killed it with a headshot.

'Status!' he demanded over his helmet link.

'Alive!' the voice of Sar Af snapped back, a vox crackle.

Holofurnace didn't answer, but Eadwine knew that was because the Iron Snake always had something better to do. Eadwine could see him, thirty metres away across the piled and burning rubble, fighting at close quarters with a dozen of the surviving loxatl. Holofurnace's spear circled and stabbed, killing them one by one, leaving arcs of xenos blood in the air behind it.

According to Eadwine's visor display, they had lost one of the gun servitors, crushed under the fall. Regrettable, but an acceptable loss. He activated his helmet's vox-record.

'Note for posterity,' he said, turning to despatch

another pair of lunging reptiles. 'The selfless sacrifice and attention to duty of–'

Eadwine paused, shooting out the spine of a leaping loxatl. He couldn't remember which ancient pilot servitor had been assigned to the Caestus for the mission. It would be on file. He would amend the citation later.

Eadwine clambered forwards. Two flechette rounds punched his shield. He turned and fired a bolt round that detonated a xenos head.

Ahead of him, beyond the strewn wreckage, he saw that the White Scar had made it to the far exit of the depot chamber. Cunning and shrewd, Sar Af was always moving, always looking for a path.

There were loxatl all around the old bastard.

Eadwine ran a couple of steps, and leapt off a pile of steaming scrap metal. Despite the added weight of his revered boarding armour, the bound cleared a significant distance. He landed, leaping again, and came down a short distance behind Sar Af.

As he made this second landing, Eadwine cleared three targets with killshots. Sar Af turned, smacked a loxatl aside with his shield, and stamped on its neck to kill it.

'You moved ahead,' said Eadwine. 'We cannot cover each other if we are too widely spaced.'

'There are matters to attend to,' Sar Af relied. 'They will not wait.'

'They will wait forever if you are dead,' replied Eadwine. 'The creatures defending this site are reacting with surprising speed to our attack.'

'If your throat is cut,' said Sar Af, 'it does not matter how fast you react. We must get on and cut the throat.'

Sometimes, there was no arguing with brothers of the Fifth. Holofurnace, still locked in close combat behind them, seemed determined to methodically kill every single Archenemy in Salvation's Reach one by one. The White Scar, however, appeared quite content to leave them all standing provided he could cut ahead and decapitate their command structure.

Both were respectable combat ethics. They were entirely incompatible. That was why Eadwine had charge of the mission.

'We move ahead,' he said. 'We stay together.'

Sar Af nodded.

Eadwine activated his helmet link.

'Strike Alpha lead to Guard formation. Are you deployed?'

'Confirm, lead.'

'Who speaks?'

'Major Kolea, Tanith First.'

'Where are you, Kolea?'

'Scaling the breach now, advancing into the depot compartment.'

'You need to close the gap. We are pressing forwards. Be advised, a high density of loxatl mercenaries are present. Are you familiar with loxatl, major?'

'Yes, lead. We're just a few minutes behind you and progressing rapidly.'

'Very good. Lead out.'

Eadwine and Sar Af turned to the hatchway. The White Scar had just finished two more loxatl. Alien blood spattered his pearl-white plate.

Charges took out the hatch. In a fog of blue smoke, Sar Af and Eadwine advanced, shields raised, bolters propped over the right-angled corners. Holofurnace was closing at their heels.

They moved into a hallway, a main access way. There was blood and wreckage on the floor where personnel had fled the ram strike and sealed the hatch behind them. The structure and age of the walls and ceiling, and the machine components fixed into them, was such that it looked like the corridor had been built from scrap cannibalised from several different starships.

Shots started to snap at them. Holofurnace had joined them, his spear at his shoulder, his bolter back in his fist.

They formed a line, three abreast, shields up. A moving wall, resilient and formidable, they advanced, almost filling the corridor from side to side.

The gunfire smacked into their rigidly held shields. It wasn't xenos fire from some exotic flechette blaster. It was las-shot.

Up ahead, the first human defenders appeared, blasting down the smoky corridor with lasrifles and helguns.

Shields up, the Space Marines walked into it, blasting as they came. The mass reactive rounds streamed away from them and cut the hallway apart. Bodies fell. Wall panels blew out. Parts of the ceiling caved in.

The firefight exchange grew more intense.

The Space Marines didn't slow down for a second.

THE GHOSTS OF Strike Alpha pushed forwards across the depot through a jumble of burning debris. Zhukova reported that her company had engaged with some loxatl and were in the process of subduing them, though the bulk of the loxatl force had been wiped out by the Space Marine spearhead.

Kolea wondered if there would be more. He wondered what other wretched things lay in wait in the junk habitat.

He heard the heavy .30 crank up and start to fire. Bool and Mkan were getting busy. What the gak had they seen?

'Hostiles!' Caober yelled over the link. The scout had pushed forwards to the left-hand edge of the chamber. Kolea hefted his shield up and started to run. The shields had barrel slots cut in the top right-hand corner of their shapes, so the wearer could carry the shield on his left arm and brace the weight of his lasrifle barrel across the slot. Effectively, he could fire from behind cover. Kolea hadn't used a boarding shield in combat before, but they'd been training hard en route. He still believed they were cumbersome and ineffective.

He was running forwards with five or six other Ghosts, leaping blazing debris. A crippled loxatl flopped out of hiding into their path and ratcheted off two shots with its flechette. Kolea's shield stopped the first, and the second blew up against the deck. Derin's shield saved his legs and groin from the deflected splinters of shrapnel. Firing from behind his shield, Kolea slew the loxatl with a burst of shots.

His attitude towards the boarding shields warmed slightly. In the enclosed space of boarding action, the danger of deflection shots was dramatically increased.

More gunfire streaked their way. Kolea saw what Caober had spotted. Sally ports had opened on the far side of the depot chamber: heavy trapdoor hatches concealed along the welded line where the bulkhead wall met the deck. Archenemy troops were clambering out of them, firing as they came. Kolea wasn't sure if the hatches had been deliberately designed for defensive actions, or if the enemy was making smart use of engineering crawl spaces.

All he was sure of was that they were suddenly taking heavy fire against their left flank.

The enemy troops were big, human males. Their battle dress was not uniform, but it was all the same general mix of richly ornamented armour plate and yellow breeches and coats. Boots, gloves, belts, armour clasps and bindings, along with packs and webbing, were made of a dark, rich leather, polished a caffeine brown like mahogany. The leatherwork, especially the wide and heavy waist belts, was interwoven with purple silk bindings and silver wire stitching. The yellow of the material under the brown leather wargear was hot and acid, like a fusion beam. The warriors had tight, buckle-on metal helmets covered in brown leather that had incorporated visors: narrow, single-lens oblong frames that covered both eyes and emitted a dark blue glow. The buckled chinstraps of the helmets, fashioned from the same dark brown leather as the belts and webbing, were oversized, and designed in the form of life-sized human hands that covered the entire mouth area below the nose.

Kolea knew what he was seeing. Servants of the wretched anarch, whose voice 'drowns out all others', demonstrated respect for their master by covering their mouths.

These warriors were Sons of Sek.

EIGHTEEN
The First Cut

THE SHRIEKING OF the Hades drill was becoming unbearable. Gaunt felt as if his teeth were about to shatter. The atmosphere in the lateral holdspace was thick with exhaust fumes and the reek of burning metal and oily water. A fine vibration, transmitted through the deck by the drill, was making everything tremble.

He retreated to just outside the hold hatchway so he could hear Beltayn over the vox.

'Major Baskevyl reports six companies deployed at the primary zone,' Beltayn said. 'More coming in, but it's tight.'

'Have they kicked the door in and made a lot of noise?'

'Yes, sir,' said Beltayn.

'Opposition?'

'Loxatl. Now Major Kolea reports contact with what he believes are Sons of Sek.'

Gaunt took a deep breath. Loxatl made his skin crawl, but Sons of Sek were something else. The anarch's rumoured response to Gaur's Blood Pact. Sworn soldiers, cult devotees of the Ruinous Powers, yet disciplined and organised. Zealot warriors. Gaunt felt a particular type of fear whenever the Archenemy appeared to operate with intent. Their unpredictable insanity was bad enough. But for the Blood Pact, the Sabbat Worlds Crusade would have been prosecuted and done years before.

'Keep me appraised,' he said.

He suddenly realised the drill had shut up.

'We're through,' said Mkoll.

Gaunt walked back into the hold. Servitor crews were pulling back the protective baffles. The troop company of Strike Beta was on its feet.

Gaunt waved the lead team forwards. Mkoll, Domor, Larkin and Zered. Each one carried the tools of his trade. They buckled on rebreathers and adjusted lamp packs.

The chief artificer was staring at Gaunt, waiting.

Gaunt took the vox horn from the set operator.

'This is Strike Beta,' he said. 'Be advised, we are beginning insertion. Hull is breached, repeat, hull is breached.'

'The Emperor protect you,' Spika's voice replied over the link.

Gaunt nodded to the chief artificer. The man turned and beckoned urgently with both hands. With a mechanical grumble, the Hades backed into the hold again, treads clattering on the deck. Its retreat unplugged the hole it had bored, a huge tunnel in the hull of the Reach the size of a decent hatchway. The edges of the cut were bright silver metal, whorled and flaked like shredded foil. Approaching, Gaunt could see the cut was under four metres deep. Cold and undisturbed air leaked out towards him from the darkness inside, like the slow bleed of heat from a tomb.

Artificers and servitors were fussing around the hole with tanks of sealant.

'What are you doing?' asked Gaunt.

'The edges will be razor-sharp in places,' replied the chief artificer, 'hazardous to touch. We are preparing to seal them with–'

'No time,' said Gaunt. 'We'll just be careful.'

The artificer's crew backed off.

Mkoll and Domor led the way, and Gaunt fell in behind them with Larkin. Zered brought up the rear, his flamer lit.

Gaunt drew his bolt pistol. Larkin carried the old solid-round rifle he had been training with. His longlas was in its cover across his back.

Mkoll stepped forwards into the gloom, lasrifle ready. Beside him, Domor adjusted his headphones and extended the sweeper broom of his detector set. Gaunt could hear the sweeper's little portable auspex ticking like a radiation counter.

They advanced down the cut, through the bored hole, carefully avoiding the razor-sharp sides. The skin of the hulk was dense and thick. Light from the hold winked off the milled and sawn edges of the tunnel.

Beyond lay darkness and silence.

They moved slowly. Even by Mkoll's wary and calculated standards, they were being cautious. Gaunt's eyes slowly began to adjust to the gloom.

A greyish half-light was revealed ahead of them, a dusk. They were coming through into a cavity that had the dimensions of a hold space, but none of the regularities. The ceiling sloped down at one end. This wasn't a space that had been designed, it was a chamber that had been partially crushed into its current shape: the internal compartment of one of the ancient vessels that had fused to form the Reach, deformed by slow gravitational pressure.

The deck was uneven. Panels had popped their rivets and sat like displaced flagstones. Cables, ancient and powerless, hung down from busted roof plates. The air was ominously dry. Gaunt noticed that Zered's flamer began to suck hard, and the trooper had to adjust the mix rate to compensate for the oxygen-poor atmosphere.

Domor swept steadily to and fro, passing his broom

across the walls and low ceiling. Gaunt could see the blue glow of his set's display screen. The ticking was steady.

'Anything?' he asked.

'I'm calibrating,' said Domor. 'There's a lot of bounce. So many different densities and intermixed alloys.'

Gaunt didn't envy Domor's task. A quick look at the walls and ceiling showed extraordinary levels of gross compaction, with structural fabric and mechanisms crushed along with circuits and energy filaments into scrap filler. Getting any meaningful discrimination through the auspex was going to be a challenge.

'Steady,' said Mkoll. They climbed over a fallen beam and ducked around a fractured metal arch, the remains of some giant hatch, which stuck up out of the mangled deck like a broken tooth. Mkoll waited while Domor scanned both, and marked them with yellow chalk as items to be cleared from the route. Beyond the arch, the compartment seam had ruptured open like a scar. The metal looked molten. Through the rupture lay a service-way.

They went through. The service-way was long, and only slightly deformed. It was wide and high enough to drive a cargo-6 along. It had been built for humanoids, but not by any human. Curious designs along the wall sections had been defaced and over-marked by Archenemy sigils.

'This area's in use,' said Mkoll. 'The dust on the deck shows footprint scuffs. Not recent. I'd say six months, though environmental conditions are so stable, it could be six years.'

'Or six hundred,' said Larkin.

'They come this way often enough. They didn't like looking at these markings,' said Domor, nodding at the defaced walls. 'They scratched them out, changed them.'

'Or altered them to leave instructions of their own,' said Gaunt. 'Like "Keep out". Check the deck. Wires, anything.'

Mabbon Etogaur had been quite specific about the

ways in which the extremities of the Reach were protected. No wards or warp magic, no infernal devices or
daemonic mechanisms. Anything like that might be too
easily triggered by the sensitive study and development
being undertaken at the facility.

At the Reach, the Archenemy was relying on good, old-
fashioned mechanical booby traps: mines, explosives,
lethal anti-personnel defences.

Domor scanned ahead, adjusted his settings, and then
did it again.

'Nobody breathe,' he said. 'I'm getting something now.
The deck plates ahead are hollow. Wait… yes, feth. I've
got cables, active-fluid hydraulics and an electric charge.
We've got a pressure trigger. The deck's live.'

Mkoll pulled a scope that matched the one screwed to
the top rail of Larkin's rifle. The chief scout put it to his
eye, and Larkin raised his weapon, hunting.

'Cable wire comes out eight metres down, to the left,'
said Domor.

'I see it,' said Mkoll. 'That look like storage drums to
you?'

'In the alcove?' asked Larkin, squinting through his
rifle scope. 'Yes, it does.'

'The sniffer's getting fyceline and promethium gel,'
said Domor. 'About a tonne volume.'

'Throne,' said Zered, genuinely appalled.

'Detonator?' asked Gaunt.

'Looking for it now,' said Mkoll, training his scope. He
had it set to low light. 'Got it. I see the trigger pin. The
cable's cleated up the wall along the bulkhead seam. It
goes in at the top of the left-hand drum.'

'Yes, I see it,' said Larkin, aiming.

Gaunt wondered if they should back off. The target
was tiny and the light levels were poor, but eight metres
was comfortably within Larkin's effective range. If the
shot failed, and the device detonated, no amount of
shelter or cover would save them. A tonne of fyceline

compound explosive would create an overpressure blast in the confined environment that would suck through the narrow apertures of the compartments, pulp their internal organs to soup and their bones to jelly, and probably burst the improvised atmosphere seal between the *Armaduke* and the Reach. Even the rest of Strike Beta, waiting in the later hold, would probably be killed by focused atmospheric concussion.

Hiding in cover when Larks took the shot might make them feel better, but it would have zero practical safety value.

'Let's get this done,' said Gaunt.

Larkin knelt on one knee, settling his position, shaking out his shoulders. He chambered a single saline round, slammed it home, and then took his aim. Mkoll crouched beside him, and activated the passive tagger on his scope, so that the pencil-thin light beam indicated the precise target. As shot caller, Mkoll wanted to make sure he and Larkin were both appreciating and agreeing upon the same exact spot.

'Got it,' said Larkin, locking up his scope.

Domor lowered his broom and murmured a silent prayer. Zered hooked his flamer head to his waist belt and, to Gaunt's amusement, put his hands over his ears.

'None of you were actually planning on living forever, were you?' Larkin asked.

He took the shot.

THERE WAS A dull, distant boom. It was muffled, but big. It resounded through the thick, deep hull of the *Armaduke*.

In preparation seventeen, a dingy cargo hold space, Blenner heard it and looked up. Some of the Ghosts around him had also noticed the noise.

'What the hell was that?' asked Wilder.

Blenner looked at Ree Parday. She'd been looking pale ever since they'd kitted up earlier in the day.

'Go ask, would you?' he asked.

Perday jumped off the wheel arch of the Tauros where she'd been sitting and ran towards the main hatch.

Blenner looked around the chamber. Three companies of the regiment, including the marching band, had been placed as combat reserve under the command of Captain Obel, with Captain Wilder as his second. In full combat gear, they were standing to in the hold space ready to deploy as required. They had eighteen Tauros assault vehicles ready and laden with spare munitions, with further re-stocks prepared on cargo pallets. If the word came, they could deliver munitions by truck down the *Armaduke's* main spinal to either of the lateral holds, and even cross into the Reach via the bore holes to support Strikes Beta or Gamma. Alternatively, they could transport the munitions to the main excursion to reload the Arvus lighters and other drop ships if Alpha needed reinforcement or replenishment.

The reserve unit was edgy, mainly because they were the only part of the regiment not directly deployed. Obel was sour – he'd drawn the duty by lot, and he wasn't happy about it because he'd been hoping to lead J Company in with the Alpha run.

No one, especially Blenner, was surprised that the band had been grouped into the reserve section. If anything, Wilder was more pissed off than Obel. J Company had pulled an unlucky duty. Wilder's mob hadn't even been entered into the lottery. They'd been put in reserve, the assumption being they were only worth deploying in the fight if it was really necessary.

Blenner didn't care. Waiting to fight was his kind of war, and he had no wish to see the band company trying to prove itself, even though it really wanted to. The results were likely to be messy and ultimately disappointing.

Blenner also wasn't surprised to see that Gaunt's boy, Chass, had been placed in reserve. That must have been a damn hard call for Gaunt. He wouldn't have wanted to be seen to be showing any kind of favour, but how could he throw his son into the line when he was seriously undertrained? That was the card that Gaunt had played in the end, to justify his decision. Felyx was not yet certified at basic. His place had to be in reserve.

Sitting alone at the far end of the hall on the tow-bar of a Tauros, Felyx Chass looked even more unhappy about the arrangements than Wilder. Maddalena lurked nearby.

Perday returned.

'Something explode?' asked Blenner brightly.

'It was the main airgates opening on the excursion deck,' Perday said. 'The first of the lighters are returning for restock. They want us to start shipping munitions down for loading.'

Blenner got up.

'We've got a job to do at last,' he called out. 'Let's look lively!'

LARKIN'S SHOT WAS perfect. The frangible saline round punched clean through the firing mechanism, shattering as it did so and drenching the trigger circuit with a desensitising flood of salt water. It was anticlimactic: a little puff and a spatter of water.

Mkoll and Domor edged forwards across the decking. The rigged plates shifted and there was a click, but the pressure trigger was no longer connected. They approached the stacked drums, Domor sweeping for secondary triggers.

Once he reached the drums, Domor put down his broom, pulled on a pair of leather gloves, and dismantled the shattered trigger mechanism, gingerly sliding the core up out of the socket in the drum top. He tied off all the bare wires, taped them to prevent conduction, sprayed the interior of the socket with inert gel and insulated the internal plugs with petroleum jelly.

'Safe as it's going to be,' he said.

Gaunt nodded. Mkoll marked the drums and the sur-rounding floor plates with red chalk to indicate a bomb made safe but still dangerous. They moved forwards. All of them had stripped off their clumsy rebreathers, pre-ferring the mineral stink of the Reach's dry atmosphere.

The service-way broadened. Domor's scans detected a cavity ahead of them. Gaunt could feel cold air moving against his face.

The service-way ended in a hatch, followed by a brief section of some other corridor that had been brutally severed in some ancient time. Beyond that, the ground dropped away in a deep ravine, a metal chasm lined with compressed junk. A ragged metal bridge with par-tial handrails crossed the gap.

On the far side, there was a landing space, and then several spurs of corridors or tunnels.

'Wait,' said Domor. His auspex clucked every time he swept the bridge.

Mkoll got down and peered.

'Big charge,' he reported. 'Halfway across the span, wired underneath.'

'You see the trigger?' asked Larkin.

Mkoll had his scope out. 'Yes, but it's a really bad angle. It's facing away from us. I think it's hooked to the bridge walkway. Motion detector.'

'Let me look,' said Larkin. He'd already reloaded. He got down on his belly at the lip of the chasm, and rolled on his side to squint along the underside of the bridge. He had to take his longlas off and hand the cased weapon to Zered because it was getting in the way.

'Nice,' he said. 'Lucky I'm so good.'

He started to ready his rifle. He was sprawled in a posi-tion that looked both uncomfortable and less than ideal for marksmanship.

'Let me tag it for you,' said Mkoll.

'Don't bother,' said Larkin. 'Just hold onto my legs and stop me rolling, or I'll fall right off this fething ledge.'

Mkoll knelt down and physically braced Larkin's body. The marksman had to lie almost flat with his rifle under his chin and a foreshortened grip supporting the barrel. It was the posture of a stage contortionist. Gaunt felt his pulse rate rise again.

The rifle cracked, the sound of the shot echoing oddly down the gulf below them, a small sound in a vast space. Gaunt saw the impact, the spray of glass-like shards from the round casing, the mist of saline droplets.

'Blew it clean out,' said Larkin, getting up and ejecting the brass. He was collecting his cases, putting them in his pocket.

Sweeping as he went, Domor edged out across the bridge, checking for secondaries. From the look on his face, the metal structure felt none too secure. Cold air kept breathing up from below in gusts, as if the vast and crushed structure of the Reach were respiring. Each gust of cold air turned their breath to steam.

Domor lay down on his front, reached under the bridge, and disengaged the dangling firing pin. It was wet from the shot. As he brought it up, it slid from his fingers and fell away into the depths.

Everyone realised they were holding their breath.

'It's fine,' said Domor sheepishly. 'We didn't need it.'

Reaching down again, he squirted gel into the pin holder and the wiring junctions. Mkoll marked the bridge with red chalk.

They crossed the bridge. It looked precarious, though Gaunt guessed it would probably take a light vehicle. Ahead of them, past some clutter and scrap metal, lay the three spurs. One was another service-way, the second led through into a dank vault that seismic action had split into three different levels. The third turned right and joined a rusted gantry that crossed a sunken chamber full of rotting and long-dead machines.

'Charges in the roof here,' said Mkoll, indicating the second service-way.

'Clear them,' said Gaunt. 'I'll drop back to move the rest in. If we're getting alternative routes, we need guidance.'

He started to walk back towards the borehole. Larkin began lining up on the third device.

Gaunt used his link to signal to Strike Beta. The first few units met him in the service-way.

The first clearance team to follow them in was led by Criid, with Leyr as scout and shot-caller, Banda as marksman and Mklaek as sweeper. Their flamer was being lugged by Domor's adjutant Chiria. The second was led by Mktass, with Preed as scout, Raess as shooter and Brennan as sweeper. Sairus came in support with a flamer. Gaunt gave them instructions to proceed, and to link with Mkoll's squad before dividing to open up the alternate access points. He underlined the need for caution, discipline and constant vigilance.

They listened carefully, and then moved up.

Sergeant Ewler appeared next, leading in the first of the combat troops from A and K Companies. Ezra was with them, and so was Kolding, carrying a medicae pack. Curth, as acting chief medicae, had insisted on riding with the Strike Alpha deployment, where the highest casualty rate was anticipated.

Behind them came the Suicide Kings.

Rawne had allowed Mabbon to lose everything but the manacles. The foot shackles had gone. Around the pheguth, Varl, Bonin, Brostin and the others stood ready.

'How far have you got?' asked Rawne.

'Not far, and three devices disarmed already,' replied Gaunt.

'That's good,' said Mabbon.

They looked at him.

'It's what I would have expected,' he explained, 'so it suggests things haven't changed much since I was last here. Also, it suggests that they're relying on unmanned defences for these layers of the Reach.'

Gaunt nodded. This had been Mabbon's assertion all along. The main Archenemy strengths guarding Salvation's Reach were positioned around the primary docking areas and facilities. Subsidiary levels of the colossal structure, most of them unused, and many of them uncharted, had been mined and booby-trapped then left as unpatrolled deadzones. The Archenemy expected any significant attack to come from the front, which was why Gaunt had sent Strike Alpha in to knock on the main door and attract as much attention as possible.

The Archenemy did not particularly anticipate anyone having the patience, discipline, skill or technique to cut through the hull of the Reach and attempt an insertion through the mined levels. Even with the requisite levels of skill and discipline, such an undertaking would still be doomed to failure.

Unless you also had inside information. Unless you had reasonably accurate experiential data that told you where to cut, where to insert, and what to expect when you did.

Unless you had an etogaur of the Sons of Sek.

'Let's move forwards,' said Gaunt. 'Show me the way you'd take.'

They headed back in, overtaking the waiting troop advance and crossing the bridge. Mkoll's squad had begun to clear a significant distance along the second service-way, neutralising three more devices in the time it had taken Gaunt to backtrack and lead the rest in. Criid's team had begun to disarm bombs in the split vault. Mktass's team was crossing the corroded gantry into the chamber full of dead machinery.

'I think your man Mkoll has the best idea,' said Mabbon.

'He usually does,' Gaunt replied. 'It's a gift.'

He turned to Rawne.

'We'll follow Mkoll's team, but the other two routes

may be viable. Let's divide the troop force here and spread out.'

'Maximising our chances?' Rawne asked.

'Minimising our losses,' Gaunt replied.

'STRIKE BETA IS deployed,' said Beltayn over the vox. 'Full strength inside the Reach structure, though moving slowly.'

'Understood,' said Daur. He was pacing in frustration. The drill was taking forever to make the second cut.

'Can't they increase the rate?' he asked Major Pasha.

She shook her head.

'They say it would burn out the cutters,' she replied.

'It's burning out my patience.'

She laughed, but there was a serious look on her face.

'Please try to stabilise your mood, captain,' she said. 'Once we're inside, we're going to be moving through an environment loaded with improvised explosive devices, most on trembler or pressure switches. Patience is going to be our greatest virtue.'

'I know, I understand,' Daur replied. 'But if we don't cut in soon, we will be badly behind schedule. If Strike Beta reaches an impasse or hits opposition, and we're not advancing as an alternative, then this mission is going to be a failure.'

'Sometimes missions are failures,' said Pasha. 'That's the nature of war.'

'Forgive me, no,' said Daur. 'I mean no disrespect, and I understand a decent officer needs to keep a philosophical perspective on such matters. But you haven't served with Gaunt before. You need to appreciate what he expects.'

Major Pasha frowned and nodded.

'I also believe,' said Daur, 'that when a mission is this critical, it can't be a failure.'

Nearby, behind the baffles and bombarded by the

hideous screech and rattle of the working drill, Merrt
rubbed at his neck.

'What's the matter?' asked Maggs.

'It's… gn… gn… gn… wearing off,' said Merrt.

He'd shot the numbing agent into his jawline when
the drill started up, so he'd be ready to take a shot the
moment they were through. But the drill had been cutting
for almost forty minutes, and the numbness was ebbing
away.

'You got another?' asked Raglon.

'A couple. Three I gn… gn… gn… think.'

'Don't waste them,' said Maggs.

There was a sudden bang from behind them.

'What the–?' asked Merrt.

'I think we're through,' Nessa mouthed.

'You sure?' asked Questa.

'We're through. We're through!' Hark called, ushering
the strikeforce back to position. 'Ready, now. First team
up and ready!'

Major Petrushkevskaya was to lead the first clearance
team. Her days in the scratch company had taught her
plenty about booby traps and bomb disposal. Nessa, Zel,
Marakof and Raglon moved up with her. Raglon had the
sweeper broom ticking ready. Nessa checked her antique
rifle. Marakof, one of the new Verghastite scouts, took a
deep breath and winked at Major Pasha. They'd served
together on the Zoican War and knew how one another
worked. Zel was another influx Verghastite, hand-picked
by Pasha. He jogged over to join them, his flamer lit.

'Steady and wait,' Pasha told her clearance squad. The
artificer crews were removing the baffles and protective
screens while the drill team prepared to disengage the
drill.

'Hurry it up,' cried Daur. 'Places, please! Major Pasha,
you're up first. Pollo, you'll follow them in when I give
the word. Then Haller, your team. I repeat, clearance
teams first! Commissar Hark, if you please. I know we're

all eager, but get the troop elements back out of the way.
We need room to move!'

Hark barked some orders and herded the waiting troop
sections back. Haller traded knuckle slaps with the members of his squad.

Daur turned to look at the drill.

'What's taking them so long?' he asked Pasha.

'The artificer there says the cutting teeth have bitten in,
caught on something,' she said. 'They're just freeing it.'

The drill was attempting to retract from the deep socket
it had bored. Something had snagged the cutting head.
The engine was revving hard, coughing up puffs of sooty
smoke. The operator was engaging the cutting head for
quick screaming bursts, forward and reverse, trying to tear
free so that the insertion could begin.

'Oh, come on!' Daur cried in exasperation.

Whatever flaw or imperfection, whatever ultra-hard
seam of adamantium or ceramite in the hullskin had been
snagging the drill-head, it finally and abruptly gave way.
The Hades lurched backwards violently, its cutting head
squealing across the inner surface of the borehole. The
operator had just shifted the rotation into reverse again.

The brutal release threw the drill operator off his station
onto the deck. Racing, the power-cutters scythed sideways
into the rim of the borehole and sheared away a large
chunk of hyperdense metal, which it shredded into razor-
fine fibres and slivers and ejected backwards into lateral
hold thirty-nine.

The flying metal shards blew back with the penetrative
force of a dozen loxatl flechette blasters. There were no
longer any protective baffles around the cutting site.

One flying shard decapitated an artificer. Another two
tore clean through the torso of a servitor. Other whizzing
scraps struck the deck and the roof.

The rest ripped into the clearance teams waiting to go
in.

NINETEEN
Bleed

'OH, HOLY THRONE,' Daur gasped. 'Medic!'

Bodies littered the deck of lateral thirty-nine. Torn and bloody, they were strewn about like discarded dolls. The deck was spattered with blood as though canisters of scarlet paint had been indiscriminately spilled.

Mohr ran forwards.

'You're cut,' he said.

'What?' Daur reached up and felt blood on his face. A shard had sliced his temple above the eye. Another had gone through Mohr's sleeve. His left hand was soaked in blood that was running out from under his cuff.

'Oh, gak, what a fething mess,' Daur stammered.

Lesp was the medic assigned to Gamma. He was already struggling to cope with the volume of simultaneous injuries, yelling for help from troopers in Gamma who had corpsman training or any first aid skills. Soldiers were setting down their weapons to run forwards and assist. Others looked on at the devastation, aghast. Blood spray from the injuries had dappled the faces of many of them. One unlucky lasman in the front row, a

new influx man called Gorgi, had been killed outright by
a fragment between the eyes.

All three clearance teams were decimated. Some were
alive and struggling to get up, dazed. Others lay still,
apparently dead. All of them were soaked in blood.

'Strike Gamma, Strike Gamma!' Daur yelled, grabbing
the vox from Mohr. 'We have multiple injuries in lateral
thirty-nine. Multiple injuries!'

'Say again, captain,' Beltayn responded. 'Are you under
fire? Are you reporting hostile contact?'

'Negative! Drill accident. Multiple laceration casualties. We need medics from the ship's infirmaries here
now!'

'Captain, can you proceed?'

'Assessing now. Stand by.'

Daur gazed around in horror. Major Pasha's team,
the primary, had been slashed to pieces. Lesp was trying to staunch injuries to Pasha's throat and face while
the corpsman Fayner applied compression to wounds in
Nessa's upper arms and legs. Both women were bleeding profusely. Raglon was curled in a ball, gasping and
choking, yet barely had a scratch on him. A razor-sharp
filament had gone through his torso, puncturing a lung.
Zel and Marakof were dead. Marakof's head had been
sliced in half diagonally, from the left corner of his jaw
to his right temple, like some immaculate biological
sample. The missing piece of his head lay a few metres
behind him, internal side down on the deck, so it looked
like a small part of someone surfacing out of a pool.
Zel's torso was shredded and his left arm detached. Daur
stepped forwards, numb, and killed the feed of Zel's
fallen flamer.

The second team, Pollo's, was as bad. Pollo had suffered a huge scalp wound that was bleeding copiously,
as well as significant wounds to his arms. Bright red
blood beaded his dark skin. Questa, the marksman, had
taken lacerations to his hands and thighs. A needle sliver

of metal the length of a man's forearm impaled his hip.
Maggs was whining in rage and frustration, clutching a
bloody stomach wound. Pollo's sweeper man, Burone,
had been cut in two through the waist. Nitorri, his flame
trooper, was also dead, so covered in blood it was impossible to tell which of his wounds had proved lethal.

The third team, Haller's, was covered in the blood of
the first two. Haller was looking down at his battledress,
astonished at the gore spattering him, amazed that none
of it seemed to belong to him. Merrt had taken a scratch,
but had rushed to Nessa's aid. Vahgner, the scout,
was virtually unmarked. His mouth was open as if he
couldn't find anything adequate to say. Vadim put down
his sweeper broom to help Raglon, but immediately fell
over. A flying shard had cut his Achilles tendon. Belloc,
a usually cheerful new influx Vervunhiver, was ashen as
he tried to unbuckle his flamer unit so he could assist.

'Leave that on,' Vadim hissed.

'What?' Belloc replied.

'He's right,' said Daur. 'Team three's got to move in
first. Haller? Haller!'

Haller jumped.

'What? Yes,' he said, blinking.

'The door's open,' Daur said, glancing at Pasha.
Despite her miserable wounds, she managed to nod.
'We've got to move in before this prong of the assault
collapses completely. We have to proceed. Haller?'

'Yes, all right,' said Haller, trying to regain his wits,
incapacitated by shock. 'But… but Vadim's out. I've got
no sweeper man.'

Daur breathed deeply to control his panic response.
'I need a replacement sweeper here. A volunteer. Right
now!'

Most of the Strike Gamma force had come forwards to
help the injured. Those that couldn't actually help were
just looking on in dismay. They glanced at each other
dumbly.

'That's an order,' Hark yelled, moving in beside Daur. A flying filament had nicked his cheek, like a nasty shaving cut. 'The Emperor expects! Captain Daur needs a sweeper. Come on!'

'A good one,' Daur added. He could see the problem already. Gamma and Beta had selected the six best sweepers under Raglon and Domor. There were other Ghosts who understood basic operation, but the most skilful operators in the lateral hold, and the best trained, were the ones lying dead or hurt on the deck in front of him.

'I can do it,' said Maggs, wincing.

'Shut up and wait for the medics,' Daur snapped.

'I'll do it,' growled Hark. 'I know how they work.'

Haller coughed. He wiped specks of someone else's blood off his pale skin.

'No, it has to be me,' he said. 'I was the first reserve on the training list.'

Daur nodded. Haller was right. When they'd been making the selections for the clearance teams, Haller would have been made a sweeper if he hadn't worked so hard for a team command.

'You're right' Daur said. 'Take Noa's kit. Check it works. I'll lead you in.'

He turned to Hark.

'You and Spetnin have acting command here, Hark. See if you can assemble a functioning second clearance, and send them in. Then bring the troops in if I signal.'

Hark nodded.

'And for Throne's sake get more medics.'

'I will,' said Hark.

'Come on, Ghosts, move!' Daur said.

He turned and walked towards the bore hole. Merrt followed, with Vahgner and Haller. Belloc buckled his flamer tank and went after them. Vadim's auspex set had been damaged, so Haller had taken Raglon's instead. Daur heard Haller quietly promising Raglon he'd look after his precious kit and bring it back, though Raglon was probably too far gone with pain and disorientation to hear him.

Daur reached the bore hole. He glanced up at the ragged tear around the rim, the silver split of metal that had just compromised Strike Gamma's effectiveness, perhaps beyond any hope of recovery.

He activated his lamp pack.

HOLOFURNACE WADED INTO the Sons of Sek. He had harnessed his boltgun and, with spear and shield, was laying waste to them. Body parts and fragments of severed weapons flew out from his spinning blade.

Shields up, Sar Af and Eadwine continued the advance into the withering enemy fire. Firing over their shields, they were trying to break the Sons holding the next hatchway section. Their boarding shields quaked and shook under the deluge of fire. Most of the surface decoration, markings and the purity seals had been seared off.

Eadwine reloaded. He issued quick vox commands that brought the gun servitors in at their flank.

'Rush them?' he suggested to the White Scar.

'While the Snake is holding our left flank? Why not?' Sar Af replied.

'We need weight behind us,' said Eadwine. 'The damn Guard are slow. Adequate supporting fire would allow us to push ahead.'

'They will get here in their own sweet time,' replied Sar Af.

'Their own sweet time is not good enough,' said Eadwine.

KOLEA WAS PINNED behind a processor unit, enduring some of the worst crossfire he had ever known. It whined and streaked around him, slamming off the metal casing of the unit, puncturing and buckling it. Two Ghosts had already died trying to cross the open depot floor to join him. The Sons of Sek were intent on containing the invasion force in the outer compartments that the Caestus had penetrated. They were positioning to block them, shut them out, and then drive them back into the hard vacuum. Kolea had several company strengths behind him, but none was in any kind of position to advance and deliver firepower.

As for the Space Marines, they had plunged ahead regardless. Kolea was physically unable to render them any support. Indomitable as they were, the Space Marines would soon be cut off, surrounded and ultimately over-whelmed. They were the spearhead of the weapon, the tip of the sword. It didn't matter how sharp it was, a sword still needed a strong arm behind it.

Kolea had no doubt the Space Marines would pile body on body before they finally fell.

But in the end, they would still die.

Electromagnetic distortion from the torrential gunfire, especially the hellguns and plasma weapons fielded by the Sons, was chopping all vox exchanges. Kolea could barely coordinate with the other squad and company leaders. He'd lost sight of Rerval during a particularly fierce barrage, and he hadn't got a reply from Eadwine or the other Space Marines for twenty minutes.

The focus of the enemy fire shifted away from him, like a rainstorm passing overhead. He looked to his left, across the burning litter and destruction of the ravaged depot space, and saw Ferdy Kolosim's company being driven back into cover behind a row of huge steel bunkers. They left their dead on the deck behind them.

'Kolea!' his vox crackled.

'Go!' Kolea responded.

The vox burbled something else indistinct. He looked to his right in time to see a couple of shoulder-launched rockets whoosh up from the Guard lines into the upper part of the depot chamber. They blew out a row of

generator pumps and hurled the bodies of several Sons
into the air. Heavy, clacking fire, some of tracer rounds,
zipped from .30s and .50s. Baskevyl's company, D, was
attempting to push forwards from the hangar space. They
hadn't come through the hole the ram had punched.
They'd forced the internal hatches and surged through
under the cover of gantries and service walkways.

The Archenemy line taking D Company's fire withered slightly and tried to retrain. Kolea saw Baskevyl
get up and lead a rush towards some heavy manufactory engines that stood in a row across the centre of the
depot's decking.

Plasma fire streaked into them immediately. Kolea
winced, head down, as he saw three or four Ghosts cut
down. Then some rockets fell too, screeching down out
of the vault, and the gritty blast wash knocked Kolea
back.

The last thing he glimpsed was Baskevyl's burning
body thrown, headless, into the air.

Blinking, dizzy from the concussion, Kolea looked
around. Fury was filling him, rage at the losses and the
helpless state of their situation. He saw Meryn and some
of his force pinned around another row of processors.

'Move up. Move up!' he yelled. 'Into the fethers,
captain!'

Meryn didn't appear to be able to hear him over the
roar of the firefight. His men were pinking off shots in a
feeble manner, their heads down.

Something snapped.

No longer really thinking rationally, Kolea got up. He
hefted up his shield and ran at the Archenemy position,
leaping debris and bodies, firing his lasrifle through the
shield's slot.

Somehow, he didn't die.

Afterwards, he could not account for it. It was a story he
would tell, when suitably persuaded and after an amasec
or two, for the rest of his life. Kolea was destined to live

out a soldier's life, so that wasn't a terribly long time, but
it was long enough to make that day, that moment, an
old story. Others told it in turn, after his death: Kolea,
running the line like a madman, shield up, gun blasting.
He was yelling something as he went and, depending
who was telling the tale, what he yelled varied.

Some said it was the Vervunhive battle cry, others the
Founding Oath. Some said he was cursing the names of
Daur and Rawne, and everyone else who'd drawn the
easy option of the Gamma and Beta insertions.

The truth was he was probably yelling the name of his
friend Baskevyl.

It was a wild action, and utterly lacking in discipline,
especially given that Kolea was the force commander
and should have been setting a measured and sober
example to the ranks. Caober said it was exactly the sort
of fething idiot stunt Colonel Corbec used to pull.

That was why Caober got up and followed him. Derin
did too, and Lyse, Neith and Starck... and Irvin, Bewl,
Veddekin, Wersun and Vanette. Ludd, who should have
been ready to reprimand Kolea for reckless deportment,
got up and charged as well.

'Men of Tanith!' Ludd yelled. 'Straight silver!'

Most of C Company broke and charged after their
commanding officer, and so did a decent section of D
Company and Kolosim's H Company. Meryn's company
was mostly pinned, but a chunk of that also broke and
sprinted after Kolea. Dalin led these men, bayonet fixed.

Some versions of the story, later ones, insisted that not
a single Ghost who took part in that gloriously foolish
and improvised charge – *Kolea's Charge* – fell or took so
much as a scratch. This was not true. Plenty died or were
maimed. The Sons of Sek were not so astonished that
they forgot to keep shooting. The charge left almost forty
dead or injured on the depot floor.

Nevertheless, it hit the Sons like a tidal wave and broke
their line. Kolea was first over the barricades. In his

mindless haste, he had forgotten even to fix his silver, so he shot the enemy instead, point-blank, smashing with his shield, clubbing with his stock. The men behind him were slightly more composed. They came in with bayonets up, stabbing and spearing the Sons of Sek from behind their pock-marked shields. Some lobbed grenades over the front row into the support groups, blowing yellow uniformed brutes off their feet. A couple of flamers belched spears of liquid fire into the Archenemy ranks. Figures staggered, on fire, like ritual straw doll offerings, shuddered, fell.

Kolea killed eight of the enemy troops before he ran out of strength and dropped to one knee, panting, astonished by the sudden realisation of his own madness and, more, at the fact that he was still alive in spite of it. The charging Ghosts swarmed in around him, fracturing the enemy masses and driving them back along the defence barricade in both directions. Kolea had renegotiated the map of the battlefield and broken the impasse.

'Are you alive?' asked Dalin, helping him up.

Kolea nodded.

'I mean, *sir*,' Dalin added.

Kolea laughed.

'That was madness,' Dalin said.

'Yes, well, it runs in the family, so be warned,' Kolea replied.

Ghosts jostled past, forcing deeper, securing the position and firing on the retreating Sons. Ludd and Kolosim supervised the new deployment, yelling orders.

'You're quite insane,' said Baskevyl, slapping Kolea's arm. 'Probably get a bloody medal, though.'

Kolea stared at him.

'You–' he began.

'What?'

'You were hit. I saw you.'

'Not me,' said Baskevyl.

'The rockets! They came down right in amongst D. I saw you. You–'

Baskevyl grimaced.

'I lost eight men. Gudler was right beside me. Got his head blown off.'

'I thought it was you.'

Baskevyl laughed.

'Damn it, Gol. You charged the Sons of Sek because you thought I was dead?'

'I was angry.'

'He probably wants to marry you,' said Kolosim, running past them.

'Major Kolea!' Ludd shouted. 'We need some orders here.'

Kolea ran over to Ludd, assessing how best to disperse the Ghosts from the new positions that had just taken. Though in hard retreat, the enemy was still laying down heavy fire.

'We need to find exit points,' Kolea told Ludd. 'Drive on through. The Space Marines expect us to support them and we're lagging badly.'

Ludd nodded.

'Maybe we can bring up some tread-feathers,' he suggested, pointing. 'Punch a hole there and there, by that silo. Then we could advance under shields–'

He broke off. Just ahead of them, Sons of Sek were moving. Their unit discipline had vanished.

'Feth me!' Ludd exclaimed. 'Are they counter-charging us?'

'No,' said Kolea. 'They're *running*.'

A whole section of the retreating Archenemy line had broken and scattered towards Kolea's force. The advancing Ghosts began picking them off, amazed by the sudden opportunity. Explosions drove the Sons forwards into the Tanith field of fire. It was a brief but sustained slaughter.

'Look!' Ludd cried.

The White Scar, Sar Af, appeared out of the smoke, driving the breaking Archenemy troopers in front of him. He was blasting with his boltgun, disrupting their unit cohesion and driving their line around so that it buckled and withered under the Ghosts' fire.

He spotted Kolea.

'What is keeping you?' Sar Af bellowed.

'We were occupied,' Kolea yelled back.

'With what?'

'The usual,' shouted Kolea.

Sar Af shrugged his huge shoulderplates. He turned and blasted bolt rounds into the weakened enemy positions to his right.

'Come on if you are coming!' he yelled. 'We will not wait any longer. I told Eadwine I would come back to find out if you had a good excuse for not keeping up.'

'Like what?'

'Like being dead! Now come on, Emperor curse you!'

The White Scar began to move towards the depot's main rear hatches. The deck was covered in enemy dead. The hatchway was broken and buckled. Smoke threaded the air in dense, noxious walls.

Kolea turned to the advancing strike force.

'Double time,' he yelled. 'Put your backs into it. We've got a battle to win, and I don't intend to fight it on my own!'

'Despite evidence to the contrary,' said Baskevyl.

THE DEEP INTERIOR of the Reach was dark and cold. Daur's team moved through dank chambers and rusting tunnels, edging a few metres at a time, picking a path. Merrt's rebreather had become a hindrance, and he'd taken it off. Soon afterwards, the others had ditched theirs too. The chilly, metallic air was infinitely preferable to the sweaty, claustrophobic limits of the masks.

Haller was edgy. He was painfully conscious of how much depended on him reading the sweeper's scope right. He played the broom back and forth with infinite care.

'Just do it right,' said Daur. 'Don't overdo it.'

Haller nodded to his friend, loosened his collar, and moved on.

Eerie breezes murmured along the ancient, twisting tunnels. The burner of Belloc's flamer jumped and fluttered. In some places it was so dark that even the twitching light of the flamer cast their shadows up the rotting walls.

'Wait!' said Haller suddenly. His scope had started clucking. They held position while he moved the broom. Merrt quietly loaded a saline charge into his old rifle. He'd injected the muscle relaxant into his jaw again, and it was numb, but the second dose made the muscles in his neck and lower back ache.

'There,' said Haller, studying the scope while he pointed. 'Left side, wired along.'

'Left side, wired along,' Vahgner repeated, looking through his hand scope and running the passive tagger.

'Whoa, you've overshot,' warned Haller. 'There. Behind that bulkhead.'

They got the lamps on it. Twenty metres away, four squat munition boxes were stacked up behind a bulkhead support. Cables ran back under the seam of the deck to pressure plates directly in front of them.

'One more step would have been bad,' said Haller.

Daur nodded.

Vahgner was moving the tagger beam around.

'Look, there,' he said. Closer to the device, a hair-thin trip line was threaded across the deck at ankle height. If somehow you stepped over the pressure trap, a second surprise awaited you. Vahgner put the tagger back on the firing pin screwed into the top of the boxes.

'Twenty point one eight metres,' he said.

Merrt lined up and locked his scope to the tagger Vahgner was supplying. Twenty point one eight metres.

A breeze came up in their faces with a slight lift to it. He wanted to swallow, but his jaw and throat were too numb.

He snuggled in, the rifle held firmly but not too tightly. Everything in his life since that moment in the jungle on Monthax, everything had been about this moment, this shot. He felt sick.

'Good,' said Daur. 'Good shot, Rhen.'

Merrt blinked. A wisp of smoke was trailing from his rifle. He'd taken the shot. He'd been in the zone so completely he hadn't even noticed it.

'Perfect,' said Vahgner, checking through his scope. 'You sheared the firing cap right off.'

Haller moved forwards. The deck plate trigger was dead. He disengaged the tripwire, removed the trigger and sprayed inert gel into the device. Then he marked out warnings in red chalk.

'Think you can do that again?' Daur asked Merrt.

Merrt signed an affirmative. He wanted to whoop with satisfied delight, but his jaw was too numb.

'Let's make up some time,' said Daur.

'Got another one here,' Haller called out, sweeping the junction ahead of them.

Merrt chambered a fresh round.

'THIS SHOULD HELP with the pain a little while we get you to the infirmary,' Dorden told Nessa. She nodded and tried to smile at him as he gave her the shot. Her multiple cuts were field-dressed. Patches of blood were already showing through the bandages.

'You shouldn't be here,' Hark said.

Dorden got up from his patient, unsteady for a moment. He looked up at the commissar and gestured to the scene that lay around them in lateral hold thirty-nine.

'The dead and dying surround us, Viktor, and barely enough medics to cope. How better could I spend my time?'

'You know what I mean,' said Hark.

'No, actually,' said Dorden. 'Should I go off some-where quietly and wait to die so I don't become an inconvenience, or can I use what little life and skill I've got left to help the regiment?'

Hark shook his head. There was triage and field surgery going on all around them. Lesp was fighting to save Raglon's life. Medicae from Spika's crew were working on Maggs and Vadim.

'I was sitting in the infirmary, Viktor,' said Dorden. 'I heard the casualty alert. Old habits.'

'We appreciate your efforts,' said Hark.

'Let him work,' said Zweil. 'He just annoys the shit out of me when he hasn't got anything to do.'

The ayatani bent down to whisper last rites to Marakof.

'When do you go in?' Dorden asked.

Hark shrugged.

'We're running way behind schedule thanks to this mess,' he replied. 'Captain Daur's taken a clearance team in. We're waiting for him to signal us to follow.'

Hark glanced over at Mohr and Captain Spetnin. Both shook their heads.

Dorden fished in his medical satchel to get some dressings for Major Pasha.

'Waiting's the worst part, isn't it?' he said.

Hark agreed, but he had a queasy feeling he knew what the old regimental doctor was really talking about.

MERRT TOOK HIS fourth shot in fifteen minutes. The saline round punched the trigger cap clean out of the suspended tank of explosives. Perfect. Four for four.

Haller moved forwards to make the device safe and mark it up.

'Major tunnel route opening up ahead,' said Vahgner.

'We've cleared quite a way,' said Belloc.

Daur nodded. Maybe they had caught up a little time on Strike Beta after the disastrous start.

'I'll signal them to follow up,' he said. He adjusted his link.

'Daur to Gamma, Daur to Gamma.'

'Gamma here, captain,' Mohr answered.

'Instruct Hark and Spetnin to start leading the strike inside,' said Daur. 'Follow the marked route and go slow.'

'Understood.'

'Inform command we are deploying.'

'Understood.'

Daur looked at the others.

'Let's clear a little more of this path, shall we?' he said.

'STRIKE GAMMA!' SPETNIN yelled in his thick, Verghastite accent. 'Get up and get ready to deploy!'

'We're going in!' Hark called out, walking the line as the Ghosts assembled. 'Squad order. Get ready!'

'The Emperor go with you,' Major Pasha croaked to Hark, her throat bandaged. Hark nodded.

'Come on!' Spetnin cried.

'Where are you going?' Hark asked Dorden.

'Intending to advance without a medicae?' asked Dorden.

'Oh, Throne. Come on, doctor, I haven't got time for this.'

'Lesp can't leave his patient,' Dorden said quickly. 'He's got his hands full. I trained him well, so he's not about to walk off in the middle of surgery. I'm your only option. And the rulebook states–'

'Don't quote regulations at me, doctor,' said Hark. 'You're not strong enough, and you're not fit enough.'

'Of course he isn't!' snapped Zweil. 'He's dying, you pompous arse. Look at him, he's wasted away. He's almost see-through, he's so skin and bone. Let him have this much for feth's sake.'

'Father–' Hark began.

'Don't you get it?' Zweil asked. 'He doesn't want to die

idle, and he doesn't want to die on his own.'

'Show him some respect, father!' Hark growled.

'Actually, I couldn't have put it better myself,' said Dorden. 'That's all I'm afraid of, Viktor. Dying in bed and thinking there was a little more I could have done.'

Dorden stared at Hark.

Hark found the pale, bright eyes hard to look into.

'I swore,' said Dorden, 'on the Founding Fields at Tanith Magna, to serve the Imperial Guard and the Tanith First for the rest of my days. Are you, an Imperial fething commissar, really going to stand in the way of me performing that sworn duty? Because if you are, that's one staggering irony.'

'Get your things,' said Hark.

Dorden looked at Zweil.

'The Emperor protects,' said Zweil. 'Even stubborn old bastards.'

'That's why I never worry about you,' said Dorden. 'Look, I'll… see you later.'

'Of course you will,' said the old priest.

'MEDIC!' KOLEA YELLED.

Curth ran forwards along the line of cover, her head down in an instinctive posture that anyone who spent time on the battlefield quickly learned to adopt. She dropped in beside him. Fairly continuous gunfire ripped over their heads from the Sons of Sek positions in the vault chamber ahead. Crew-served weapons on either side of them rattled out return fire. Flamers roared.

'Are you hit?' she asked.

'Not me,' Kolea replied. He pointed at Fazekiel beside him. A shot had clipped her shoulder and flecked her face with blood.

'It's nothing,' Fazekiel said.

'It's light, but it's bleeding a lot,' said Curth, leaning in to dress it. 'You're no use to Gol if you're faint from blood loss.'

'Exactly what I told her,' said Kolea, turning back to his scope.

'Yes, well, from what I hear, you're hardly demonstrating the most rational behaviour today,' said Curth. She torn open a gauze pack.

'You heard about that, did you?' asked Kolea.

'It was the most amazing thing I ever saw,' said Fazekiel, wincing as Curth packed her shoulder. 'I intend to have him shot for it later.'

'Are we winning yet?' asked Curth as she worked.

Kolea shrugged. After the charge had reestablished contact with the Space Marine push, Strike Alpha had made some serious ground, breaking through into a series of vast internal compartments beyond the hangar bay and the engineering depot. These vault chambers were towering spaces like the insides of bulk manufactories. Huge machines filled their cavities. Kolea supposed they had something to do with atmosphere or gravitics.

The Archenemy had fallen back to dig in here. Sons of Sek, some loxatl, along with cult troops and weaponised servitors, held the line across three vault chambers, and harried the determined Imperial assault via the networks of ducts and sally ports. Loxatl were also using the roof spaces and conduits to gain advantageous firing positions.

Kolea's response was to systematically mine or burn out all ducts and hatches as they advanced, and scour the ceiling vaults and pipework with flamers. It slowed the whole force a little, but it was worth it.

It was costly, however. H Company, under Elam, was busy ferrying munition restocks up through the line from the hangars, where the landers and lighters that had delivered the troops for the assault were returning with cargoes of ammunition, flamer tanks, charges and rockets. Some of the lighters were turning around to make their third run of the day.

Jan Sloman scurried up.

'The brother-sergeant wants you to know that he and his brethren are about to make another push,' said Sloman.

'He could have told me on the link,' said Kolea.

'He tried. Distortion's even worse in here.'

Kolea knew this was true. He'd had to send Rerval back through the depot to keep the vox-link open with the *Armaduke* and the other strikes. Rerval had seconded a team of runners to keep messages flowing.

'Did he give any idea how long before this would happen?' Kolea asked Sloman.

There was a punishing roar of cannon-fire from the left of their position. Kolea knelt up to look behind his shield and saw the three Space Marines striding towards the thickest part of the enemy line. Their gun-servitors came with them, weapon pods blazing. Withering fire rippled along the ranks of the Sons.

'That answers that question,' said Kolea. He gathered up his lasrifle.

'Four! Nine! Twelve! Thirteen! Ready on my left!' he shouted. 'Eight! Fifteen! Vanette, your mob too! Get up and get ready! Suppressing fire on my order! Rockets, please! Objective is that processor hub!'

'You heard the commander!' Fazekiel cried, getting to her feet and buttoning her coat. 'The Emperor's watching you! He's watching us all. He's relying on you today so don't let him down! Numbered squads as ordered. Load and get ready!'

'For Tanith! For Verghast! And for the fury of Belladon!' Kolea howled. 'Into them!'

TWENTY
Salvation's Reach

'WAIT,' WHISPERED MKOLL. '*Wait.*'

'It was clean,' Larkin protested, lowering his rifle.

'Yes,' Mkoll agreed. He adjusted his tagger beam. 'You hit the pin, but look.'

The beam from the chief scout's scope lit up a fat black cable wrapped in tape running down the side of the device Larkin had just crippled.

'Secondary trigger,' he said.

'Feth,' murmured Larkin.

'What's it set to?' asked Gaunt.

Domor was busy with the auspex.

'I'm reading some kind of sack under the deck flooring there. To the right. I think it's a compression bag. Put your weight down and it squeezes air or fluid into the trigger cable. Throne, I almost missed that.'

'Secondary triggers suggests tighter security,' said Gaunt.

'We're about a kilometre and a half inside,' said Mkoll. 'If our friend's plans and memories are accurate, we're close.'

Larkin had reloaded.

'I can sever the cable. The trigger's partly obscured.'

'Do it above the trigger,' said Domor. 'Even if you only partly snap the line, the pressure will vent backwards out of the breach. Do it under the trigger, and the force of the shot could blow fluid or air up into the trigger anyway.'

'Thanks for the tip,' said Larkin, taking aim.

'It should work,' said Domor.

'"Should"?' said Zered.

'I like to leave room for circumstantial variability,' said Domor.

'Yes? Go feth yourself,' said Larkin, taking aim.

Mkoll waved Gaunt to one side.

'Larkin's getting tired,' he said quietly. 'His hands are unsteady.'

'He's all right,' said Gaunt. 'He was born unsteady.'

The rifle popped. There was a thick slap of water and glass.

'*Aaand* we're still alive,' said Larkin.

'He's taken out eighteen devices so far,' said Mkoll. 'The sustained stress is taking its toll.'

'We all trained for this,' Gaunt replied.

'And part of that training and planning involved an agreement to sub out shooters or sweepers if they started to show signs of fatigue.'

'Sub them out for whom?' asked Gaunt. 'You heard what happened to Gamma. Pylar and Curo were the two reserves with lanyards, and they've been called in to support Daur.'

'We've got other shooters.'

'Nobody who's trained this hard. Nobody this good. That's why we had so many wash-outs during preparation,' said Gaunt.

Mkoll marked off the device with red chalk. They began moving up again along the rusty vault. The walls were so corroded they looked like they were dripping in green and white ooze. They'd barely gone forty metres when Domor called in another hidden charge. Larkin began to mark it out.

Gaunt signalled to the main force advancing at a distance behind them to stop and wait.

'Raess then, or Banda,' said Mkoll quietly. 'Get Criid or Mktass to break off and regroup with us.'

'Raess and Banda have both done a dozen or so shots each,' said Gaunt. 'They're no fresher than Larks. We're committed and we're out of options.'

Mkoll sniffed.

'It's your call. But I don't think Larkin's got more than three or four sound shots left in his finger.'

Mkoll turned to help Larkin line up. Gaunt walked back to the main force.

'The pheguth says we're close,' said Rawne.

'How close?' asked Gaunt.

'He recognises this corrosion. He says two or three chambers on, we'll reach a hatchway that leads into the complex proper.'

Gaunt looked at the etogaur. Mabbon was flanked by Brostin and Varl. The rest of the S Company detail was nearby. Mabbon had been allowed to make notes on a data-slate. He showed Gaunt his sketched plan.

'You see?' said Mabbon. 'We're very close. You should get the troops ready.'

Gaunt chewed his lip.

'How sure are you?'

'About ninety per cent,' said Mabbon. 'This is a vast structure, and my memories are not perfect. But I spent several years here, and everything on this route has looked familiar. It's been what I expected. No surprises.'

'Ninety per cent?' Gaunt asked.

'Yes.'

'If Larkin was ninety per cent accurate,' said Gaunt, 'we'd all be dead by now.'

'Then it's a good thing I'm not the one shooting out the triggers,' said Mabbon.

There was a pop behind them, another saline round. The world did not dissolve into light and concussion.

They had survived another step.

Gaunt waved up the vox.

'This is Strike Beta, Strike Beta. I want transport ready to follow us in. The route is marked, do not deviate. Wait for my word.'

'Understood,' Beltayn replied. 'I'll signal Captain Obel.'

Gaunt turned to the long, waiting line of Ghosts that formed his fighting strength.

'Get ready, straight silver,' he said. 'It seems we're coming up on it.'

The Ghosts fixed their warknives in place.

In the Armaduke's preparation seven hold space, they were waiting by the Tauros units when the call came through. Obel listened to the vox, nodded a few times, and handed the horn back to his operator.

'Unload the munitions,' he ordered. 'These eight vehicles here. Load them with the empty carry crates. One driver, one spotter in each. Come along!'

Blenner walked over to him.

'Orders?'

'Strike Beta's called in transport. They're about to get their hands on what we're looking for.'

Blenner nodded.

'I'll lead this, then,' he said.

Obel frowned.

'I've been waiting all day for a chance to–' he began.

'I know you have. But this is just a transport duty. In and out, lugging freight. My kind of job. I'll use bandsmen who can drive a unit as crew.'

'I… I would like to voice my objection,' said Obel.

'I hear you, I do,' said Blenner. 'But I outrank you in this circumstance. Look, Obel, any minute we could get the call to send active fighting reserves to the excursion deck to support Strike Alpha. Combat drop, man. That's your kind of job. Let me take the band in to drive the cargo. That's just grunt work. Don't waste your time with it. Wait here for your chance to do the thing you actual heroes do.'

Obel made to reply, and then stopped.

'I just paid you a compliment, captain,' said Blenner.

Obel shook his head and laughed.

'Good luck, sir,' he said.

'Oh, I won't need that,' said Blenner.

Blenner walked over to Wilder. His heart was pumping harder than he really liked.

'Time for work, captain,' he said.

Wilder looked at him.

'Really? Another munition restock?'

'No, something much more stimulating. We're going in to support Gaunt. Select eight drivers and five spotters.'

'Five?' asked Wilder.

'The others will be you, me and the boy there.'

'Shit, commissar!' Wilder hissed. 'Gaunt's son? Really?'

'He needs to do something before his confidence withers and dies entirely,' said Blenner.

'Come on now!' he called to the bandsmen. 'Let's look like we know what we're doing. Perday? You'll be my driver.'

Felyx approached him.

'You want me for this?'

'It's just a little trip. You'll enjoy it. Something to do, Meritous.'

'I'll ride along,' said Maddalena.

'There's no room, so you can't. Sorry and all that. I'll bring him back in one piece. Promise.'

'No,' said Maddalena.

'Yes!' Felyx exclaimed.

'You are bound by Imperial Guard law,' Blenner told her. 'It was a basic condition of you remaining with this regiment. I know that as a fact. So I have authority and I'm exercising it. Go away. Let the boy do something today so that when it's all over he can look his father in the face without feeling ashamed.'

Maddalena Darebeloved stared at him. Her jaw was tight.

'I do not like you, Vaynom Blenner,' she said.

'They all say that at first,' he replied. He stared right back at her. 'My dear mamzel, if I worried about all the things in this fething galaxy that didn't like me, I'd never get out of bed in the morning.'

He turned away.

'Shall we go?' he asked.

CRIID SHONE HER lamp pack into the darkness overhead. Her clearance team had entered a vast cavern that seemed to be a natural formation because time and compression had crumpled the walls and ceiling so much. Micas and alloys glittered and wrinkled like rock. The deck beneath their feet was rusting plates forming a path across oil-stained rockcrete surfacing.

'Hold up,' Mklaek called out. He tuned the dial of his sweeper. 'It's mined,' he said. 'Under the floor plates.'

Banda wiped sweat from her forehead.

'Great,' she said. 'How do I shoot out the trigger, then?'

'Can we lift the plates up?' asked Leyr. 'Disable the mines manually?'

'That sounds like a gigantically bad idea,' said Criid.

'We go around then,' said Leyr. 'Off the path, onto the rockcrete.'

Mklaek shook his head.

'I'm getting nothing at all off the rockcrete. Too dense for a clear return. There could be filament charges or remote triggers that I'm just not picking up.'

Criid breathed deeply.

'So we find another way,' said Chiria, easing the weight of her flamer pack. 'Go back to that last junction, take the other spur.'

Banda put down her rifle and leaned against the cavern wall. She was trying to regulate her stress.

'Listen,' she said. 'You never mine an area you can't disarm. That's a scratch company basic rule.'

'That's not always true,' said Leyr.

Banda shrugged. 'All right. Maybe not on an open world where you've got the luxury of space. Space to go around. Space to detonate from a distance. But not here.'

She looked at Criid.

'Think about it, Tona,' she said. 'They wouldn't wire up a main route like this if they couldn't unwire it again later. In case they needed to. It stands to reason. They couldn't set this off safely to clear it. The concussion would blow right through the tunnels.'

Criid thought about it.

'Which means,' said Banda, 'these charges *must* be defusable. We can lift the plates.'

Mklaek nodded eagerly. 'Because they won't have pressure releases,' he said. 'They won't be triggered by weight coming off them. Just weight being applied.'

'Can you do it?' asked Criid.

Mklaek nodded again.

'It'll make a change from taking pot shots,' said Banda.

Criid looked at Chiria. 'Go back to the troop support and get them to back off at least fifty metres,' she said.

'That won't do any good if we set this off,' Chiria objected.

'It'll make me feel better,' snapped Criid. She looked at Banda and Mkleak.

'You're up,' she said.

They put on gloves and got down on their hands and knees. Mklaek slid the sweeper set alongside him as they crawled along, keeping an eye on the auspex unit.

'This is the first one,' he said, halting.

Criid and Leyr stood watching, intent.

Banda drew her warknife and fitted the tip of the blade under the edge of the corroded deck plate.

'Steady,' said Mklaek.

'Really?' Banda replied. 'I was just going to flip it up.'

Mklaek got right down so the side of his head was on the ground. The moment the plate lifted, even a finger width or less, he could see under it.

'Do it,' he said.

Banda began to lever up the edge of the plate. It was thick and very heavy, and the knife blade was polished so finely the plate looked in danger of slipping off it. She prised the edge of the plate up about two centimetres, and very quickly got three fingers under it before it fell back onto the pressure trigger.

'Throne alive,' muttered Leyr to Criid. 'I can't bear this.'

Banda swallowed, adjusted her grip, and slid the knife out. Mklaek still had his head pressed to the ground.

'Ready?' she asked.

He nodded.

She started to lift. It was heavy. She wouldn't be able to hold it for very long.

'Stop,' said Mklaek.

'What?' Banda asked. The plate was no more than three centimetres clear on the side she was lifting.

'Don't move it any higher,' said Mklaek.

'Oh right, just sit here? Holding it?'

'The underside is wired,' said Mklaek quietly. 'It's got a pull-away wire hooked to the trigger cap. Lift it any higher and it'll fire.'

'*Now* you tell me,' said Banda.

RAESS TOOK A sip of water from his flask. His throat was as dry as Jago. There was a soreness in his right arm that he didn't like.

'Fit?' asked Mktass.

'I'll do,' said Raess. He stoppered his flask, put it away, and got up. 'Where is it?'

Mktass's team had advanced into another engine room, a giant, rusting metal box full of rusting metal machines. It was the third in a row that they had slowly picked their way across. Preed speculated that they were all parts of a

ship, a shiftship, that had been compacted into the mass
of Salvation's Reach centuries before. It reminded them
of the corroding, jury-rigged hulks the greenskins used.
Every surface was a drab, flaking autumnal shade of rust.

They were coming out on a gantry halfway up the
height of the chamber. The gantry became a metal bridge
that stretched out to a hatch on the far side. Support was
from metal bars that descended from the ceiling. It was a
long way up and a long way down.

Brennan had swept the chamber and located an electrical source on the bridge, halfway along. The central
span was wired up to pressure plates under the approach
span. A major charge lurked under the bridge, secured
in a fuel barrel and lagged with swathes of oilskin sheet.

Raess chambered a round. He had officially lost count
of how many shots he'd taken that day.

'Line me up,' he told Preed.

The scout took out his scope and put the tagger beam
on the trigger mechanism, which stuck out of the bundle
under the bridge like a spigot.

'Got it?' Preed asked.

'Yes,' said Raess, setting his rifle scope.

Mktass waited behind them, with Sairus. Sairus had
turned his flame unit right down to the slowest rate.
Mktass glanced back to the troop element, waiting a
hundred metres back down the corridor. The Belladon
sergeant, Gorlander, at the head of the column, shot
Mktass a quick nod.

Brennan edged forwards beside the shooting team and
swept again. Just his weight and movement on the gantry made it stir and creak.

'Feth!' Mktass breathed.

Small scabs of rust fluttered down from the pins supporting the structural bars. Most of them billowed away
like dead leaves. Preed gently caught one of the largest
before it could land on the wired bridge span. He was
pretty sure it would have been too slight to activate the

pressure plate, but there was no sense tempting fate.

'Take your shot, please,' said Mktass.

Raess lined up.

'Wait,' said Brennan. His scope was showing something else. 'There's a second charge at the other end of the bridge. It's wired up to the same pressure pads as the first.'

'Feth,' Raess whispered.

'What do we do?' asked Preed.

Brennan took a deep breath, thinking.

'Take out the first as you were,' he said. 'Reload fast, take out the second. In between times, pray that the impact of the first shot doesn't throw the second trigger.'

Raess took out a second saline round and stood it on its brass base beside his knee.

'Line up both shots in advance,' he told Preed. 'We'll plug both sets of range parameters into our scopes so I can take the shot, load and switch to the second.'

Preed nodded.

Raess's palms were sweating.

THE BLAST HATCH was scarred and coated with dust, but it held power. Mkoll touched the release and raised his weapon as it whirred open.

Silence.

He took a step forwards, weapon still aimed. Bonin and Ezra were by his side, with Brostin just behind them.

Mkoll felt warmth on his face. Heated air, circulating, an atmospheric pump. There were pendant lights in wire cages hanging from the brushed metal ceiling of the hallway. Some were lit. Some were dead.

He stepped through the hatch. The hallway was ribbed. The wall panels, battered old slab-cut metal sheets, had been painted with crude yellow symbols that made him feel uneasy. He could smell foul biological waste, oil and heated metal. He could hear a generator chugging close by, and deeper more faraway sounds of major machines at work. Patches of the floor were scorched as if fires had been lit and left to go out. Piles of discarded junk, unidentifiable fragments of rubber and metal salvage, were heaped in the corners.

Bonin edged down to the first junction. Ezra checked the nearest doors. The metal swing doors opened into little stone cells, like a jail without locks, sleeping quarters, monastically simple and spare. There were dozens of them, and then others above them, accessed by makeshift metal ladders, and others above that; a honeycomb of cells that stretched away into the darkness of the roof space.

They advanced a little further. Gaunt had followed them through, trailed by Rawne and Varl and the pheguth.

Gaunt shot Mabbon a look. The etogaur nodded and pointed ahead.

Gaunt holstered his pistol and drew his sword. He signed for *silent approach*. The Ghosts slung their rifles over their shoulders and drew their blades.

Two figures emerged from a hatchway up ahead of them. They were soldiers in brown leather webbing and yellow coats. Sons of Sek. They paused to mutter at each other. They turned to head in different directions. Mkoll took one down with his knife, cradling the corpse all the way to the deck. Ezra put a reynbow quarrel through the spine of the other.

Gaunt approached and glanced at the bodies as Bonin checked the hatch the enemy troops had emerged from.

The Sons were big and corded with muscle built from punishing training regimes. They stank of spices and dust. Their uniforms were bleached faded Guard surplus, patched up and dyed yellow. The belts and leatherwork they wore were finely made and polished. Their weapons were freshly stamped lasrifles, probably from some hijacked forge world shipment heading for the front line.

The masks were curious, the helmet chinstraps ornately broadened to cover the mouth with a life-sized simulacrum of a human hand.

Gaunt looked again, more closely. The leather hand had fingernails. It wasn't a simulacrum. The ornate boots, belts, straps and other leatherwork worn by the Sons was tanned and cured from skinned victims or enemies.

Gaunt got up, and they moved on. The chambers felt like crypts. Wall paint was flaking and only half the light sources worked. There was a litter of junk and signs of scorching everywhere. Somehow, Gaunt had been imagining something more organised, something less like a slum or a derelict hive-hab occupied by vagrants.

All the metal surfaces flaked with rust, scabs of brown and black and yellow. Old wire braziers fluttered with open fires. Wires hung down from the galvanised metal ceiling frame.

They crossed a broad area like an open yard that was piled almost knee-deep with old, worn, faded and discarded rebreather masks. The cracked eye-slits seemed to stare at them. Then there was another bank of monastic cells, climbing like a cliff-face into the mangled junk vault of the chamber. A hatch opened into another hall. The space was filled with huge zinc baths, glass sinks, glass flagons and metal cooking pots. They were placed side by side on the floor, as if they had been arranged to catch drips from a leaking roof. All of the vessels, large or small, were filled to a greater or lesser extent with blood. The stink was terrible. Much of the blood was old, decomposing, clotted with rafts of mould and decay. Some of it seemed fresh.

Beyond that there were more of the monastic cells.

Leading the way, Bonin, Mkoll and Eszrah had silenced two more Sons along with some kind of robed official who was dressed like a hierophant. This creature's malnourished, pallid form, replete with tattoos, was wrapped in a crude wire-and-metal armature under his robes, a frame that seemed designed either to support him or torture him. The joints had chafed and cut his flesh. The frame reminded Gaunt a little of the wire-wolves of Gereon.

Gaunt glanced at Mabbon, quizzical.

A weaponwright, Mabbon wrote on his data-slate. Mabbon had told Gaunt that the weaponwrights were a fraternity of technical adepts who operated the Reach manufactories and had served the malign Heritor, Asphodel. They would now be serving a new Heritor, enabling him to function as Sek's principal arms provider. Their prowess was likened to the tech-priests of the Adeptus Mechanicus, though they relied far less on augmetic body modification and far more on esoteric and forbidden lore.

Gaunt nodded. He checked behind him. The troop element was advancing into the active section at their heels. Mkoll had made sure that the bodies of the Ghosts' kills were dragged out of sight and thrown in the cells.

Mkoll signalled. He and the scouts fanned out.

'These cells are where the weaponwrights rest and meditate,' Mabbon whispered to Gaunt. 'We are remarkably close to one of the main colleges. The *colleges of heritence.*'

'The manufactories?' Gaunt whispered back.

'Yes, but more like labs,' said Mabbon.

Mkoll returned.

'There is a suite of chambers up ahead,' he reported. 'An extensive complex. Bad light in there, a weird light. There are people at work, men like the one in the robes. Servitors too, but not like any I've seen. There's stuff there. Benches of it, shelves, alcoves. I saw artefacts, books, charts, data-slates.'

'That's the target,' Gaunt replied. 'Decide the order of attack. We need this to be discreet.'

'We'll never do it silently,' said Mkoll.

'Quietly, then, and quickly.' He looked back at Mabbon. 'Will there be defences? Things that we can't handle?'

Mabbon shook his head.

'Some of the things the weaponwrights craft here are so volatile they have to be kept inert for fear of interreaction. The Reach's principal defence has always been its inaccessibility.'

Gaunt looked over at Mkoll. The chief scout had finished briefing the men. He gave Gaunt the nod.

Gaunt signed *execute*.

Three prongs moved forwards, fast and quiet. Mkoll led one, Rawne the second and Bonin the third. They ran down a long, paved hallway with towering walls the colour of mud, and under the broken stained glass dome of a large circular chamber that rivalled many temples. The floor was littered with fire-burns and blackened rubbish. This area of the Reach had been deliberately designed and constructed. Compartments and rooms had been cut and dressed with stone, decks had been paved or bound in iron. On the walls, strange murals had been painted: abnormal views that were barely intelligible and curiously disturbing. They seemed to be views of alien landscapes or records of macabre ritual ceremonies. Gaunt felt as if they were invading a cathedral precinct, a cathedral precinct that smelled like a library and a machine shop and a latrine and that had been buried deep underground, lit by the ruddy glow of simmering lava.

The college of heritence was a trio of long, high halls, linked end to end, with a series of side chapels and annexes to either side. Its floor was hammered copper, and its walls were carved ivory inlaid with silver threads and bio-organic mechanisms. Strange objects stood in alcoves or on bench consoles. There were shelves of books and data-slates. Some of them had been chained down or welded shut. A vast and ornately carved bank of wooden pigeonholes along one wall contained millions of hand-numbered scrolls. Larger devices, some partly disassembled, lay in the side bays and machine-shop chambers, shrouded by mirror-glass screens and silk canopies. The copper floor was blanketed with junk and salvage, like a garbage dump.

The Ghosts rushed the area, entering from three sides. A weaponwright, his head braced and held painfully erect in a frame of wire and brass, lifted his gaze from the cogitator he was dismantling at a bench and looked at them. His fingers had been amputated and tools implanted in their place. Machine oil trickled out of the corner of his mouth.

'Voi shet jadhoj'k?' he asked, perplexed by the appearance of people he didn't recognise.

Mkoll put his dagger through the wretch's heart.

Other weaponwrights nearby, looking up from their study or delicate manufacture, were killed quickly with blades. Others got up, and made to run or cry out. The first shots were fired: quick bursts of las that cut robed figures down. Bonin hit one who fell and overturned his work bench. Delicate wirework creations, glassware and brass instruments crashed onto the copper floor. The acolytes and servitors assisting the weaponwrights were distressing confections of machine skeleton and grafted human meat, fused through an amalgam of augmetics and artificial tissue. The Ghosts shot them too. They died with shrill, squealing cries. Some tried to scurry away or raise the alarm. They fled in every possible direction through the long, bizarre halls of the college.

Strike Beta was thorough.

Several Sons of Sek appeared at the far end of the first hall, disturbed by the cries. Varl killed one, and Cardass clipped and then finished a second before serious gunplay could begin. A third ran for cover and began to return fire. His head vanished in a pink mist.

Larkin had made the shot from the main entry. He

hadn't even had time to take out his longlas and put away his rifle. He had simply slotted a hard round into the old gun's breech. Forty-three metres, a target moving into partial concealment.

'Who says I'm tired?' he muttered.

Inside five minutes, the Ghosts had the college area secure.

'They will now know we're here,' said Mabbon.

'Of course,' Gaunt noted.

'Simply from the cessation of activity and processed data,' Mabbon added. 'But with the primary raid going on, I'd say we have half an hour before they properly realise they have a second crisis on their hands.'

'Let's get to work,' said Gaunt. 'Mkoll, bring the transports up as close as they can come. Bring the empty crates in. Two squads. Rawne, set up a perimeter. Etogaur, tell us what to take, and how it should be correctly handled. The rest of it we burn. Then we get the feth out.'

'But we do burn it?' Brostin asked.

Gaunt nodded.

'Just checking,' said Brostin.

THE EIGHT TAUROS vehicles rumbled into lateral sixteen and drove through the bore hole into the Reach.

Inside, the rate was slower. They were following the route that Mkoll had marked out, picking up his chalk marks with their headlamps. The ship's artificers had moved in after the troops and cleared some areas, but space was still tight in places. Where devices had been secured, the drivers had to use extra care not to snag or disturb the packed explosives.

Blenner rode in the first Tauros. He felt the sweat on his back, smelled cold air and exhaust fumes. It was times like this, he thought to himself, when a bottle of sugar pill placebos just didn't cut it. Where was that nice medicae Curth when you needed her?

'Easy, easy,' he urged Perday. Her hands were clenched

on the wheel, her eyes wide with concentration and tension.

Two vehicles back, Felyx held onto the cabin cage with one hand and cradled his lasrifle in the other. The empty carry crates rattled in the back of the vehicle.

He was actually doing something, for the first time in his life. He was engaged in an activity that could lead anywhere, and that his mother couldn't absolutely control with her power and money.

Now it was happening, he wasn't sure exactly what he thought of it.

'MY ARM'S TOO big,' said Mklaek.

'That's fantastic,' Banda replied through gritted teeth. Sweat was beading her face. Her arms were beginning to shake through the strain. 'I can't hold this much longer, and I can't lift it any higher.'

'I just can't get my arm in under the plate far enough to reach the wire,' said Mklaek. He looked at Criid. There was panic in his eyes.

Criid got down on her knees beside Banda, pulled off her gloves and rolled her left sleeve up. Her arm was more slender than Mklaek's. She had a better chance than either Leyr or Chiria.

'What do I do?' she asked, gently sliding her hand in under the heavy metal plate.

'Find the wires,' said Mklaek, *without* pulling them out. Gently.' His hands were bunched tightly together, fingers interlocked, as if he was praying all the while he watched her.

'Go really slowly,' he implored her.

'I *am* going really slowly,' Criid replied, reaching further.

'Not too slowly,' Banda grunted. 'I can't do slowly.'

'Holy feth,' Leyr said to Chiria.

'I can't look,' said Chiria.

'I've got them. I've got wires!' Criid said. There was no

way to reach in and see what she was doing at the same
time. She was groping under the metal slab blind.

'All right,' said Mklaek, nodding. 'Trace them up to the
slab. Up. Do it really gently. You do not want to pull
anything out by accident.'

'All right,' said Criid. She bit her lower lip in
concentration.

'Don't follow the wires back to the firing cap,' said
Mklaek. 'Go up.'

'Yes, I understand what "up" means!' Criid said.

'Do any of you understand what "quickly" means?'
Banda gasped.

'I've got the wire,' said Criid. 'I've got it at the top,
where it meets the plate.'

'Is it soldered?' Mklaek asked.

'No, it's wound onto a metal terminal.'

'All right. Good. So, without pulling it, unwind the
wire and detach it.'

Staring at the deck, her arm in the hole, Criid grimaced. 'That's easier said than done. I can't get hold of
the end.'

'When we're done here,' murmured Banda, 'I've
decided to kill everybody.'

'If we don't do this right,' said Mklaek, 'that won't be
necessary.'

'I've got it,' Criid said. 'I've picked the strands loose.
Wait. Wait...'

She looked at them.

'It's off,' she said.

'Are there any other wires?' Mklaek asked.

'Oh, *what*?' cried Banda.

Criid gingerly felt around.

'No,' she said. 'No, there's– wait. No. No other wires.'

'Then we lift it off,' said Mklaek.

Criid drew her arm out. She and Mklaek got their fingers under the plate beside Banda.

'On three,' said Criid.

'Three,' said Banda.

They lifted.

As it came away, the deck plate exposed a dull grey anti-tank mine buried in soil beneath. A wire trailed from the pressure pin on the top.

They put the plate down on the path beside the hole.

'I have to make it safe,' said Mklaek, taking out a pair of pliers and kneeling beside the mine.

'I do not want to do that again,' said Criid.

RAESS FIRED. THE shot was perfect. The saline charge blew the firing cap assembly out of the device under the bridge span.

But the recoil also made the gantry shiver unpleasantly.

Preed lined the tagger up on the second trigger cap quickly. Raess scooped the waiting round up off the deck beside him and reloaded.

He reset his scope and locked on the point that Preed was tagging. His finger curled around the trigger, ready to squeeze.

Small flakes of rusty metal trickled down from overhead, disturbed by the recoil. Mktass caught one before it landed.

A second, no bigger than a rose petal, landed on the first span of the bridge.

'Oh f–' Mktass began.

The pressure switch clicked. The second charge, at the far end of the bridge, blew.

The force of the detonation instantly shredded the entire length of the bridge into rust particles and ignited the first charge. The combined blast lit the chamber like a supernova.

Mktass, Preed, Sairus, Brennan and Raess were simply atomised. Concussive pressure split the chamber walls and forced a titanic shockwave back down the access tunnel. The pressure blast liquidised Sergeant

Gorlander and the troop element waiting in the passageway behind them.

The rushing, sucking fireball that squirted up the tunnel incinerated the pulped remains a millisecond later.

TWENTY-ONE
Salvation Lost

THE CONVOY OF Tauros vehicles had reached the inner hatch that led into the occupied section of the Reach. Blenner, Wilder and their team stood guard by the vehicles. Gaunt had sent troops back from the college to collect the carry crates and begin the extraction of sensitive materials.

Wilder was pacing.

'Calm down,' Blenner told him, but only because the pacing was making him feel more tense himself. They were exposed, literally right on the doorstep of the enemy holding. The smells of squalid decay and putrefaction coming out of the hatch were horrifying.

He looked at Felyx. The boy was standing by the tail board of his vehicle, watching the dark cavities around them for movement. He was holding his weapon too tightly.

Blenner tried to think of something encouraging to say, but he had used up all his banter on Perday on the ride in.

The bang made them jump. The ground shuddered.

Pressure shock popped their ears so hard many of them cried out and dropped their guns.

A second later, they felt the rush of hot wind come at them down the tunnel, and smelled the grit and fyceline.

'Damnation,' said Blenner. 'What just happened?'

MERRT WAS LINING up to take a shot when the ground shook. They all felt it. Pieces of junk trickled down from the roof. The distant boom came a second later and then, like a feverish sigh, the rush of burned air.

The team members looked at each other.

'Feth,' said Vahgner.

'Somebody just got unlucky,' said Daur.

IT WAS LIKE a grenade going off behind them. A violent tremor ripped through the floor, and a shockwave of noise, heat and pressurised air slammed through the chamber into them. Criid, Banda and Leyr were all knocked over. Somehow Chiria kept her feet.

They all knew what it was. They knew instantly. One of the other clearance teams had set something off. It was close by, too. Who? Mktass's bunch? Mkoll's?

It was the noise, the blink of annihilation, that they had been dreading all day, the thing they had been braced for, the thing they had been yearning and willing not to happen.

It hadn't happened to them. Someone else had got unlucky. It hadn't happened to them.

But it might as well have done.

Mklaek had been in the process of removing the firing pin from the floor mine they had finally exposed. Keeping his hand as still as possible, he had been lifting the pin he had unscrewed clear of the socket, slowly and cleanly, making sure no extra wires were attached. Criid was rolling her sleeve back down and putting her gloves back on. Banda was trying to flex life into her fingers and arms from holding the deck plate.

He had been a millimetre or so away from lifting it clear when the blastwave hit them.

'Mklaek?' Criid cried, getting up.

Mklaek was prone on the deck, belly down, his face over the anti-tank mine. His hand was on the trigger pin, still holding it. The blast had made him touch it against the rim of the socket. He didn't dare move. He didn't dare break the contact.

'Mklaek?' Criid repeated. She and the others moved towards him.

'Don't come any closer,' he hissed, trying not to move. 'Don't come any closer. Run. Get the detachment running.'

'Feth that!' said Banda.

'I'm not kidding!' Mklaek whispered, his eyes wide. 'Run, you stupid bastards! Run now. I think this has gone live! I think it's live and I can't hold it forever. Run!'

'No way–' Criid began.

'Run!' Mklaek rasped, almost a wail of desperation.

They looked at each other.

'We can't–' Criid began.

Leyr and Banda grabbed her and bundled her towards the passageway behind them. They started running, Chiria too, labouring with the weight of the flamer tank. The troop detachment saw them coming and needed no encouragement to turn and run as well. They fled down the tunnel, full sprint. Leyr and Banda had to virtually drag Criid.

Mklaek held on for as long as he could. When his fingers finally began to give out, he lifted the pin away from the socket.

Nothing.

'The Emperor protects,' he murmured, tears of relief in his eyes.

The tank mine exploded.

* * *

THEY FELT THE detonation rather than heard it. The copper flooring of the college hall shivered. The lamps rattled and stirred.

Gaunt turned to look at Mkoll, and as he did so they both felt the pressure shift of air passing through the chamber. Gaunt could taste the heat and the dry stink of explosives.

'That was big,' he said.

Mkoll didn't reply. He knew they'd just lost someone. A lot of people, probably. Perhaps that had been the sound of them losing the fight, the mission, and everything they'd come for.

Bonin came in.

'That came up the tunnels,' he said. 'One of the disposal teams made a misstep.'

'Which one?' asked Rawne.

Bonin shook his head.

'If we felt it here–' said Gaunt.

'Sir?'

Gaunt turned. With Varl guarding him, Mabbon had gone over to one of the control panels wired into the wall of the college chamber. Behind a dingy glass panel, a strip of stained paper was scrolling through a chart recorder, six claw-like, spring-loaded arms leaving scratchy lines on the graph.

'It's a motion recorder,' said Mabbon. 'They're commonplace. The magirs and etogaurs of the facility will have detected it.'

They felt another smaller but definite thump through the ground. The graphing arms recorded a sudden and steep spike.

'Another one?' said Gaunt.

'Available time just reduced considerably,' said Mabbon. 'No matter what is happening on the main approach, your enemy will now be sending units to investigate.'

Gaunt strode back to Rawne and Mkoll.

'Strengthen the perimeter,' he said. 'I want to know the moment they arrive.'

Members of the troop detachment were bringing in the first of the empty carry boxes.

'Let's get these filled. Quickly,' said Gaunt. He glanced back at Mabbon.

'Take everything you can,' said Mabbon. 'Papers, books, document cases, tubes, data-slates. Use gloves. Seal the boxes when they're full.'

'Don't sort,' said Gaunt. 'In fact, don't even look at what you're grabbing. The Inquisition can worry about decoding and understanding it all. We've just got to deliver. Pick it up, ship it out, move on to the next box. Anything you're not sure about, leave it or ask me.'

'Come on,' said Domor, clapping his hands. 'Grab and go.'

Gaunt took an empty box, moved to some dirty metal shelves, and began to take the pamphlets and books off it. He could smell book mould and damp. Some of the page edges had stuck to the metal. He took each handful and packed it into the box, filling it neatly and efficiently, the way his father had taught him to pack a foot locker.

He never imagined he'd be handling this sort of material. It was his imagination, no doubt, but his flesh tingled despite the gloves. What were they disturbing? How were they being contaminated? This stuff had power. This knowledge, this *learning*, it had a potency of its own. The books, the bindings, the materials used, the very words, dictated through the warp by lisping, gleeful, inhuman voices. Under any other circumstances, they would have been burning the stuff.

He moved to another rack. Scroll cases. The tubes were made of the same nut-brown, glossy leather as the belts and straps of the Sons of Sek. He knew what it was. He kept packing anyway.

The box was full. He closed the lid, secured it with

the straps, and turned to hand it off in exchange for a fresh one.

Felyx Chass was offering him the empty box.

'What are you doing here?' Gaunt asked, biting back his alarm and managing to keep his voice low.

'Following orders, sir,' said Felyx.

'What orders?'

'Conveyance transport duty, sir,' the boy said. His face was pale.

'Take this crate back to the transports. Load it securely. Come back for another one,' said Gaunt.

'Yes, sir.'

'Are you all right?'

Felyx nodded.

'In duty we find true fulfilment, sir.'

'That's Ravenor,' said Gaunt.

'I took the liberty of reading some,' said Felyx.

Gaunt handed the sealed crate over.

'Get moving,' he said. 'We've got to go quickly.'

Felyx hurried towards the exit with the box. Gaunt picked up the empty carton he'd left behind.

'You look troubled,' said Mabbon. Gaunt turned. Mabbon had wandered over to him. Varl and the other Suicide Kings were busy packing boxes and watching the outer exits.

'This is a precarious situation,' said Gaunt. 'We prepared for so long, and invested such effort, and now we're here... I'm not sure it's worth it. We're stealing secrets that we don't want to hear, and laying the blame on another.'

'I see,' said Mabbon. 'I thought you might just be worried about your son.'

Gaunt narrowed his eyes.

'You leave him alone.'

Mabbon raised his chained wrists.

'I'm not in a position to do anything to anyone.'

'How did you know?'

Mabbon's face was impassive.

'I hear things. I don't get much opportunity to do anything except listen. I am not regarded as human, colonel-commissar. People talk around me as though I'm not there. They gossip to pass the time when they guard me. I could tell you all sorts of things about your Ghosts. I choose not to, because it would be impertinent and inappropriate, and I have no desire to damage the fragile relationship between us. On this occasion, I was merely expressing concern for you because I respect you.'

Gaunt was silent. Then he nodded and began packing the second box.

'I worry that we're tainting ourselves. Just handling this material, bringing it back to the *Armaduke*...'

'That is simple paranoia, sir,' said Mabbon. 'Perfectly understandable. As I explained, the material in the college is inert. It is simply data. Oh, some of it is fairly unpleasant – records of abominations, atrocities – but it is not toxic of itself. It can be handled and removed quite safely.'

Gaunt began to put bundles of old data-slates into the box.

'Would you like me to help?' asked Mabbon.

'I'd prefer it if you didn't touch anything.'

Mabbon nodded.

'There are,' he said, 'other areas, crypts and vaults not far from the colleges of heritence, but kept separate, where true evil lurks. They contain artefacts. Devices. Books that need to be weighed down and chained, and which can only be read with surgically adapted eyes. Those are the things you need to avoid. Even the weaponwrights and the servants of the Heritor treat those with care. The warp is in them. But the Imperium is so afraid of the influence of the Ruinous Powers, it chooses to ignore vast amounts of data like this – data that is perfectly sound and reliable – and thus blinds itself to its enemy.'

'I understand the brief,' said Gaunt. 'That's why I supported the proposal. That's why I volunteered my regiment. The removal and review of this material will give us insight into enemy operations that most likely will shift the course of the Crusade. If we cripple this facility, we also deprive the Archenemy of a vital resource.'

'Even those two fine reasons are secondary to our goal,' replied Mabbon.

'Sir!'

Gaunt looked around. Sergeant Ewler had found something. Gaunt and Mabbon went over to him. Ewler and two other Ghosts, all of them with half-packed crates, were standing in the doorway of one of the college hall's annexes, a small circular room lined with wooden shelves. There was a brass display case and analysis console in the centre of the floor.

'These aren't books, sir,' said Ewler. 'Do we take them too?'

Gaunt looked around the shelves. There were small objects everywhere, individually boxed in wooden frames, or stoppered in specimen flasks, like catalogued museum items: small ikons, pieces of technology, idols, figurines, amulets, strange items of jewellery, ritual athames, wands and beakers, playing cards, samples of powders and compounds, fragments of bone and fossil, pots of liquid. Gaunt saw a few old Imperial medals, a broken aquila, an Inquisitorial rosette, some pieces of augmetic and Imperial tech that he could not identify. He saw items that seemed unmistakably eldar in origin, and the blunt teeth and fetishes of greenskins.

'Do we take this?' he asked the prisoner.

'Take it all if it's portable,' said Mabbon. 'A great deal of the material here comes from salvage efforts in the Reach. The weaponwrights plunder the debris field, harvesting material from a thousand cultures and a billion years. There are several more side chambers like this. Strip them all, along with the written material.'

'Do it,' said Gaunt.

Ewler and his men started to clear the shelves.

Mabbon had crossed to the central display stand.

'Look here,' he said.

Gaunt went over to him.

Inside the glass-topped case lay eight damaged stone tablets. Each one was about the size of a data-slate, and they had been cut from a heavy, gleaming red rock. All of the tablets were chipped, and one had a significant piece missing. They were covered with inscribed markings, a language that Gaunt had never seen before.

'These are important,' said Mabbon. 'We must take them.'

'Why?'

'I remember them being brought in, years ago. They were found at another site. One of the Khan Worlds, I believe. Xenos script, very old. The weaponwrights were very taken with them. They considered them to be important. They described them as the Glyptothek. A library in stone.'

'Then we'll take them for Imperial savants to study,' said Gaunt.

'Good,' said Mabbon. 'Look where they are.'

'In that case, you mean?'

'They're being studied. See? The analysis devices. The transcriber? This alcove was the workplace of a senior weaponwright. A *magir hapteka*. He was concentrating his studies on this.'

'Your point?'

'Think about it. These objects were brought in years ago, and were considered significant then. They're still under close and detailed examination. They are important.'

Mabbon looked at Gaunt. His eyes were fierce.

'Your Emperor must be with us today. Your Emperor or your beati. In the act of undertaking this mission, he has led us to a discovery of singular value.'

'Maybe,' said Gaunt. 'I'm not convinced, but we'll remove them too.'

He nodded to Ewler, who opened the case and packed the stones into his crate one by one. Gaunt watched for a moment, and then went to the analysis console. It was a battered but recognisable Imperial cogitator. Gaunt pulled out his data-slate and connected it to the console's memory socket. He began to export the console's archived data. The screen of the slate flickered as information flowed into it.

He'd almost finished when the first shots rang out at the far end of the college precinct. A few single blasts at first, then sustained fire.

Mkoll appeared in the doorway of the annexe.

'Sons of Sek. Full order, eight companies, moving this way to secure the college,' he said.

Gaunt drew his bolt pistol.

'Deny them,' he said.

BASKEVYL LOBBED A grenade around the hatch and stood aside.

There was a hard bang and two cult fighters were thrown headlong into the open in a spurt of debris and smoke.

Baskevyl swung back into the doorway and fired his lasrifle into the smoke. He spotted two other cult fighters, dazed and bloody from the grenade, and cut them down before they could react.

On the far side of the hatch was a machine bay and a loading ramp. Baskevyl killed another fighter on his way down, and then came under fire from a fireteam of Sons.

Gansky's squad was moving up to his left. They covered the fire team with rifle fire and drove them back from behind a row of punctured, dented fuel drums. Baskevyl reached for another grenade, and realised he'd just used his last.

'Flamer!' he yelled.

'Waiting for refill tanks, sir,' Karsk shouted back.

'Damn,' Baskevyl muttered. They'd advanced, hard and fast, behind the Space Marine assault, but the Archenemy forces had native knowledge of the facility's layout and kept striking at them from the flanks, weaving their way through the complex and cluttered geography of the depots and engineering spaces. The Sons of Sek had laced Salvation's Reach with sally ports, false walls, blind hatches and artificial dead ends. The junk architecture of the ramshackle site was working to the enemy's advantage, allowing them to sidestep, double-back and ambush.

It was costing the Tanith First men, and the munition expenditure was immense. Baskevyl didn't think they'd ever lit off so much firepower in such a short space of time. The lighters had just jockeyed back in with a second ammunition restock.

The Sons fireteam had found new cover and was firing at a steady rate. Baskevyl hoped they didn't have any grenades, or fresh throwing arms.

A sudden burst of lasfire split the air from above. Baskevyl glanced up to see that Dalin's squad had found a way up onto a raised gantry. They had an almost unobstructed view of the Sons' position, and were making best use of it. Nine of the Sons of Sek died where they stood. Two more broke and ran, and Baskevyl's squad knocked them flat.

In the middle distance, a series of hefty explosions tore across the compartment, knocking down several cargo-lift gantries. Brother-Sergeant Eadwine and his weapon servitors had finally vanquished and destroyed a grotesque and ugly war construct, something that scuttled along on black wire like an arachnid as it fired its belly-slung lascannons. Baskevyl heard some of the Vervunhivers describe it as a 'woe machine'. It wasn't the first one they'd seen that day, and the Vervunhivers claimed it was like a small version of the constructs they'd fought during the Zoican War.

Huge flames sprayed up from the dying machine, scorching the compartment roof. Eadwine was already moving on. From his position, Baskevyl could still see the White Scar fighting his way forwards, but he'd lost track of the Iron Snake.

Kolea's company began moving up alongside him. They'd brought fresh rockets and grenades with them, and at least four re-tanked flamers.

A shout went up. Two more large woe machines had rattled into view, supported by light stalk tanks and a detachment of Sons of Sek. They had come in through a bulk hatch from a derelict hangar and were punching the Ghosts back with the speed of their strike.

Kolea and Baskevyl called their tread-feathers up, and began to advance through the jumbled yards of the machine shop to get a better angle on the deadly constructs. Baskevyl could hear the chugging crack and whicker of their heavy guns. Something was on fire, weeping a curtain of thick, black smoke across the yards. Dalin's squad switched to dealing with an enemy sniper who was taking potshots over the line of advance.

Kolea and Baskevyl reached an archway, hoping it would give them a good shot at the woe machines, but the sound of heavy gunfire had stopped. There was no sign of the lumbering machines or their support.

'Where have they gone?' asked Kolea.

Several runners arrived, bringing reports of a significant fall-away in the enemy resistance. Sons of Sek units had been seen breaking off and retreating.

'Could they have been pulled back deliberately?' asked Baskevyl. 'Redirected?'

Kolea looked at him. He didn't like where Bask was going.

'I think it's possible they've just discovered they've got a more vital problem to deal with,' Baskevyl said with a shrug.

'How would they know that?' asked Kolea.

'Sensors? Detectors? Plain bad luck?' Baskevyl suggested. 'Maybe Gaunt's forces have got right inside, and it's kicked off? We can't know.'

'If they know what we're doing,' murmured Kolea, 'they know we're just the sound and fury. They'll know what's really at stake.'

He called to the nearest runner.

'Get to a vox,' he said. 'Signal the *Armaduke*. Message reads "Enemy may be aware of the secondary strike forces. Strike Beta and Strike Gamma must, repeat, must make ready for serious assault. The enemy knows what the target is." Got that?'

'Yes, major.'

'Then run.'

THE SONS OF Sek threw themselves at the college of heritence. They came up in squads a dozen strong, armed with lasrifles and hellguns. Officers carried long, curved swords. They advanced out of the maze of inner tunnels and chambers that made up the Reach facility and fired rifle grenades at the doors and windows of the college to unseat the Imperial force. Stained glass exploded in glittering fragments. Fire took hold of ancient benches and shelving. Lamps fluttered and went out.

Under Gaunt's direction, the Strike Beta detachment used what cover they could: the bulkheads and shelves, the annexes, the heavier metal desks and benches, and set up resistance fire.

Sons officers, yelling in brisk, curt accents, sent howling cult fighters forwards ahead of the battle troops to soak up the fire. The bodies of these poor wretches began to pile up around the outer steps and hatchways of the college precinct. Well back from the fighting line, Mabbon watched grimly.

They were exactly the tactics he would have employed.

'How much longer?' Gaunt asked Blenner.

His old friend paused, lugging a carry crate that he was taking back to the transports.

'How long is an Imperial crusade?' he replied. 'We've cleared a little over half the rooms. Quite a quantity of stuff. If we gather too much more, we'll have to send back for more transports.'

'Keep going for now,' said Gaunt. 'Get as much as you can.'

'Maybe two dozen or so crates before the last Tauros is full,' said Wilder.

'Good. Do it,' said Gaunt.

'Could we not just leave?' asked Blenner. 'Leaving sounds like a wise tactical move.'

'Like bringing my son here?' asked Gaunt.

Blenner snorted, and started emptying another case of shelves into a fresh crate.

Gaunt moved forwards, into the part of the college where the fighting had intensified. He passed Kolding, who was patching up three Ghosts caught in the opening gunplay.

He saw Eszrah Ap Niht.

'Histye,' Gaunt said. 'Watch over my son.'

Eszrah nodded, and melted into the shadows.

Gaunt heard ugly animal noises over the heavy gunfire ahead of him. He ducked in beside Varl.

'What is that?' he asked.

'Feth knows,' Varl replied, slapping in a fresh cell. 'They're bringing things in. Animals. Like packs of dogs on leashes, but–'

'But what?'

'I think they made them, sir. I think they sewed these things together, stitched them from parts of different creatures. And humans.'

Mabbon had mentioned a fascination with surgical and genetic experimentation amongst some of the Reach's weaponwrights.

Something was scratching and pawing at the doors

and hatches. Gaunt could hear claws and hooves. He could hear whining voices and throbbing growls. He could hear human mouths making pitiful animal sounds.

Part of a wall blew in. Sons of Sek charged at them through the smoke, scrambling over the rubble, trying to capitalise on the hole they'd made.

Gaunt got up to meet them, scything his power sword around, taking off a head. He blew another Son off his feet with a bolt round, painting the rubble and the ceiling with blood from the detonation. Varl was beside him, shooting point-blank and stabbing with his bayonet. In a second, two more Suicide Kings – Cardass and Nomis – had reached them, firing single shots at selected targets. Gaunt ripped in with his sword, carving a path through the troops to face the officer, a massive brute with a power axe.

'Drive them back. Plug the hole!' Gaunt yelled.

Varl was too busy taking headshots to make a sarcastic reply.

Gaunt reached the officer. The axe swept at him, but he blocked it with his sword and levered the Archenemy warrior back a step or two. Gaunt had to duck the next chopping swing. He struck with the sword, ripping open the officer's left thigh. Then, as the officer lurched forwards in pain at the injury, he tore his torso open with a massive upswing cut.

Twenty metres away, through the smoke, Ezra bundled Meritous Felyx Chass away from the breach. Felyx tried to shake off the firm grip of the mysterious heathen. He could see his father, the fabled People's Hero, the man he had heard stories about since he was old enough to understand them. He could see him fighting, outnumbered, a determined blur with gleaming sword, spraying the walls with blood, cutting and slicing.

Felyx watched for a second, wide-eyed. He realised that, when all was said and done, there was precious little difference between being a hero of the people of the Imperium and being a ruthless, brutal killing machine. To be the former, one had to accept much of the role of the latter.

'Come, soule,' Ezra whispered.

'I need to help,' Felyx began, pulling away and trying to get his lasrifle off his shoulder.

Ezra didn't reply. He picked Felyx up as if he were one of the carry crates ready for removal and strode towards the exit.

Varl switched to full auto, smacking two Sons and two cult fighters back out of the breach. Their bodies fell across the dust-swirled rubble. Cardass tossed a grenade out through the gap that exploded amongst the enemy squads still trying to force their way in. Gaunt joined Varl and Nomis at the top of the rubble, firing out into the smoke and darkness. Bayonet bloody, Rawne joined them.

'Our options are limited,' he said. 'Our position here is narrow, just the hall area. They're coming at us on three sides. We can't overlap fire, or lay down anything to protect the right flank.'

'Those windows?' asked Gaunt.

'Too high,' said Rawne.

'Get ready to pull out, then,' said Gaunt. 'I don't think we'll be staying here much longer.'

'If we stay much longer, it'll be permanent,' said Rawne.

A cry went up outside the college wall. A huge force of Sons bayonet-charged the main hatch, firing as they came. The Ghosts barricading the main door and the side annexes were driven back, heads down. A storm of lasbolts tore through the hatchway and ripped apart benches and consoles. Gaunt saw two Ghosts cut down. He cursed.

Their grip on the college precinct, tenuous to begin with, had slipped entirely. The Sons of Sek were upon them so tightly, there wasn't even a possibility of disengaging.

VAHGNER BECKONED THEM on. The tunnel network Daur's clearance team had penetrated was a jumbled mix of stonework and rusted metal.

'Can you hear that?' asked Vahgner.

They stopped and listened, weapons ready.

'Gn... gn... gn... fighting,' said Merrt.

Daur nodded. Through the thickness of stone and compressed void junk ahead, they could hear the sounds of a serious firefight. Salvos of gunfire, lasweapons, grenade bursts.

'I think someone's got there first,' said Haller. He grinned. 'Should we lend them a hand?'

Daur wiped his mouth, thinking hard. Hark and the troop detachment hadn't yet caught up with his team. What good could the five of them do, even with a flamer?

Some good, he decided. Maybe *just enough*. The biggest fight often turned on the smallest margin. They'd go in. Hark couldn't be that far behind.

Vahgner brought his rifle up. Something was moving ahead of them. Something was skittering in and out of the rubble and junk piles that filled their path. It was getting closer.

The something lurched into view. It bounded towards them, with a long, loping gait. It was a dog, a big hound of some sort, a bloodhound perhaps. Its tan coat was shaved very short, and it wore a thick, spiked collar. It stopped and stared at them.

It sniffed, drool leaking from its loose black lips.

Its coat was not short. It had no coat. Now they saw it properly, they realised it was just bare flesh. There were suture marks around the spine and some of the major muscle groups. It was skeletally canine, but had a human skull, with face attached, had been grafted onto the thick neck.

Its eyes were white and dead. It whined.

Vahgner killed it.

'What the sacred feth was that?' he asked Daur.

Vahgner's blood spattered Daur's face. The scout fell backwards, dead, his head destroyed by a las round.

Sons of Sek came out of the darkness past the body of their slain creature. There were a dozen of them, firing rifles and pistols.

Haller dropped his sweeper and reached for his rifle. A shot clipped his shoulder and threw him into the wall. Daur returned fire, cutting down two of the attackers with a fierce burst. Merrt fired almost instinctively, crippling a Son with a saline charge he had loaded. A second later, he felt searing pain. A sledgehammer of momentum hit him in the chest and knocked him over.

'Get back!' Belloc yelled. 'Get him back!'

His flamer gouted a spear of flame down the passage, torching one of the Sons. The man lit up and ran, consumed with white flames, into the passageway wall. Belloc fired again, filling the passageway with a hot orange light. A shot blew his throat out in a spray of blood. He staggered backwards and a round went into his chest, another into his hip and a final one into his eye. He fell on his back, his flamer gasping and flaring spurts of untrained fire.

Haller got up, bleeding, firing his laspistol.

'Get Merrt!' Daur yelled. 'Get Merrt! Drag him back!'

Merrt was staring at the ceiling, his eyes wide, his augmetic jaw opening and closing uselessly. His chest was a bloody mess.

'Get him!' Daur yelled. He turned to fire again, and las rounds found him too.

TWENTY-TWO
Departures

'BAN! BAN!' HALLER yelled, firing wildly. He couldn't even reach Daur. He could see that his friend had been hit badly. Daur wasn't moving.

Haller also knew there was no way he was going to hold off a Sons of Sek assault on his own with just a pistol.

The enemy charged him. A piercing plasma weapon beam blew the leading officer apart. Lasfire ripped in, cutting down several of the others. The gunfire was coming from behind Haller. He ducked down. The las and plasma fire streaked over his head, punishing the Sons, driving them back down the tunnel.

Hark appeared, plasma gun in hand. The rest of the Strike Gamma detachment came up after him.

'Emperor damn it, Haller,' Hark said, looking in dismay at the fallen men. 'Decide to start without us, did you?'

'They just came at us,' Haller replied.

'Medic!' Hark yelled. Dorden came forwards. He groaned sadly at the sight that greeted him, and knelt

down to examine Daur and Merrt. Vahgner and Belloc
were way past saving.

'We can hear fighting up ahead,' Haller told Hark.
'Captain Daur was pretty sure that Strike Beta has
engaged. It sounds like they're in the thick of it.'

'We'll move up to support,' said Hark. He looked at
Dorden. 'How long, doctor?'

'Move ahead,' said Dorden, busy. 'I've got my hands
full here.'

'I'm not leaving you,' said Hark.

'Well, I'd also prefer it if you didn't carry two critically injured men into a fight with you. Let me patch
them up. If you can spare Haller, we'll move them back
down the tunnel as soon as they're stable.'

Hark looked at Haller.

'All right with you?'

Haller nodded.

'Get them to safety,' Hark said. He leaned closer to
Haller. 'All three of them, all right?' he whispered.

He stepped back.

'Well done,' he said. 'You've opened the way up for
us. Strike Gamma? Ready weapons. Look lively! We're
advancing against hostiles.'

There was a clatter of weapons.

'Forwards!' Hark ordered. The troops began to file
past. Hark looked back at Haller.

'Get done here and get back. I'll see you on the other
side.'

'Good luck, commissar,' said Haller.

'The Emperor protects.'

Haller watched as Hark's force moved out of sight
then he clambered over to Dorden.

'Can we move them?' he asked.

'What's wrong with your shoulder, Haller?' Dorden
asked.

'It got shot. It's nothing. Can we move them?'

'Not yet. Maybe soon.'

'Can you save them?'

Dorden looked at Haller. In the dim, twitching light cast by Belloc's fallen flamer, his eyes seemed fathom-less. He was exhausted. He couldn't pretend any more

'I don't know, Haller. I can't even save myself. Merrt's chest wound is severe. His heart is damaged. Daur is... who am I kidding, Daur's critical too. An infirmary is their best chance. An infirmary and a better medicae.'

'You're the best doctor w–'

Dorden shook his head.

'Hush, Haller. I can barely walk. My hands are weak and clumsy. I am so tired and addled with pain-suppressing drugs I forget basic techniques. The ridiculous sentiment and affection of men like Gaunt and Hark has allowed me to continue serving long past my competence. I shouldn't be here, Haller. Hark should have seconded a medic from the ship's crew. He was humouring the last wishes of an old, dying fool.'

'That's not true,' Haller replied.

'Trust me, Haller. I forced my way into this because I wanted to matter one last time. I'm an old man and I should have known better–'

'Stuff it. You know what you're doing. All the while you've been spilling out that self-pity, you've been working. You know what you're doing. Tell me what I can do. Compression or something. Let's get them fixed and get them out. *Now.*'

'WE'RE NOT GOING to hold them off much longer!' Mkoll yelled, firing out of the college's main hatchway.

'I can see that,' Gaunt replied, loading another clip of ammunition into his pistol.

Rawne appeared beside them, standing against the corner of the wall, firing his rifle. Las rounds whined past them or blew chrome punctures in the rusted metal.

'This turned out so well,' he murmured.

'If we can break their onslaught, just for a few minutes, we can pull out,' Gaunt said.

'Have you seen how many of them there are outside?' Rawne retorted. 'It's like the whole fething habitat is trying to kill us!'

'Rawne's right,' said Mkoll. 'If we're going to break off, some of us have to stay here to cover the rest.'

'No,' said Gaunt.

'Last ditch,' Mkoll said.

'Suicide Kings,' said Rawne.

'No. To both of you,' snapped Gaunt.

'Then this mission is going to fail,' said Rawne.

The Sons of Sek threw themselves at the college precinct with renewed fury. They had brought up rockets, and heavier, crew-served guns. Gaunt tried to assess numbers through the smoke. Everything was about to end, and very rapidly.

'Remember Tanith!' a voice boomed across the concourse outside the college hatchway. Gaunt watched in disbelief as concentrated small-arms fire smacked into the Sons' deployment from the right. Despite their superior numbers, the Sons seemed wrong-footed by the counter-assault. Half of their advance positions were suddenly exposed to the side.

'It's Strike Gamma!' Varl yelled.

'Daur?' asked Gaunt.

'I don't see him,' said Domor. 'I see Commissar Hark. They're coming out of the vents down there.'

'Keep firing!' Gaunt yelled. 'Use this! Hit them hard while they're reeling.'

'Yes, sir,' said Rawne.

Gaunt scrambled back from the hatchway. He looked at Blenner and Wilder.

'The last of the transports are loaded,' said Wilder. 'Everything we can carry.'

'Get moving. Get back to the ship. We'll follow on foot.'

Wilder nodded. He and Blenner turned.

'Signal the *Armaduke*,' Gaunt called to Blenner. 'Begin withdrawal now.'

'Understood,' said Blenner.

DALIN CAME RUNNING through the debris field to the spot where Kolea and Fazekiel were in cover.

'We're ready for the next advance,' said Kolea. He pointed. 'Through those hatches there, into the yards on the far side, and–'

'No, sir,' said Dalin. He handed Kolea a slip of paper. 'Just received by Rerval. We've been given the order to disengage and pull out.'

Kolea studied the piece of paper. He handed it to Fazekiel.

'It's authentic,' said the commissar.

'All right,' said Kolea. 'Contact all section and company leaders. The order is disengage and fall back. Systematic, just like we trained. Fall back by unit, covering fire. No unnecessary risks. No one rushing for the transports. Any charges, explosives, grenades left, use them to good effect. Bring the place down behind you if you can.'

Dalin and Fazekiel nodded.

'Get the order spread quickly,' said Kolea.

BASKEVYL FIRED A couple of shots at some cult fighters dug in ahead of his position.

'We've got the word, Bask,' Kolosim yelled. 'Pull back!'

'Because we have to or because we're done?' asked Baskevyl.

'Let's hope it's the latter,' yelled Kolosim.

'TIME TO GO,' said Gendler.

Meryn tipped his head back and blew out a deep breath.

'You sure?' asked Costin.

Gendler ignored him.

'You sure?' asked Meryn.

'Word just got passed up the line,' said Gendler. 'We're out of this shit-fix.'

'Suits me,' said Meryn. In the last half an hour, the enemy strength had depleted a little. Things weren't as hellish as they had been right after the drop, but they were still pretty bad. A steady stream of fire was coming their way, and Kolea had ordered his company to take a particularly inaccessible storage area.

Meryn could smell sour milk and crushed mint. He had no intention of taking any storage area. E Company had sat down on their arses and dug in for the last ten minutes, claiming to be waiting for restock before following the order to assault.

'Let's go then,' Meryn said. 'E Company, out now! Fast! Head for the transports. Move your scrawny arses!'

'Orders said something about systematic retreat and covering fire,' said Gendler. He looked at Meryn. They both snorted with laughter.

Costin tried to join in too, faking a laugh.

'Shut the feth up,' said Meryn.

They began to back off, scrambling over the smouldering wreckage and heaped debris in the direction of the hangar bays and the drop site.

MERRT COULD WALK, very slowly, with Dorden supporting him and using the autorifle as a walking stick. His skin was sallow from blood loss. Each step he took was a massive effort. Daur was still unconscious; Haller was obliged to carry him. Every ten metres or so, Haller put his friend down to rest his arms.

'Maybe we should wait for Hark's squad to come back this way and help us,' said Dorden.

'What if they don't?' asked Haller through gritted teeth. 'You heard that fighting. Like the West Wall at Vervunhive.'

'You're right, you're right,' said Dorden. He was

behind Haller, so Haller couldn't see how sick he was or how badly he was faltering. Already tired and wrung out, the effort of supporting Merrt was sapping the last dregs of Dorden's strength.

Merrt was ailing too. He slumped against the passage wall, dropping his rifle. Dorden tried to help him slide down to the ground without further damaging himself. Blood welled up over the lip of his augmetic jaw.

'Gn... gn... gn... can't do it,' Merrt whispered.

'You can,' said Dorden. 'You can, Rhen.'

Merrt shook his head.

'Get him up, doc!' Haller urged.

'He needs a moment to rest,' Dorden replied. *So do I,* he added, under his breath.

Haller cursed and put Daur down again. He sat down, rubbing his arms.

'How much further, do you think?' he asked. They'd already passed half-a-dozen of the devices that Merrt and Haller had disarmed and marked up with red chalk.

'Not far,' said Dorden. He gave himself a shot in the thigh that no one could see, a huge and desperate hit of pain-killers.

'Too far,' Merrt whispered, sitting with his back to the wall, his eyes closed. 'Tell me the gn... gn... gn... truth, doc. I'm done, aren't I? I'm bleeding inside. My heart... It feels like I'm gn... gn... gn... torn up.'

'You're fine,' said Dorden. He couldn't avoid Haller's eyes. Haller could see Dorden was lying. The old medicae no longer had the strength to fake a confident bedside manner.

'Leave me here,' said Merrt. 'You'll be gn... gn... gn... a lot faster without me.'

'We're not leaving you,' said Haller.

'No, we're not,' Dorden agreed. He looked at Merrt. More blood was seeping through the dressings on his chest. Slowly, painfully, Dorden got up and crossed to Haller.

'You go on,' he said quietly.

'No, doc.'

'Yes. I'll follow on with Merrt when I've got my breath back. Please, Haller. Get Daur back to the ship.'

'I'm not leaving anyone behind,' Haller insisted, frowning.

'Haller, Ban's your friend. Your good friend. You've known him for years, since before the Ghosts. He's got a brand-new wife waiting for him. Sweet, sweet girl. She needs you to bring Ban back to her. Decent surgery on the ship will save his life. Do you understand what I'm saying, Haller?'

'I'll carry you,' said Haller. There were tears in his eyes.

'All of us?' Dorden smiled. 'Daur can't walk. Neither can Merrt. And I can't carry Merrt. I can barely get up, Haller. Go on. Do this for me, Haller. Pick Ban up and carry him home.'

'What about you?' asked Haller.

'I'll follow you, with Merrt. As soon as we've both pulled ourselves together and had a little rest. All right?'

There was a noise in the tunnel behind them. Something moved, dislodging debris.

'It's Commissar Hark! He's moving this way!' Haller cried, starting up.

Merrt had opened his eyes.

'It's not Hark,' he said. He reached out for the rifle that had fallen on the ground beside him. His hand was unsteady. It took him a long time to grasp it.

'Haller,' said Dorden. 'You've got to go now.'

'THE TRANSPORTS ARE all away!' Domor shouted to Gaunt.

Gaunt nodded.

'Get ready to follow them out,' he yelled back. He looked at Mkoll and Rawne. 'We need to pour everything we've got left at that line there. Give Hark a chance to get his men into the college so we can exit.'

'That's going to be tight,' murmured Rawne. 'Can't

we just leave them here? I've really grown to dislike the commissar.'

'That's a lie,' said Gaunt.

Rawne shrugged.

'You're right. I didn't like him to begin with.'

'Where the hell is that gunfire coming from?' asked Bonin.

They turned to look. A second layer of weapons fire was ripping into the Sons of Sek. It was coming from an entirely different angle, meshing with the efforts of Gaunt's force and Hark's detachment like an interference pattern.

'It's Criid!' Varl yelled. He whooped.

'Feth me,' said Rawne. 'There really is an Emperor.'

Criid's strikeforce, smaller in size than Hark's but still packing a punch, was storming out of air shafts and tunnels on the far side of the concourse. Chiria's flamer was roasting the Sons of Sek out of position, and Hark's front-line shooters were making the most of the pickings. In less than five minutes of intense gunfire, the three prongs of the Imperial position had driven the Archenemy units back into a distant line.

'They won't hold there for long,' said Mkoll. 'They'll take reinforcements and–'

'Long enough,' said Gaunt. 'Let's move. Signal Criid and Hark to get their forces in here.'

Criid's mob was the first inside the shot-up, ruined college hall. They were dirty from their trek and many were carrying minor injuries.

'What happened to you?' asked Gaunt.

'Tank mine,' said Criid. 'Lost a few. It wasn't pleasant. But there was an up side. The blast cleared the path for us. Opened up those old airshafts that brought us here. We followed the sounds of a desperate last stand.'

'Your timing, as usual, is impeccable, Criid,' said Gaunt. 'Get moving. Domor, show them the way out of here. Double time, Ghosts. Come on!'

Hark and his force began spilling in through the front hatches.

'What the hell is this place?' Hark asked, looking around.

'You can read the report later,' said Gaunt. 'Move your men out that way. Follow Criid. Fast as you can, Viktor.'

The Ghosts force was exiting fast. The scouts held the front hatches, taking steady shots to discourage the Sons from making another push. Gun teams were breaking down crew-served weapons and carrying them away. At a signal from Gaunt, Domor started to wire up the satchel charges every member of Strike Beta had brought with them.

'Burn the rest,' Gaunt told Brostin.

Brostin smiled. 'You're too good to me, sir,' he said.

Brostin turned his torch on the annexes first. Flames licked up, lighting the college halls. Paint flaked away like dried skin or dead leaves. Objects caught in the fire popped and cracked and burst. Gaunt watched the flames for a while, basking in the heat. The fire was purifying. It marked an end, a baptism, a re-entry into the war. Most of all, it seemed to mark an accomplishment that he hoped would be truly significant.

The effort of making it happen had come with a price for his Ghosts, a price he had not yet counted.

He turned to find Mabbon Etogaur watching the flames.

'We've done what we can,' he said. 'Let's hope it's sufficient.'

Mabbon nodded.

'Shipmaster Spika will have been broadcasting the prepared transmissions for the last half an hour. He will continue to do so as we leave the system. They were all prepared according to the codes and language you supplied. When the benighted anarch comes to pick over the ruins of what we leave here, and when he plays back the transmissions captured during the attack, it will

appear that his facility was raided by the Blood Pact, and
that his treasures were confiscated to prevent him over-
reaching himself.'

'You have lit a fuse,' said Mabbon. 'The Gaur. The
anarch. Neither one will stand for the accusations that
will follow this raid.'

'If we have gone part-way to engineering a divisive
internecine war between the Sanguinary Lords, I believe
we have expended worthwhile effort.'

Gaunt looked at Mabbon.

'It's time to leave.'

Mabbon looked puzzled.

'Really?' he asked.

'Of course.'

'I thought–' Mabbon began.

'What?'

'I presumed you would leave me here. Leave me to
burn. I presumed I had served my purpose.'

'I'll decide when your duty ends,' said Gaunt.

Mabbon nodded.

'Major Rawne!' Gaunt yelled. 'Have your Suicide Kings
escort the prisoner back to the ship. Mkoll! Prepare to
break off. It's time to leave. Brostin! I think that's quite
enough.'

'WHAT ARE YOU doing?' yelled Ludd. 'We're falling back to
the lifters. The order's been given!'

The Space Marines turned to look at him. Their ancient
armour was covered in dents and scratches, and they
were drenched in blood that was not their own. Holofurnace had lost his shield. Sar Af was taking shots at
another depot structure while the others stripped usable
ammunition from the last of the operational weapon-
servitors to fall.

'This is the next target,' said Eadwine. 'The assault will
continue. Go to your ship.'

'Major Kolea sent me to find your personally,' said

Ludd. 'The order to withdraw has been given by the operation commander.'

'We do not take orders from the Imperial Guard,' said Sar Af.

'So I've noticed,' said Ludd. 'But we have to jump to yours.'

'I believe you have just described an abiding principle of the Imperium,' said Sar Af.

'The order is to withdraw,' said Ludd. 'Please follow it.'

They turned their backs on him.

'What? That's it? You're just going to carry on? Are we supposed to wait for you?'

'Leave us,' said Eadwine, without looking around. 'We expected this. Our commanders expected this when they sanctioned our collaboration in this effort. The Guard may leave when it wishes. We will keep going until this place is obliterated.'

'Really? And then what?' asked Ludd.

'If we have survived to that point, we will endure in the debris field until such time as a vessel detects our signal.'

'That could be years,' said Ludd.

'We are more patient than you,' said Eadwine.

'Go,' said Sar Af.

'I won't,' said Ludd. 'I am an officer of the Commissariat, responsible for discipline and correction. We don't want this place obliterated. That's the whole point. We *want* there to be traces left behind. We want to leave clues. We want the enemy to know. If you keep going, you will undo and undermine the entire purpose of this endeavour. You will be breaking orders and the authority of the Imperium. You will be in breach of duty and your sacred trust, and–'

'Silence,' said Holofurnace. He looked at his brothers. The blood of his enemies trickled down the dented gold fittings of his helm.

'The boy has a point,' he said. 'The logic is solid. To

continue would be counter-productive.'

The other two nodded. All three turned and walked away, their massive boots crunching over the scattered debris.

Side by side, they began to trudge back towards the distant hangar bays.

Sar Af turned and looked back at Ludd.

'Hurry up, now,' he said.

THE LANDERS WERE coming in as fast as they could. The problems of space that had affected the original drop remained. Only a few at a time could set down, and most had to ditch their payloads of munitions once they had. They had all been making a restock run when the orders changed.

Baskevyl and Kolea were supervising the dust-off, getting as many lasmen into each Arvus and Falco as they could.

Kolea saw Dalin.

'Where's Meryn?' he asked. 'Where's the rest of E Company?'

'They're coming,' said Dalin.

'From the looks of it, Meryn pulled back too fast,' said Baskevyl, checking the tactical display on Rerval's voxcaster. 'He's let enemy units get in behind him. They're coming out of the depot under enemy fire. Not the neatest extraction I've ever seen.'

'Meryn's not the neatest soldier,' said Kolea.

Kolea looked at the chart.

'If we force open these hatches, his mob can get out and clear without having to come through the breach.'

'Makes sense. Let's go.'

'Keep the pull-out moving, Bask,' said Kolea. 'I'll do it.'

KOLEA TOOK A squad with him back to the edge of the engineering depot where the Caestus had finally come to rest. Last groups of F and H companies were making a solid and dignified withdrawal through the huge ram-wound in the depot doors.

Kolea's squad could hear the gunfire beyond the doors. The whine of las-shot and the thump of flechette blasters. Meryn's company had got themselves into trouble all right.

'Come on!' Kolea yelled. 'This way!'

He led his unit down to the passenger hatches set in the far corner of the depot's vast vehicular shutter. It took a few moments to locate the lock mechanism and cut through it with a plasma torch.

Kolea opened the hatch.

'Meryn. Meryn! Fix on my signal and move this way!' he voxed. 'We've got an exit for you. Come on!'

'Read that, Kolea. Nice work.'

Meryn's troops quickly appeared, running across the littered floor of the depot towards the hatch. Some were turning and firing from the hip as they ran. Enemy fire chased them.

Kolea's squad laid down a little covering fire and then pulled back as Meryn's men started to reach the doorway.

'Get through. Go on!' Meryn yelled. His men dashed through the hatch in twos and threes. Weapon fire spattered off the shutter. Meryn stayed outside to see his men through. He yelled through the hatch to Kolea.

'Get them up to the landing zone. I'll get the last ones out!'

Kolea nodded and headed off.

'Come on!' Meryn bellowed at the stragglers. 'This is not a good place to be!'

He fired off a few shots. Some Sons of Sek had appeared in the distance, and he could smell mint and milk again.

Gendler reached him, unfit, red-faced and out of breath.

'Here come the last of us,' he panted.

Meryn took a look. The last four or five. Eklan. Mkgain. Fozol. Rozzi. Costin.

Meryn wiped his mouth on his sleeve.

'No, Didi,' he said. 'You know what. I think we're all here.'

They stepped through the hatch.

'Captain!' Eklan yelled, the closest of them, running as fast as he could to reach the door.

'What are you doing?' Costin yelled. 'Where the feth are you going?'

'You're right,' said Gendler to Meryn. 'I don't see anyone left unaccounted for.'

Meryn and Gendler shut the hatch and slid the manual bolt across.

The last few members of E Company reached the hatch and began to hammer their fists against it.

'What are you doing?' Costin wailed. 'What the feth are you doing? Open the hatch. Open it! Open the hatch, you bastards!'

On Meryn's side of the door, the banging fists made the faintest of sounds.

Costin staggered back from the unyielding hatch. He was so scared he threw up. Eklan and the others were caught in a blind and disbelieving panic.

'You bastards. You bastards!' Costin screamed at the door, his fists balled at his sides.

He turned slowly. The loxatl had reached them. He heard their alien chir and chatter. He smelled their milk and mint, and threw up again. Rozzi howled in terror. Eklan fired at the xenos monsters.

The reptiles were closing in from all sides, chattering, slipping across the deck. Their dewclaws were extended.

They had no need to waste blaster shot on these kills.

Costin began a scream that he never finished.

THE SONS OF Sek were getting closer. Merrt could hear them approaching along the tunnel.

'Gn... gn... gn... get behind me, doc,' he murmured.

Dorden took a long time to reply.

'Don't be daft, Rhen,' he said, his voice as thin as upper atmosphere. 'Get up. You can walk. Get after Haller. Leave me.'

'I can tell when you're lying, doc,' said Merrt. 'Be truthful now. This gn... gn... gn... wound I've got here. It's not one you come through, is it?'

Dorden looked at him. He shook his head.

'No,' he admitted.

'Then I'm gn... gn... gn... gonna stay here with you, aren't I?' Merrt said. He reached out with a bloody hand and turned Dorden's head to look into the old doctor's eyes.

'It's all right. I know you can't tell, but I'm smiling,' Merrt said.

The first of the Sons had appeared. Their lamps bobbed as they came closer. There were dozens of them.

Merrt took the saline round out of the old rifle, and chambered a hard round instead. He pushed Dorden back against the wall behind him and sat up, aiming his rifle at the approaching enemy soldiers.

'You've only got one shot, Rhen,' murmured Dorden.

'I gn... gn... gn... know,' said Merrt. Blood dripped over his metal lip. 'And I've used up the last of those gn... gn... gn... muscle injectors too. Can't shoot for shit now.'

'Just make sure it counts,' said Dorden. He was clutching a loop of votive beads Zweil had given him.

Merrt took aim. The Sons brought their weapons up.

'Hey!' Merrt yelled, snuggling the rifle in. 'Hey, you bastards! You know what? I used to be a gn... gn... gn... great marksman. I had a fething lanyard. Not any more, though. These days, I aim at something, I miss it every time! You understand? I'm not a very gn... gn... gn... good shot!'

Merrt fired. The round passed through the Sons of Sek fireteam without hitting a single one of them. Nor did it strike the firing pin of the massive barrel charge twenty metres behind them. It missed the pin socket by the distance of a middle finger, and punched into the side of the barrel just above the red chalk marks Haller had made when they disarmed it earlier.

The hard round punctured the metal shell of the container.

There was a spark.

TWENTY-THREE
Out of Reach

SHIPMASTER SPIKA NODDED the instruction to execute to his steersmen. With a grinding shudder, the *Highness Ser Armaduke* pulled away from the mangled skin of Salvation's Reach. All the lighters and landing ships were aboard, and the hatches of the lateral holds had been shut. The ship's departure broke the atmospheric seals around the boreholes cut by the Hades drills. Explosive decompression ripped up through the lower and uncharted cavities of the Reach, voiding vacuums and collapsing compartments like eggshells.

Parts of the vast structure were already on fire where massive explosions had torn through them, the blasts of carefully laid satchel charges, or of ditched munition loads ignited by departing landing ships.

Some of the damage was the result of booby-trap devices in the lower depths spontaneously detonating.

Tiny cavities in the Reach glowed from within like the heat inside a coal. Explosions and firestorms continued to rumble through the habitat for several days.

Shields up, the *Armaduke* powered away from the

target zone, plotting a hard acceleration line through the dense junk fields towards the nearest viable Mandeville Point. It continued to broadcast the streams of chatter, accusation and insult in Blood Pact battle code until the moment it translated.

TWO HUNDRED THOUSAND kilometres behind it, cloaked and hidden in the debris field of the Reach, the monstrous and night-black daemon ship watched the *Armaduke* depart. It listened to the vox-chatter the Imperial ship had scattered in its wake.

It lit its weapons and its drives and sped forwards, tracking its prey.

As it moved, it whispered its name, a sonic crackle like a hushed curse.

Tormaggedon Monstrum Rex!

'I WILL DO everything I can,' Curth said. 'The prognosis is good. Haller brought him into the infirmary in decent time.'

Elodie nodded.

'Thank you,' she said. The beds of the infirmary chamber were full. There were so many injured personnel that some of the crew infirmary facilities had been co-opted by the Ghosts too.

Only one bed concerned Elodie. She sat down at the side of Daur's cot and held his hand. He was very pale against the old, poor quality bedding. He did not stir.

'With rest and good care, he will recover,' said Curth. She was exhausted and empty inside, but she stayed with Elodie until the woman seemed calmer.

Curth went back into the medicae offices. Dorden's desk was as he had left it, his instruments laid out the way he liked. Lesp had done that, as he did every morning. The familiarity of the work area was almost unbearable.

She sat down in the chair that had been Dorden's since

they had boarded for the mission. On the desk, in an old, worn frame, was a faded pict of a young man and his pretty young wife. She was pregnant. He was a newly qualified county doctor. Behind the smiling couple, sunlight shone through a stand of handsome nalwood trees.

Curth wiped her eyes.

The door opened. Blenner came in. He shut the door behind him and looked down at her.

'I don't know what to do now,' she said.

'Then we'll have to think of something,' he replied.

'The silly old feth,' she said. 'He was never going to die in bed, was he? In bed, being cared for, where he belonged.'

'I don't think that's where he actually belonged, do you?' said Blenner. He plonked a bottle of sacra and two small glasses on the desk, opened the bottle and poured shots.

He handed one to her and took the other himself.

'I'm no good at this,' she said.

'At drinking?' he asked. 'By the Throne, lady, the other night that certainly wasn't true.'

'At saying goodbye,' she said.

'Ah,' he nodded. He raised his glass.

'To the best of us, who leave us too early,' he said, 'and to the worst, who outstay their welcome.'

'You look sad,' said Felyx.

Gaunt did not reply. Slowly, carefully, he cleaned and oiled the blade of his power sword.

'I thought we… won. We won, didn't we?' asked Felyx.

'The mission was accomplished,' Gaunt said quietly. 'There is every decent prospect that we achieved something of lasting value.'

'Then why do you look sad?' asked Felyx.

'I lost men. A lot of men. They gave their lives to become Ghosts. That's always painful for a commander to bear, even in victory. And some of them… one especially… was very dear to me.'

Gaunt looked at Felyx. Gaunt's quarters were quiet. Maddalena was sitting in the outer room, reading. She appeared to be studying Gaunt's copy of *The Spheres of Longing*. Gaunt watched her turn a page.

'There's a reason you like her,' said Felyx.

'I'm sure there is,' said Gaunt.

'The most valuable lifeguards of House Chass receive very sophisticated body modification. Maddalena's face and voice, they were designed to resemble my mother's. The similarity was supposed to reassure and comfort me. I imagine it has an effect on you too.'

'I imagine so.'

'Is that the sword of Heironymo Sondar?' Felyx asked.

'It is. Would you like me to tell you how I came to own it?'

Felyx shook his head.

'I saw you use it today,' he said. 'That's all I need to know.'

RAWNE CHECKED THAT Mabbon's shackles were in place and locked to the deck pin. He took one last look at the prisoner and moved to the cell door.

'A good day's work, pheguth,' he said and closed the hatch.

By the light of the single lamp he was permitted, Mabbon sat back in his chair and allowed the tension to slip out of his muscles.

For the first time in a long while, he smiled.

IN DRESS UNIFORM, with the power sword strapped to his hip, Gaunt walked onto the excursion deck. The place was silent. The ranks drew up to attention. The regimental retinue looked on, wordless and still. Outside, warp space scratched against the hull, but inside there was a solemn hush.

The band, in full ceremonial finery, stood ready to

play the memorial march of the Imperium.

Gaunt got up onto the podium. Zweil stood there already, ready to conduct the formal service. The ayatani looked old and tired and sad.

Gaunt had a list in his pocket, but he didn't need it as a prompt. He knew it by heart. He looked down at the regiment and at the three Space Marines ranked at the front, side by side and impassive. They had returned their battered boarding plate to the storage caskets and donned the power armour they had been wearing when he first met them. Silver, Snake and Scar.

'We gather to commemorate the end of this undertaking,' said Gaunt in a strong, clear voice, 'and to acknowledge the contributions and sacrifices made. At my discretion, a number of decorations have been recommended. Some of them are awarded posthumously.'

He took off his cap and began to announce the list of names. The Ghosts bowed their heads. Holofurnace raised his spear up straight in a salute to the fallen.

High above, looking down from its perch on a cargo gantry, the psyber eagle listened to the roll of honour.

A perfect aquila, it spread its wings.

Special thanks to
Ead Brown, Richard Dugher, Nik Vincent,
Nichola Loftus, and Bruce and Michelle Euans.

ABOUT THE AUTHOR

Dan Abnett is a novelist and award-winning comic book writer. He has written almost forty novels, including the acclaimed Gaunt's Ghosts series, and the Eisenhorn and Ravenor trilogies. His latest Horus Heresy novel *Know No Fear* was a New York Times bestseller, and topped the SF charts in the UK and the US. In addition to writing for Black Library, Dan is highly regarded in the comics industry for his work for both Marvel and DC, and has written a number of other bestselling novels, including *Torchwood: Border Princes, Doctor Who: The Story of Martha, Triumff* and *Embedded*. He lives and works in Maidstone, Kent. Dan's blog and website can be found at *www.danabnett.com*

Follow him on Twitter *@VincentAbnett*

WARHAMMER
40,000

DAN ABNETT

RAVENOR VS EISENHORN

PARIAH

An extract from Pariah
by Dan Abnett

On sale November 2012

I HEARD THE crack, the crack of metal on flesh, the sound of an axe smacking a ripe tuber. Saur's head was snapped aside, his body rotating after it. Blood flew. It was in his dirty white hair. He crashed backwards into the railings of the upper ring, and knocked over a spit bucket. He half-fell, yet somehow kept his feet, but he was done. The stranger was following in, the *salinter* going for the throat while the guard was dropped.

You have to remember the speed. You have to appreciate, as I tell you this, that virtually no time at all had passed since I first entered the room and saw them fighting. Three, four seconds, enough time for them to trade two dozen blows. I had come in with just enough time to grasp the basic situation and see Saur fall.

I never liked Thaddeus Saur. It's safe to say my feelings towards the cruel bastard were stronger and more negative than that.

But he was of the Maze Undue, and so was I, and this could not be permitted.

I started forward. I shouted out a great cry, and snatched a buckler from the pegs. My cuff was turned to *dead*, so the force of my bluntness came with me and my shout.

It can be like a slap to have a pariah come at you, aggressive, un-limited. To even a non sensitive, a regular human, the psykanic null of a blank mind can be disturbing, if only fleetingly.

He recoiled. The stranger recoiled. It was enough of a surprise to stop him cutting out Saur's throat. My interruption wasn't going to stop there. I hurled the buckler like a discus.

The small, circular shield missed him, but he was obliged to duck. Saur was far from finished. He kicked out, savagely, and caught the stranger on the inside of his thigh with his heel, throwing the man sideways, clumsily.

The stranger landed, hands on the canvas, but was ready as Saur propelled himself forward and kicked the mentor's legs away. Saur slammed onto his back.

And I was, all this time, still running at him. I turned the run into a flying kick.

He rolled under me, flat to the floor, and sprung up as I landed and turned.

I think he wanted to say something to me, but he didn't know what. Perhaps he wanted to tell me to flee, to back away from a fight I had no part in, but he couldn't. If he wanted Saur dead, he had to kill me too, or the whole house would come down on his head.

I could sense his conflict. Unarmed as I was, I drove at him, using his reluctance against him. Fighting Saur was one thing, but he didn't want to engage a young woman. His response was half-hearted. He tried to shove me away. He tried to spare me his blade, though it was still in his hand. I think he hoped to clip me with the hilt or pommel and perhaps knock me out.

I would not let him off so easily. I grasped his wrist, turned it and, with my other hand, punched the pressure point in his upper arm.

The *salinter* flew out of his deadened fingers.

'Who are you?' I demanded.

With both hands, he rammed me aside. I staggered and fell, knocking down a rack of wooden exercise staves.

I got up, gripping one stave and kicking the others out of my way. The stranger was backing from me, his hands up.

I think he was intending to cut his losses and flee.

He doubled up as Saur's *cutro* tore into him from behind. The short sword went through his coat, through his robes, through his under-jack and mesh, and sliced into his waist. Saur ripped the blade free, and blood squirted out across the canvas. The stranger stumbled away, his head wobbling like a drunkard, his feet unsure. his eyes confused. He had both hands clamped to his waist, but even tight together, they could not plug the hole in him. Blood poured out, like red wine from an jug. His hands and sleeves were soaked with it.

His mouth opened and closed, without managing to form words.

He fell down on his back. Saur just stood there, watching him bleed out, the bloodied *cutro* low at his side.

Blood formed a huge, dark red mirror on the canvas around the stranger. The mirror crept out. Blood soaked his coat and robes, covered his hands, and flecked his face. He stared at the ceiling, mouth fluttered open and shut, his legs twitching.

I bent over him.

Perhaps he didn't have to die, I thought. We could hold him, bind his injury, call for the city watch. I tried to apply pressure to his ghastly wound, but it was open, and as big as a dog's mouth. My hands were no better at stemming the flow of blood than his had been.

He suddenly, finally, saw me instead of the ceiling and the lights. He blinked, refocused. Tiny beads of blood had lodged in his eyelashes.

'What is this? Who are you?' I asked.

He said a word. It came out of him like a gasp, more breath than sound.

It was a word I had not heard before.

He said, 'Cognitae.'

There was a bang, right in my ear, and it made me jump because it was sudden and close and painfully loud. A bark of pressure clouted me along with the noise. I flinched as bloody backspatter hit my face, throat and chest. I had his blood in my eyes.

Mentor Saur put another round through the stranger's face for good measure, then holstered his snub pistol.

Order from *blacklibrary.com*
Also available from

and all good bookstores